Adrian Hitt

The Grant Poem

Containing Grant's Public Career and Private Life from the Cradle to the Grave

Adrian Hitt

The Grant Poem
Containing Grant's Public Career and Private Life from the Cradle to the Grave

ISBN/EAN: 9783744711654

Printed in Europe, USA, Canada, Australia, Japan

Cover: Foto ©Andreas Hilbeck / pixelio.de

More available books at **www.hansebooks.com**

THE GRANT POEM,

CONTAINING

GRANT'S PUBLIC CAREER AND PRIVATE LIFE FROM THE CRADLE TO THE GRAVE.

General GRANT, what a Volume in a Name, an Army in a Man.

BY

ADRIAN HITT,

AUTHOR OF "LOS CINCO MASUS SONER," "SHAKESPEARE'S BONES," ETC.

Designed, Illustrated and Engraved by the Author.

The reason why I wrote this book was to get money for an expedition to the North Pole by an entirely new and novel scheme, which is too simple and positive to ever fail. *May the sons of Uncle Sam be the first to view that curious, long-sought object of the frozen realm.*

NEW YORK:
NASSAU PUBLISHING CO.,
122 NASSAU STREET.
—
1886.

The place where my compositors
  Worked and growled so strong,
Was No. 1 New Chambers street,
  A street not very long.

Set by Hawley & Flanagan, employed by H. L. Williams, in the
  office of C. H. Crysler & Co., as
  directed by Nassau Publishing Co.

This book needs
      No introduction ;
It's the poetic side
      Of a bloody ruction.

The Author's writings here,
  According to Congress served,
He has them copyrighted
  With all their rights reserved.

The date of this book's
  Copyright we'll fix
In the year eighteen hundred
  And eighty-six.

DEDICATION.

To the dead soldiers of the lost cause,
And the living ones of the Union laws.
To the dead heroes of a mighty nation,
To them I seal this dedication.
To the GRAND ARMY OF THE REPUBLIC, who gave
Their life and limbs the nation to save.
To those, and those alone.
To the living now, and the ones that are prone.
To all the late warring nation I dedicate these lines.
To those from the northern snows, or southern pines
    To you-alls and we-uns alone,
    I set this monumental stone.
May none in this poem see any harms,
But just the power of American arms.
    It shows how the southern rebs,
    With their swords disaster spreads.
    It shows the Yankee in his cause,
    Supported by a nation's laws.
    It was horror, disaster and dread,
    O'er a lovely country spread.
    But who was right, or who was wrong,
    Should be told in prose and song.
    So no more a neighbor's war,
    This mundane sphere shall ever mar.
    The Yankees, in long chanted song,
    Claim the rebel hosts were wrong.

DEDICATION.

The Yankees think—ah! let us see,
Was it the rebel hosts, or we?
Must all those horrid wars and moan,
Be yoked to but one side alone?
Did not both, the reb and Yank,
Tread on one disastrous plank?
Oh, that black plank of the southern cause,
Oppressor of the northern laws,
    You've fell;
And may you wiggle straight to hell.
Such is the prayer of one,
A republican of democracy's son.
I hope this is dedicated to fit,
By the best ability of

        Adrian Hitt.

CONTENTS.

EIGHTEEN HUNDRED AND SIXTY-THREE.

EIGHTEEN HUNDRED AND SIXTY-FOUR.

GRANT'S TOUR AROUND THE WORLD.

PROEM.

Grand Nation, stop and lend thy ear;
Help me our Grant a monument to rear.
May the power of his arm never be forgot.
For weak is my pen to describe his mighty plot.
As he marched along the world echoed with his tread.
And bannered armies before him in chaos fled.
O, had I the pen of Campbell, Burns, or Moore,
Then up to his true genius it's probable I could soar.
For it truly takes a genius to designate a seer,
Then it can be done without an ostentatious bleer.
[name :
But the history of his country will ever hold his
It will ever stand out bold on the pages of its fame.
Grant was a man like Moses in the Bible, for
He could not talk, but was mighty in a war.
Eloquence of speech can often charm the mind,
But all good qualities in a man we very seldom find.
It is grand by imagination to soar in dazzling flight—
[fight.
But it is a greater thing to unsheathe a sword and
When the sword in a proper place can fall,
Bathed in destruction the enemy to appall.
From the cradle to the grave;
Before the foe and o'er the wave;
All in verse,
I will rehearse,
His actions so bold and free.

He was a character all alone,
The likes of him was never known,
Till Illinois,
Among her boys,
Pointed him out to me.
Ever since then I have been craving,
To write his life, my pen's been raving,
And now
I trow
The chance I've overtook.
In justice everything I'll deal him,
And as a hobby I'll never speal him,
But fair,
And square,
All in an honest truthful book.
May his life, so rich and rare
Lead me like a wandering prayer,
To dare
Deal square,
For the sake of all others.
He was a giant in my estimation,
The greatest captain of our nation,
In true
Manly virtue,
And he classed all men as brothers.
In truth and justice he ever dealt,
Pangs of remorse he never felt,
Blood and war
He did abhor,
And all his life will teach us so.
Beyond the water, 'mid kings and queens,
He treated them as common scenes;
In any crowd
Was never proud.   [and low.
He treated alike the rich and poor—high

HIS PARENTAGE.

Jesse Root Grant, long live thy name,
Deeply engraved on the pages of fame,
The son that was fondled with pride in your arms,
Preserved his country from ruinous harms.
That sturdy young man of Scottish descent,
To Clairmount County, in Ohio went.
On the banks of Ohio's bold flowing river,
Stopped and immortalized it now and forever.
(For on Ohio's bold flowing stream
Grant was born, the hero of our theme.)
He came to that place of low, humble station,
Drifting along on the tide of emigration,
For westward in emigration
Pours the Empire of our nation.
And many a youth of rare intent,
Westward for a fortune went.
For Illinois so broad and bold,
Would entrance a hero's soul.
Where prairies so broad and grand,
On either side through space expand.
There's bread enough to make one sigh,
Stretching far beyond the viewer's eye.
And Indiana, just as grand,
Lies this side that prairie land.
But the land of rugged stones,

Ancient tales and Indian moans.
Lovely dales and romantic scenes.
Powerful oak and evergreens,
Lovely flowers of every hue,
Beneath a sky eternally blue.
(Except when storms, or rain-clouds blast
A shadow o'er the heavens cast.)
Where springs so pure and cold,
Have flown for ages, ages old.
Where many a dusky Indian queen,
Roamed at will, o'er wood and stream.
Where many a panther sat and growled,
And bears upon each other scowled.
Where many a wolf in solitude,
O'er his miseries, howled and brued.
Where the Indians shot the mate
Of many a deer with eyes elate.
And the coat dame Nature wrapped them in,
For moccasins was tanned that skin.
And upon them many an Indian tread
To the haunts where white man bled.
Where many a scalp dripping with gore
By their sides on belts they wore.
Many a woman of grace and beauty,
Was carried off as Indian booty.
To become the wives of Chiefs,
Or other such marauding thieves.
With tomahawks uplifted high,
Bathed in sunlight from the sky.
To descend on the head of captive man,
Or with powder prime his flint-lock pan.
To hurl a missile of misery,
As he sits cowering behind a tree.
Such was Ohio in early days,
Ere it turned to white man's ways.

Here the father of our hero came,
Without a farthing, without a name.
Ere he started in the distant to roam,
From Pennsylvania, his dear native home.
He fastened on his buckler and shield,
To dare the world in an open field,
Or beard the de'il in his den,
Hovering near the haunts of men.
For the Bible was his staff and stay,
His lamp by night, his guide by day.
The sword by which he smote his foes,
The club by which he struck his blows.
It was almost his board and bed,
By its holy precepts he was led.
The Bible on him made its innovation,
He became a Christian of Methodist persuasion.
He floated along through the woodland waste,
All dangers alike he calmly faced.
He drifted along till Clairmount County
Offered him rest with its frugal bounty;
And at Point Pleasant, high and dry,
Towering up towards the azure sky,
There a home he founded neat,
In hearth and bride it was complete.
A rail fence before it stood erect,
Such neatness in the wilds could one expect?
In one end a fire-place stood,
The house, though small was seemingly good.
There in Point Pleasant he met his lonely mate,
She came from Pennsylvania, his dear old native state;
She came with her parents to this far and distant place.
Where civilization must soon unmantle its face.
"Hannah Simpson," was this fair maiden's name,
An honest virtuous maiden, unknown to buds of fame.
It was said of her by those who knew her best,

She was a fearless, daring, true maiden of the West.
And would one suppose in this great land of kings,
                                        [things?
A man born of such a mother would stoop to little
When this lovely miss was wedded to her Jess',
I have at hand no record and therefore cannot guess.

CANTO.

Now may I rate,
The day and date
When baby Grant was born;
The night was run,
The day begun,
And it was in the morn.
They sent for Mother Cumons,
And the doctor they did summons,
That day a day of all others.
All this din and clatter,
Oh, what is the matter
With Hannah?
She will soon, soon be a mother.
The weather it arose
In wild tempestuous blows,
As though it would hurl away the land,
The storm it was furious,
How grand and curious,
Surely the de'il had something on hand.
The rains poured,
And winds roared,
Oh, what a cuffing the oaks received;
Poplars were rattled,
Elms were battled,
The De'il played his hand, **or I'm deceived.**
Let us see
What the spree
In the elements are on,
That they rage,
Then assuage,
And in an instant are gone.
Let it blow,

Rain or snow,
This poem must be ended,
For history and mystery
Never can be blended.

SECOND.

From Mount McGregor away to the West,
To that cabin on nature's fair breast,
Where the Ohio eternally flows,
And modern sleighs glide o'er soft Winter snows.
Now almost three score and ten,
Lies between this time and then.
That cabin, who built it?   None can tell,
But preserve it long and protect it well.
It was there in Ohio, at Point Pleasant Town,
Where Our Hero was born, a soldier of renown.
Who thought on that early Spring morn,
A Prince! a Soldier! a Statesman was born.
The Spring in its infancy was putting forth green,
Its hue on the woods, in the distance was seen.
The day and date of April need I here to name it,
So in future ages another race can claim it?
Minus one, two times two times seven,
He was born exactly one hour before eleven.
That stormy April morn, a day of all others,
Brought a son to the proudest of Christian mothers.
The morn that he was born, please remember it well,
Rain from the heavens, in spouting torrents fell;
The wind through the forest frantically howled,
And heaven an' earth for a moment scowled.
The winds through the forest so mightily sweep,
The oaks bow down as though they would weep.
The doors of the barn shut to with a bang,
While the fence about it tumbled down with a clang;
And the most indolent might readily understand

That old Gabe or the de'il had something on hand.
The moments swept on till the hour of ten,
When a captain was born to a nation of men.
The elements that reveled in hopes of his birth.
Instantly vanished from the face of the earth ;
And when he opened his eyes to the light of day,
The storm-clouds and rain had vanished away.
Oh! that hour, that hour of all others on earth,
That immortalized a cabin. and gave Grant a birth.
No man of genius on a cabin should frown,
From them have come men of eternal renown.
(I myself was born in a cabin small,
On a towering hilltop rocky and tall,
Where the towering oaks to the heavens reach,
And the ground was shaded by the boughs of the beach.)
The rain that came down with the blast of the storm,
On the tender grass lay like gems to adorn.
The diamonds of wealth may flash on the fair,
But naught like dew on grass can compare,
For what is more lovely or rich to be seen
Than rain-drops glistening o'er a fresh virgin scene.
In such a robe no princess can adorn
E'en the beauty of a dew-drop hung on to a thorn.
On such a scene the infant's eyes first strayed,
For the beauty of Nature for all were made.
He was no extraordinary infant at all, .
Than to the common lot of man may fall.
His intellect was solid and true to be sure,
And why should a man e'er ask for more?
His delight was a horse, from an infant small,
He was a hostler from the time he could crawl.

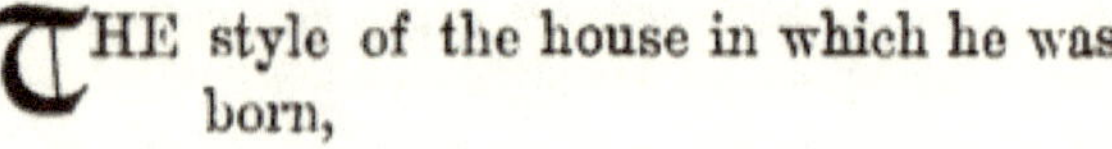

HIS BIRTH-PLACE.

THE style of the house in which he was
  born,
  Aristocracy of to-day would hold it in
    scorn;
  It was known by the home-like appearance
    that it wore,
  A shed-kitchen behind and two windows
    before;
  A door is located the windows between,
It stands facing a romantic, fair scene.
It lovingly stood inviting to all,
That longed to visit, or wished to call.
It was a home of welcome, no one can doubt,
With its latch-string hung invitingly out.
Locks and bolts never barred the door,
And a carpet never disgraced its floor.
Such was the home of the then wild West,

And home-made jeans were their Sunday's best.
Each man raised his pork and his bread,
And each man's shote from his own crib fed.
In those days there was very little fakin',
Each man cured his own hams and bacon.
In front of the house a wood-pile arose,
Snaked in on a sled when deep grew the snows.
The blaze on the hearth danced merry and gay;
Winter snows were sweeter than blossoms of May.
Nuts from the woods in plenty were gathered,
Oh! many a long Winter in the country I've weathered.
Many a corn shucking I've seen that was grand,
Which you never will see in this fair eastern land.
In Ohio, is the state where they do it the best;
Or in Indiana, a state farther west.
A corn shucking's the place to drive away care,
With a pumpkin beneath you to serve as a chair.
Stories were their glory, as they labored late and soon,
          [moon.
The only lantern that they had was the glimmer of the
Each one told a story, his dearest favorites then,
For daring deeds by women were done as well as men;
For the bold pioneer, with his whetted knife and gun,
Started in the chase ere the rising of the sun;
And his cabin was protected by a fearless, daring dame;
While her lord alleged chased the frightened game.
They feasted on the turkey, the bear and the deer,
         [squaw in fear.
While the Indians with terror held his long knife
Many a warrior in dust have been laid low,
In provoking the squaw of his long knife foe.

   Then an old hunter, grown old in the chase,
   Would tell them a story that once was his case;
   How, when a young man, pioneer in the State,
   He killed ten Indians and frightened off eight:

It was on the Ohio, a clear purling stream,
Where happened the fight of my pioneer's scene.
He was in bathing on its sand-paved shore,
When a peroge of Indians down on him bore,
He had no chance to escape to the brush,
So to the peroge he dived with a rush,
So over he turned it, their huge canoe,
And its occupants into the water he threw;
He drew a large knife from a belt that an Indian wore,
For his on the sand lay far on the shore,
He stabbed them to death as they tried to escape,
Their powder was wet and that ended their fate.
Ten braves it cost the chief of that clan,
In trying to capture a single white man;
And eight more were frightened half out of their wits,
To see their companions slashed up into bits,
See how he done it so easy and cute,
To turn o'er their canoe and kill them to boot.
They hung to the edge of the canoe to save them,
And that is the way a white man braved them.
The hollow beneath it furnished him breath,
While his Indian blade carved them to death.
When one was carved so he had to pass under,
He gave them a roar, a pattern of thunder.
A dim red spot was all that told
That an Indian had left his chieftain's fold.
The voice of the Ryor had made a demand
For the soul of the warrior in the Spirit Land.
So he hastened away without bidding adieu
To those around him, so simple a few.
Thus he laid down with no spirit to infest,
For it got away through a hole in his breast.
Then up spoke old Morgan, a rough of the woods,
Telling of Indians, how he dealt in such goods.
Many an Indian, he knifed them till dead,
Then lifted the hair from the top of their head.
Left alone on the ground they rested,
Whose flesh in the crop of ravens digested.
The crows picked out their eyes as they lay,
And buzzards filed apast in long array.
But many a white man, ere this was done,

Was laid low in the dust by an Indian's gun.
    Many a tale of daring and deed,
    Where Indians died and white men bleed,
        Was told;
    To the youthful mind it was feed
        From the old.
    Many a bear-hunt was there related,
    Many a chase from a panther stated,
    While all but the talker in silence waited
        For the end,
    So by another it could be mated
        To extend.
Then up spoke a hunter, while yet in his teens,
That told of the wonders of Western scenes;
Where the prairies west of the Wabash roll,
Where in the distance looms the wood-covered knoll;
Where buffaloes grazed like herds that are tame,
With numerous deer and other small game.
Many a buffalo I've carved and fried,
And many a cold night slept warm in his hide,
Where rabbits like kittens are playful and spry,
And the song birds are distant and shy;
Where the chickens of the prairie in springtime hoo-oo,
And the doves plaintive voice in the distance coo-oo.
Now back to the buffalo with mane shaggy and long,
With his wide set horns so dumpy and strong.
Many a red man to death they have gored,
His horns are his weapons, his chief battle sword;
The hump on his shoulders gives him power in motion;
A coming herd roars like the waves of the ocean,
In traveling, he goes for battle incog.,
He moves as solid as a down-stream log.
He travels with his horns in position ready,
His movements are graceful, his motions are steady;
His nose almost sweeping the ground at his feet,
And he moves with a steady, long galloping leap;
The hair of his head grows long on his for'd,
And there it is kinky, with dust matted hard;
His tail is bushy, like that of a cow,
And high he holds it when engaged in a row;
He's dangerous to meet on prairies that roll,

No man is able his power to control;
There is but one style this beast to lay,
And that is to feed him on rifle-ball hay.
The buffalo story is dragging too long,
Oh, the beautiful West, how it holds me in song.
A story that I should have told long before,
Happened on the banks of the wild Missour':
When a gang of us boys went out for sport,
Fishing and hunting far from the fort.
Somehow or other I sauntered along,
Charmed by the flowers and the birds' gay song.
Until I raised my eyes to scan,
But where had fled my fellow-man?
Before my eyes no human I seen,
But a lonely buffalo fed on the green.
Beautiful and grand the spot where he fed,
Joy knocked at my heart as I thought of the lead
That lay in my gun, all ready to fly,
As soon as I raised it to my shoulder on high.
With machinery all ready to kindle a fire,
That would the sluggish lead inspire,
And sent it out to rip and scouder,
Riding along on the wings of powder.
I looked along the barrel, through the sight to steer,
Then let go the lead in its wild career;
It went tearing along with plunge and bump,
And settled in the top of that buffalo's hump;
He plunged after me as I started to go,
With all the madness and fury of a deadly foe.
Now, what could I do with an empty gun,
No time to load it and less to run?
No brush to hide in nor trees to climb,
I tell you my safety was sad and sublime.
    Nothing to save but the wild Missour',
    Dumbly beating the low clay shore,
    It was take to the water, and nothing more,
    Though little I'd ever swam before.
So thus I lost all hopes of shooting,
And in an instant commenced unbooting.
    Thus boots and gun together lay,
    No time had I with them to stay,

But to the water went rushing away,
To shun a desperate and wild affray.
So with leaps and mighty stride,
I soon was in Missouri's tide,
Swimming for the other side,
O'er its waters dark and wide.
I'd went far enough for to make me blow,
When hard on my heels pressed the buffalo;
He came up till his nose could rub me,
Then with his horns he tried to club me.
And as he lowered his horns to gore,
He could not see me then before,
For the water got into his eyes,
And filled his nose, to his surprise.
My furious strokes gained little length,
And the looks of the bull gave me little strength.
How long could I stem its mud colored tide?
How long could I safely o'er its billows ride?
The bull was as fresh as in the start,
Which sent a quivering to my heart.
In my mind I then decided,
By strategy I would be guided;
Various thoughts my mind engaged,
As the furious race for life was waged.
At length I had the plan complete,
To turn and my pursuer meet.
To keep him from running me down,
Scarce had I time to turn aroun';
And as I met him face to face,
I thought of who should win the race.
As against my face his cold nose pressed,
To clench his hump I done my best;
First his ears I caught onto,
Then to his back myself I drew;
When my fingers clutched his hair,
All his power I then could dare.
He then turned to gain the shore,
Never to roam the prairies more;
For as I clenched my trusty whittle,
Deep in his sides I drove its mettle.
He, dying, staggering, reached the bank,

While behind in the waters I cautiously sank
'Till I knew that death had claimed him,
And life went out where I had lamed him.
Then o'er the prairie distant and low,
I saw my friends o'er a dying foe;
They came to aid me when all was done,
We shook hands o'er his carcass 'neath a setting sun.
Never on earth was I gladder at seeing
The return of friend or a fellow being.
This is but one escape of many I run,
From bears, buffaloes and Indian gun.
This is but one story of many that's told
By our pioneer fathers in time of old.
So this is the way night chased eve into morn,
Telling wild stories an' shucking long ears of corn;
Then break up with a dance or a fight
To celebrate the long eventful night.
Not a fight because they were mad,
But a luxury they used to indulge in when glad.
  Gone, gone are those days,
  With all their old rejoicing ways,
   Beyond the reach
  Of all the power men can teach.

HIS CHILDHOOD.

"I SOMETIMES CATCH MYSELF A-WISHIN'
FOR POWER OF RANK TO GIVE POSITION."

The birds chirped gaily as they listened
To the baby's name as he was christened;

          [other,
The father suggested names, first one and then an-
Then the tender parent assumed the right of a mother.
So the father took a stand, oped his ears and listened,
Thus, Hiram Ulysses the baby first was christened.
When o'er his head twelve months had spun around,

          [ground.
They moved up the river from their old accustomed
It was a score of miles up the river to Georgetown,

Seven miles back from the river, and the county it
[was Brown.
In the same old state, here the little family found,
That a people more thriving and intellectual did
[abound.

T was to this village school, where first
    Ulysses went,
He, for an education to the village school
    was sent ;
Here's where he obtained rudimental
    education,
(That was some day to quell the rebels of a nation.)
At this early age there was nothing about him grand,
He was said to be inferior to the others o' the land.
Now I'll relate some anecdotes which of him are told,
Though they may have been performed by renowned
[men of old :

He delighted in a great big noise,
Along with the other village boys.
    Pistol reports,
    And all such sports
Delighted his infant mind.
    In his life, we are told,
    While an infant two years old,
    As his father in his arms
    Protected him from village harms,
A boy came along with a pistol loaded,
With the father's consent the baby exploded.
It was just the father's desire
To see how the baby would stand the fire.
His tiny finger around the trigger was bent,
But little power to the force he lent.

So through life some people say,
In the hands of others a dummy he lay;
He only bowed to the nation's way

Was all.
He was a paw to the cat in the affray
That couldn't fall.
If he's the general that fought our fights,
Where is the soldier's humble rights,
Where is the hound that bit the bites
That poisoned so?
Where is the man that lit the lights
That burned so?
Where are the men that dealt the blows.
That laid low the rebel foes;
If Grant's the only one that arose,
God help our seas!
He's one of ten thousand that goes
To quell a breeze.
Where are the men that bled and died?
Where are the men that death defied?
Where is the man of the champion ride?
Were they all shot?
Liberty go then and abide
By that sacred spot.
What countryman first drew the sword,
With fury attacking the rebel horde,
And drove them o'er the muddy ford
To fields beyond?
Who was it made the rebel horde
So soon abscond?
Who first supported freedom's cause,
And trampled o'er oppressive laws,
Or gagged the rebel's yawning jaws
With grape?
That let no foe from his claws
Escape?
Show me, noble men of earth,
The champion freemen of our hearth,
Where does his native land of birth
Exist.
It's in Uncle Sammy's land of mirth,
Be it never hissed.
Such are the questions always asked,
Such generals are always tasked
By some one in ignorance masked,

Or fraud,
Won't let them be asked
To applaud.

The hammer came down as the trigger swung back,
Then loud and sharp came the powder's crack;
We are told that he stood it just like old men,
And he simply asked them to " *Fick it agen'.*"
A man that stood by the report did hear
His remark on it showed the sight of a seer;
Said he to the father of baby Ulyss',
"He'll make a general, or all signs will miss."

No one can say that that seer has lied,
Or that his predictions were not verified,
What thousands mourned in butchered death,
That a seer might breathe a truthful breath.
Many a factory in Uncle Sam was run,
To manufacture missiles to kill her warring son;
And almost unnumbered were her working hordes,
[swords.
Standing by steam grind-stones a-whetting up her
Then many a daughter of nature's fairest mold,
Manufactured death and bartered it for gold;
Manufactured death in shape of powder, caps and ball,
Then off by railway power to warring men they crawl;
[tories runs,
Thus by women and cripples the country and fac-
[guns.
With the able-bodied men in front to bear the nation's
[wheels,
The factories side by side turned their ponderous
[steels.
One would be grinding drugs and the other grinding
To cure and to kill seemed the people's occupation,
Of women and men throughout this curious nation.
Oh! medicine factories, shot and shell,
Has Uncle Sam turned into hell!
Has all her people, sons and brother,
Turned into murdering one another?
While mother, daughters and lover's maid
Stay at home to whet their blade,

Oh! who can e'er forget the days of eighteen sixty-two,
When all the nation to one grand centre flew?
The sons of war and liberty their power of genius tried,
On carriages of steam to the battling front they ride;
[wire,
The terrors of heaven they tamed, and guided it by
[fire.
That thought might travel along on wings of electric
It only took a nation's few to weld a mighty chain,
[links in twain.
But it took ten hundred thousand strong to rend its
For many a husband left a weeping mother,
And many a daughter wept the loss of a brother.
To verify a saying once said,
Battle fields were heaped with dead.

THE BOY'S MOST PROMINENT FEATURE.

The ledger's account,
From his father's fount,
Pours out in one long, mighty stream,
But horse, and horse alone is the theme,
Horse, horse was all his tricks,
Nothing but horse with him would mix.
Mare or colt, were also beasts he would take hold;
[them;
And like a gem, though they run or rear, he stuck to
His grasp, upon a horse was sure to last;
What he said, they obeyed though trudging in a sled;
His pride, was a drive or horseback ride.

Look at Alexander in his eventful course,
He learnt to rule men by learning to rule a horse,
Till beast or man beneath his sway,
To all sullen stubborness gave way,
This great bandit in blood and flame,
Sword and bridle he handled the same.
But the power of his pen,
Never stirred the souls of men,
But him and his bloody horde,

With their fire and naked sword,
Devastation was their only aim,
And their only hell-tainted fame.
Among the civil haunts of men,
A sword's less frightful than a pen.
          A wit,
          That is a hit,
Never can be smothered down,
And will stand longer than a crown.
But a sword must lose its trust,
Give way to years and crumble in rust.

THE FIRST HORSE HE EVER DROVE ALONE.

Kind Providence his father sent
To Ripley, twelve miles off he went,
And thus, a chance to Hiram lent
          To drive ;
And it was industriously spent
          To thrive.
Was it a heavenly chance,
That ordered Hiram to advance,
And give his tender hands expanse
          In hostler's art,
To make a horse proudly prance
          In sled or cart.
Or was it a sly inclination,
To be at some good occupation,
Or was it a childish deviation
          To obey
The rules of the vast creation
          That will not stay.
Or was it just because he knew
His father off to town had drew,
And offered a chance that was rare and few,
          To work the nag,
With nothing else at hand to do,

But drag.
For well he knew his father's stay,
Would occupy the livelong day;
And there was nothing in his way,
    But mother,
And well he knew she'd yield her say
    Without bother.
He knew by his father's former trips,
As children are apt to pick up chips,
And notice their parents' slides and slips,
    So he sported,
Matured his plans for his daddy's grips
    He never courted.
So thus by history we are told,
When but seven and six months old,
The first horse he then controlled,
    Hitched in sled.
Whether the horse was tame, fierce or bold,
    It never said.
That horse by Hiram first was hitched,
Beneath the harness by Hiram first was switched,
But whether lame, blind or bewitched,
    We cannot tell.
But after being with harness enriched,
    Worked he well.
Though it was said of the horse before,
No collar or harness had it ever wore,
Or served in harness of coach-and-four,
    To draw
Some blithering fiend to roar
    In law.
Nor at his heels e'er drew a divine,
With a hung out de'il for a sign,
Wearing a plug hat tall and fine,
    To attempt

To pierce the sinner's sin-bathed rind
   With divine contempt.
But one thing history does entail,
And its statements does not fail
To say that it had carried mail
   Over streams,
Led the lonely shade-covered trail
   Through pleasant scenes.
That horse was of a coltish mold,
And scarce had left the foundling's fold,
In years it was three summers old,
   But worn down
By somebody's rough control,
   To mailing boun'.
But rough and tough the falls it had seen,
Mid-winter's snows and summer's green,
Or whether it was lank or lean,
   Or minus fat ;
Through the hide the bones were seen,
   It ne'er told that.
Another thing history has given,
By a single line the horse was driven.
But in that horse, power was his'n
   To run away ;
For what power to a child is given
   That horses should obey ?
That horse driving he turned to good,
Upon a sled in hauling wood,
That for a warming purpose stood
   In hand,
Or for a cooking purpose stood
   In demand.
Driving where the trees were chopped,
Then branches from the trunks cropped,
Dangling o'er the runners lopped

Toward the ground.
Marks o'er the road it moped,
Homeward bound.
Till beneath his sturdy blows,
As from history I suppose,
A pile to the size of a cabin arose
In the wood yard.
But to whether the ground was soft or froze,
It pays no regard.
All day long from sun to sun,
That sled in constant motion run.
It seemed that work with a will was done,
For when his father home had come,
He had ceased his sliding fun
And unhitched.
For he quit as he had begun,
And littie as he was he had moved a ton.
It seems like a mouse hitched to a gun,
Or a prize by a sparrow won,
Or am I bewitched,
Or to a loaf have I turned a bun,
Or used for a cable a thread that was spun,
Or poisoned flies with a half made pun
That was ditched;
Or am I to pleadings of nature dumb,
By plucking a big imported plum
That was stitched
On a thing that was cold, lifeless and glum,
By sugar enriched.

MUSINGS ON THE FIRST HORSE HE EVER DROVE.

History does not deal us square,
For whether it was horse or mare,
History does not presume to tell,

From lids of history it never fell.
Would that I knew that horse's name,
So I could hand it down to fame.
A nail from that horse's shoe would applaud,
A nail that Hiram himself had drawed,
It would be a trinket of might and main,
That well could adorn a golden chain;
A lock from its mane would surpass a gem,
And a hoof be greater than a diadem,
Among the free-born races of men.

THE SLED IT DREW.

If that sled we now could collar,
It would bring us many a dollar;
It could be cut into mites and morsels,
And peddled out in tiny parcels,
To make sets in jeweled rings,
In ear bobs and precious things.

SERVING AS A STAGER, *A LA* HACKMAN.

When years had lent him ten in age,
He run a half-way country stage;
For in it he carried man,
And everything that wagon can.
From Cincinnati to Georgetown then,
Two horses he drove to carry men.
Along that road he was no wonder,
Driving horses. drawing plunder.
Though they say he was a child,
Does that prove his darings wild?
From Cincinnati to Georgetown then,
In miles was two times, two times ten.
But now, to tell its distance lies beyond my power,
For things are growing so at each receding hour,
For how truthfully the present sayings trow,
That ancient little streams have grown to rivers now.

When Hiram ran his forty miles of stage,
He was said to be *about* ten years of age;
But I suppose *abouts* varied then,
As they do at present, among the sons of men.
                                        [hosses.
Now when the country shows came along with tricky
                                        [bosses;
They never could throw Hiram with orders from their
For many a tricky pony beneath the seat of Grant,
Lopped his ears as if to say, to throw that boy I can't.
Hiram Ulysses rode all the ponys that came,
                                        [the same.
Whether they threw other boys or not, to him it was
But along came one that was a regular sounder,
                                        [pounder;
It went flying around the track, just like an old ten-
But all its flying movements producing no effect,
He did not tumble off as the master did expect;
The pony tried to shake him off, but sadly it did fail,
It just as well have tried to run off from its tail.
He froze on to him as close as macaroni,   [the pony.
One not used to horses would have thought him part
The pony rushed around with all his fiery speed,
But to his furious movements he paid but little heed;
                                        [Jack the Hurcle,
Then out jumped a hideous monkey, they called him
And mounted behind Hiram to help him sail the circle,
Into the pony's heels it put more fire and mettle,
                                        [settle;
But closer to the pony's back young Hiram seemed to
Then the monkey, to fill him with disaster and chagrin,
Dismounted from the pony by mounting upon him;
That monkey seemed a fiend, a de'il to do and dare,
                                        [hair.
He stood on Hiram's shoulders, and hung on by his

Ring-master, pony and monkey all tried to bluff him
                                          [out,
But he proved to that show he was no common lout.
O, he was an oddity. just like a fifth wheel caster,
For at a tender age he was a riding master.
He was a ring-master where'er he dealt his blows,
                                          [shows.
Though it was in battle fields or common country
Now, all ye readers please tumble to this fall,
He never rode the pony unless there was a call,
He kept up the practice, never thinking of being lamed,
Until he grew so large he finally grew ashamed.

AS A HORSE-DEALER

So by tradition we are told,
When Hiram was scarcely twelve years old.
              His father bade,
"Go, son, and close a standing trade,
Which with neighbor Ralston I've begun;"
And instructions like this he gave his son:
"Offer him fifty dollars, and if he wishes more,
Raise it nine dollars, minus four,
If this the trade does not fix,
Give him ten multiplied by six."
So in tradition it is said,
The son to the neighbor's sped.
When Ralston put the question direct:
"How much to pay, does your father expect?"
(Hiram, at this age, tradition goes on to relate,
Had not learned e'en to prevaricate,
He was then as pure as a polished gem,
Untainted by the sins of men.)
The truth he then went on to state,
What his father said, he gave it straight.
Said he, "father told me of course,

To offer fifty for the horse,
And if fifty would not buy it,
At fifty-five I'd better try it;
And the highest number he did fix,
Was ten, just multiplied by six."
So Mr. Ralston did straight reply:
"It takes sixty dollars the horse to buy."
Then Hiram made a bold assay,
Saying, "Sixty dollars I'll never pay,
For since I saw him I've set my mind,
A better horse elsewhere to find."
Old Ralston's wits to keenness lent,
Knew Hiram spoke just what he meant.
(He was a boy of bold decision,
And never heeded keen derision,
His fist was just as fast to play
As his mouth was bold to say.
In youth he never knew retreat,
In age he never felt defeat.
He was like the bear that wins his prey,
Not like the wolf that skulks away.
He was like a lamb when the fight was ended;
In noisy tumult he never blended.
In Sunday school he never taught,
In church affairs he never wrought.
But at a dog fight he would stay
From the last of April to the first of May.)
Old Ralston, mixed with some chagrin,
Took just a lonely fifty in,
        And of course,
Hiram rode home a purchased horse.
  (Of all the stories passed o'er I'll say,
  You can believe as few or as many as you may.
  Perhaps he did things both foolish and thin,
  But it's foolish to believe all that's told of him.

In the days or Hiram, when things went to smashes,
They put on their old clothes and soaked their heads
                              [in ashes.
        He spent his days in good old times,
        With virtuous things that now are crimes.
        But strange it seems, among the seers,
        The past has been the glorious years.
        In the coming years I see beyon'
        The glorious years begin to dawn.)
Now Hiram had an uncle, a brother to his father,
That settled in Canada, on the creek of Bolleywather.
There was no school in that Dominion settlement,
So out to Ohio young Johnny Grant was sent,
                              [tended,
To board with his uncle, as a Georgetown school he
Among the girls and boys of Uncle Sam he blended.
John and Hiram were age and age together,
                              [weather.
Each one had seen as much of summer and winter
Johnny was a Britisher in deviltry and birth,
                              [mirth.
To call old "Wash" a rebel would fill him up with
(Now Johnny was a whooper whenever he was riled,
And Hiram was a rapper whenever he got wild.
They were not old enough to pass along as misters,
But in sparring they were pretty clever fisters.
One could hit a lick, the other just as hard,
                              [fore'ead.
They always caught their subject upon the chin or
    "Washington was only just a boasterous thing.
    A rebellious traitor, he fought against his king."
    That was the insult that Johnny offered Hi.,
"Just repeat that o'er again, I'll knock your face a-wry."
Thus Hiram, the American Eagle,was ready to assail,
He 'lowed no English Lion to fondle with his tail.

The Lion at the Eagle was looking darts of steel,
One would not retreat, the other wouldn't squeal.
The Eagle to be sure, received some heavy blows,
But the Lion as well was punctured in the nose.
     Hiram and his cousin
     Gave each the other a buzzin'
      For all they were worth ;
     They caught it in the lug,
     And pounded each other's mug,
      In their demoniac mirth.
  After years in toil and joy spent,
  When their ages on the wall of manhood leant,
  And to tell the truth,
  They had only scaled the outer walls of youth.
From boyhood it seemed their fathers' homes diverged,
Between their homes the great St. Lawrence surged,
The Niagara also poured her endless floods
Between Hiram and Johnny's native woods.
  But as years roll on they meet again,
  Each on the footing of a man.
  Beyond the St. Lawrence, in a foreign clime,
  Is where they meet the second time ;
  And as they together pleasantly chat,
  Said John to Hi, "Do you remember that,
  The thrashing you gave me while at school,
  For calling Washington a rebellious tool ?"
  "Yes," said Hi, but all the while,
  The skin on his face stretched to a smile,
  "And just as sure as he ruled a nation,
  I'd do it again under the provocation."*

---

*Believe all of this you dare to swallow.
Through a loose and flabby collar.
Grant was said to ne'er provoke,
To never give or take a joke.
He was said to ne'er get tight,
Was never known to have a fight.

HIRAM ULYSSES BECOMES ULYSSES SIMP-
SON AND A CADET.

CANTO.

As a cadet,
You can bet
Ulysses now assails us
Among the cadets,
(Credulous set,)
Ulysses never bewailed us.
He went to train,
In battle reign,
And governmental power.
Oh! may wars,
National catarrhs,
N'er o'er us lower.
Cruel war
I do abhor,
It is a murderous slaughter,
It's where man
Really can
Court the de'il's daughter.
Love and justice
Always cuss'd us
With their olive branch of peace,
Until Swartwout
Found the route out,
And snatched it from the de'il's lease.
Sheath thy sword,
Ye bloody horde,
Ne'er sound a war's alarm,
The sword stroke,
And bugle note,
Is but a veteran's charm.
May Uncle Sam,
(The pious lamb,)
Never turn to a battering-ram.
All nations list! my ditty hear,
Peasant, sages, king and peer,

Sheath your war swords, bloody blade,
And rest forever in peaceful shade.
For now its been in constant wear,
Draining blood and whetting care.
Since the earliest dawning day,
It has been in constant play;
It is time, it now should rest
To let its bloody gorge digest.
Through all our historic ages,
A bloody sword drips on our pages.
Let swords no longer sustain our power,
Wave the olive branch in a trying hour.
May Swartwoutians win the day,
And drive all swords from earth away;
May all nations forget the part,
That swords sustain in nation's art.
May a dove the emblem be,
Peace o'er every land and sea,
    May the sword in its sheath lay,
    From the coming races hid away.
May the coming race in peace be staid,
May they never find that bloody blade,
May they never learn their father's trade.
    For if its found by boys or mother,
    They'll try it on some lusty brother,
    Or be whittling one another.
For it's man nature to prod and pry,
And every new-found thing they try;
For every fraud that works our land,
Much its wanted, big in demand.
Stop your militia on every shore,
Teaching soldiers to kill and doctors to cure.
Look at man in his exalted station,
What a wonderful hallucination.
To sum up war, its done in brief.
By one extended page of grief.
All the deeds of Grant have been expanded,
Since on this terrestial ball they landed.
From the pods of his life, deeds have been hulled,
            Picked and culled,
To make him more famous and great,

Than all the pilots at the wheel of State.
He was a great man in a great position,
The country's stay, and the law's physician.

COMPARISON OF WARRIORS.

Look at Napoleon, Oh, what a death was his'n,
He died upon an island, that island was his prison;
Ceasar, Oh, that Ceasar, note ye the death he died,
He died by a dagger, for daggering was his pride.
Oh Alexander, Alexander, the buccaneer for pelf,
He conquered the world, then finally quenched himself.
He must have died a death glorious and fine.
Deep he drank his death in a herculean bowl of wine.
Napoleon was a man who loved to wade in blood,
Ceasar was a captain who loved a crimson flood;
Alexander was a man of glory and renown,
And all his glory lay in tearing kingdoms down.
Each one of these heroes was a bold and daring bandit;
Grant raised no war but coolly stood and scanned it,
Until his mind had grasped the bloody situation,
Then he coolly took the reins and pacified a nation.
He was the same wherever chances found him,
Though the bloody field or cabinet surround him.
Oh, Grant, he was the same wherever he has been,
Whether dressing rebels, or a calf's soft and tender skin.
He died in time of peace with a country full of friends,
                                        [amends.
The solid south mourned his loss, to make sincere
                Such is the tone of papers,
                And all such civil rapiers,
                That stab so very deep,
                With many a fiendish sweep.

THIRD.

WEST POINT.[*]

At West Point, Hiram gained admission,
By another man's official position,
He went to ask the situation,

---

[*] In Hiram's family, besides himself, there were two girls and boys,
They lived long and all grown old—partook of many joys.

So he could change his occupation.
He was so low in public esteem,
That he that gave it thought him mean.
He remarked at Hiram's request,
"You'll lose it at your very best."
Old Hamer, with a twinkling eye,
Told him all the reasons why.
A youth of more than his talent had
Gone in good and come out bad.
Therefore he could not stand the press,
Much more a youth with talent less;
"And if your visage does not gull,
I think you are extremely dull."
But never wilting, Hi' insisted,
And at West Point was enlisted.
And as old Hamer gave his consent,
Thus he condoled him ere he went:
"Ere you enter that hopeless place.
I'm sure you cannot win the race."
But Hiram counselled like a seer,
Saying, "Of my future have no fear
I will capture state with little treasure,
And study West Point at my leisure,
The power of enemies I will defy,
On myself alone I will rely,
I'll do what duties in my power,
And use my time to every hour."
He went—was ushered in,
A place surrounded with military din.
But as he entered West Point gate,
Changed was his name from that date.
Mistakes could change his humble name,
But he unaltered, was the same.
Let us stop a moment to moralize in,
To change his name, was it surprisin'?

They scarcely noticed him at all,
Except his name upon the wall;
And as they read it o'er in jest,
In merriment it was expressed.
He told them that it was a rake,
The handiwork of some mistake,
His name was not U. S. at all,
As ledgered down upon the wall.
So he was bound to let it stay,
As entered on the books that day.*
His progress at West Point, as a rule,
Was sturdy, as at the Georgetown school;
Never brilliant; but steady he rose;
One by one he conquered his foes.
One thing his progress made complete,
He never was know to retreat.
His mind was like a mighty clasp,
It covered all within its grasp.
Never brilliant, always solid:
Never brilliant, never stolid.
In every duty faithful and true,
Well representing his navy blue.

The four years at West Point hunting education
Were four years of intense application.
He studied all the arts and sciences of war;
It was to know exactly what things were for.
He was led by close, studious application   [tion.
Through the various branches of an English educa-
By hard study, lessons he also wrung
From the French and the Spanish tongue.

---

*At West Point, when he was ushered in
The Hiram part of his name got straggled in the din;
Hiram into Simpson somehow got strained,
And why it was done has never been explained.
By a great man it never was expected,
How Hiram into Simpson was so curiously converted.
[See book, 'Remarkable Remarks on Grant.']

He also filled his warlike maw
With constitutinal, national, and international law.
Experimental chemistry and philosophy he did digest,
In mineralogy and geology he did his best.
In infantry and artillery was thoroughly drilled ;
        [guns, was filled.
With the uses of rifled, mortars, seige, and sea-coast
In the use of other arms he was uncommon wise:
Such as small-sword and bayonet exercise.
Along with the others he advanced as far
In field-works, fortifications, and munitions of war.
Then we find him wrapped in another tex',
Learning the art of drawing and dabbling in ethics
  Thus by long and severe training, he
  Was able to meet the foes by land or sea;
  For human woes and passion's wrath,
  Lies stretched across each mortal's path.

Such are the legends floating down on the river of say,
Swelling in volume, as it sweeps to the present day.
From to-day a hundred years, they know more of him,
Than ever was known in his war-battling din.
They'll make fun of us for not knowing our men,
They'll stuff our skeletons with the paint of their pen,
They'll discover points in a far distant time,
That I dare not pen in this truthful rhyme.

 Finally his love military was satiated,
 In June, Forty-three, he graduated.
 Of course he would ordinarily pass,
 Ranking about the middle of his class.
 The United States army he immediately entered,
 His rank in brevet second lieutenant centered.
  As a supernumerary Infantry lieutenant,
  Far to the west to join a company he went.
  On the frontier of Missouri's wild territory,
  Where the Indians roamed in scalping glory.
  In the neighboring years of Forty-three,

The west was a carnival of murderous glee.
All acts were due to meanness then,
Hateful deeds were done by vagish men.
The Indians in their degradation,
Knew no art of discrimination.
The guilty and innocent both alike,
Fell under the tomahawk and pike.
In ambush they often laid,
Many a victim they burnt or flayed.
To look on their vengeful strains,
Curdles the blood within my veins.
Their war costume was painting red,
With gaudy feathers on their head.
What grand progress they had made
In counterfeiting, the de'il's trade.
The Indians got it down so fine,
The de'il knew not the genuine;
Which made him stretch his goggle eyes
In consternation and surprise.
It seemed that hell on earth had scowled,
Women and children were embowelled.
At many a scene, bold pioneers
Bathed their cheeks in salty tears;
Turning youthful hearts of tender mold
To butchering fiends, stern and cold:
Until the Indian race at last,
Is but a horror of the past;
Passed into a wild unknown,
Where spirits people it alone;
Where it is, or where it lays,
No Indian bible ever says.
Our bible as a book contains
The spirit resting-place of man's remains.
(For Indian bibles, blood or war,
Is not what this poem's for.)

Oh, wandering pen now return,
And all bloody subjects spurn,
Oh, spurn to note the bloody trade
That causes man to wield the blade.
Oh, butchering fiends of the human race,
Why will you your souls disgrace?
Why will you in mighty deeds,
Proclaim the sword a king of creeds?
Let every man in justice deal,
And fling away the murderous steel;
Let love in its true courses run,
And fling away the murderous gun.
But it's no use of moralizing,
And dull my pen in its exercising;
For it seems but few people heed me,
And for advice but few e'er need me.
Lieutenant Grant, almost two years passed,
In Missouri's solitude, dreary and vast,
　　Where Indians and buffaloes roamed at will,
　　And murder was committed along every rill,
　　And blood shed, streamed from every hill.
Of Lieutenant Grant it was truly said,
"He never shot an Indian nor scalped a red."
　　　But in the distance, far beyon',
　　　A cloud was gathering on our horizon.
　　　In the southern distance, see it grow
　　　O'er the boundary lines of Mexico.
Death and disaster lies among
The people o'er which this cloud is hung.
Texas, with a fierce and motley horde,
Shines up her gun and draws her sword;
And without a declaration,
Commences pounding at a nation.
To this place, infantry Grant was sent,
As a full commissioned second lieutenant.

And history says he did arrive
In Eighteen Hundred and Forty-five;
And long he did not have to wait,
For tumult clamored o'er peace's gate.
Upon the banks o' the Rio Grande,
Two sword-drawn armies stand:
And as her floods rush along,
It keeps the mighty from the strong;
For plain in history it is seen,
The river pours her floods between.
But a small American garrison without a town,
Got up a fort and called it Brown.
But Mexicans with warring sport,
Hurled lead and iron upon their fort;
And their bomb-shells of modern size,
On wings of powder rode through the skies;
And then to make the Americans shiver,
The Mexicans boldly crossed the river;
And in front and rear of Fort Brown they thunder,
Those cut-throat greasers, six thousand in number;
Then twelve miles away, at Fort Isabel,
Taylor knew that Brown was catching hell:
For well he knew the greasers were strong,
Their knives were sharp, and their bayonets long.
Old Major Brown you may well guess,
Burnt much powder in distress.
At intervals he heaved a sounder,
A well-loaded eighteen-pounder;
And they came at stated times,
Loud and bellowing were his signs;
For well he knew that greaser knives,
If taken, would rip out their lives.
All Americans were treated as a spy,
If captured, they were doomed to die.
All night long, old Brown, the major,

Distress signals loud did wager.
He was a'feared,
Himself and men were scared.
Lieutenant Grant then of course
Was with General Taylor's force,
And between, around and among them,
There were twenty-two hundred men.
At the dawn of day,
On the eighth May,
Showed that rear and van,
Marched man to man,
For Brown must be saved,
And the greasers caved
At once.
The greasers were no bubble,
And their comrades were in trouble
Could be seen.
As they press on eager and hard,
They hear the Mexicans' loud bombard ;
It tells them plain that their comrades are pressed,
To reach them they're doing their best.
The loud and bellowing cannons roar,
Proves that death o'er their comrades lower.
As the echoing boom of the cannons rebound,
It has an awe-inspiring, strange, weird sound
On the prairies vast as the storm-beaten sea,
O'er which the cannons roar with fantastic glee.
Not a tree on the plains to rest the eye,
Its a wide stretch of green, 'neath a blue, azure sky.
Such was the scene near the day's dinner-time,
When they encountered the Mexican's long battle line.
Taylor filed promptly into a long battle row,
Half a mile in front of the fierce, bloody foe.
Oh, what a plain, so vast, level and true,
Not a thing, not a thing to obstruct the view.

But the long prairie-grass, by the breeze kept in motion,
Like the low, gentle billows that ripple an ocean ;
Not long did the foes expectingly stand
In idleness to view a scene so grand.
So still and silent they scarce draw a breath,
As they nerve themselves for the harvest of death.
The drawing of the sword, with its small auxiliary,
And the booming reply of the fierce artillery,
Showed that the reapers of death had begun.
In the wave of the sword and breath of the gun.
Artillery was the main weapon used,
And the common soldier was the main man bruised.
Among their missiles and dangers of war,
Artillery was the only thing that carried so far.
The best generals among the Americans did rate,
And their guns carried metal of much more weight.
With this 'vantage, our round shot, grape and shell,
Tore through Mexican ranks with a deadlier tell.
Greater safety the American infantry found
In throwing themselves flat, face first on the ground.
O'er their head, sung many a Mexican shot,
And many more fell far short of the spot.
The Mexicans stood it with stubborn despair
On their part, what a suicidal, foolish affair.
Their blows on the Americans fell scattered and light,
As they stood up for targets, in their efforts to fight ;
For the Mexicans were not aware that their shot
Didn't reach, go over or fall on the spot.
But at this juncture of fierce battling strife,
The prairie-grass started into wild, hideous life ;
Its flames leaped up and soared on high,
Turning to darkness, the clear, azure sky ;
Darkening the sky to a deep, sullen gloom,
Smoking the sun till it looked like a moon.
Its flames leaped up with a sparkling and roar,

Like the surge of an ocean, on a rock-bound shore.
Its flames resembled a storm-beaten ocean,
When its waters are heaving in wild commotion.
Its flames leap, they twist and extend,
As if Satan alone were its intimate friend.
No power had man to look at his foes,
As the covering of smoke o'er the armies arose.
One army knew not how the other was rating,
Enveloped in smoke, to the verge of suffocating.
The sun on the work looked shabby and mean,,
It descended with night, and closed o'er the scene.
Now let us look o'er Palo Alto's plain,
To number the missing and count the slain:

> The greasers in death that turned up to view,
> Numbered two hundred and sixty-two.
> Now, notice ye how the Americans were billed,
> Thirty-two missing, and only four killed
> Ah, heed ye well the bloody sequel,
> As foe to foe they numbered equal.
> All this din and hideous rattle
> Only shows us Grant's first battle;
> And little chance had he to wield
> Glory upon such a battle field.

Oh! for wood to try my tools
Upon this warring lot of fools.

> At night the Mexicans ceased to fire,
> Then back to the rear they did retire;
> The dewy night was fresh and balmy,
> As they posted in Resaca-de-la-Palma.

In that ravine, with dwarf oaks surrounded,
So numerous the oaks in denseness they abounded.

> Taylor went cautiously hunting for them,
> With drawn sword and guns, to war them;
> He stumbled into them, stirring up their picket,
> Snugly stowed away in an impenetrable thicket;

He dusted that brush with cannon-ball,
Then the soldiers charged in and took it all.
Decided was the victory that the greasers lost,
Killed and wounded, a thousand was the cost.
Though fiery and sharp is the American disposition,
                                        [pedition.
Yet they lost one hundred and fifty in this gunning ex-
It took all their gunning, racket and rattle.
For the greasers to get up Grant's second battle.
Then when the greasers thought it complete,
They got up and skipped in a lively retreat.
The Americans on the left bank o' the Rio Grande,
One hundred and forty miles footed it on land.

> And then crossed o'er
> To the other shore,
> As down they bore
> > On greasers;
> And then advance
> O'er prairie's expanse,
> > Like a band of Cæsars.
> Ah, they march down
> On Monterey town,
> And there they foun'
> > Ten thousand troops,
> > With shouts and whoops,
> And swords and gun,
> They tried to make the greasers run.
> > The Mexicans staid,
> > Were not afraid
> > Of gun or blade.
> The Americans tried,
> Fought and died,
> > Their blades were long,
> > Their arms were strong.
> The men Taylor led,

Fought and bled,
But never fled.
    Six thousand then,
    Two-twenty men
Firm and determin'
To whip the vermin.
    And they, we suppose,
    Could whip the foes,
    And reek them woes,
And take the town,
And tear it down.
    Near which they loiter,
    And reconnoiter,
The town they spied,
Well fortified,
And would be tried,
    If men would labor
    With gun and saber,
And bring them to bear,
Their walls to tear.
    It was a decender,
    And well I remember
    Sunday noon, September,
The twentieth day,
And here I will say
    After a fashion
    Of roaring and smashin'
In a four days conflict,
The dead were ricked,
And the greasers licked.
    Whipped, so it's stated,
    Till they capitulated.
The city was smashed,
Bombarded and crashed,
Where the cannons flashed,

The natives were hashed,
Where the small arms clashed.
The wounded greasers lay scattered around,
Vast destruction everywhere did abound.
Grant in this battle, we are told,
Showed himself useful, fearless and bold.
(By esteem, in West Point he could rule
The boldest riders in that academic school.
Of him, it was said, in the far away East,
While sitting the horse, he was part of the beast:
And he lost none of his horsemanship in the territory,
Among the Indians, in wild Missouri.)
The brigade at Monterey, in which he commanded,
The powder nigh exhausted, more they demanded.
[all,
They were in the heart of the city, with no egress at
Only by a narrow street, under a gun-covered wall,
Which the Mexicans held in barbarous pride,
Shooting footmen and all that may hitherward ride.
For they held one side of the street of egress,
While the Americans hard on the other side press.
[your.
They longed for the Mexicans, their strength to de-
While death and destruction hung dark o'er the hour.
Who ever went to order ammunition's supply,
On running this gauntlet they had to rely.
The general in command, gave orders to none,
A volunteer he called for this gauntlet to run.
So up stepped Grant and offered to serve,
Determined to go, but never to swerve.
So mounting a steed, fleet as an eagle's wings,
He spurred through the streets, for Walnut Springs,
Which was in the suburbs, four miles away,
Behind the horse, like an Indian, in safety he lay.
By the mane he held on, also his foot,

Steadied his body fast to the crup.
In an hour he returned, according to all wishin',
With an escorted wagon, loaded with 'munition.
On the greasers, the Samites wreaked vengeance of war,
Corpse-strewn was the city, and blood ran afar.
                                        [awful,
The carnage among the greasers was tremendous and
                                        [unlawful.
And e'en to describe it nears the verge of something
Heads and arms lie scattered in the ditches,
Gnawed by dogs and their mother bitches;
And great was the number of Americans consumed,
To lay wrapped in dust of a romantic land, entombed,
                For then
Fell twelve officers and one hundred and eighty men;
And many more were sabered, shot and scared,
Many wounded light and many wounded hard.
(Oh, strange is it that man in war will delve,   [helve.
Bathing their daggers in blood, from reeking point to
Strange is it that man, with all his loving nature,
By contrary words turns to a deadly creature.
Take reptiles, snakes of all the poisonous kind,
                                [poison combined.
And they are naught to man's deceit, with all their
                But in war or peace
        Man loves to serve in a deadly lease.
        Soldiering man honors the trade,
        To work a gun or use a blade.
        My thoughts to exercise, are out a canterin',
        Viewing nature by the moon's great lantern;
                And here let me own,
        The nature I view is man alone.)
But it's the third in which Grant e'er took a hand.
        Thus he was led through flame and fire,
        To cap the climax of man's desire.

But little then did the world suppose
He was the man to strike such blows,
That a nation wept and armies bled,
And the world shook with his martial tread.
He scattered rebels, with great disaster,
And proved to the world he was their master.
But time on his pinions bears rewards
In hatching statesmen, soldiers and bards.
Thus, Grant was a man the times had hatched,
And never by a military man was matched.
High on the rocks of fame's bold cliffs,
He plowed his name in artillery rifts;
He plowed it deep on the surface of fame,
So deep and lasting, it will ever remain.
But little then did the nation dream
In one man there was such a team.
A team in one man so mighty to haul,
The world stood gaping at a thing to appall.
With artillery planted across his path,
And faced by a nation's rebellious wrath.
He was the same in facing all,
Born to fame, and not to fall.
As a part of General Taylor's detached force,
In the capture of Vera Cruz, he helped seige it of course.
There it was the greasers caught it fierce and hot,
By lead and iron, from the lines of General Scott.
As the army was preparing to march to the interior,
(To the Montezumean halls, to palaces superior.
Something superior to any halls erected,
That from such a nation could ever be expected.
Halls that surpass our generous age,
That seem like a romance on history's page.
Where gold and silver was bounteous as tin,
But what is it now, where that luxury has been?
    The dagger and sword, cross and creed,

Destroyed the country, caused her people to bleed.
Her gold and silver vanished with utmost speed,
To quench the thirst of a christian greed,
    Oh, that ancient bible and holy cross
    Is mouldering away to worthless dross.
    The cross has turned to a whetstone grand,
    To sharpen the sword in the christian hand.
    And the bible has turned to a holy oil,
    To make the christian cauldron boil.
    The copper worked in that ancient clime,
    Assumed a luster with eternal shine.
    Now, this art of which I allude,
    Was an art of vast magnitude,
    Their copper of old was curious wrought,
    On it rusting canker never caught.
Her copper was wrought with a cunning hand.
Long corroding ages it could withstand;
But the power of her people was doomed to fall,
And strangers possess Montezuma's Hall.)
An honorable appointment to Grant was given,
To a regiment quarter-master he was risen;
Which brought him more into general view
Of the private men and commanders too.
At the bloody battle of Malino-del-Ray,
Fought the eighth of September, a bright sunny day.
Now I'll go on in this poem-i-zation,
And give you the facts of realization:
It was a day, a day of all others clear,
The nineteenth century's forty-seventh year,
Grant was promoted by his bravery that day,
On the bloody field of Malino-del-Ray.
That day on the greasers he so furiously smote,
To first-lieutenancy, grew his promote.
Always active, as a quarter-master, he would not yield
To stay in the grub-tent, and forsake the field,

He rode the fiercest, the fastest and the strongest,
The first to the front, where he stayed the longest.
        Better time than any he always made,
        The first to come, and longer stayed.
        He was the first the foe to meet,
        Would march forward, but never retreat.
        Thus the soldier's endless praise,
        In the civil war's latter days,
        But now you must expec'
        The battle scenes of Chepultepec.
                In that fierce strife
                Of wasted life,
                Where guns and sword
                And cannons roared,
                Where devastation
                Reeked deadly vengeance o'er a nation.
    Fought was that battle, the thirteenth day,
    Same month of Malino-del-Ray.
    His tactic sagacity while under fire,
    To a brevet of captain he arose still higher.
The greasers in courage were not exempt,
But what was to shield them from Samite contempt.
        Cannon-balls at them, the Samites threw,
        On wings of powder, along they flew.
        As they flew along, the earth they spurned,
        They mangled greasers, but never returned.
        Death and disaster followed each bomb
        That rode from the muzzle of each Parrot gun;
        For the American guns were long and dangerous,
        And were well manned by Texan rangers.
        The greasers drew the sword from its sheath,
        And threw it away to administer death.
        The Mexican's savage plundering son
        Gave no quarter, nor asked for none.
        Death seemed to be their only master,

With death they gloried in disaster.
When fell the city of Mexico,
Beneath the Samites conquering blow,
Then they faced their foreign guest,
Inviting him in peace to rest.
Then that bold, impetuous horde,
Looked up a scabbard to sheath their sword;
And since then they have never drew,
A sword on Uncle Sam, to hew.
The greasers were not slow to learn
To sue for peace which did return.
The Samite soldiers were recalled,
And back to New York harbor hauled.
Homeward they with joy drew,
Under wings of canvas, o'er the ocean blue;
Then in the city of New York,
From their vessels disembark.*

CANTO.

Now in brief.
A short relief,
From cannon ball,
And armied hall,
Surround us.
In tents of ease,
Free from disease,
The old veteran,
Fights his battles o'er again,
To astound us.
Wheeling here, and charging there,
Driving greasers in wild despair.

---

* Grant's service was commenced and ended,
And all his promotions that service ascended.
Was with the United States Infantry fourth,
That on Mexic', bore down from the land of the north.
Along the frontier of New York and Michigan,
Its companies were scattered, as only a regiment can.
Captain Grant, with his company in command,
At a point of defense, took up his stand.

THE LIFE OF GRANT.

On his arm a wound behold,
The greaser who did it in death lies cold.
They rehearse the scenes on Mexican fields,
The rattle of swords and crunch of wheels;
And the cannon-ball that screams afar;
The deadly missile of an armied war·
Also the soldiery's veteran hards,
Relate their success dealt in cards.
And how they stole from the greaser women,
And with their daughters went in swimmin',
And all the tricks that accompany war,
Three-card-monte and what it's for.

The deceiver,
Gold fever,
Rich and forlorn,
All started off for Californ',
Where old Cap. Sutter linked his name
And his servant, Marshall's, to a golden fame.
And that old mill-race
On Sutter's place,
Shall hold a page
In historic age,
It was the biggest find the world e'er knew,
The seeming worthless sand rich as a Jew.

On every hand
The country abounded in golden sand.
But lots of it has since been known
To have been pounded from the stone.
Every hill and every field
Seemed to produce a bounteous yield.
People thought one time their future kettle
Would be made of the precious metal,
It was so vast,
In abundance massed.
In the territory beside the pond,
Grant was stationed in Oregon.
Like a blear.
On the sluggish, wild frontier,
Grant resigns,
As the fortune-seekers delved in the mines.
Then of himself a farmer he made,

Working with the breaker, shovel-plow and spade.
                        Then a while,
He tried a business more mercantile.
Laying away his plow and spade,
He commenced business in the leather trade.
Educated by Uncle Sam he therefore could well afford
To quit his leather trade, and buckle on his sword.
And he would have been a very ungrateful whelp,

                                          [help.
To not have buckled on his sword when his country called for

FOURTH.

Marshall's shovel handle turned to a golden wand,
                                          [land.
The find he made for Sutter in that far away, distant
Oh, California! the land of romantic scenes,
To delight a painter's eyes, and fill a poet's dreams.
                Facts do not grow old,
                But damned and cussed
                Is he whose stay and trust
                        Is gold.
                Rich, glorious, precious gold,
                The worth of sand, the price of mold.
                It figures in field and fold,
                On its turnpike, wagons are told;
                Machinery by it is rolled,
                The government by it's controlled,
                Old age by it is consoled,
                The young by it are oft condoled,
                Many votes by it are polled,
                Bright, stern, beautiful gold;
                The scarcest of the worldly mold,
                Heavy of weight, lifeless and cold,
                Hard to get, and harder to hold.
        California, the hub of creation,
        Streams rush to it from every nation.

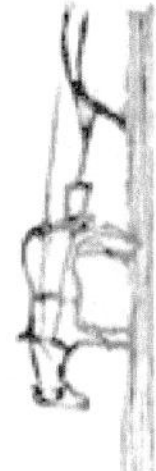

Gold! gold! was the one absorbing theme,
                                    [their dream.
It was their thought by day, the blossom of
For it, they dared the scorching of the sun,
                                    [be won,
To reach the land of gold, where fortunes could
For it they dared the inclements of life,
                                    [scalping-knife.
And crossed the Indians' country, beneath a
Gold! gold! was chanted in their lay,
Gold! gold! was their staff and stay.
Those gold-seekers knew no earthly friend,
Only what aid a shot-gun power could lend.
The gold-seekers, in rushing o'er the border,
Left behind them all semblance of order.
Old Judge Lynch predominated o'er all,
Death carried away the many he dared to call.
                                    [order,
To make those adventurers remember eastern
                                    [border.
To Oregon Grant was sent, way on the distant
Grant, with his vets' of Mexican fame,
Established himself in a wilderness of game.
The Indian's dance was war's infernal glory,
Near Fort Dallas, in Oregon Territory.
                                    [whites,
In the darkness of the eve, they crept to the
                                    [nights.
Then lurid were the scenes that illumined the
                                    [chased them,
But history does not tell us that Grant ever
                                    [to deface them.
Or that his sword leaped forth in revenge,
At Fort Dallas, the days were all the same,
Monotony ushered them in and drove them out again.

Dreariness ruled by day, and also ruled by night;
Dreariness was all the soldiers had to fight.
The active spirit of Grant, no pleasure there could find,
In short, it's said, he therefore, soon resigned.
From Oregon to St. Louis, we find he was a comer,
In the beautiful month, the month of middle summer,
                                            [dish, in
And the nineteenth century's fifty-fourth year, is the
                                            [mission.
Which he handed o'er to Uncle Sam his Oregon com-
In it he threw away the dagger to mortal bloody strife,
And turned his attention to a better and active civil life.
But first of all he persuaded Miss Dent to be his wife.*
And that happened just before a farmer he became;
                                            [name,
By occupation he was a farmer, but never deserved the
                                            [Missour',
He tried to farm near St. Louis, in the State of old
On its frontier he had soldiered many a year before.
Then what a sight that glorious general did show,
It proved that cadets into farmers seldom grow.
Being raised a soldier, he therefore, could not farm,
He liked it, but dimes were too scarce to charm.
                                            [toil,
He did not know how to succeed in raising bread by
                                            [to spoil.
For ere he got one side complete, the other was sure
His corn forgot, his wheat would rot, his potatoes spoil,
            Treasured beneath the loomy soil.
        Thus, by endless waste and pains,
        He found many troubles, and few gains.
        Then he threw it up not knowing how
        To wield a spade, or shove a plow
                To succeed,

* See book of " Remarkable Remarks on Grant."

In farming for all that he should need.
Then with his father in the leather trade,
He threw away forever the plow and spade.
In it he won some leather renown,
In Illinois at Galena town,
And that leather firm began to run.
The year before the bloody sixty-one,
The year that peace melted into war,
When the insulting blows on Sumter growled afar.
  The men that fired the first tragic cannon-ball,
  With wild, wide insults it smote on Sumter's wall,
  It was the key-note to a long and bloody ball.
  And the managers of that long and bloody dance.
  Some have gone to hades, and others visited France.
Oh, it was a dance, a civilizing riddler,
Where every one in turn stepped up to pay the fiddler.
And Grant, it seems wore the laurels of a master,
For where'er he led, the ball grew furiously faster;
Though in his fights of each succeeding day,
To win, he'd cast a thousand lives away.
In that mighty civil war, an hundred fields ran red,
                        [gled dead.*

And an hundred thousand people mourned their man-
Educated under the patronage of the stripes and stars
Grant thought it right to be foremost in her wars,
To abandon all civil and domestic life,

---

*As I write,
This stormy night,
I see the papers say,
McClellan died but yesterday.
Stop a moment, let's enumerate,
 The great men that's met their fate:
Three great generals of the war,
That drove the rebels wild and far,
McClellan, Grant and McDowell.
Death on great men seems to scowl.
Of great poets, three or four,
And of painters, half a score;
Also a dry goods prince, or two,

And buckle on his sword when rebellion blossomed rife.
When rebellion fired on the national flag,
And insulted Fort Sumter, at the base of the rag,
    The fury of Grant run to a white heat,
    He unsheathed his sword, to never retreat.
    He was ready to obey his country's call,
    In the open field or behind the wall;
    He was ready his country's law to support,
    To dare the field, or storm the fort.
  Said Grant to the people and country at large,
    Had I a sword like the gunwales of a barge,
    And a cyclone, to wield it in time of a charge,
      It would be felt
    In a murderous, bloody, death-dealing gorge,
      At every pelt.
    My sword in the Mexican war I drew,
    I'll buckle it on in this one to.
    Uncle Sam, in this war I'll see him through.
      Though death and disaster,
    At our country and fire-sides may hew,
      We must be master.
Staunch and determined, in the streets of Galena,
That might awe the Flora soldiers imported from Xenia,
He speedily raised a company of volunteers,
Farmers, merchants, boot-blacks and auctioneers;
    And all his ambition in this motley band,
    Was to lead them as captain in command.
    In person he led them to Springfield, Illinois,

A greater than Claflin, there were but few;
Also Louis Riel, the rebel chief,
On a Canadian gallows, died like a thief.
Are present times going to deceive us?
Are all the great men going to leave us?
All this, death has done,
Since a few short months have run;
And none can tell what death may do
For the world, e'en me or you.

And offered his services along with the boys;
    And of course, Governor Yates accepted,
    What else of a great man could be expected.
Governor Yates at once recognized his station,
And desired his help and his coöperation.
In the wild excitement of volunteer organization,
        Which then
Was to be his untiring occupation
        Among them.
To rebeldom at once he became a pesk,   [desk.
When Yates, in the executive office, assigned him a
    His military perception was so very fine
    In military regulations and all its routine,
    That invaluable services he rendered at once,
    To the Adjutant-general, who was no dunce.
      He was so deep, so gentle and wise
      To regulate and reorganize,
      The world at large he did surprise,
          By the fact,
      That rebeldom, by his power, was racked.
      As a field commander, high he stood,
      In qualities, both stern and good.
      As in after days told his led,
      How the rebels from him fled;
      Their horses 'neath their saddles fretted,
      As the sabers against their haunches whetted
      From the field he could not be spared,
      Where shell and sword he boldly dared.
      His education in that line, so rare,
      In the field it placed him there.
      At first he held a wandering station,
      Commanding several camps of organization.
      The twenty-first regiment of Illinois,
      Was a volunteer lot of demoralized boys,
Through circumstances peculiar, they'd been wrecked,

From them, no great thing could the state expect.
Governor Yates was stern in his demand
For efficient officers to assume the command.
The colonelcy to Captain Grant he gave,
He promptly accepted it like a brave.
Here, his commission in dead earnest begun,
The fifteenth of June, eighteen sixty-one.
That regiment, beneath his touch,
In ten days was strengthened much.
Up to a thousand men it come,
To a regimental maximum;
And in discipline, it quickly gained
What volunteers ne'er yet attained.
This regiment started on its trip
To Missouri, o'er the Mississipp',
To guard the Hannibal & Hudson rail,
That wild and lonely, dangerous trail,
That led through Missouri's northern land,
Where John Pope was then in command.
Than this no rail in the state grew harder,
That run through the state, to Kansas border.
To usher this chapter in,
One thing was sure of Grant,
He never knew the power of can't,
In wars infernal din.
When Grant arrived at this position,
To own a high-titled, sound commission,
He knew exactly how to use it,
And by law to not abuse it.
It was no magic or a ghost
That made him commander of a post,
But Congress and our laws.
He was a soldier, keen and strong,
And wore a blade sharp and long;
With a foresight keen and far,

To see the shape of a coming war.
He turned his claws to meet the foe,
And dealt them one long, bloody blow
　　　　With eagle-like determined claws.
But by the law's infernal rope,
He was a colonel, under General Pope.
John Pope was the Missouri lad
That made bushwhackers feel sore and bad.
It was Grant, with his well-trained mob,
That fortified and garrisoned Pilot Knob;
Then from there to Ironton, Mo.,
Thence to Marble Creek did go,
Which it garrisoned in state,
Then for the rebels laid in wait.
Thus his time was wholly consumed,
Before into generaldom he had bloomed.
When his generalship really begun,
Was May the seventeenth, sixty-one.
From his regiment he was detached,
Then from Missouri he was snatched,
And then to Cairo was despatched.
For that was a point of all others in the world,
Where rebels into a neutral state were hurled.
Cairo held beneath her guns' iron grip,

　　　　　　　　　　　　　　[sissipp';
All the rebel navigation that climbed the Mis-
It was a key to the long and broad Missour',
And all the waters that mingled with her before.
It was a point, the grandest in the nation,
And to general over it the highest occupation

　　　　　　Of any in the army.　　　　[stormy,
Because the rebels were determined, rough and
When Cairo first, by General Grant was led,
Kentucky was a neutral state, so politics have said.
So at once Kentucky became a bug-a-boo,

For in that state was a rebel rendezvous.
Columbus and Hickman they fortified,
In all the glory of an infant rebel's pride.
And Bowling Green, on the big barren river,
They fortified it, to make the Yankees shiver.
When all this was done beneath our general's nose,
He prepared himself to strike some heavy blows.
Paducah, he struck her in the face,
And drove away all the rebel race;
Then on September sixth, he occupied the place.
Paducah, it is plain to you and me,
Is in Kentucky, at the mouth of Tennessee.
And within ninety well generalled days,
Glory be to Federal arms and ways.
They took Smithland, and blockaded southern land;
[helping hand.
And kept the northern sympathizers from lending a
And I really think, I do surmise,
They were good bases for supplies.   [hag,
When Grant struck Paducah, and captured the rebel
O'er many a residence floated the rebel rag.
These flags were waving in the breeze, of course,
Expecting to welcome a rebel force,
Which was said to be hurriedly marching along,
In a column, nearly forty hundred strong;
And this mighty, rebellious, gunning band,
They supposed were almost, right at hand.
But with cheerful, joyous whoops,
In rushed the jolly Yankee troops.
The loyal citizens kicked the rebel hag,   [rebel rag.
And, from o'er their erring brothers tore down the
I think I should go on, and tell as much as
All the important points fell into the Yankee's clutches.

PROCLAMATION.

All ye, about this rebel station,
Read ye this civil proclamation.
I come here with a few fighting men,
Not as an enemy, but a fellow-citizen.
I am not here to annoy or maltreat,
Or trample civilization beneath an army's feet.
But an army in rebellion against our common laws,
Have taken possession of you with her bayonetted claws.
They have planted their guns right upon your ground,
And have already flung their deadly missiles around.
Columbus and Hickman are in the rebels' hands,
And they are stationed there, in deadly, daring bands.
They might come out and chase themselves this way,
And fall upon your city and take it if they may.
I am here to defend you, and every righteous cause,
And support the government and all its common laws.
Opinions, I have nothing to do with them,
Only with armed, rebellious, fighting men.
And all their aids and abettors,
With their spotters, and their setters.
All the loyal, without molestation,
You can pursue your usual avocation.
The government's arm is powerful and long,
Her swords are sharp, her bayonets are strong.
It is here to protect its friends,
And on the rebels to make amends.
When you are able to protect yourselves
Against those rebellious, marauding elves,
And run your government as you ought,
And as your law-books long have taught,
I'll withdraw the forces under my command.
Note ye this, my seal and hand.
Late from Cairo landing,
U. S. Grant, Brigadier-general commanding.

The tone of the above proclamation,
Shows well the soldier and his station.
He used no power, only enough,
He gave none, and took no guff.

GENERAL GRANT AT CAIRO.

In flim flaws,
And gewgaws,
Grant would never attire,
His clothes would lay,
Thrown on as one may,
While under a chafing rebel fire.
They seemed to be flung on,
Caught as they hung on,
And never adjusted.
In place of a military hat,
An old stove-pipe sat,
Gay trappings he never trusted.
No military hat, with golden cord,
Ever pressed his thoughtful for'd;
But a "stove-pipe," old and worn.
None of his subordinates
Would have dragged it o'er their pates.
But few knew Grant's greed
For the Havana-Indian weed.
Between his teeth he always kissed 'em;
From his lips, one never missed 'em.
Grant would smoke his cigars
At home, in or out of doors;
He smoked them for all they were worth;
He was a smoker from his birth.
Between his teeth they loosely fit,
And always brightly were they lit.
With now and then, a smiling cup,
To gently wind his spirit up.
I may be wrong, but yet I'm right,
Grant's was surely, a smoky "stove-pipe."
Beneath its brim, it always fumed,
From his mouth it always loomed,

He thought oftener of the cigar at hand,
Than this and all the rebel land.
As he smoked, he always thought,
Therefore, miracles among men, he wrought.
Several reconnaissances now were made,
Common to the warlike trade.
And many skirmishes ensued
With prisoners it did include.
Both sides had prisoners taken,
As o'er the country, each went rakin'.
Which caused the roaring rebs
To correspond with fighting Feds.
Each one for his victim laid,
Each one had some men to trade.
Man is currency in time of war,
Man for man is traded for.
When politics need a physician,
They call for men, grub and 'munition.
And when together an army hoards,
They shine their guns and whet their swords;
And swear at their opposing foes,
And march about the camp in rows.
And in their mind, from post to pillar,
They chase their foe from rock to willer.
And every tree they hide behind,
The searching foe is sure to find.
Chasing them from oak to pine,
Capturing the army to break their line.
Thus, the rebels for Grant laid,
Therefore Grant at Cairo stayed,
Until things grew more complete,
Until he dared the foe to meet.
He will meet them in due time,
And fall on them, in battle line.
When foe to foe will unsheath the sword,

And meet in one vast, bloody horde.
When sons shall their fathers gall,
And brother on a brother fall.*
   October the sixteenth, sixty-one,
   Colonel Plummer's march begun,
   From his station, Cape Girardeau,
   Way out in the barbarous State of Misso.
Orders from Grant made him march down,
   Through Jackson, Dallas and Fredericktown.
While Colonel Carlin moved in another direction,
To catch Jeff Thompson's north-bound section.
   On October's day, number thirty-one,
   The rebels were licked, into a run.
The position of Jeff Thompson's rebel force, [course.
Was all Grant wished for, he therefore, learned of
He found the rebels collecting like type flung in a font,
In Missouri State, at the station of Belmont.
He thought he would go o'er and give them a rehearse,
To scare the rebels and make their men disperse.
He had no love for them, prowling around Missour',
To help their brother rebs beat the Yankees soar.
   So two brigades he took along as guards,
   To disperse the Belmont rebel hordes.
He commanded one brigade, McClernand took the other,
Upon the battle field .they backed up one another.
   From Cairo, November sixth, they left,
   By steamboat prows, the waters then were cleft.
   In the highest spirits they moved along,
   Each soldier a host, determined and strong.

---

* What's all this blood and carnage for,
To christen it a civil war?
Show me in it something civil,
And then I'll prove each saint a devil.
I'm no doctor, judge or jury,
But sin, I'm sure, is mixed with glory;
That is if glorp to be good,
Must be bathed in human blood.

To protect the right, and punish the wrong.
The next morn, at eight o'clock,
Grant and McClernand unloaded their stock;
Their precious stock, of two brigades,
With loaded guns and sharpened blades,
A line of battle at once they form,
As deadly as death ever painted a storm.
At once they advance, the foe to dare,
And deal him death in his dangerous lair.
They found the rebels there to meet them,
In force commanded by General Cheatham;
But they knocked the rebels through their camp,
And sent them off on a rapid tramp;
While a twelve gun battery they took,
As they, the rebels, their camp forsook.
The rebel baggage, by the Yanks was not forsaken,
Their camps were burned. and their horses taken;
And several prisoners were captured for
The Yankees to boast about prisoners of war.
I vow those prisoners were right in the way,
Why didn't they chase them off, and not let 'em stay
To eat up the Yankee's salt-pork and beans,
And devour their salad, in shape of greens.
I'd made them prisoners till Gabe blew his horn,
And left them to sleep till time's last morn.
From Kentucky, in Columbus Town,
The rebels o'er the rivers came pouring down.
Belmont was covered by Columbus guns,   [tons.
Where she could hurl her metal, to the weight of
Columbus blockaded the broad Mississip',
And was dangerous to Yank's on a Belmont trip.
But for all that, Grant made them fag,
He whipped their soldiers, and got the swag.
His three thousand men, to the Belmont courts,
Were carried over in five transports.

Two gunboats convoyed them along,
To see that nothing to the steamers went wrong.
Many a shell in the convoy's hole was stowed,
That through the rebel lines, on powder rode.*

GRAND THANKS TO HIS SOLDIERS.

After Grant returns o'er the rebel border,
His soldiers from him receive an order;
He thanked them for brave deeds done,
And for the battles they had won;
He thanked each and all of them,
Prisoners, private and commissioned men.
And the dead, be it their lot,
Never their valor be forgot,
Until old Gabriel blows his horn,
On the eve of time's last morn.†

* GRANT TO HIS SIRE.

All of my colonels were brave to a fault;
They rushed to the fray, without stagger or halt;
The privates followed where they dared to go,
And ready to strike their heaviest blow.
Oh! such men, I am proud to command,
They're a brace and a stay to any land.
The horse beneath me sank and died,
Diseased with bullets, under the hide.
They played McClernand just the same,
They shot his horse and got their game.
We found the rebs no sneaking knaves,
They are a well-armed band of braves.
    About the fight,
    Am I right?
        Ah, listen,
Wounded, five fifties, killed and missin'.

† Grant's soldier's grew so bold,
A cannon-ball they would take hold,
    And chuck it in a cannon.
But rebel soldiers beat them bad,
A bridle and saddle to them they'd add,
    And ride them o'er an army;
    And as they sped,
    O'er the army's head,
They'd note the army's bearing,
    Some liked the fun,
    But every one
Declared it was quite wearing.

GRANT'S TROOPISTICAL ORDER.

In all the battles that Scott and Taylor fought,
Along with them, 'gainst Mexico I wrought,
Except in the battle of storming Buena Vista,
But the battle there, somehow or other missed me.
Sure at Belmont I found the rebels game,
Fighting Mexicans by the side of them are tame.
I never saw such gallantry on any battle-field,
To such gallant soldiers, be every battle sealed.
U. S. Grant to L. Polk,
Where arose Belmont's smoke.
Grant to Polk, on the Belmont fight,
Asked him to deal his wounded right;
Bind and splint their broken limbs,
And get them again upon their pins.
Show no inhumanity to man,
Deal him right whene'er you can.
The rebels to Grant, Polk this at him,
From the field I've gathered them in,
And every man
I will take care of, best I can
To help the wounded and bury the dead.
You can assist as your message said.
Such a boon I grant with pleasure,
According to a warlike measure.
With a flag of truce high o'er your head,
You can entomb your mangled dead;
And help the wounded, all you find,
Keeping my wounded ones in mind.
When General Halleck reached his glory,
In commanding more territory.
General Grant's true warlike vim
Was quickly recognized by him.
Halleck went the rounds of an organizing tour,
Then Grant got more territory than he ever had before.

"The district of Cairo," the one that Grant commanded,
A foreigner might say it was "immensely landed."
 It took in all the counties of warring old Misso',
 That extend south of wild Cape Girardeau;
 And all of southern, or Egypt Illinois,
 That turned out so many warlike boys;
 And all of Kentucky, west of Cumberland,
 Whose waters roll over shining sheets of sand.

DRILLING SOLDIERS.

  It was surprising
How Grant at once began reorganizing.
He moved like a magic. ruling vision,
All were under his copious supervision.
At all the training and rehearsin',
Grant was always there, in person.
When recruits understood command,
He dropped them from his moulding hand.
Some place then, for them was picked,
Somewhere in his wide district.
Therefore, all of his command,
Was directly in his hand.
  Now, the year of sixty-one
  Have begun, we've seen it run,
  Old sixty-one, a long farewell,
  See what sixty-two can tell.
  Let sixty-two be ushered in
  'Mid a war like battering din.
  Bloody fields and cannons are
  The aspects of a cruel war.
 It seems to me that nations sinned,
 When with blood they are begrimed.
 But ever since the world has stood,
 Contending armies fought for good.
 (Where is all the good they've gained?

Nought but the sword have they maintained.)
And every army invoked God's aid,
To inspire its dangerous blade;
Or assist them in their trade.
But I'm sure it is not right,
I cannot see it in that light,
God made man, man made his blade,
But God assists in no such trade.

1862.

Now, sixty-two, we'll introduce,
Her bloody sword is no excuse;
War and famine it does produce,
        Where e'er it camps;
And men in peace it does confuse
        Where e'er it tramps.
Where cannon-ball screams through the air,
Like hell-bound spirits in dark despair,
Submerged in brimstone's hottest fire,
        To roast ;
Or is it a heavenly God's desire,
        A spiritual toast.
If God made hell for man to swim in,
God bless the army and Mormon women,
May they kill one another, to keep from sinnin',
        To purge the earth,
    And burn the flax to destroy all linen
        For holy mirth.
    There's nothing good, or nothing bad,
    If shooting men don't make one sad,
    And make the world at large feel mad
        At one another.
    It makes even a tender lad
        Despise a brother.
    But it seems that warring must be done,

To quell some war that has begun,
When a brother shoots a father's son,
        Hard is the scene.
And after once such deeds are done,
        They're hard to wean.
But let the world run as it may,
Wars have conquered to this day;
Always one side must give way
        To death's disease;
And some vast, long wrought affrays
        Are won with ease.
In every place, midst army hordes,
Disease destroyed more than swords;
Death goes for privates, well as lords,
        What a bore.
Death is sure to clip all earthly cords,
        If nothing more.
There's nothing in this world that's safe,
From a palace, down to a café;
One is a sea-sick homeless waif,
        Where sins are found.
All cash accounts with God are safe
        On sinless ground.
There's nothing in this world to trust,
Everything is bound to lust,
Or rot away with cankering rust,
        There's nothing strange.
Time's old-aged corroding dust
        Sticks like a mange.
Let us all do what we can
To peacefully aid our fellow-man;
And let the strife of warriors' wane
        And pass away.
The earth through warhood's almost run
        To welcome Millennium's day.

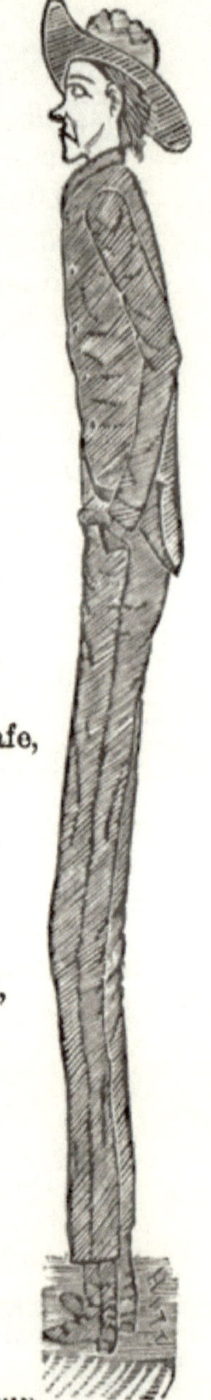

January 10, 1862.

ENERAL McClernand and all of his com-
        mand,
    Left Cairo in transports for another stand,
    Convoyed by two gunboats that went
        along,
To do the shelling, if things went wrong,
At Fort Jefferson, is where McClernand staid,
And off the Fort, the gunboat laid;
But Mr. Confed., with three armed vessels.
At them hurled some oblong deadly missiles,
That excited the Yankees to such a degree,
From Yankee wrath they had to flee.
They threw the shot without estimation,
Which threw the Yankees into devastation.
Wildly they flew from Yankee balls,
To a refuge neath the Columbus walls.

January 11, 1862.

The powers of Satan, to citizens lent,
Caused picket shooting to a frightful extent;
Blessings unended the pickets got,
Four of them that morn were shot.
Shot by some assassin's hand,
Defending by gun, their native land
Now, read ye Grant's noble orders,
Driving natives from his borders.
All citizens must now obey,
Leave my borders six miles away;
(Or come to our camp with your subsistance and stay).
This includes all ages, sex and size;
It's a shield for shot, a cure for spies.
Any one found in said territory, woe to his lot,
His property destroyed, and himself shot.
    Grant well knew it did behoove,
    That no spy should pipe his move;

He made three columns of his force,
Each under an able commander's course.
Hear ye the commanders that worked the same,
C. F. Smith, McClernand and Paine.
Thus, Grant for rebels went a-fishin',
In person he commanded the expedition.

GRANT'S ORDER.

Before venturing on his venture, which I venture to call an adventure.
This is my fervent wishin'
While absent on this expedition,
Almost wholly in a land of rebels,
We'll travel only thorns and pebbles,
And here we are, to now suppose
All we meet to be our foes;
All marching troops must keep in ranks,
O'er hills, dales, morass and banks,
All stragglers are charged upon
The company where he may belong.
No fires will be allowed in camp,
While on this long, dangerous tramp.
No, not a single bit of fire,
Only what duty may require
While in camp,
On this long and rigid tramp.
No privileges will be granted to officers or men,
Privates, captains, colonels, or any the rest of them.
Hard will be the reckoning day,
Tough on those that disobey.
Some brave boys have been disgraced
By a habit, I want erased.
As through the country, you march along,
Rob not the weak. because you're strong.*

---

* Oh, it's hard
That I must stop to just record
How death has kilt
William Henry Vanderbilt.
He did some mighty rousing things;
He was the prince of railway kings.
Are all the great men going to close
Their career in earthly woes
Before my pen
Finishes this book for the use of men.
December 20, 1885.

Destruction in a wanton way,
Such destruction cannot pay;
Private property, which lies along
The road we pass so very strong,
Destroy nothing, although
Nigh the road that you may go.
It demoralizes all that steals,
In towns, or lanes, or battle-fields.
One sympathizing with the south,
Why rob him to shut his mouth?
It's sure to make a deadly foe,
Into the rebel ranks he'll go ;
And pay you back with death and fire,
To satiate the man desire.
Man will not be trodden on,
When wealth and friends are gone.
Treat them well and make a friend,
Then their rebel mood will mend.
If they take no arms to fight us,
They are harmless and cannot bite us.
On them try no army patents,
Make them friends or non-combatants.
Quick the punishment, hard the fate
To those who steal or confiscate.
Privates shall pay for it dear.
And the officers much more severe;   [burn,
For they must leave the army, though sore their conscience
And leave their sword behind, to never more return.

An advance cavalry guard will lead
A flank guard, we also a rear one need.
To see that nothing drops in the rear.
Disabled soldiers, teams, baggage or cavalier.
Each day go into camp, every member accounted for,
Is the only true way successful in a war.
Such orders on the borders of rebeldom red,
And to be sure, nothing more than rightly said.
To obey, they say, an army should,
To last the blast and make it good,
For disorder is harder to cure than prevent,
And stealing is a feeling of sad discontent.
Unless their jaws and paws are full they will growl,

Then officers and men alike will howl.
Let us of, my soldiers, for rebels pant,
By Commander Brigadier-general Grant.
Grant goes out reconnoitering, thirty thousand strong,
All opposition before him, is onward borne along.
He went out among them, to view the rebs at home,
For he was well aware they ne'er could fight alone;
And well it's known they must have something to shoot,
And they must also be shot or killed to boot.
That is what constitutes a war,
The only thing they kill each other for.
Ah, what ruin and devastation,
Do such mighty armies cause within a nation.
Blood must pour,
And cannons roar
When two such armies meet;
The earth must scorn
That man was born,
When foes chase in retreat.

[man gore,
The saber's thud, and splashing mud mixed up of hu-
It is a sight, a horrid fright, to view a battle o'er.

[shapes,
The dead and dying fall, as they're lying in all imagined
Fire the cannon, hide the scene,
Behind one mighty smoke-wreathed screen.
Draw no pictures imaginary,
To the rules of war contrary.
McClernand leaves Fort Jefferson again,
Also from Paducah, moves Smith and Paine.
Their columns move in harmony,
It is one living human sea.
Flooded with ice was the Mississipp',
When Grant commenced this memorable trip.
But few can imagine the extent of the job,
To cross the river with such a mob.

The transports were hard to control,
Amid the ice that Gulfwards roll.
McClernand growled in Columbus' rear,
To fill the haughty rebs with fear.
The rebels thought the Yanks would come,
They could almost hear the flying bomb,
They make a feint to storm the town,
And tear the rebel raggery down.
The pole gently bending in the breeze.
That scarce would stir the leafy trees;
How boldly it flaunts its stars,
The rag that holds the hellish bars.
But Columbus, you must tumble down,
And every gun-infested town.
At the village of Blandville, K - y.
To fight the rebs, a ruse they try;
It was a success, far as it went,
The rebs were frightened and the Yanks content.
As McClernand's forces marched along,
Regiment by regiment was added on;
They were the troops under Smith and Paine,
The two commands were joined again.
The fifteenth of January, foggy and drear,
Encamped were the Feds in Columbus' rear.
Their camps a line of battle form,
As if ready to rush to the coming storm.
It was here General Grant fell in,
From Paducah, where he had been;
And in person, he superintended,
So right or wrong could be defended.
Back of Columbus, ten miles at most,
By two roads, they threaten that post.
Here, Grant divides his army,
The rebels think it will be stormy.
By the cloud the army casts,

It seems impossible to evade a blast.
The first division, so we learn,
Next morning, started for Milburn;
And then, their march they did extend,
As if to Mayfield, their way to wend.
But they didn't go, of course,
Cut southward, to Paducah's force.
Then onward, onward they clamored still,
Within eight miles of Lovelaceville.
And the day they did arrive,
Is the sum of twelve and five.
The nights of the eighteenth and nineteenth day,
They encamped at Bladesville, one mile away,
The next day they returned again,
Through mud and mire, sleet and rain.
Fort Jefferson received her troops,
With yells of love and friendly whoops.
Between the fourteenth and twentieth day,
Battle-equipped, and in camp array;
Eighty miles the infantry made,
One hundred and forty to the cavalry laid.
Many a time the soldiers tire,
Over roads of ice and mire.
The expressions of the soldiers were stronger than jolly,
The roads were but a string of soft loblolly,
The inclements of the stormy weather,
And frightful roads combined together,
Made it hard on such a lengthy tramp,
As performed by the troops under General Grant.
Their reconnoiter developed one pleasing fact,
                              [not packed.
That west of Paducah and Mansfield the rebels were
The power of Columbus it also did disclose,
A shadow of strength that we did suppose.
By roads, which on no map of the time appear,

Columbus could be attacked by several in the rear;
Along which large forces could move or haul
Guns to Columbus, and batter down her wall.
The fact is, the general truth to tell,
Columbus was a fort, of just the merest shell.
As soon as General Grant the facts about it learned,
He, with two columns, back to Cairo turned.
While McClernand's column kept along its course,
To show the enemy a mighty determined force.
        The reason that General Grant retired,
        He had learned all the facts desired.
    Many a gunboat was commenced in sixty-one,
    Which was finished now, and ready to be run.
    Above Cairo, they were built on the Mississip',
    Out of the reach of rebel's bold and daring grip.
To get men to float these monsters, mighty dangers',
For those gunboats were e'en salt water strangers.

CIRCULAR.

January 20, 1862.

        Oh, what a grand wholesale war retarder,
        Read ye this, Grant's important order.
    All of ye regimental commanders,
    Though born in Ireland, or far-away, distant Flanders·
        Hearken to this order, and immediately obey,
        Hand in your report, bring it right away.
        How many sea-faring men it does contain,
        And how many river men each can name.
        Let no officer raise an argument,
        But silently report, quiet and content.
        All of the men that may thus volunteer,
        Shall be discharged the ending of the year;
                Or I suppose,
                Sooner, if the war shall close.
        Seeing how important every boat may be,
        Steaming along the river, from interior to the sea.
                Then haste,
        E'er rebeldom, this country has defaced.
        We are all striving or warring to the knife,
        To put down rebellion or end its hateful life.

By war's peculiar moves, and battle's changing luck,
        [Kentuck',
In a few days, McClernand's force withdrew from old
And at Cairo, once more rendezvoused, [sloughed.
Where many an old soldier on whiskey-straight was
The district of Cairo, by military demand,
Temporarily o'er it, McClernand held command;
He was commander, so various authors say,
During the time that Grant is going away.
Grant is not driven, nor therefore is he decoyed,
But it is a journey he cannot well avoid.

FORT HENRY AND DONELSON.

A few days developed Grant's whole scheme,
And what was meant by the west Kentucky scene.
        [weary mile,
Where McClernand and his men marched many a
Through sleet, rain and snow, o'er roads of every style.
It must not be forgotten at this, or any date,
          [wait.
That at Smithland and Paducah the Yankees laid in
The rear of Columbus, they kept pelting at it,
Always moving amiss, just to make a hit.
The moves on Columbus, all were dummy ones,
They cared not for Columbus and all her mighty guns.
The gunboats in her front, the army in her rear,
It really filled the rebels with vigilance and fear.
When the gunboat's shells rode o'er, in howling proof,
Or descended on her, to try her sheltering roof.
No wonder then, that the rebs felt a shaking,
When the foundation of their very fort was quaking.
All the available troops that they could command,
To Columbus, immediately they did demand.
At Columbus, it was there, of course,

They concentrated all their available force ;
It was there that Grant had planned to toll them,
So he could more easily in another place control them.
    Grant had his men all well under hand,
    To strike another place in old Kentucky land.
    Grant issued an order here, read ye how tame,
    Issued to the army, also brigading the same.
    How many men now alive,
    Remember general orders, number five,
    For a temporary brace and stay,
    Is to know how an army at any moment may lay.

The first brigade with cavalry, artillery and all that at hand,
Will be under Senior Colonel R. J. Oglesby's command.
The second brigade, with all its necessaries in line,
With four siege-guns, to Colonel W. H. L. Wallace I do assign.
It takes those two brigades to make the first division,
Which shall be under John A. McClernand's supervision.
    (The third brigade is out, under E. A. Paine,
    But its hoped they'll all return again.)
The fourth brigade is similar to the others in its standing.
Only that it has Colonel Morgan tending to its commanding.
Cairo and Mound City are assigned to E. A. Paine's command,
With Bird's Point, to Colonel Morgan upon the other hand.
        By order of U. S. G.—B. G. C.
   JOHN A. RAWLINS, A. A. G.

To command Cairo, the power to Paine was lent,
By an order, an order subsequent.
    This order being publicly announced,
    So if it ever was to rebel fingers bounced ;
    (Of which the chances were very small.
    As you closer look there were none at all.)
    Then the idea would be plain to rebs,
    That above were all the trooping Feds.
So it would not in their vivacious memories bloom,
That this Yankee trick would leave them in the gloom.
Us, and our Yankee doings, to mind they'd never call us,

Or think of Paducah and Smithland, with C. F. Smith
[and Wallace.*
    Cairo was the army supplying place,
    And you may be sure Grant well secured his base.
        Second of Feb.,
        Woe to ye's, reb.
        Destruction soon must spe'd
        From Yankee's sword and flying lead.
        Oh, when will Fort Henry's walls grow red ?
        That rebels on her walls have shed ;
        Which from dying men have bled ;
        Where man to eternity is wed ;
        Death howls, and but little's said ;
        Where death on human life is fed ;
        With clay for winding sheets and bed.
Grant, from Cairo, in the darkness crept ;
If the rebels had known it, few would have slept,
They moved with a stillness that would baffle and scorn
The stillness that leads the approach of a storm.
From Paducah McClernand and Smith's division, also,
Shortly afterwards buckling on their trappings to go.
Onward they move to Fort Henry in front, aye,
Where rebels in ditches, lay snugly stowed away.
Here's an explanation I freely give thee :
Fort Henry's in Kentucky, near the line of Tennessee.
On the Tennessee River, there, like some daring beast,
[the east.
Fort Henry crouches on the bank, the one that's to
The gunboats had advanced to help in the great melee,
Down the river of Ohio, and up the Tennessee.
    Oh, such a dangerous and a mighty foe,

---

* Ex-Governor Hendricks, Vice-President,
  Has gone the road all great men's went ;
  He has crossed beyond the bourn,
  From whence no travelers e'er return.
  Death disturbs my pages oft,
  But honest death should ne'er be scoffed.

Fort Henry must fall beneath its blow.　　[o'clock,
On the morn of Feb. the sixth, at half past eleven
　　　　　　　　　　　　　　[knock.
The gunboats, with shells, at Fort Henry began to
Of course Fort Henry worked her every power;
And hot they made it two and one-quarter hour;
But they had to beneath our boats succumb,
For Foote, from his boats, hurled no little bomb.
Then the rebels thought they would get up and slide,
But at last they found they couldn't if they tried.
　　By that time Grant was in their rear,
　　Ready and prepared to give another scare.
　　So they lowered their stars and bars on rag,
　　And with their garrison surrendered up the swag.
　　One hour after Fort Henry capitulated,
　　Grant arrived, as all accounts have stated.
　　Over Fort Henry no one need to boast,
　　For it was like a picket to a post.　　　　[done,
It was only a commencement to things that must be
It was only a skirmish, compared to battles to be won,
For her troops had moved to support Fort Donelson,
General Tighlman and staff, with sixty men they won.

ON TO FORT DONELSON.

　　Grant had no time to rest upon his laurels,
　　If he would be teacher, teaching peaceful morals.
　　He ordered all the available troops at hand.
　　Against Fort Donelson, to join in his command.
And to join him on this perilous trip,　　[landed strip.
Between Cumberland and Tennessee, on Kentucky's
　　　　On the eleventh of February, so it's said,
　　　　Reinforcements from Cairo were quickly led.
　　　　As doll-babies are handled by maids,
　　　　He quickly disposed of them in brigades.
　　　　McClernand, the first division led,

The second by Smith was onward sped.
From Smithland moved the third division,
Under Lew Wallace's supervision.
    To Fort Donelson, is the cry,
    On sword and musket all rely.
    Sword and musket, blood and fire,
    Is a soldier's wild desire.
The Union forces were many thousand strong,
But as one man, determined, on they marched along.
Freedom! Freedom! was their only thought,
Bunker Hill and Concord's plain will ne'er be forgot.
    The flag that their forefathers gave,
    Was a gift, an emblem of the brave.
        And in no nation, friend or foe,
        Dare insult it with a blow.
        From Fort Henry, so they say,
        All the roads that lead that way,
        Whether metal, sand or clay,
            Armies fill them.
        Fort Donelson must fall a prey
        To the armies bound that way,
            Or kill them.
        They are moving, night and day,
          Horse and men.
The Union troops in line of battle form,
With determination as deadly as a storm.
The first division, the mighty right wing forms;
The second division, in line of battle warns.
All the rebels they fall upon, are cleft;
Then in line of battle, from Dover, on the right,
To a creek on the left, the army passes the night.
(Oh, battle-field, show me thy many charms,
Men in line of battle, slumbering on their arms.
In a line of battle, where all must stick together,
Through rain or snow, all inclements of weather.)

On February thirteenth, alas, for rebel power,
O'er Fort Donelson, there rained a deadly shower.
Fort Donelson's mighty guns had all her triggers set,
When up crept a gunboat, the Yankee, Carondelet ;
Then like the elements of warring weather,
They mixed their wreathing smokes together.
Thus, gallant men, by gallant deeds inspired,
Where many a man to the unknown world retired,
The Carondelet threw many a blazing bomb,
That sent many a rebel into kingdom's come.
                    Thus the sport
                    Between boat and fort,
                    For two long hours lasted ;
The boat well stood the iron showers,
Which seemed an age, those two long hours,
                    She then withdrew.
This gunboat racket most sublime,
Was only a racket to kill time ;
They did not only kill time alone,
But time and rebels with one stone.
The troops belonging to division third,
And gunboats yet had not appeared.
But all arrived that evening and night,
And prepared to join in the coming fight.
On Feb. fourteenth, at two o'clock.
At her walls, the gunboats flung their shot.
Their gunners then in sad dismay,
From the water batteries fled away ;
But the upper batteries' plunging shot,
For Foote and his boats grew hot.
The flagship got handled rough,
In that ugly game of bluff.
A wheel and pilot-house, entire,
Was wrecked beneath the rebel fire.
The other vessels, more or less,

Were battered into sore distress.
Thus Admiral Foote ordered all,
To follow him in quick withdrawal.
Thus, wound up the fourteenth day,
No rebel victory, or Yankee dismay.
Grant was determined the fort to infest,
To watch the rebels, while hunger did the rest.
But he had to change that very plan,
There was work next morn for every man.
    Charges bold, the rebels made,
    With bayonet and saber blade.
    On Grant's extreme right they fell,
    Like the surge of an ocean swell.
    It seemed as though they charged to stay,
    Two batteries of guns they carried away.
    The Union troops had to retreat,
    As on their front the rebels beat;
It seemed as though they couldn't be rated,
Where the rebel force was concentrated.
Where they fell in battle rank,
It seems all opposition sank.
(The ground, it was blood red,
Each soldier a fiend for bloodshed.)
But reinforcement their progress stayed,
They pruned the rebels with their blade;
A common work in a soldier's trade,
        For low,
In death many a soldier laid,
          By saber's blow.
The Yankee swords, by rebel blades were crossed,
Except three, they got back all the guns they lost;
But the rebels also reinforced their horde,
Then once more put the Yankees to the sword.
And like the ocean's surf a-beating on the sand,
The Yankees gave way because they couldn't stand.

On rushed the rebels, with all their main and might,
O, see the Yankee soldiers, how they retreat and fight.
The rebel's frightful yells, like mighty thunders roll,
Wiping out all music that enchants the warrior's soul
Other Union regiments were hurled against the reb.,
But they fell upon their friends, their comrades instead,
It was there a friend upon a friend descended,
O, it was a mistake that never can be mended.
    For it was there
Confusion was the only charm left them to inspire.
  So another brigade was hustled along,
  And fell into the same mistaken wrong.
  Before that rebel mass, they all retreated,
  And the Yankees were all but defeated.
    (For old Buckner,
     Bucked the Yankees out of fear.)
  But in another part, under Grant's command.
  On a rebel's footing, the Yankees stand.
  The rebels before the Yankees lay,
  But the Yankees drove the rebs away.
    And in their stead,
    Took their footing, by force of lead.
  The price of the day, this, the cost
  To the Yankee's it seemed the day was lost.
  In the Union lines, from front to rear,
  To an observer, things looked drear,
  But in them Grant saw no fright,
  The future seemed a rosy light.
  For as reports of various commands
  Fell into the General's hands;
  After they were compared and read,
  "Good," in joyous tones, he said.
  Oh, how quick we'll now deface them,
  In a better posish', chance couldn't place them.
He then ordered C. F. Smith to strongly assault,

And carry the left without default.
No matter at what sacrifice, carry the position,
On the right he showed the same disposition.
The lost ground he intended to gain,
And a solid position in front maintain.
With the rebel works direct before,
Where death could multiply its score.
Smith advanced without firing a gun,
His bayonets forced the rebs to run.
It was a hand to hand, a bloody fight,
Where Yankees and rebs exerted their might.
The assault was a destructive, daring deed,
Of one to excel it, we seldom read.
The works were carried, and the flag of the brave,
Floated o'er the works, with a joyous wave;
But the expense of its purchase, was dear,
It cost many an orphaned and widowed tear.
But it inspired the troops with courageous hope,
Burst enthusiastic cheers from every throat.
The heights were all, all carried by storm,
But the rebels received them spirited and warm.
But, notwithstanding the morning disaster,
The Union troops seemed to be the master.
Their position was much better than bad,
It was far better than they'd ever had.
The soldiers' bed that night again
On their arms slept every man.
So at the morn's break of day,
They could commence their deadly play.
By the tune of the musket's hum,
And the buzzing sound of the flying bomb,
On which rebeldom rode to kingdom's come.
Oh, what a din,
With an accompaniment of fife and drum,
To just fill in.

The soldier's groan and frantic curse,
Too horrible to e'en rehearse;
It was all bad, but might have been worse
　　　　For all.
New Andersonville prison's accursed force
　　　　Could appall.
For death it seems was prone to wander
All around, both here and yonder,
And seldom soldiers e'er stop to ponder,
　　　　How or when.
Death, for soldiers are fonder,
　　　　Than other men.
But when the morning sun arose,
To the Union troops it did disclose
A white rag flying o'er their foes,
　　　　To tell
Them of their dire, distressing woes.
　　　　The fort fell.
Buckner's letter, short and strong,
Seemed to Grant entirely wrong;
Or clearly I shall state to boot,
In no wise would Buckner's wishes suit.
The answer to Buckner, from Grant is noted,
On the breeze of the past to the present it's floated.
"To you, Buckner, one chance I'll tender,
And that is an 'immediate unconditional surrender.'
I'm no old dilapidated fogy of the ancient quirk,
I propose to move immediately upon your work.
　　"My men are a furious lot of bleeders,
And might have beaten you, if they hadn't changed their leaders.
This, and your overwhelming force,
Compels me to surrender now, of course
To your unchivalrous, ungenerous terms."
Thus the messenger, to Grant, with a letter returns.
　　　　So all that army, vast and grand,
　　　　Fell into the Yankee general's hand.

Buckner's lines were grand and long;
Of men alone, thirty thousand strong.
Floyd* and Pillow understood the lay,
So with a brigade† in the night they stole away.
And left General Buckner, with the total sum,
To do as he pleased, fight, surrender or run.
Frightful was the rebels' cost,
Three thousand horses in animals lost.
Of gun metal they lost their tons,
Seventy heavy, and forty-eight field-guns.
Of arms, twenty thousand stands, or more,
With a large amount of commissary store.
Of rebels, two hundred and thirty-one
Were shuffled off to kingdom's come.

But,

They had one thousand and seven shot, crippled or cut,
Of Union soldiers, four hundred and forty-six,
With dead soldiers of antiquity, did mix;   [five,
And wounded a thousand seven hundred and thirty-
                                                  [vive,
Many of whom were wounded so, they never did re-
Now, the Yankees, they did the thing up thrifty,
As prisoners they lost but one hundred and fifty,
      Talk about your fabled wars,
      And all such bloody frightful horrors;
But there were two regiments of Tennessee rebels,
That beat all soldiers that e'er tread on pebbles.‡

---

† 5,000 men. {* Was Floyd a thief because he stole away,
               { Or Buckner ignominious 'cause he lost the day?
         ‡ While I write,
            This storm-brewing night
General Hancock lies dead on Governor's Isle.
            For yesterday
            He passed away,
In true heroic, yet easy manlike style.
            February the time,
            The day is nine,
One thousand eight hundred and eighty-six.

Of the officers and men, strong and alive,　　　　[five;
There were one thousand, four hundred and seventy-
They marched along with their rag on high,
With their bands playing a bold defy;
They had been ordered to Donelson's Fort,
The rebel cause they went to support.
They had not heard of Buckner's beat,
Or Floyd and Pillow's coward retreat;
They had not heard that the Union men
Had jumped the rebel's claim from them.
But they marched right into the Yankee's core,
And learnt a trick they'd ne'er learned before.
The Yankees let them march into their ranks,
And captured that whole army of cranks.
Not a gun was fired, not a sword was drawn,
But their arms were taken, and their freedom gone,

REMARKS.

M[markable row,
ARKS and remarks about this re-
　　　Then and now,
　　　When and how,
　　　Dead and livin',
　　　All's been given.

Grant, the fiery and bold gossoon,
Played them a fearful and wild old tune.
He played it for the Confederate dance,
All rebeldom in yellow pants.
Sand lapper, secession and the Jew,
Oh, wasn't it a motly crew.
Their was but one lady invited to dance;
She has a statue on Bedloe, imported from France.
The imps of the south insulted the maid,
Therefore the soldier plied his trade.

The arrangements unmade
Where he's to be laid,
But all of those arrangements they'll eventually fix.

And sabered the south till they thought it wise
To comfort the maid, and apologize.
Her southern lovers, she grasped their hand,
And forgave the wrongs of their daring band.
What countless thousands of mankind,
Their graves in flying lead doth find.
And nigh them a mighty horde,
That bared their bosom to a sword ;
And in it what was their find,
Only to be destroyed by their kind.
For he that doth a-swording go,
Must perish by a sworder's blow.
War is now on tottering pegs,
All nations have drank of its dregs;
Ah, it harrows up my soul,
It makes the very blood run cold
To see men in such disaster,
Kill them slow, or kill them faster.
The image of a power divine,
Fellow-mortals of mankind.
Grant's mind was a great one, and soared on giant wings,
And showed he was a soldier, and far from little things.
All ye peaceful nations, waken,
The first millennium steps are taken.
See the infant try its toes,
Why does it wear such scanty clothes?
All the world seems to court it,
But not e'en a paper will support it.
All the world calls it a dude,
Because the creature is so nude.
And whether it's a lad or lass,
All kinds of judgement on it pass.
It will some day get wide and long,
And powerful as the world is strong.
Ah, the laureled wreaths that a soldier wears,
Are pruned by swords, and watered by widows' tears;
But all of this, in time of war is needed,
For in time of carnage can blood or death be heeded?
A bleeding country, in the hands of soldiers lay,
For truly, a soldier is his country's staff and stay.
Smiles to the soldier, his grim and sunburnt face,

It's he that teaches the world to know his country's place.
    Oh, sages and seers, stop a moment and rate,
    What countless thousands died to make Ulysses great;
    And the waste the country suffered then,
    Can ne'er be calculated by mathematic men.
    Men craved their fellow-mortals' flesh,
    And all that caused it was Union and "secesh'."
    Small those phrases, but wide as Uncle Sam,
    One was to enlighten, the other doomed to damn.
    But ere the chains of slavery could be rent asunder,
    The world was shook by ponderous, crashing thunder,
    And countless shells went screaming through the air,
    Leaving in their wake, destruction and despair;
    And many a solid shot, on wings of powder rode,
    Through a human mass, a swath of misery mowed.
The rebel fountains flowed at General Grant's command,
Like Horeb's rock, beneath the prophet's hand.
    Fountains that washed slavery's chains away,
    And shook the world with their mighty spray.
Remember, it was Grant, with stupendous cannon-balls,
That crept up to Fort Donelson, and thundered down her walls,
    Oh, wizard Jeff, of the southern land,
    Will Yankees retreat at your command,
    Can you lull the wild cyclone to sleep,
    Stay the rolling world, or chain the deep?
    The North, like the cyclone or rolling main,
    Holds the puny power in disdain.
    You can fire your guns at Fort Sumter's wall,
    Will that rend the fabric, so Uncle Sam will fall?
    Oh, wizard of the south, you do mistake its power,
    It braces up the country to stay some future hour.*

---

*SEYMOUR.

    The monster of the scythe and glass,
    Once more through our country pass.
    More hearts with sorrow filled,
    Governor Seymour, he has killed.
    It was two days before to-morrow, they say,
    He did the deed in broad, open day.
    Before rolls on an hundred years,
    He'll murder off our sages and seers.
    Why don't Congress pass a law,
    To break his neck, or crack his jaw,

This victory was more important than one could well suppose,
For Fort Donelson was the backbone of our foes;
Which left the two wings without a center to hold them,
Therefore, in a few days, the Yankee troops controlled them.
For, from Columbus, to Bowling Green,
Was a continuous, vast, rebel scene;
And they stood ready, in long, bloody files,
To heap the Yankees dead in piles,
In length, one hundred and twenty miles.
When the news of this victory reached Washington, D. C.,
The folks there were tickled so, they almost took a spree;
And below the despatch that told of glories bold,
On historic pages, may that passage be enrolled:
Wave, flag of the free
O'er Tennessee,
Never to be
Removed.
For this victory Grant received
A title, o'er which he never grieved,
A major-general of volunteers,
Slightly dated in the rears;
For, his commission, it begun
At the fall of Donelson.
Here, why not tell the story,
About the plunders of his glory.
The news in the papers seemed to spread,
Faster than balls of Yankee lead;
And the horrid tales they told,
Some were reckless, fierce and bold;
And one yarn they gloried in,
Was Grant's tippling at the gin;
Because now and then he took a dram,
Was it supposed to ruin Uncle Sam?
They gloried, as they loudly said it,
In every paper they tried to spread it.
So at last, a delegation from Illinois,
Went to have him removed from o'er her boys;
So to Halleck in St. Louis they went,
Upon this one grand object bent.

Or banish him from out the land,
Such murder, we cannot stand,

But when they got there, curious to say,
They found Halleck unwilling to obey;
Saying, I like Grant, he exactly suits me,
Like myself, undoubtedly, you soon will be.
While the deputation were lying in wait,
And thinking o'er the soldier's fate,
Fort Donelson fell with a crash,
Then the news to St. Louis went with a flash,
Where the deputation at the hotel staid.
Halleck, with the news, straight for it made;
On their bulletin board Halleck nailed the news
(Or maybe he fastened it up with screws);
Saying, if Grant was such a drunkard as represented to be,
All St. Louis to-night should join in one grand spree;
And if any in the city in drunkenness should fail,
He should be fined a dozen times, and locked up in the jail.
If Grant is such a drunkard, and so glorious in battle array,
I ought to issue an order to read that very way.
So the people of St. Louis immediately took a hitch,
And that city, in the morning, was independently rich;
For the people there, at once, with their friends and their frows,
Got into a mighty long drunken carouse.

So Grant was the man all over town,
Grant was a man of great renown;
And whether he drank from jug or demi',
For the rebel cause he was to many.
Oh, it was a great night to barter and to dicker,
To those who dealt in ales, also beers and liquor;
Also that honored, pious delegation,
Drank whiskey raw, to the health of the nation.
They owned Grant a man of mighty sense,
A man of rare intelligence.
Down in the land of corn wine,
But fairer the land of the muscadine.
Further south, where the cottons grow,
And the yams lay large in the sand below;
Where blossoms in the winter come,
That is the land of niggerdom.

DISTRICT OF WEST TENNESSEE.

ALLECK gave Grant more room in ter-
ritory,
To wallop rebeldom in all her martial
glory.
With his headquarters at Fort Donel-
son, Tennessee,   [be.
Or any other place where the General may happen to
Grant's territory was bounded on one side
By the Mississippi, flowing broad and wide ;
And the Tennessee River formed another line to rate,
From Cairo to the Missisippi State.*
Cumberland and Tennessee navigation reclaimed,
Now, to settle the rebellion, was all that remained.
So Grant took a short rest, and then he went at it,
The southern Confederacy, he aimed to combat it.
So Foote and his gunboat command,

---

*GENERAL ORDER NO. TWO.

Dear soldiers, hear my congratulation,
For the bloody work in your occupation ;
For four successive nights you've stood,
And did your work so strong and good.
At night the snow and sleet would pelt,
And shot by day from rebels felt.
From their safety that nature made,
Made more strong by scienced aid.
Prepared all times to meet the foe,
With musket shot or saber blow.
You drove them from their position,
And made them surrender without condition ,
Capturing the largest army yet,
That ever did in battle set.
(Now understand it as its meant,
The largest on this continent).
In after years the battle you've won,
Will make noted Fort Donelson.
Fort Donelson in capitals will stand
On the map of our united land ;

Pushed their way up the Cumberland,
While a foot force followed on land.
A strong division of General Grant's army,
To make the south, in red battle stormy.
February the twentieth, Clarksville without a fight,
To the Union army, gave up all military right.
With it the stores they there obtained,
On it, twenty days,Grant's army was maintained.
A garrison at Clarksville, laid,
Grant's division, the ones that stayed ;
And on the spot,
Devoured the grub they got.
But the gunboats, to Nashville opened the way,
So the army of the Ohio could go in and stay.
The Union army by efforts grand,
Had hewed their way into the rebel land ;
So that it had been necessary, before they'd farther go,
To place a binding law upon both friend and foe.
It was necessary to keep the army grand,
And to save its morals from a guerillerous band;
To place it under rigid discipline,
Strong as a jack-oak, and long as a pine.
So read this extract,
Not an exact,
Number seven general order,
Inside of rebeldom's bold border,
It will state the time and when,
In February, at Fort Donelson, Tenn.,
Which is head-quarters all can see,
For the western district of Tennessee.
For, where General Grant is found,
There head-quarters does abound.

And the boys that fell in the strife,
Will be remembered in after life ;
And from a grateful country's heart.
The soldiers that fought it will never part.
U. S. G.—B. G. C.

Rebellious Tennessee doesn't care a damn
About the laws made by Uncle Sam.
So to the citizens, I must declare,
Only martial law can be brought to bear,
    Until citizens can return,
    The power of rebel law to spurn.
    Until then, the martial arm
    Will protect you from rebel harm.

J. A. Rawling, A. A. G.   By order of   M. G., U. S. G.

    Another order followed close,
    To all soldiers, mild or verbose
    From the head department it came to hand,
    Purposely for Grant's command.

Head-quarters, district of Missour',
At St. Louis on a mud-washed shore,
    And such occurred,
    On February twenty-third.
    Let good order and discipline
    Save the army from a cripplin';
    It preserves from a hellishness dire,
    More awful than the rebels' fire.

From our actions let our fellow-citizens learn,
We come not to plunder and to burn,
But to return the flag that waved o'er them and their slaves,
Yes, to plant the flag o'er an hundred thousand graves.
The plebe, from their rebel leaders learn,
That the nature of our army, is to plunder and to burn.
Now, let us undeceive them and hoist the flag again,
Hoist it in love and truth, so it will forever remain.
Have nothing to do 'tween master and slave in any way,
For that's not for military but civil law to say.
    No slaves of the forced or fugitive,
    About our camp, must stay or live,
    Unless the general in command,
    Offers them a friendly hand.
    All private property must be regarded,
    Where the Union has not been retarded.
    When private property is taken away,
    Its value in full you must repay.
    All that's captured from the foe,

Into Uncle Sammy's hands must go.
But those who steal, transfer or hide,
By martial law they must abide.
Fellow soldier, officers and all,
Let no excess on your illustrious glory fall.
    The above order must be read
    At every regimental head;
    And the army must obey
    The rules that in them lay.
For Its Major-general Halleck's command,
From Adjutant-general W. H. McLean's hand.
                So read it off,
                By order of   M. G.—U. S. G.
J. A. R.—A. A. G.

The gunboats, after Nashville fell,
Down the Cumberland, returned a spell.
From the Cumberland River to Tennessee water,
The gunboats went up to reconnoiter.
They went up it with their gunboatish ram,
To northern Mississippi and Alabam'.
The natives advanced, the boats to meet,
And opened their throats, in roaring great.
The woods and the river resounded with noise,
As the natives come out to greet our boys.
They yelled themselves most nigh to a spasm,
In trying to vent their enthusiasm. |covered,
The feelings of the people were therefore, quite un-
And no large rebel forces were seen or e'en discovered.
    After all those facts were learned,
    When the gunboats had returned,
    Grant moved his head-quarters o'er,
    On Tennessee's Fort Henry shore.
To fit out an expedition, the hopes of his dream,
To operate o'er ninety miles further up the stream.
About this time, Grant's detractors tried
    To have his commission set aside;
    And even 'twas calculated on every hand,

That he was deprived of his command.
It was, perhaps, some pious old tumor,
That originally started the ridiculous rumor.
Or it may, perhaps, have sprung from the cause
Of the army's uncivilian and warlike laws.
When C. F. Smith commanded the field,
So Grant his burdensome job could wield.
Transporting his troops up the Tennessee River,
With bombs to shake rebeldom till it would shiver.
And at Savannah, in the State of Tenn.,
Is where he landed his warlike men.
Oh, honest men, stop and learn.
Smith commanded till his return.
At Fort Henry, where the General got his board,
He was presented with a handsome, bran new sword;
And he received it from the hand
Of the regimental officer in command.
It was a fine sword, to be sure,
And manufactured from the best of ore.
The handle was Ivory, inlaid with gold,
Of the richest shape and finest mold.
Two scabbards were with the blade,
One was for service, and the other parade.
Both were gilded by the handy designer;
One was fine gilt, and the other much finer;
The box that encased it was strong and good;
Made of seasoned rose, a highly polished wood.
With a sash and belt suitable, ah yes, and more,
On the blade a single inscription it bore.*

Here's an articls that rips to the center, you bet,
And it's found in the Florence, Alabama Gazette:
It was designed to seethe and scorch
In that gazette, on the twelfth of March.

---

* "Presented to General U. S. Grant, by [officers contented]
J. W. Graham; C. C. Marsh; John Cook and C. B. Lagow,
The date I'll name it now, March 11, sixty-two."

"At Savannah, in the State of Tenn.,
	The Yankees have landed their bloody men,
	To fall on our good men, and kill what they can,
	For it's always the good men that lead in the van.
For the Memphis & Charleston railroad they're lurking,
But e'er they get it they'll do some tall working;
And many a dead Yankee will stretch on the sand,
E'er they get that road, the chief of the land.
Arise, fellow-men, and stand by your hearth,
The land of your forefathers, the land of your birth.
		Hold to the railroad, if the river is lost,
		At all hazards, though heavy the cost.
Our great thoroughfare, it musn't be blocked,
Or our country is ruined, and our cause is locked.

								[out,
As the Tennessee operations were thus being carried
								[about;
Grant was not unmindful of home, that rebels lurked
	So he sent expeditions. wide and long,
	O'er the country deep and strong,
		With reconnoiters far and near,
		O'er the country, front and rear.
		To see where the rebels laid,
		Their stronghold, and where they stayed.
		So on the twelfth of March, they found,
		A rebel force, within their bound,
		Near Paris, burrowed in the ground.
	So an artillery mob and a cavalry gang,
	Went for them with clatter and clang.
	The rebels were driven from their hold,
	By the Yankees, firm and bold.
	The rebel force was badly shaken,
	Three fifties crippled, killed or taken.
	The Yankees got there along the road,
	'Mid screaming balls and bombs explode.
They drove the rebels from where they spied them,
And the works, themselves, they occupied them.

All the armies of the west,
Down the Mississippi, they pressed.
Towards the Gulf, their columns ran,
The Union army and border man.
So it was important to the whole,
That one chieftain should control.
So all the combinations could move,
Like greased pulleys in a groove.
And connect where e'er they aimed,
And not have the army maimed
   By mistakers,
Or commanders that formerly served as bakers.
So the department of west Tennessee
Was extended from the Gulf, beyond to the sea.
       [it wore

"The Department of the Mississippi," was the name
So Grant's territory was larger than before.
For, of this department, he commanded the most.
Except now and then a powerful post.
   So the rebel host,
   Began to boast,
   And to create,
   And concentrate,
   To do their best
   In the southwest.
With a powerful man to lead them,
And a Union force in front to bleed them.
The man that led the south-west force,
Was Albert Sidney Johnston, of course;
A powerful man in brain and arm,
And gloried in a battle storm.
General P. G. T. Beauregard collected a band,
Against the Yankee troops to stand.
He was the commander of all the host
That the Mississippi Valley could boast.

With his head-quarters at Corinth town,
Apast it the Mississippi floods rushed down,
On the surf of which no boat could ride,
With Yankee name of gunning pride;
For the river was blockaded by rebel men,
Along its banks, and at number ten;
With guns of stupendous bore,
Powdered up to a thunderous roar.
Sure their balls were powdered to ride afar,
And meet the enemy advancing in war.

The balls rode along like a fierce dragoon,
Humming a low and a murderous tune.
Beauregard, at Corinth, camped in the pine,
To guard the Charleston & Memphis Line,
And keep the Yankee's daring force confined,
North of where the Tennessee may wind;
And if a chance should cross their luck,
To cross o'er, into old Kentuck',
And then get o'er the Ohio River,
And make the north in vengeance shiver.

Up the Tennessee River, to Savannah Town,
The rest of Grant's troops, south moved down,
And at that place, went into camp,
To Corinth, a twenty long miles to tramp,
Where the rebels, fearless and bold,
Lay encamped in their stronghold.
Grant's third division, to work its trade,
On the fifteenth of March, a march it made;

 And into McNairy County it went,
 On destroying rebels, determined and bent.
 At Purdy they struck a railway line,
 Constructed so level, so smooth and fine.
 It was the Corinth road to Jackson, Tenn.
 Dealing in war munitions and rebel men.

The Union force,
The bridge of course,
　　They burnt it ;
And the railing pries
Loose from the ties
　　(For a distance or more).
It delayed the course
Of the rebel force,
　　But that was all.
For the road they controlled,
Except where it was "stoled"
　　(By the Yankee boys in blue).

CANTO.

The Shiloh flood
Of human blood,
Where it occurred,
And why preferred.
Who're the leaders,
　　And fiercest bleeders ;
What generals led,
And how many of them came out dead.
That battle was fought,
To death, sold and by blood bought,
　　　　Dear !
How many soldiers perished there ?
They think they know,
And have books to show,
But them I doubt,
It's a mystery not so easily found out.
Life on that field, was chances to many,
Like heads and tails in flipping a penny ;
With a partner, for instance, you I choose,
Heads, I win, and tails, you lose.
Now, behold the size,
You'll lose, 'less it sets edgewise,

FIFTH.

On April first, the rebel command
Had forty-five thousand men on hand,
(And were all armed with swords or gun,
Prepared to give the Yanks a run.
Chase was both armies' solemn oath,
But ah, to chase, how could they both,
One wanted to see the other run,
Therefore, fled they, sword and gun.
So the hindermost could follow behind,
To pick up the things that they could find.
Such things as jolts out of an enemy's train,
When traveling along with might and main.
As men that travel with such alorum
That their backs try to get before them :
As if some fright might take a wind,
And hurt it if it stayed behind.
Men in such a hurry, wouldn't stop for shirts or pants,
Or from a mud-hole, to pull their dearest aunts.
Let alone their soldiering fellow-man,
And the government goods do the best they can.
They care not how other things may fare,
It's of themselves they're taking care).
But notwithstanding wind and weather,
Grant's force was nearly all together,
Therefore, concerning creeks and drains,
Muddy roads and swollen streams,
His troops were nearly all under hand,
Awaiting for his stern command.
They had better've given their spades a try,
In lifting dirt, to fortify.
It seemed as though they acted the dummy,
More so than any Egyptian mummy.

Why did they coolly wait for rebs.,
Instead of digging bullet-sheds.
Spades, there employed, could have won,
Or had more power than swords or gun.
If I am judge or justice, fair,
Grant surely must have missed there.
It seems as though I haven't rated
Where Grant's troops were concentrated.
It was Pittsburgh landing, or at Shiloh,
Where Grant awaited the coming blow.
The cavalry pickets, without whine or boasts,
Were occupying the outer posts.
  It was on April's second day,
  The Unionists were driven away.
Driven away from the landing of Crumps,
With the rebels hewing at their horses' rumps.
 They came in without supervision,
 The videttes of the third division;
 They rushed in the best they may,
 Those not captured. by the way.
 For the skirmish was short and quick,
 And wounds rained o'er them fast and thick,
 And several soldiers were carried away
 In this short and fierce affray.
  It was the third of April, when
  Johnston thus addressed his men:

 Ye mighty armies of the Mississipp',
 I lead you forth on a perilous trip;
 To fall upon the agrarian Yanks,
 And cut to pieces their mercenary
  ranks.
 Coming now to invade our land,
 Fiends collected in a fiendish band.
 Fall on them with deadly aim,
And drive them from our broad domain.

In my vision, I can behold
The Yankees crushed in your deadly fold.
Fight till the last bloody fiend departs,
Tear from their bosoms, their treacherous hearts.
We'll take their hearts, the de'il their souls,
To mix among his brimstone coals.
Strike for vengeance and heaven above;
For mothers, daughters and the women you love;
Strike as though it's the last to deal,
Let the sun shine only on death-reeking steel.
May the Negro hounds bark at their fugitive heels,
And tear down their carcasses to enrich our fields.
Oh, the South! for chivalrous daring she's my pride,
Has the spirit of Marion's men in your bosoms died?
The same old spirit is there, full well I know,
But rouse it up, to meet the coming foe,
May their horses run riderless on that sunny bank,
And our cavalry sabers after their fugitives clank.
Strike as never man struck before,
Swell the tide of the river with hirelings' gore;
Strike terror to the hireling, blood-covered foe;
Strike the crime-bathed, Lincolnite hirelings low;
Strike for the cause you would sustain;
Strike for freedom, your country and name.
By death, their ranks must be dissolved,
For remember the precious stake involved.
Defeat? Oh, fellow-soldiers! remember what a cost,
A broad domain will weep, if the coming battle's lost.
The eyes and hopes of twice four millions rest
On yon bloody field, we must so soon contest.
If a failure, our country is proned and bleeding,
But if we win, we'll behold the Yanks receding.
Be equal to our women, which no country has ever done,
　　　　　　　　　　　　　　　　　　　[first begun.
They've lived a band of heroines, since the war was

May heaven assist us, one and all,
May Yankeedom break, and its power fall;
May I lead you o'er all coming fields
Of clattering balls and clanging steels,
To victory and nothing less,
To all, I feel assured success,
    Notwithstanding.
General A. S. Johnston commanding.

A. S. Johnston first in command,
Then Beauregard next under hand.
The first corps to prod and croak,
Was under Lieutenant-General Polk;
The second corps to tote the rag,
Belonged to Lieutenant-General[Braxton] Bragg;
The third corps moved to obey
Lieutenant-General Hardee, W. J.;
Major-General Crittendon, G. B.,
After the reserve, he had to see.
Opposed to this great, big rebel force,
Small was U. S. Grant's, of course.
The army marching or a standing,
Was under Major-General Grant's commanding.
The first division pursuing rebels, or returnin',
Was under command of Major-General McClernand;
The second division, where'er their chances fell,
Was run by Brigadier-General Wallace, W. H. L.

                [rows,
Where e'er the third division meandered her lineal
Major-General Wallace directed all its blows;
Whenever the fourth division went out to kill and hurt,
They were led by Brigadier-General[S. A.] Hurlburt;
When the fifth division went out a rebel warmin',
They were led by General W. T. Sherman.

On the evening of April four,
Rebeldom came out to roar.
With two regiments wide and long,
They reconnoitered deep and strong.
They came to the Yankee lines to grieve them,
And foand the Yankees to receive them.
Then back they wriggled off the stage,
For the men were not ready to engage;
For Generals Price and Van Dorn
Had not anteed up their corn.
Their corn of wretched, rebellious mold,
To stronger make a very strong hold.
When rebeldom was rushing on,
And Shiloh's first blood was drawn;
Ere Shiloh's mighty death-like flood
Washed her fields in human blood.
As rebeldom poured out her foes,
On Union lines to reek them woes.
At Adamsville, division third,
A rumbling racket around them heard;
It was rebel hordes advancing,
To set the Union troops to dancing.
It was a cavalry dash so fierce,
It struck the Union force in tiers.
This fierce cavalry dash was made
With carbine shots and saber blade.
It was to hold General Wallace from
Helping Grant with sword or gun.
You can see in those lines written before,
As Shiloh's battle began to roar,
Rebels held advantages, from peel to core.
They had force, two-thirds of Grant's numbered twice,
Without the assistance of Van Dorn and Price.
Johnston determined Grant's doom to be sealed,
Ere Buel and his soldiers could arrive on the field.

For the rebels learned from their spies among the
[Yanks,
What the Union soldiers done, all their movements
[and their pranks.
So April the fifth, was the day set apart,   [heart.
To stab the Unionist deep, with a thrust through the
That ere they commenced their death-dealing trade,
Another day, in the woods for Van Dorn they layed.
That should be a day, a great day, of course,
For that day in waiting, saved Grant and his force.
It saved Grant from ruin, and his forces from disaster,
And the bloody field of Shiloh from a secession master.
For Grant, with all his cunning and glorious might,
Couldn't have equalled Johnston in that unequal fight
But that one day of waiting gave Buel a chance,
To assist Grant with his heavy advance.
    That one day of waiting, was all that done it,
    That one day of waiting, is why Grant won it.
It ought to be a day that our nation should praise,
It ought to be one of our national days.
    Oh, what a great thing it is to be lucky,
    But its a greater thing to show one's self plucky.
    If Johnston's mind could thus have strayed
    O'er the proverbs that never fade,
    He'd known to-morrow cannot repay
    The chances of slaughter lost to-day.
    For, as to-morrow's richest treasure,
    Can but fill its proper measure.

SHILOH IN BLOOD.

Now, we'll behold fierce scenes of Shiloh,
Where human blood like rivers flow,
Bright April sixth, early Sunday morn,
Marched out rebellion, death to adorn.
The Union pickets rushed in with a charge,

As the Union officers were shot at large
By the sharp-shooters of the rebel cause,
According to the custom of national laws.
The rebels advanced like a world set in motion,
Or the waves on a wreck from a merciless ocean.
The rebels advanced, furious and strong,
Their soldiers were many, and their swords were long.
Many of our men fell dead in their track,
As foot by foot they fought their way back.
For foot by foot the ground was contested,
As inch by inch it was digested.
When they found our troops retreating slow,
Fast and furious their war-whoops grow.
The rebels gained vigor and vim,
As the Yankees fall back to the river's brim,
Till the field was alive with dead men strewn,
That from powerful ranks were hewn.

THE FIRST DAY.

The following is an account
Of Shiloh's bloody fount
Reviewed.

O'er battles of modern days,
This surpasses in all its ways;
But it wound up to a close,
And fleeing from us are our foes.
The rebels attacked us Sunday morn,
Ere the sun arose, the hills to adorn,
Then blood and carnage, the whole day long
Beat on our ranks, deadly and strong.
The whole day long, without intermission,
From the desperately bold secession.
The trumpets trumped their loudest blast,
As rebeldom murdered furious and fast;
As though it was her only chance,
Through blood and carnage to advance.

The gates of hell seemed ajar,
And fiends came out to give us war.
Hung to their bodies, long and lank,
The trappings of their weapons clank.
They clanked with a doleful rattle,
Suggestive of a bloody battle.

THE SECOND DAY.

On Monday morn, the scene renewed,
The foe upon a foeman hewed;
With bloody din and cannons roar,
Monday slid to the hour of four.
Then the army of the Mississipp',
Had her glory pruned, and her pinions clipped.
For the Union army was mighty and strong ;
Their swords were sharp, and their points were long.
Making the rebels to Corinth stir their course,
Hard pursued by our cavalry force.
They rushed along, with racket and rant,
And speed that made the soldiers pant.
The cost of the victory was immense,
And purchased at a sad expense.
For fifty thousand soldiers lay
Inanimate as their couch of clay.
The Union lost in this mighty affray,
A vast army for an early day.
Twenty thousand beyond caring for.
Ten thousand more, as prisoners of war.
The rebels numbered their butchered dead,
At the rate of thirty thousand head.

THE COMMENCEMENT AND ENDING REVIEWED.

The regiment, Twenty-Third Missour',
Of her soldiers, fifteen score,
They attacked the rebels' hard,

Beating back the advance guard,
Of course those soldiers, where and when,
Were part of General Prentiss' men.

The rebels, at once on Prentiss fell,
Like purgatorian fiends from hell.
Their musket, shells, canister and grape,
Did the union camp a fiendish rape.
The engagement, soon a general one,
Brought to play the heavy gun.
The battle scene, from end to end,
O'er four miles it does extend.
The rebels seemed to hold the sway,
The center of our lines gave way.
Then Hurlburt's division ran, for
To support those battered men of war.
A bloody conflict then ensued,
Death, it seems, whole dozens wooed.
There, there advance, motion slack,
As death and soldiers beat them back,
But they rally, to advance again,
With vengeance and a deadly aim.
Thus, undecided the whole day through,
The ranks upon each other hew.
The rebels held within their grip,
Remarkable good generalship,
Of which I cannot here relate,
For room is lacking here to state.
The rebels did some desperate work,
As the afternoon drew on its mark;
For well they knew their only chance,
Lay within a fierce advance.
Major Taylor's artilery from Chicag',
The throat of death it seems would clog.

This Tree represents in the timber the marks of war.

His grape and canister rode on death and pains,
As through rebel ranks, it mowed wide lanes ;
But, again those lanes with men were filled,
Which were again as quickly killed.
Taylor's guns were regular mowers,
They raked the rebels down in scores.
The rebels done some fighting, tall,
To pin the Yankees to the wall.
Grant must be licked ere Buell came,
Or rebeldom would lose its name.
They could almost hear Buell's army trappings clank,
As it marched upon the opposite bank.
Fretfully waiting the river to cross,
To help multiply the rebel loss.
Had they from Nashville, marched so far,
To stand idly, gaping at a murderous war?
With only the river to keep them out it,
Or they'd draw their swords and be about it.
The rebel soldiers saw them there,
Therefore roughly the Yankees fare.
They made a swoop to drive them like mist,
Ere Buell's soldiers could assist.
For well they knew when Buell crossed,
At once, by him would the field be bossed.
Therefore, fearful the carnage grew,
The rebels butchered, shot and slew,
Until the Yankees on the river hovered,
And the rebels, two-thirds of their camp had covered.
The rebels tried to drive them in the river,
And thus to end the quarrel forever.
First, the right was banged and battered,
Then the left was sorely tattered ;
Tattered with bayonet, sword and gun,
But still the Yankees would not run.
As rebeldom did shoot, cut and hew,

Extremely critical their position grew.
Large numbers of men panic-struck,
Rushed to the rear for better luck;
Where many skulkers there they found,
And hard-worked, worn out men abound.
Grant and his staff rushed along the lines,
Where grape and canister mowed the pines.
He incited his men to deeds of daring,
Where he could hear the rebel hordes a swearing.
He begged the soldiers to stand the charge,
Till reinforcements crossed the river at large.
Here chief of staff Webster, the colonel,
Worked a racket that dealt infernal.
He brought the heaviest guns into play,
To sweep the rebel ranks away.
Their black mouths, dark as night,
Spewed metal o'er the rebel's right ;
And all the guns of heavy weight,
Was brought, the rebel lines to break.
Thus, along our whole line, entire,
Artillery belched forth a deadly fire,
Such cannonading or hellishment,
Was never known on this continent.
With musketry mixed in the clatter,
Made more devilish a hideous a matter.
The gunboats " Taylor " and " Lexington" poured
Metal and death o'er the rebel horde.
The rebels vigor soon decay,
As their last efforts die away,
And ere night puts on its veil,
Quiet reins throughout the dale.
Blood and carnage cease its awful strife,
In frightful misery and wasted life.
The men sank to rest from their awful fight,
Slept on their arms throughout the night

General Lewis Wallace then arrived at last,
When darkness o'er the sun was cast.
On the right, a position he took,
The fury of rebeldom to brook.
From o'er the river and Savannah town,
Buell's troops to the battle-field got 'round.
(But Buell, we must understand,
Was on the field ere the battle began.)
General Buell's soldiers took the left hand wing,
With the morning sun to hear the bullets buzz and sing

THE SECOND DAY.

Monday, April the seventh, the second day in battle,
[rattle;
My pen cannot describe it with its deadly scenes and
A pen cannot describe it and a canvas cannot hold it,
[mold it.
The thought of man in vision can never be brought to
In the morn, ere the sun had risen at all,
General Nelson on the left, opened up the ball.
The racket was commenced simultaneous in the fight,
By Nelson on the left, and Wallace on the right.
Nelson's division worked a galling fire,
Following up the rebels, as they sullenly retire.
[extend,
Then the fire became general, along the whole line to
[bend.
But the rebel lines were tough, and hard they were to
[before,
All of General Grant's soldiers that fought the day
They rallied to the racket, and helped to make it roar.
The rebel resistance would make the de'il pause,
They fought with a resistance worthy a better cause.
[would appall,
The rebels butchered, and they stood it in a way that

Their bravery and their vim was surely grand and tall.
[wrath,
But our army, brave, undaunted and towering in their
Would allow no obstacle to stand, within their path.
At every belch that our artillery gave,
It swept scores of rebels to hades or the grave.
For well the rebels knew, defeat here would be sore,
So with all their force on the Union ranks they bore.
The Unionists did all they could in true heroic gunnage,
Ere the rebels would take up a line of regular rummage.
[deadly power,
They battered at the Yankee's front, with such awful
[hour.
That they shook and wavered till the afternoon's fifth
Then the Union soldiers came to a deadly stand,
[hand.
And each one grasped his weapon more firmly in his
As they rallied with all their bleeding power,   [hour.
Forced was rebeldom to retreat, that very, self-same
General Buell followed, to see what he could find,
[behind.
And shoot that part of rebeldom that showed itself
The two days,
War and its ways,
(The facts in the case, the truth to tell.)
The gallantry of the battle, is without a parallel.
Grant and his staff were in the thickest of the din,
Until it ended, from the time it did begin.
[Pherson,
As along side of Grant, rode Lieutenant-Colonel Mc-
Shot dead was his horse, without injury to his person.
[responder,
As Captain Carson rode between Grant and the cor-
[to squander.
His head rode off on a cannon-ball, with nothing left

And that same cannon-ball unaimed by sire or mothers,
Murdered a few, and wounded several others.
Generals McClernand, Sherman and Hurlburt,
Got balled through the clothes, and neither one hurt.
Among the rebels' dead, was their commander-in-chief,
[lief.
A Yankee cannon-ball brought him quick and sure re-
[deads,
As General A. S. Johnston was with the murdered
[Feds
General Prentiss was wounded, and with the captured
The Yankees got some prisoners, and also lots of guns,
But the rebels got the largest lot of runs.

[ing,
The accounts of this battle, so awful dire and frighten-
[ning.
Rode all o'er the country, on electric wings of light-
The Halls of Congress soon received the news,
["blues."
They rejoiced at the victory, but its cost produced the
[hard,
Congress thanked Grant and Buell for striking rebels
[eral Beureregard;
Down in Tennessee, at Pittsburg landing, under Gen-
Also to boot,   [salute.
In Washington, an hundred guns they fired at one
Beauregard reported to Richmond and his master,
But Grant had little to say about the fierce disaster.
The rebel fathers came to beg the bodies of their sons,
[and guns.
That were slain by Yankee power, in shape of swords
[line,
Their butchered sons laid within our martial picket
[a crime.
And to refuse such a request would surely have been

Beauregard and Grant, the correspondence of the two
[men,
Each one claiming to the other that he is more humane.
To listen to them, you'd think them 'postolic saints,
And battle is all smoke, colored up in paints.
General Sherman, division fifth commander,
[grander.
He went out to reconnoiter, in a style that's seldom
Of infantry he'd two brigades, and cavalry in force,
To wipe out all rebeldom that lay along his course.

> The roads, the Feds were sure to find,
> Doth o'er the country, to Corinth, wind
> Along which many a rebel tent,
> Their canvas in the breezes bent.

But their camps were deserted and the rebels fled,
Except the butchered and mangled dead.

> O'er their tents waved the hospital flags,
> A lie imprinted on worthless rags ;
> A lie to protect them from ravages of war ;
> A lie to check the foeman's car.

But Sherman advanced with the stride of a giant,
To protect the name of his chosen client ;
> And skirmished the rebels from the field,
> Who rode away but would not yield.
> To the rebel tents he applied the torch,
> The housely duds to ashes scorch.

He destroyed the ammunition for the rebel guns,
All their flanneled powder and deadly bombs.
> On the road to Corinth, Sherman found,
> Trinkets of war strewn o'er the ground ;
Such as wagons, limber boxes and ambulance,
That the rebels flung down in the Union's advance.
The rebels injured the batteries, so they say,
By leaving a score of limber boxes along the way.

The rebel moans
In delirious tones,
Were bread and bones.
Sticks and stones
To the Yankees.
When Halleck read the fearful news,
Of Shiloh, and her trusty blues,
He at once determined to go,
And view the scenes of Shiloh's blow.
To take the field and its command,
And see who's monarch of the land;
To see what Grant in battle, done,
See whether the rebels fought or run.
So on April thirteenth, at Pittsburgh, Tenn.,
He thanked his generals, and their men.
Of course his praise was fast and furious,
As were his sayings old and curious.
Loud were his thanks to Grant and Buell,
For heaping hades with rebel fuel;
And all that aid in the cause,
To throttle the Confederate laws.
From the generals in command,
To the ones who shoveled sand,
All were blessed,
Kicked or caressed,
In some stupendous manner.
Every rebel that crossed Jordan's stream,
Was accompanied by a Federal team;
Every rebel that bathed in hades' fire,
It took two Yankees to get him there.
They were so tough, lank and lean,
The Yankee bullets slid between.
But when plenty of grub was found,
The flesh upon their bones abound.
When e'er they crossed o'er Jordan's stran',

They took along a Yankee man.
They held so tight beneath the skies,
Those that tore them loose would paralyze,
Their hold on earth, was so secured,
To get them loose it took a sword;
And when one of them was killed,
With them, a foe or two was billed.
    Halleck, from the field did not return,
    But engaged the whole concern.
    Each commander did remain,
    Their old "posish" they did retain.
    Out-post skirmishes intervene,
    Till April ran to seventeen;
    Then the whole Union force,
    To Corinth stir their deadly course.
No army e'er marched in a line so long,
With a movement so powerful and strong.
Winding along, o'er hills and vale,
O'er their country's foes to soon prevail;
Winding along under noonday splendor,
Their gun-barrels gleaming bright and slender.

MOVEMENTS AND SIEGE OF CORINTH.

Cavalry-Chief Brigadier-General Smith started out
On the seventeenth, to reconnoiter, broad and stout;
    Roads all o'er the country run,
    But Halleck took upper one.
    He took the one which led along,
    Where seemed rebeldom most strong;
    He found priest and plebe in a mighty wrong.
    With whetted swords, keen and long.
Unmolested they marched through the country,
Until within two miles of Monterey.
    Dismounted men served as a scout,

To spy the line of marching out.
They found the enemy in force, his position and his
[place,
They turn then, backwards, their footsteps to retrace.
[four,
Also, when April, in spending days, had run to twenty-
[time before.
The same reconnaissaince went out as had gone the
And on the Pea Ridge elevation,
They found a rebel station.
The Yankees for this tramp,
Got some prisoners, and destroyed a rebel camp.
The gunboats, with their never-tiring men,
Opened up the Miss', below Island Number Ten.
(It is the biggest tramway that ever trunneled dirt,
And it does it up so calm, it's really cunning and pert.
It trunnels off enough of dirt and carries it below,
To choke a Jordan River or build a Mexico).   [mand,
On learning this, Beauregard, who had assumed com-
Of troopel Dixie all o'er the Southern land;
Because he was the boss, and monkeyed with the helm,
[realm:
He thus addressed the planters that dwelt within his
[clatteries,
"By the casualities of war, and the Yank's infernal
[batteries;
The Miss' has opened up to their monstrous pegleg
And, now, the time's arrived to try each loyal breast,
[test.
Now full at hand, the time has come to put you to the
All ye planters, that be in reach of the Federal march,
To your cotton on hand, at once apply the torch.
This rebel leader thought that if there was no cotton,
[gotten.
That the so-called Yankee Union at once would be for-

If there was no cotton, there was nothing to lure them
[forward ;
If the cotton was destroyed, he, at once would have
[them bowered

The rebel planters they believed,
The rebel planters they were deceived.
The torch applied, the cotton gone,
But straight advanced the Yankees on.
On they advanced, on they came,
Filling village, country roads and lane.
Till the rebel toughness bowed,
Trampled beneath a Yankee crowd.*

When Tennessee, was Yankee soldier ridden,
And April days to twenty-seven had "slidden,"
Purdy was vacated because the rebels fail
[rail.
To hold that little village on the Jackson & Corinth
Near Monterey, a cavalry skirmish close,
By the Yankees making prisoners of their foes.
Then we'll look at Monterey, two days further on,
[gone.
The rebels lost their camp, with their men as prisoners
Then upon the following day,
After Monterey camp was carried away,

---

* That rat
And its pity pat,
I've got 'em now both in a trap.
It's annoyed me many a night,
When alone in peace I longed to write.
Its life, you may suppose it,
Cat or dog or I will close it ;
For I've trapped and waited for it too long,
To part with it for just a song.
It must run the gauntlet for a' that,
Between a terrier and a cat.
Besides a row of boys with clubs,
And Chinamen with washing tubs.
And if it 'scapes with hair or hide,
It will die from being terrified.

General Halleck's force went out to reconnoiter,
Looking for rebels to capture or to slaughter.
  They treated the rebels fierce and cold,
  And chased them into their stronghold.
  They took possession of Purdy town,
  And burnt the railroad bridges down.
  Thus cutting off all communications
  Between Corinth and north-western stations.
  But whether the rebels would stand or run,
  The siege of Corinth here begun.
  From rebel prisoners it was found,
  That Beauregard entrenched his ground.
  Strong fortifications were created,
  All available troops were concentrated.
Here the rebels claimed, with desperate resistance,
They'd fight till death ended their existence.
  So General Halleck, to have an invincible clan,
  Called to his assistance every available man;
  So in case of a battle winding up the affray,
  He could sweep the rebel lines away.
  Thus all the extras under his commanding,
  Were concentrated at Pittsburg Landing.
  For Pittsburg Landing was a station,
  Supply and base of operations.
  As a special honor to Grant, you see,
They christened it "Grand Army of the Tennessee."
  Into three armies it was divided,
  By three successful generals guided.
  The *Ohio* as a centre, was led by Buell,
  Pope, o'er the *Missisippi*, as left did rule;
  The *Tennessee*, as right was wide and long,
  With Grant for commander, was wide and strong.
  Into sixteen divisions, this Grand Army divided,
  Over half which General Grant presided.
Generals McClernand and Thomas were right up to biz.

Each one helped Grant, commanding the whole of his.
   General McClernand was lucky, for
   He held in command, the reserve of war.
   The opposers of Grant smoldered, but not to die,
   Broke forth in almost universal hue and cry.
   His command, they tried to take it away,
   And he was christened the butcher of the day.
   The charges, I will a few of them relate,
   He had no capacity, and was inebriate.
   In Galena, Washburn was his neighbor,
   In Congress, to save him, he wielded manly labor.
                   [loud,
Their howls at him in Congress, were e'en long and
Went to Halleck, Western Governors in a crowd.
                  [wrought,
The Governors, unlike Samson, at Pittsburgh landing
For there the jaw-bone asses non-effecting fought.
For unto Grant, Halleck stretched a friendly hand,
And on May the first, made him second in command.
(Now, here understand soldiers, friend or thief,
                  [chief.)
That Halleck stood high, the army's commander-in-
   General Beauregard, by being advised.
   By Union arms was ne'er surprised,
   But he expected the Union troops,
   Would attack him in deadly swoops.
      So with rebel desperation,
      He commenced a concentration.
   So at Corinth, on the second of May,
   Thousands of rebels were hurried away.
   There, Beauregard, his soldiers impress,
   With a long and spirited address.
   Around Corinth, all o'er the lan',
   Strong Union reconnaissance ran.
   And thus upon the eighth of May,

The rebel pickets were driven away.
Our cavalry bore the rebels down,
To within one mile of Corinth town. [one and a half]
As on the other hand the rebels dash,
Fell on our lines with many a crash.
Some forces on our right were forced to retire
From before the rebels' deadly fire.
Halleck and his officers, so facts doeth say,
Held a long consultation on the eleventh of May,
And they agreed to agree on a grand advance,
And the whole Grand Army to aid in the dance.
Then soon the advance commenced, steady and sure,
Down on to one common center they bore.
All to one center, this grand army drew,
Their swords all drawn, on Corinth to hew.
At every command they were eager to go
Down into Corinth, to strike at the foe.
The enthusiasm of the Union cause,
Seemed unbound by any laws.
In battle our boys were determined and firm,
Knowing full well all couldn't return;
And the rebel boys seemed as determined as ours.
Oh, when they meet what devastating powers.
No wonder the fields ran rivers of gore,
When veteran armies fling missiles of ore;
And each draws his sword to chase in defeat,
Or die in battle honor, too proud to retreat.

But the Union hard,	Pressed Beauregard;
They reconnoitered,	Shot and slaughtered.
But the rebels determin'	As hungry vermin,
Struck hard at our cause,	Uncle Sam and his laws,
But rebeldom raced,	As Yankees chased
At every chance,	To kill or advance.
Thus Sherman's troops,	At Russel's house swoops,
The rebels gave way,	But Sherman did stay.
When from rebeldom wrenched.	The house he entrenched.
Thus at every approach,	The Union encroach,

Till nearly every road to Corinth town,
By Union forces are fastened down.
Fastened down from tread of foes,
Fastened down for seiging woes.
Allowing Beauregard no recreation,
But beat his men by just starvation.
Now, Beauregard was well aware
Of siegery and its rough affair.
Of all the guns the Yankees bore,
A siege would frighten ten times more.
Thus Beauregard made up his mind,
Along some open road to wind,
For he knew the city of New Orleans
Had weakened to the Northern fiends;
And should Memphis follow suit,
And Vicksburg fall in line to boot,
His army would surrender itself and hold,
Ere they'd stand a siege, with its miseries untold.
His army could be captured, but not surprised,
For it was growing demoralized.
So thus to gall his Yankee foe,
He struck them many a deadly blow;
They made some bold and daring swoops,
To check the advance of the Union troops.
That ridge to the north of Phillip's Creek,
The strong must take it from the weak.
So T. A. Davis took the job in hand,
With the second division of Grant's command.
So on the twenty-first of May,
On the rebel camp began to play;
He found them no shyster shirks,
But strongly posted in their works.
To drive them, he couldn't at all,
By saber's point, or musket ball.
But to deceive a foe it is so sweet,

So thus in feint, he ordered a retreat.
The rebels from their garrison sally,
And for the Union troops they rally.
They did their best in warring din,
But could not scoop the Yankees in.
In this sharp contest the rebels were outed,
And in the end completely routed.
Of course the battle had its charms,
In captured campage, men and arms.
The Yankees took the garrisoned heights,
Subject to approaching fights.
Around Corinth in constant lurk,
The reconnoiterers kept at work.
The rebels as an outward sign,
Put forth a strong, determined line.
The Union lines, around Corinth hovered,
Their guns, almost the city covered.
Powder along the whole line extended
Skirmishing, both armies befriended.
Old skirmishers arrived with the rising sun,
And were welcomed with a smoking gun.
No rebel then, dared show his pate,
Or from that instant death would date ;
And the Yankees, just as well,
Secured themselves from lead that fell.
When the month of May, in flowery glee,
Had run to three times, three times three ;
Sherman's division tried to entwine
Itself around the rebels' line ;
But it is plain to be seen,
It caused a flight both sharp and keen.
Though half as many, the Union won her,
And the rebels were the soonest runner.
It was then plain, at a glance,
A mere check on Sherman's advance.

SHERMAN'S REPORT.

　　　　Let Sherman tell
　　　　How many fell.
　　　　"Surprised was the foe,
　　　　And they laid low
　　　　　　　But two;
　　　　And then nine more
　　　　Were wounded sore.
　　　　Ere the rebels run it.
　　　　To the ridge's summit;
　　　　Then took a stand,
　　　　Batteries in hand.
Guns in the center, the right and the left,
They paused, the Union lines to cleft.
At us, they threw the worth of a farm,
Doing my brigades but little harm.
　　To death but three men they fetch,
　　And they belonged to General Vetch.
Our cannon-balls, for them went fishin'.
At 10 A. M we mastered the position.
Grant and Thomas, both were there,
Present through the whole affair.
The rebels from their place were rooted,
Well by our men it was executed.
Officers and men handled well their steel,
And kept their places like soldiers real.
The next day. three Union ranks,
Advanced against the rebel cranks;
They went in strength, to tear and rend,
With Grant in person to superintend.
They pressed so hard on Corinth's spot,
They got within a musket shot.

The rebel soldiers did their best,
Every inch of ground they did contest;
But the Yankees contested fierce and cross,
As the rebels fell back with fearful loss.
Thus, the Federals went to reconnoiter,
And they did it up with blood and slaughter.
Bruised was our left, battered and worn,
Bombshell lanes through their ranks were torn."

FROM THE CINCINNATI GAZETTE.

Now, read what we bring from yonder,
The work of a viewing corresponder.
Now, to the siege of Corinth, I'll give it entire,
May the son receive it from the hand of his sire;
May my pen be able the facts to tell,
How Corinth and her rebels fell.
But to tell how things existed,
By the pen of man can ne'er be fisted.
The pen, with the writer's inspiration,
Only paints a glimpse of the situation.
Back, the foe must now be driven,
Which adds to the dead, a list of the livin'.
Regiments sufficient, are brought in advance,
With artillery to play, main music of the dance.
When distance intervenes between the foes,
The cavalry in advance of the driving goes;
But when little distance may intervene,
About the driving, no cavalry is seen.
A cloud of skirmishers cover the lead,
To hide the advance, as well they need;
Following the skirmishers, the reserve advance,
Then the main line follows, to aid in the dance.
Then all is still as a cyclone's sleep,
As silently forward, the skirmishers creep;

Then along the advance, somewhere near.
A rifle rings out sharp and clear;
Then in the distance, another is heard,
As if an echo had only occurred;
Then the din of arms awaken,
As if the earth was cyclone shaken.
Here slow and steady, the fire has been,
Then it leaps to a racket and din;
Fierce or slow, into the distance roll.
As thunders traveling from pole to pole.
When the skirmishers onto the reserves fall back,
Fierce the noise, and louder the crack.
Then it seems the racket case had bu'sted,
Where years of fearful noise had crusted.
Then, if the reserve fall back from force superior,
The loudest cyclone would be inferior;
Then it seems that a noise-box had exploded,
Where for ages the extract of noise was loaded;
Or some other big noise-case had cracked.
Where the fuss of a thousand years was packed;
Or some over-charged racket-case had bu'sted,
That peaceful times, with age had crusted.
(Ah, its when batteries open their throat,
That living men, with death are smote.
To armies of the land, or on the sea,
The bombshell's hum is their lullaby;
The solid shot or bombshell's scream,
Is a sailor's love, a sailor's theme.
Beneath their hum, they work content,
As the muskets play an accompaniment,
The fife and drum seems lonesome and far,
When artillery and musket tunes up a war.
A cannon-ball has a doleful sing,
As it rides o'erhead, on powder's wing.
But worse the shells that curving flies,

With lurid light to illumine the skies.
Which never stops for men in masses,
But mows a lane, as through it passes.
Where e'er explodes these screaming shells,
Of misery and death alone it tells).
When the rebels are driven, and the ground is clear,
Then it's time for the workers, on the ground to appear.
When the line is selected, at a word of command,
The workers step forth, with tools in hand.
With tools in their hands, and rails on their backs,
It's the spade and pick, shovel and axe.
Thousands of rails from the fences plucked,
Breastworks of which, they did construct.
It was rails and dirt together fixed,
Dirt and rails together mixed;
It was all done so lightning quick,
One would scarce note the curious trick.
(After the breastwork reared,
And the brush was cleared.)
Then a division into the ditch was taken,
To give the rebel ranks a shakin'.
The siege-guns were taken along,
To brace the ranks, to make 'em strong.
A house of logs was torn do'n
For timbers, to set the cannons on.
And a southern lordly residence,
Was used for a fort, by our President.
Thus had our army, in a space so brief,
Hewed its way into the rebels' teeth,
And rested there on the third day's night.
To wait for the morrow's coming fight.
But it was found, by the morrow's sun,
The rebels had got up to run,
And left behind some ragged boars,
To destroy the surplus stores ;

But exploding magazines repeated,
Proved to the Yankees they had retreated
One has not the slightest sense,
What the rebels destroyed was immense
For the rebels, they were "afeard,"
And therefore, they got badly scared.
    (This is why they ran,
     All to a man).
It was Halleck's careful creep,
That made the rebels so retreat.
Though nature well protected them,
It was assisted little by men;
And when the signs of battle appeared,
The rebels then got up and cleared,

Then—W. T. Sherman, with his men,
    The works he first occupied,
On swords and guns they all relied,
That was so oft in battle tried.
These men from Shiloh to this time,
Had marched in many a battle line.
In blood, the country then was drenched,
Seven camps they had entrenched,
They did it so strong as to surprise
The expectations of the wise.
The rebel pickets, unprotected,
Looked for the foe they had expected,
Then when the morning's sun arise,
They behold him with their eyes;
Then they fled to seek their chums,
But they had fled with all their guns.
Oh! where was Price and bold Van Dorn,
Who, to retreat were specially born?
    Ah, they had fled,
    And left their wounded with the dead.

The marks of vandalism then,
Showed the spirit of rebel men.
    (The day that the rebels fled,
     May, to twenty-nine had sped).
When they moved from Corinth town,
And the Union soldiers had closed aroun',
Gracious, what a hand-shaking then.
Passed among these noble men;
And how their cheers on the air smote,
Each Yankee tried to split his throat;
And as they marched o'er Corinth's land,
It was a sight stupendously grand.
(Now's the time, here let me tell it,
Important was Corinth, to those who hel' it).
Surrounded is Corinth by a chain of hills,
Beautiful scenes and sluggish rills.
Towards Farmington, the highest land,
Than any found on either hand;
Then towards the College hill abounds
Some high and lofty pleasant grounds.
In it, when rainy, you cannot tramp
For Corinth then becomes a swamp,
  When the rebels from Corinth drew,
  The Union cavalry did pursue.
      Then cars were burned,
      And steameries turned;   [railway.]
      Supplies destroyed,
      And rebels annoyed;
      Their depots flamed,
      Their engines lamed.
Then wreck and ruin seemed to float,
And man, with sword, his fellow smote;
Then many a Confederate son,
In getting captured, lost his gun.
Then weary of foot, and tired of soul,
He trudged home on a sworn parole.

HALLECK'S REPORT.

Away down in that southern clime,
When June had chased her days to nine :
From Corinth, Halleck warned the nation,
Fifty miles were the rebels from that station ;
Fifty miles, by the steamery's nearest cut,
But seventy by the wagons' worn rut ;
And that the rebels lost so many men,
It took forty thousand to number them.
That Beauregard's army was demoralized, and,
Of them, we captured many a band.

HOLLY SPRINGS.

Read ye, the length and breadth of this .
Down in the State of swampy Miss' ;
It was in June, the twentieth day,
The sun shed forth its warmest ray ;
When Sherman plumed his daring wings,
And sallied forth on Holly Springs ;
From whence the rebels had not long fled,
Ere Sherman came to try his lead.

HALLECK CALLED TO WASHINGTON.

Here the rebel cause was stabbed and ended,
Ere warring troops on them descended.
Famine, with her dagger laws,
Seemed ready to conquer the southern cause ;
And it's strange it did not sooner fade,
Bombarded by that vast blockade.
Halleck, then, to Washington went,
In obedience to an order sent ;
And when July had slid along,
Till the seventeenth was partly gone ;
Then Halleck bid his army adieu,
And praised them for the rebs they slew.
He went to Washington to swell a reef,

And assume the position of general-in-chief.
Then General Grant's command was changed,
And the old department rearranged.
Grant's department lines were stretched,
Till a part of Missi' State they "catched."
With Corinth for headquarter town,
To tear the rebel raggery down.
Grant's department was known to be,
"The Department of Western Tennessee."
Memphis in Grant's department laid,
Important in the warring trade.
A Provost-Marshal ruled her strong,
Sometimes right, but oftener wrong,
It was a rebel place, in a rebel land,
Around which marauded many a guerilla band.
It was hard for rulers to keep it straight,
Disorders seemed its prevailing fate.
It was so hard to e'en control,
The citizens they did parole.
Then as June on in a state did ride,
Equal to three, by seven multiplied.
Then Sherman took the reign in hand,
To stop the state in contraband ;
And General Sherman as well expected,
The devilish points he soon detected.
The guerillas were dealt with tough,
And when caught were handled rough.
Grant ordered Sherman to make demands,
And rent idle Memphis as she stands.
Rent the empty houses to protect them,
Till owners returned, as they did expect them.
Owners, that to war had fled,
To strike our lines with hissing lead.
Their houses must bring the rent,
That must in warring them be spent.

The Corinthian rebelites
That fled from death or many fights,
Concentrated at Jackson, Miss',
Why they went there, the reason's this;
So they could go where they were needed,
And their officers be superceded.
To Port Hudson, Vicksburg and Baton Rou',
They were all sent, except a few.
In the Union lines, black refugees,
Seemed to be a hideous disease;
 For on the commander's hand,
 They were an encumbrous band.
 Therefore Grant put his to labor,
 With the spade, instead of the saber.
 Company cooks, and various things,
 To lighten the soldiers' drudgerings.
 And many an officer took a pair,
 To black his boots or comb his hair.
 Of course the officers then fed them,
 And from his pocket book he paid them.
 The servant was a traffic raid,
 According to the bargain made.
 Of course, slaves then were slaves no more;
 Only just a country's bore.
 Black men then became a drug,
 Sore for Uncle Sam to lug.
Their owners claimed them to be sure,
But they only claimed them, and nothing more.

GRANT'S ORDER (General Order No. 72).

Disloyal citizens around any military station,
Known to be disloyal, or in dangerous organization,
Can be ordered away, or legally arrested,
And their crops and stock by army men digested.
 But no soldier in the Union lines,
 Must dare to take whatever he finds,

Unless it is to the government given,
And turned o'er to the soldiers' livin'.
Let no legal point be supervised,
By soldiers who are unauthorized,
For thus, whole armies are demoralized.
After armies, there always drags,
A worthless lot of scallawags,
Of which Grant tried to rid his ranks,
By working on them the drafting pranks.
For they were men that would abscond,
A thieving tribe *de* vagabond.
They'd violate the army trade,
The rules and regulations made.
But if caught, their goods were ta'en,
And themselves placed under military reign,
To do duty as a soldier, private,
Until honesty they sould arrive at.

  The rebel Major-general Bragg,
  In Chattanooga struck a snag.
He issued an order, September fifth's the date,
As if it came from Sparta, the Bamialian state.
This was an order to just mislead the Yanks,
But he didn't find them such an eyeless lot of cranks.
For Grant's cavalry was constant on the lurk,
And understood the rebels and all their petty dirt.
        [tuck'.
So Grant sent reinforcements to the army in Ken-
        [bad luck.
And Bragg found out to go that way would surely be
        [times,
The rebels found it necessary, to keep up with the
        [lines.
To send some heavy columns against Grant's extended
This was to keep Grant from assisting Old Kentuck'.
But again they were mistaken and got into bad luck.
For Grant's reconnoitering cavalry party knew
All about the rebels, and what they were going to do.

The rebel General Price fixed up to strike a blow,
And crush the little camp at the village of 'Cinto.
But Jacinto arose, and trimmed herself for fight,
And sent her baggage to Corinth in the darkness of
[the night.
With troops from Corinth, and Jacinto added in,
[din.
They started out for General Price to raise a mighty
He was stationed at Iuka with his forces concentrated.
[ated.
There the Yankee met him, and his lines were renov-
[ated.
But ere the Yankees done it they were sorely aggrav-
Generals Grant and Ord and daring Rosecrans,
Through a drenching rain, onward they advance.
The roads were worked and mudded to a slush,
So along the country roads, the armies couldn't rush.
They struck Iuka in a double,
To work there Price a fearful trouble.
[Grant and Ord,
Via Burnessville, from the north came Generals
And from the south, General Rosecrans pressed hard.
It was when September had partly slid away,
And the morning of nineteen had opened up to day.
[pickets,
General Hamilton's division encountered the rebel
[ets.
Around about Burnet's Corners, stationed in the thick-
Then towards Iuka they were borne six miles down,
Until they were in but two miles of the town;
And there they found the rebels concentrated en masse,
With a warm welcome in musketry and brass.
[that;
Soon the engagement became fierce, and sanguine at

One-third of the Union force engaged, was soon placed
                          [*hors du combat.*
And when the welcome dark closed o'er the bloody
                          [scene,
Each one slept upon his arms, of battle-fields to dream.
But when darkness fled from the morning sun,
Not a foe was left to fire a murderous gun.
    For Price and all his murderous clan
    Got up and slid down to a man.
        Ere Grant upon the scene arove,
        Rosecrans had the rebels drove,
        And when the sun dispelled the night
        He was pressing them in flight.
        Of Rosecrans be it understood
        His army of the Mississip' was tried an' good.
        Grant had no hand in this battle so tough,
        But only served in the game of bluff.

A REBEL SOLDIER TO A FRIEND.

In Iuka one peaceful day we stayed,
Then we was shook up by the Yanks infernal raid.
How they got so close was a mystery to me,
When the woods full of our cavalry seemed to be.
They almost got into town itself, and
Began to crack away, on each and every hand.
The head-quarters of Price they even shelled,
And by them many of our brave boys were felled.
                          [hurt.
The musketry was dreadful and wonderful was its
As the grape and canister howled in wild concert.
                          [tune.
In hours more than two and a half, battle waged its
And many, aye, many a man, was overtook by ruin.
Early in the action fell General Little, dead.
Some Yankee laid him low with a missile of their lead.

O, it was a struggle frightful as 'twas grand,
To which the darkness of night lent a helpful hand.
Our killed and wounded o'er the battle-field strewn.
What a picture of disaster—what a field of ruin!
Saddest of all, our dead that were levelled by the blow
And our wounded all fell to the mercy of the foe.
For during the night, had we to hasten and retreat,
Or the foe's reinforcement would prove a sore defeat.
But as the night passed away, and the sun shone clear,
We found that the foe was hard pressing our rear;
    And nothing could beat them off our back,
    But the grape and canister's murderous crack.
    The vandalic system that our army pursues,
    Makes one shudder the facts to peruse.
        Cornfields were laid waste,
        With all the show of wanton taste;
        Potato patches were also robbed,
        And chickens running loose were mobbed.
    In the smoke-houses they went a fakin',
    And carried off the hams and bacon.
    Hogs were shot to death, and stabbed,
    And all the other live stock grabbed.
    With outrages in every nook,
    Too strong for record in this book.
Those things too strong for the fiends of Flanders,
Were done under the nose of the chief commanders.
Many a woman, perhaps, and fatherless child,
                      [smiled.
For what those fiends destroyed, would have gladly
They were fiends to spend
  What they should have been proud to defend.
  Oh countrymen, countrymen! are you such,
  That I must blush to call you as much.
           Rebel Soldier JOHN S. PIDLEY.

GRANT'S REPORT TO W. H. HALLECK, COM-
MANDER-IN-CHIEF.

Of killed and wounded I should suppose,
The friends were equal to the foes.
Four or five hundred on each side,
Numbering the wounded with those that died.
It was reliably related to me,
Price was going east of the Tennessee;
But he has found he couldn't make it,
Our bombshells coaxed him to forsake it.
Among the killed General Little fell,
With General Winfield wounded as well.
Of Rosecrans and his troops, I'll say my says,
Man's tongue's too puny to give them proper praise.
Towards the rebels, they pressed hard,
The troops commanded by General Ord,
But never got to play a card,
Or close,
To fire a shot at the flying foes.
They dusted out with shining labor,
To save their coat-tails from the saber.

GRANT'S COMPLIMENTS TO HIS TROOPS.

Congratulations here are given, to officers and troops,
For wreaking on Iuka rebs such wild destructive swoops.
Though the rebel forces were superior to our own,
Which was a truthful fact to every soldier known.
The troops to meet the foe, were burning with desire,
Such troops will always win, urged by such a fire.
While congratulating the living, its meet that we should sped,
In offering condolence to the friends of the glorious dead.
That fell in defence of their homes and their hearth,
Which will give the fields of Iuka historical birth.
Which will be memorable for ages to come,
Where such heroic deeds were so daringly done.

GRANT MOVES TO JACKSON, TENNESSEE.

Grant moved his head-quarters to Jackson, Tenn.,
So he could more readily handle his men.
He left Corinth to Rosecrans,
Corinth and its local commands.
The Iuka flogged rebels, to Ripley repaired,
Those who had not to hades retired.
Then with Van Dorn and Lovell struck Corinth a blow,
Where they bore down stubbornly hard on their foe;
But all of Grant's army, in waiting did lay,
At Rosecrans' summons, to rush to the affray.
(When the rebels so vigorously started for gore,
October had numbered her days up to four.)
So vigorous and daring was the rebels' attack,
That the lines of the Union were forced to fall back.
Oh, it was a sanguine, bloody affair;
And man must be stubborn such carnage to dare,
It was such a bloody battle bold nature to appall,
[ball.
Never was there such another on this old revolving
Cannon-balls plowed great chasms of gore,
And blood was the rain of cannon's roar.
And the rebels e'en charged into the town,
Then in the streets fought a fierce, bloody roun'.
[a tree,
But they were broken and scattered like the twigs of
That is struck by the surf of a wild stormy sea.
Ere morn the rebels saw a bloody defeat,
And the Yankees chasing in full retreat.
It was a Federal victory, though dearly bought,
'Mid a cyclone of arms, and a hurricane of shot,
Besides the dead and wounded, on the battlefield left,

A thousand more as prisoners from their ranks was
[cleft.

 Pursued the Yankees in deathly trade,
 On their stony hearts to whet their blade.
 (Will man ne'er quit this butchering trade—
 Men killing men for the wages that's paid.)
 The rebels fled to and o'er the Hatchee,
 For fear the Yankee might possibly catchey.
 As McPherson, Ord and Rosecrans
 In pursuing them had joined commands.
 Cannons we got several of them,
 Swords and guns, with three hundred men.
 It was, it was, a frightful bout,
 It turned the rebels to a rout.
 At Corinth is where Hackleman fell,
 And Oglesby grazed the fringes of hell.
 Grant congratulated his troops anew;
 The battle scenes he did review.

  Then Lincoln to Grant sent over the wires,
  Congratulations in a dispatch of enquir'es.
  "Give me an estimate of your knowledge crude,
  How does it all sum up, pursuing and pursued?
  General Hackleman's fall I specially regret,
  And General Oglesby, is he recovering yet?
   I feel very anxious that he should mend,
   For he's my intimate personal friend.
    But please keep the rebels clinkin'.
    Yours very respectfully,

      A. LINCOLN."

           [wag
By this time the Ohio army, under General Buell, did
           [Bragg,
In pursuing the flying, blood-stained rebel General
 Grant's lines had fought themselves to a hush,
 Except now and then a guerilla brush.

When Fall had fell to the sixteenth of October,
After Spring had summered itself down sober,
                                        [dee,
Grant's division, that made the rebels te-rad-a-dad-
                                        [see.”
Was designated as “the department of the Tennes-
        And the government so extended this
        As to reach around Vicksburg, Miss'.
        And our dashing officer, General Rosecrans,
        Was placed o'er the army under Buell's command.
        The combined troops under Grant was known*
        To out fight all others that stood alone.
        For it had many heads over it that were strong,
        And swords that were whetted keen, and long,
        And they were crossed by the government's arm,
            To crush the rebels to the damnedest harm.
            It was known by its force when seen,
            And of army corps it was thirteen.
                                        [green,
To the rebs they often played Old Patrick dressed in
                                [waltzing seen.
But when the tune smote on their ears, vast was the
Far from the enemy, out of the reach of friend,
And then they were out of hearing ere came the end.
            The government's head,
Thought that Tennessee might be tired of flying lead,
And the breeze's stench from the unnumbered dead.
And if she wished her own government to resume
On the old lay of Uncle Sammy's tune.
To the scheme was invited Grant's powerful hand,
Assisted by Johnson, the governor of the land.
            With all that did in loyalty remain,
            Without a blot of rebel stain.
            So Tennessee could rise again,

* See book of “Remarkable Remarks on Grant.”

And weld anew the broken chain.
But General Bragg determined that
It was a scheme he would strike at.
So Nashville, he moved near to it,
To make the folks about there rue it;
And at them shook his bloody fist,
And bade the people to desist.
Now, some heavy work before Grant laid,
The heft of which will try his trade,   .
And the keenness of his whetted blade.
        For aye,
It's soon in blood the troops will wade,
        In hellish play.
        For daring foes
Will meet each other in deadly strife,
        And clanging blows.
Then to kill each other is sweets of life,
And glory thrills with vigor rife,
When man meets man with murderous knife.
The glory sought in battle trade,
Under the coming age will surely fade,
When pruning hooks from the warrior's blade
        Are beaten,
May the bloody warriors peace decade,
        Then sweeten.

        Extracts from Jackson, Tenn.,
        Halleck's orders to Grant's men.
In baggage and wagons you must travel light,
And not get worried before the coming fight.
For the active troops in the coming campaign,
On the march must bivouac in sunshine or rain.
For we shall go out to make things roar,
And we must be fixed to kill and to cure.
But make everything light upon all hands,

Nothing we'll carry, only what want demands.
The trains from the lines must all keep clear,
With the moving troops not to interfere.

Grant went through and sorted his men,
And chased the guerillas off from them.
For guerillas only weaken arms,
And to the country does the direst harms.
About October's latter end it was this
Colonel[A. L.]Lee went reconnoitering to Ripley, Miss.
And twenty-four hours under his power it stayed,
Held by carbine power and saber blade.
And when November days had run to two,
Back to Grand Junction his forces withdrew.
                              All his command,
With the rebel prisoners that he had on hand.
When November's fourth day came in range,
Grant moved his head quarters to Lagrange,
And troops with him he took enough
To handle the rebel legions rough.
For at Ripley the rebels were congregating.
From the country round they were concentrating.
Colonel Lee with cavalry, fifteen hundred strong,
Went reconnoitering fierce and long,
Followed by McPherson's infantry gang,
To teach rebels the art in battle clang.
At Lamar the infantry stopped to rest,
As to Hudsonville Lee onward prest.
He met the rebels, they were conquered and foiled,
Their ranks also he plundered and spoiled.
Back to Lagrange he then returned.
Him, and the infantry, and all concerned.
Then Grant's despatch to the general-in-chief,
Gives his ideas in a space so brief.

(La Grange, November the 11th, 1862, 10:30 p. m.
{ So forth, so on, and then.
The seventh Kansas cavalry, under Colonel Lee,
One hundred and thirty-four prisoners turned o'er to me.
And sixteen more lay dead on the field,
While two of his boys got badly steeled.
All the rebel forces could not repel him;
And no cavalry officer can excel him.
He kills rebels with a sweeping devotion,
. I in earnest, therefore, recommend promotion.
U. S. Grant.

Lee's reconnoitering information was immense,
And helped to break the rebel fence.

The time, November nine.
From Grant's order extracted, read it
Which made the soldiers heed it.
Therefore from his pious ranks,
He expelled all plundering cranks.
The muster of the pay roll stood,
To make the thefts of soldiers good.
If not the individual found
The company where it did abound.
If the unknown company's in a known brigade,
On the purses of all of them it's laid.
And e'en charged to the whole command,
If it can't be found in a smaller band.
Each soldier, then, must stand his share,
With the officers in proportion fair.
Then in the hands of officers it stood,
To make all their soldiers good.
Where individuals can be found,
By this and former laws he's bound.
Now on parade this must be read,
Till three successive eve's have fled.
Major-General U. S. G.
Department of the Tennessee.

Thus by a hand firm and stout,
Most nigh all evils were plucked out.
Thus by discipline strict and hard,

Grant held his army under guard.
That's why his army in working rates,
Excelled all others in United States.
(Ye ignorant plebes, here do not laugh,
At the department's change, Grant mended his staff.)

So this writing we'll fix,
General order, number six.
Brigadier-generals first, we'll place them,
Where they're to go among the men.
J. D. Webster, he superintended
The military roads, wherever extended.
Lieutenant-colonels now come in,
To swell the jargon of battle din,
As Assistant Adjutant-general, sure.
John A. Rawlins is no common bore.
He is also Chief of staff,
Who does the work that kills the calf.
W. L. Duff,
Chief of artillery and such stuff.
J. P. Hawkins, chief of subsistence,
To keep the soldiers in existence.
C. A. Raynolds, chief quarter-master,
Who grew rich on war's disaster.
Now come colonels,
Head fiends connected with infernals.
T. Lyle Dickey, cavalry chief,
Who chased many a rebel to grief.
Now here come four noted scamps,
Colonels still, their aid-de-camps,
And other title tales so long,
That they reach clean through a song.
John Riggin, Jr., of this staff,
Military superintendent of telegraph.
William S. Hillyer, who ever heard him boast,
Though he was marshal-general provost.
Acting inspector-general, Clark B. Lagow,
Also George P. Ihrie was the same kind of a cow.
George G. Pride was a mighty seer,
Of military railroads, chief engineer.
Surgeon Horace R. Wirtz, he was snug

Chief of a department in the line of drug.
Major William R. Rowley, aid-de-camp and mustering officer
[too,
He saw many a bold man that battle carnage slew.
 Now comes the captains in,
 To get their share of slaughtering tin,
 For which they braved the battle's din.
 T. S. Bowers, aid-de-camp, or such
 That rush around in battle much.
 They are only message boys, it's said,
 Who carry their orders o'er living and dead.
 F. E. Prime, chief of engineers that plan,
 The shoveling of dirt to the glory of man.
Lieutenant James H. Willson, such his craf,'
Chief engineer of the topograph.
 In the ordnance department, then,
 Lieutenant S. C. Lyford was chief of men.
  By command of M. G.—U. S. G.
Jotn A. Rawlins, A. A. G.

Here many, a many ton of cotton
From the Secession States were gotten,
By confiscation and otherwise.
Which only the shrewdest dealer tries.
Cotton speculation was then immense,
All carried on at the planter's expense.
These cotton dealers bought to sell,
And they beat the government just as well.
 The negro now began to wear
 Into the government's affair,
 As well as an encumbrance to,
 From whence they their rations drew.
 Into the army forts they pried,
 In support of the rebel's side.
 Their old masters sent them for
 To investigate the facts of war.
 Therefore negroes oft in spite,
 Tried to weld their shackles tight.

So a camp for negroes they did organize,
To keep them away as dreaded spies.
Well those refugee negroes fared,
A chaplain respectable o'er them cared.
At Grand Junction was the place located,
Where the darkey camp should be created.
Their Uncle Sam placed a guard about them,
So no rebel foe should steal up and rout them
Where grub was given them, and meats to fry.
Though the coffee they drew proved to be rye.
There the negroes and their belongings lurk:
Just the unemployed and out of work.

Volunteer infantry regiment twentieth Illinois
Had among its soldiers some thieving boys,
  Who at Jackson, Tenn,
Broke into the stores of some merchant men.
The damage of which they had to pay
In the prescribed foregoing way.
I'll bet that regiment felt oppressed,
With the damage to all of them assessed,
Except those in hospital and other places,
That were away honorably without disgraces.
It took several dollars and sixty-six cents
     [1242.66]
To pay the seventh night of November's expense.
      [the bout,
While Captains Orton Frisbee and John Tunison in
For their work in the business got mustered out.
  The subject of trade in the States Secession
  After leading a long, wide bloody discussion,
  And after they got back into the Yankee lines
  Again they wished to trade as in olden times.
  But such would advance the southern cause
  More than it would aid the northern laws
  So the Treasury at Washington made

A firm finger-board in guidance of trade.
But, O, how rude
So rigid and crude,
To those that such pursued;
And they dared not contrary
The law military.
For one to do trading he needed a long writ,
Which is legally called a trader's permit.
Signed by the treasury and the local provost.
Then he was bound by the chains of a ghost.
And therefore I'll tell you why is the reason
[treason.
To buy ahead of the army, was counted as
They'd handle you unjust, or deal you unfair,
If you bought of a farmer e'er the army was there.
To describe the traffic law here I shall fail.
It worked under rules without head, end, or tail.
But it was like clouds in a summer of drouth,
The whole tariff law would turn to a mouth.
But of all the people to do things unright,
It was the sanctified wretches the Jew-ish-re-lite.
[expel,
So from Grant's department they got a lightning
And at once they moved, taking baggage as well.
All the trading and traffic Grant did retard,
Fearing the people at large would call him a pard.
[would wag.
He was afraid of the slandering tongue that
And call him the partner of each trading vag'.
Ah, here 'tis !
A grand advance into the State of Miss.'
Though chasms of death around Vicksburg yawn,
The object in view is to reduce it till gone.
Letting the Father of Waters, unsullied by force,
Flow unobstructed down from its source.

Nature herself at Vicksburg had planned
A place that with ease an army could stand;
Then round it the rebels threw soul and heart,
And strengthened it with all the details of art.
The reason that Vicksburg was so infinite strong
Was that nature and art worked on it so long.
                                        [send
Every victory that Grant among the rebels would
The works at Vicksburg were sure to extend,
Till she was strong throughout all her courts—
                                        [forts.
Until she was a fort built up out of layers of
She was a series of layers from end to end.
She was strengthened so far that none could
                                        [mend.
Thus she stood ready to oppose, defend or op-
                                        [press.
Surmounted or enclosed in a huge fortress.
Vicksburg had been struck all round and round,
And every one found she was solid and sound.
Commodore Foote, from the river above,
Struck her with all the ardor of a warrior's love.
As Farragut's fleet steamed in from below,
And struck her a heavy, though ungenerous blow.
While General Williams, back in rear of them all,
Was working away with one division small,
Coaxing Mississippi to follow his trail.
And leave Vicksburg isolated back in the dale.
        Oh, what a scheme,
If he could have stolen her away from the scene,
He would have closed a great chasm of death,
The spilling of blood, and the wasting of breath.
The great river then would have been unblockaded
And Vicksburg back into peace would have faded.
It failed, and she nobly stood the rubs,

Of those that struck her with inferior clubs.
And well could old Vicks' turn up her proud nose,
When assailed by an inferior number of foes.
Thus stoodVicksburg ere Grant crept up to her walls,
And thundered at its gates with steel cannon-balls.
Port Hudson lay fortified far down below,
To parry the navy from striking a blow.
Now note ye what Logan said,
Ye living few of the numerous dead.
General John A. Logan's speech was grand,
About northwestern men under Grant's command.
Who knew them from the first stroke made,
And he knew each carried a trusty blade.
He asserted in the nation's halls,
Surrounded by congressional walls,
If the northwestern soldiers had but a chance,
They'd hew their way to the gulf in a bloody advance.
No soldiers of an unjust cause,
Can clench them in their dirty claws.
So that's the size of the western men,
They are fearless now, but were bolder then.
Uncle Sammy viewed their hearty size,
And put backing to the enterprise.
Grant's department, they enlarged it then,
And multiplied his fighting men.
They backed him up in munitions of war,
And gave him all he desired for.
Thus our army prepared, Vicksburg was sure,
In battle din to hear things roar.
Parties reconnoitering, were so grand and wide,
The rebel army, entrenched, they e'en defied.
Towards November's latter end,
On rebels Washburn did descend.
Descended with all the fury meant,
Carrying off baggage, supplies, men and tent.

It was one grand cavalry raid.
The killed and captured, wounded and slayed.
This was along Cold Water river,
Where danger made the rebels shiver,
Throughout the country broad and wide.
On Tallahatchee's river side,
Vast reconnoitering parties rode,
Till the country was deemed a dangerous abode.
A special command to Garner's station,
Went there to deal them a depredation,
They went the rebels to annoy,
The bridge of a railway to destroy.
They destroyed some railroad track as well,
Then back to the command they quickly fell.
This raid, with several more succeeded,
As also several more were needed.
Then few of the many from glory fell,
And the rebels chased in a bloody repel.
Their devastation on every hand,
Marked the country wild and grand.
Panola got a Yankee fill,
As Oakland did, and Coffeesville.
General Hovey's command took short naps,
For knocking railroads into gaps.
Therefore they scarce could sleep,
For the love of making railroads weep.
With all those brushes, kicks and brawls,
'Mid saber strokes and cannon-balls.
Along Grand Junction's rail to Grenada
Grant's fearless army wound its way,
To Waterford through Holly Springs,
Where he stumbled onto some Jewish things.
Here illicit traffic was pursued,
A way o'er peace it did intrude.
A St. Louis house here done the job,

Itself to enrich, the North to rob.
   At Oxford, on December third,
   A skirmishing series there occurred.
Grant manœuvred the country into fear.
With a cavalry lead to a ponderous rear.
Grant's head quarters at those times
Was at Oxford, Miss., among his lines.
Our garrison at Holly Springs
There done some dirty little things.
A few rebel farmers to them came,
Conquered them, and paroled the same,
And also destroyed Grant's supplies;
Which to him was a big surprise,
Which displeased him quite immense,
At their cowardice and little sense.
And to him the darkest ghost—
Proven disloyalty, hurt the most.
Then Grant fell back to Holly Springs,
To regain his store of needed things.
Holly Springs surrender he did condem'
The sneaking acts of treacherous men,
Which ended Colonel R. C. Murphy's careers
O'er the eighth Wisconsin volunteers.
Col. Murphy did not then feel so gay,
With a lost command and a forfeited pay.
Grant's army now had grown so large
He changed commanders and men in charge.
And the time and date of this remember,
Was the twenty-second of December.
Lincoln, gathering men by threes and fours,
Swelled Grant's divisions into corps.

   Now monotony breaks the scene,
   In general order, called fourteen.
From Holly Springs—of small, and great, and glorious things,
   Now heed my order, for it's brief.

And under direction of the general-in-chief.
All of this department, and that of Missour's,
Operating along Mississippi's shores,
Will be made into four army corps.

1. Thirteenth army corps must be,
The size of it below you'll see.
The troops composing the ninth division,
Under Brigadier-General [G. W.] Morgan's supervision.
And the tenth division, all of its band,
That's under Brigadier-General [A. J.] Smith's command.
With all the uncorpsed below Memphis, Tenn.,
Must also be classed along with them.
Under John A. McClernand they are to go,
To storm the field or siege the foe.

2. Then army corps fifteen,
In the lines below are seen.
Morgan L. Smith, commanding fifth division,
[supervision.
And the Helena, Arkansas, troops under [F.] Steele's
With the forces in the district of Memphis, Tenn.,
[them.
And it's Major-General [W. T.] Sherman commanding

3. Read what follows things before,
Below is the sixteenth army corps.
Divisions eight, seven and six, who ran them.
[will man them,
[L. F.]Ross,[I. F.]Quinby and[J.]McArthur, the same
With the troops of Sullivan and Davis,
[S. A.] Hurlburt commands them just to save us.
To save us from wreck and ruin,
And one nation into many strewn.

4. Description of army corps seventeen,
Beginning here soon ends the scene.
Describing there who and what, how and when,
And who is commanding of its men.
[they all commanded,
[J. W.] Denver, [John A.] Logan and [J. G.] Lawrence,
[Pherson handed.
Divisions one, three and four, which were o'er to Mc-
With Colonel [B. H.] Grierson's cavalry, brigade one,
All combined like 'chinery, to make the Johnnys run.

All division commanders with reports consolidated,
To those headquarters must occasionally be freighted ;
   And to all other business tend,
     Danger to a foe, and assistance to a friend.
                Major-General U. S. G.

John A. Rawlins, A. A. G.

Sherman's expedition down the Miss.,
To make cannon balls o'er Vicksburg hiss.
It was a thing stupendous and grand,
To move on water and by land.
It was a whale attacking a minner.
And if they didn't lose it ! the de'il's a sinner.
Here's a sight for bards and dreamers,
A fleet of an hundred and thirty steamers,
And of gunboats half-a-score—
Perhaps a dozen if no more.
Sherman's men were Westerners,
Used to hardships,* unknown to fears.
Hardy daring fighters by trade,
That shunned no foe and feared no blade.
They were men of fighting—oh, how rife ?
   Bred to a rough, adventurous life.
   This expedition, like none before,
   In military character it was pure ;
   No speculators could attend,
   Or with them the river descend.
When Sherman left the Memphis scene,
He head-quartered on the "Forest Queen."
And at Friar's Point, ere the set of sun,
He arrived on December twenty-one.
But he was unaware that Holly Springs
Had disarranged Grant's plans and things.

---

* Talk of ships, stale eggs, and canvas hams !
What are hard ships but ironclad rebel rams ?
Talking of misfortune, man's slides and his slips,
But these iron-clad gun-boats, I call 'em hard ships.

For Grant was to strike Vicksburg when
Sherman pressed her with his men.
From all accounts the plan was this:
Grant was to strike Vicks *via* Jackson, Miss.
But it was impossible for Sherman to learn
That Grant from Oxford did return.
But Sherman's hopes that Grant would meet
Would help to bring him o'er defeat.
Therefore it was but moral aid
That could support his daring raid.
Sherman carried out his part of the plan
As well as could be done by man.
Under Morgan L. Smith, at Milliken's Bend,
He landed a small force the rebels to rend.
On the railway line Texward bound
They tore it in sections from the ground,
The Delhi and Dallas depots they burned.
Then back to Sherman's command returned.
This was to keep the Johnnies from running
After they gave up their gunning.
(But the Yankees found no end of shot
Around Vicksburg's deadly spot.)
Ah, the plan it was what we needed,
If it could have just succeeded.
When December had glided past her 'leven
To the day called twenty-seven,
Sherman disembarked at Johnson's landing,
With the main force under his commanding,
Near where the Yazoo river flows,
And into the Mississippi goes.
With all the power of thought he cared.
To assail Vicksburg he prepared,
To tear away at life's expense
The city of Vicksburg's north defence.
Sherman's force was fierce and long,

His command was four divisions strong,
And could do some bold and daring things.
'Twas was the right of Grant's two ponderous wings,
    From Johnston's landing to Vicksburg town,
    In hills and swamps it does aboun',
             Also bayous,
                Lagoons and sloughs.
To get an army to Vicksburg by this way,
Would be a difficult task in a peaceful day.
    One cannot picture in the mind,
    The difficulties there confined,
    With vantages that nature boast,
    Entrenched therein a rebel host,
    Had the country a chance to try,
    The world at large they might defy.
Sherman drew his men in line of battle,
Like men to slaughter beeves of cattle,
And as the eaves of dark set in
The enemy was driven two furlongs in.
On the twenty-eighth the men in arms,
Fought with all the power of bravery's charms.
When Grant's left wing did not appear
Bright things began to look most drear.
And the rebels that fled from the advance of Grant,
Filled up the lines that once were scant.
Where Sherman probed them with his blade,
But yet unconscious Grant was stayed.
Where the concentrated fire of the reb's
Played havoc among the daring fed's.
And Sherman could not make them race,
Or start them from their hiding place.
       (O, for what is war so good,
        Only wrecking brotherhood.)
   Such is the breadth of warring fate,
   So closed December twenty-eight.

And when the morning sun arose,
New scenes to them it did disclose.
The rebels had extended their lines
Far beyond their old confines.
They made a strong position stronger ;
Weak places pregnable no longer ;
Their sharp-shooters filled the woods,
A-picking off the leading goads ;
They done it at a rapid rate,
Dangerous to an army's fate.
Sherman done some charging grand.
In his captured places could not stand.
                              For the foe
Struck a long and tiresome blow.
And when Sherman got a hold,
He was thrust out in the cold.
In those fields General Blair
Made some charges bold and rare.
He tightly grasped his trusty blade,
A-foot he headed his own brigade.
They followed where he led the charge,
O'er hills and copse, through glen and gorge.
Of his eighteen hundred able men
More than a third was killed or wounded then.
O, bloodiest picture of historic pages,
You'd appal the soldiers of darker ages.*
    Under a flag of truce the dead was buried,
    And away the wounded ones were carried.

* Oh, for wood to try my tools,
Upon this murderous lot of fools !
Thus educated in their schools,
Up to all the general rules,
That swords are our country's jewels.
To innocence be it e'er concealed,
The hideous work of a battle-field.
It's a wreck pruned by a sword and fenced by a spear,
Its music a widow's moan, its water an orphan's tear.

Then Sherman gave out to his command
To return, return to safer land.

Now to our calendar,

We add twelve months, another year,

And see what twelve months more will bring;

War or peace, or anything.

May we in peace wind up this spree,

In EIGHTEEN HUNDRED AND SIXTY-THREE.

Then after all these battle marks,
Sherman and his troops re-embarks.
They boarded their vessels in river Yazoo,
Where in advancing first they drew.
But General McClernand at this fraction,
Arrived upon the scene of action.
Then as McClernand o'er Sherman ranked,
His orders into action clanked.
And his first action sure was this,
He got his fleet into the river Miss'.
And where'er his order ranged
The title of the army changed.
To fool the rebels, and give him grip,
He called it the army of the Mississip'.
Now for awhile this army grand
Was taken from under Grant's command.
Accordingly was Grant arraigned,
And by the President maintained,
The thirteenth corps, with the fifteenth along,
To Grant's force again was added on.
But in the meantime here they boast
Of clearing out Arkansas Post,

Which by the powers of arms to them
Fell garrison, stores, and ten thousand men.
But it was a three hour hand-to-hand
Contended they this noble band,
But many o'er death's stream did ferry,
That long and bloody tenth of January.*

                      [Springers
During the court martial trial of the disloyal Holly
The investigation fished up some political ringers.

                      [arms,
Which caused several officers to get bounced from
                      [charms.
That they might seek the country and rest in rural
                      ninth Illinois.
The volunteer infantry regiment one hundred and
A wild investigation was hurled among her boys.
But as a regiment disloyal it was exonerated.
To its old place of honor, again 'twas reinstated.
But the officers discharged, had many jags and jars.

                      [wars.
In wishing the enemy success in relation to the
My space here is too scant to write you all about it.
                      [got routed.
Though those officers of honor for dishonor they
        The cavalry about the country places
        Charged the rebels in deadly races,
        Such was the cavalry's occupations.

---

* A long time single, Cleveland tarried,
But to-day, that batchelor's married,
Married to one who'll live, I hope,
To see her ancient husband croak !
Then Cleveland, I hope he will, sirs,
Live longer than her at least two years,
And when this national job occurred,
Was sixty-eight on June the third.
Ah, hold, I am too fast,
It was the evening of the last,
Which makes it the second day,
Amid the flowers of June's array.

Around the Union posts and stations.
The Yankees followed the deadly cause,
Close as an eagle to his claws.
They followed the rebels to wound and kill,
Close as an indorsement on the back of a bill.
On a camp near Ripley, Tenn.   [Jan. 8,]
They raided it for fifty men.
And killed and wounded several more,
And carried off their arms and store,
With teams to haul their captured stores,
Of horses, half a dozen scores.
The rebel guerrillas would raid and spoil
The rebel citizens turned loyal.
Therefore the country was devastated,
Where foe on foe retaliated.
On January, day called twenty-third,
(Few now remember when it occurred)
The army of the Mississippi came
Back to Memphis with loads of fame,
Where Grant and his army laid,
Who from Mississippi strayed,
To work a plan for another raid;
To test the Johnnys with their blade.
And ditch around them with the spade.
The first campaign, who could expect,
Success, when the thing got wrecked?
It struck a *Murphy* at Holly Springs,
And that's what disarranged the things.
With the proclamation of emancipation,
Came the freedmen of the nation.
And Grant determined to back them through,
And equip them to fight their masters too.

Here it was Grant's infernal wishin',
To wreck the white man's superstition.
He wanted the white man to suppose,

It was the nigger, not the clothes;
And, that both of them together,
One was no better than the other.
He wanted the white man to raise his pride!
And with niggers work side by side.
Oh, fiends of hell's infernal dower,
The de'il's own smutty, right hand bower,
To equalize the nigger and whites!
Oh, when did man receive such rights?
On Divinity it has no claim,
For that sacred writ forbids the same.
White men and niggers, here I'll say,
Will mix no more than night and day.
For where one raises, the other descends,
Where one commences the other ends.
Wreck such thoughts, they will not last;
Be they buried objects of the past.
   But Grant was right,
To arm these de'ils, and make them fight;
For o'er those Afric' sons of bitches.
We have wasted uncounted riches.
Will be, was, now, and forevermore,
To our race a constant sore.

   Now for a race,
   A change of base,
   To displace,
   The rebel's cause.
   Therefore where,
   Will they scare,
   At Sherman's rear,
   Or bleed him with their claws.
On the twenty-ninth of January,
The country o'er looked dull and dreary.
And many soldiers, sad and merry,
Had tramped along till they were weary.
In transports were carried down,
Landed at Young's Point in the town.
Then Young's Point assumed renown,

For tramping rebel nuisance down.
 It assumed the loyalty of a friend,
 When headquarters did attend.
 Also on transports did descend,
 Troops that landed at Milliken's Bend.
Soon Grant followed and took position,
And threw out bait for rebel fishin'.
E'en rebels came and asked permission,
To join Grant's latest new addition.
 Grant wanted to be near at hand,
 Ready to attend command,
 When descending troops should land,
 With Yankee Doodle on a band.
  It was to drive the rebels bold,
  Dislodging them from their stronghold.
  Grant e'en viewed their works all o'er,
  From viewing now and learning before.
  Which on the water's front he found,
  That it was adamantine sound,
  And it needed tons of cannon balls
  To e'en shake its stubborn walls.
  Grant and his generals counseled long,
  O'er this structure fierce and strong.
  So at last they did confide
  The southernmost the weakest side
  On which to bring the troops to bear.
  The point was how to get them there.
  Above, the river was blockaded,
  And from below could not be aided.
  For their it was fortified,
  Port Hudson guarded the rippling tide.
  So General Grant concluded then
  Williams' Canal to try again
  And make Vickburg isolate,
  By taking land from another State.

It was a task most hirculain,
Shot by foes, and drenched by rain.
It took more to fight the water
Than the men called out to slaughter.
Secrecy was now demanded,
In sturdy accents, firm and candid.
No soldiers could go in or out,
And citizens dared not prowl about.
All had to stay within the lines
That was the limit of confines.
Not e'en a flag of truce could come
Inside the line where picket run.
It was all mute—a secret affair—
Verging on some great scheme to dare.
Articles of war was carried out,
In their relation true and devout.
The guerillas was a pest and bore,
Firing at transports from the shore,
With field-pieces, light of heft,
Easy to take, but easier left.
At all safe places they hovered near,
In all big steals they had a share.
A reconnaisance did advance,
Around Lake Providence' narrow expanse.
Many a skirmish then took place,
And the rebels led in many a chase.
Then on the tenth of February
They played the rebels bold and merry.
And at Old River, Louisian',
They chased the rebels to a man.
During the reconnaisance Captain Prime
Found a place o'er which to climb.
He was Grant's chief engineer,
And of this scheme he had no fear.
No facts in it, could ever lurk,

It was too watery a scheme to work.
Still Williams' canal extended;
Ten thousand men o'er shovels bended.
But on the eighth of March, the stream,
Overflowed and wrecked the scheme.
For the Mississippi ran with pleasure,
Where space was found to store her treasure.
This scheme was then forever left,
To hands that work the dirt more deft.

THE RED RIVER EXPEDITION.

Colonel Ellet worked a glorious racket,
Ran the rebel batteries with his packet.
It was a rack of death and disaster,
The wonder was, it ever passed her.
I must be excited out of a calm,
Ellet's packet was an iron-clad ram.
"Queen of the West" was the name she wore,
And closely on the rebs she bore.
She ran down blockaded Mississip',
And up the Red River on a trip.
The rebels now held her with their forts,
But from them she towed off three transports.
Where the lower end of Williams' canal expanded
There's where she and her transports landed.
When the month of February had run to ten,
On a second trip she started again.   [morn,
He captured a steam transport from rebeldom, one
With a few soldiers, and nine hundred barrels of corn.
And as he pushed along the river's course again,
He fell upon and destroyed, an army wagon train.
But he lost his own dear ram, in iron siding dressed,
                              [of the West."
His old, powerful, and active, but beautiful "Queen
Colonel Ellet by rebels I'm sure was never gotten,

For he navigated from the " Queen " upon a bale of
[cotton.
Then he sought his captured vessel, a thing that came
[in play,
Though loaded down with corn and things, but still
[not in the way.
This captured vessel, " Era" was the name she bore;
Upon a rebel water bound, by a rebel shore.
[is meet,
The United States gunboat, "Indianola," to tell of her
Though at first successful, she wound up in defeat.
[helm,
And all other boats that strained their steam and
[realm.
To run the Vicksburg batteries to gain the lower
Those vesseled expeditions show the weak and wise,
Where Gibraltered Vicksburg gets her grub supplies.
It showed the stones   That broke our bones,
That lay in the path,   That backed the wrath—of rebs
With grub secured,   They worked their sword,
With fierce disaster.   A tyrant master.
      The Lake Providence canal scheme,
We see it different now from what it then did seem.
In it could be heard the clang of many spades, [aids.
The privates were their backers and most stupendous
[of Vicks',
The bayous that run from the river out on either side
  · [land betwix'
So Grant could boat around. he aimed to canal the
He therefore called out his topographic seers,
A lot of blockheaded things, they called 'em engineers.
The simplest schoolboy their answer would know,
For a thing suggested. they would try to make it go.
The first grand, mighty thing that had to here be done,
From Mississippi to Lake Providence a canal must run.

Through which alas, a boat can pass,
      Thence, from whence, o'er Providence, and on,
Through bayous, o'er sloughs, into Black River,
    Through River Tensas gone.
Then along the bed of the River Red,
    She slides, and glides—and onward rides,
Along its banks, with clatter and clanks,
    Till the Mississip' has full grip on its seething tides.
Where the Red River, is lost for ever, in the grip,
    Of the Mississip'; oh! gigantic flow.
Then we could land under right command,
    With Port Hudson's blockade far below—
And troops by this course, could assist the force,
    Under General Banks.
That was fixing to take, Port Hudson to rake,
    By battle ranks.
Then Vicksurg o'er the Miss' no longer could master,
As boats could go above without traveling a-past her.
Under the cover of this canal racket scheme,
Grant curried and harnessed his great warring team.
Below Vicksburg, inland from the shore there,
In Louisiana State, he planted troops with great care.
The canal was dug with rapidity of motion
That proved the Union cause was run with devotion.
                                    [barges,
It was opened, and a steamer, with a number of
Were taken through it on orders of duty discharges.
                                    [needed.
When the middle of April came with her warm days
The water of the Mississippi so rapidly receded,
That the roads from New Carthage to Milliken's Bend
Began to get good as the weather did mend.
And the canal got so dangerously low
Navigation no longer o'er it could go.
So it was no longer used but the roads resumed.

Then for battle again Grant's wings were plumed.
Then after the canal to a failure had led,
Grant had no faith in it from the first, he said.
Grant dug that canal, he did in after years say,
To work the soldiers, to drive laziness away.
   It's now, alas,
W'ell view the expedition of the Yazoo Pass.
It was in the woods so densely shaded,
That the gloomiest gloom of all glooms pervaded.
        [up pass,
To the Cold Water and Tallahatchee it was a closed
         [mass;
Till the Yankee from its mouth dug the great levee
Which made it run one way, but never this,
And parted its water from the river of Miss'.
When the month of February had reached a score,
And to that many days add the number of four,
         [mass,
Is the day that they cut the levee's water-clogged
And commenced navigating the long hidden pass.
There many a log or tree and drift aggravated,
But it was a great deal better than was anticipated.
After entering the pass in four days more, [shore.
They reached the cold waters and its wood-bound
And when the vessels got there, they looked as hard
As if they had stood a long siege or a fierce bombard.
  The hurricane-deck was battered and bruised,
  As the big limbs o'er them plowed and perused.
  A smoke-stack, or two was raked from the deck,
  And a cabin or two was turned to a wreck;
  And an old contraband nigger was slain,
  As in a sick-bunk he was laid up with pain.
  By a big limb that came down through the deck,
  And left that old nigger and bunk a dead wreck.
  Take the Dismal Swamp and an Indian jungle,

And the John Brown tract all in a jumble.
The three extracted and together combined.
But in them but a shadow of the pass you'll find.
If in looking for compound crooks doubly refined.
The Yazoo Pass is the chief one? Bear it in mind!
No hundred feet in it that goes along straight.
Or I have stretched here at a hundred fold rate.
The banks of the stream meanders together,
Each fifty to a hundred feet off from the other.
And the boats in it travelled in Yazoo styles,
Three days and a half to make twenty miles.
Aided by an army to cut away the brush,
With a big head of steam through saplings to crush.
The point was to reach the Upper Yazoo,
With light gun-boats and a heavy armed crew,
To keep the rebel country from aiding their forts.
And clear from that section all rebel transports.
But ere they got there the rebels were charmed
At the daring feat that the Yankees performed.
For they had heard of their deeds and daring tricks.
And came out to meet them like a thousand of bricks.
The Tallehatche river with a fort was closed,
So that's the way the rebels welcomed their foes.
Fort Pemberton that place was called. [March, 1863.]
There General Ross and his force got stalled.
After his forces mastering such unbeatable places,
Have rebels to shove cannon into their faces,
And forbid them progressing any further at all,
For fear of destruction from steel cannon ball.
But Ross tried hard to conquer the site,
To drive out the rebels and capture 'em in flight.
But they were troops from Vicksburg lent,
Armed and equipped against the Yankees sent.
Armed and equipped to aid in the chase,
But had no desire to lead in the race.

The balls from Ross's guns were hurled,
Like comets around a dying world.
The fire in the powder so quickly expanded
That death-telling missiles in the fort was landed.
The land forces here couldn't land at all,
For the high water swept to the very fort's wall.
When March to the twenty-third day had extended,
                                        [scended.
Ross went back up the stream the way he'd de-
It was a scheme that assisted Grant's own plans
For on Vicksburg rebels it made heavy demands.
        Now the expedition of Bayou Steele,
        Shows a movement strong and real.
It was ordered by Grant and strangely maintained.
Backed by Porter and powerfully sustained.
For both of them viewed it e'er they begun,
Through Bayou Steele their boats to run.
The infantry travelled both by foot and steam,
As there was few transports for so small a stream.
The infantry received their solid strong tuition
                                        [ammunition.
That they were to carry nothing but arms, grub and
But from Young's Point,Grant, therefore, did not go.
                                        [the blow.
Sherman, Steward and Porter are the ones that struck
They struck hard, both officers and man,   [off again.
And it was hard and active work that brought them
It was in March, late on the sixteenth day,   [way.
That the expedition was prepared and started on its
The road was to the Yazoo, above old Haynes' Bluff.
                                        [snuff.
Or by that way it was proposed to give the rebel's
        Sherman cleared and opened a passage
            With his pioneering corps.
        He cleared the trees, and sawed the stumps

As they passed along before.
And the reasons the expedition failed,
   Why not I here describe it?
There was none along that knew the country,
   Well enough to guide it.
That's the reason it got into
   Several rebel wrangles,
And in navigating through the woods
   Met with several tangles.
When almost within our grasp
   The object of the scheme,
Then it vanished from before us,
   Like an object in a dream.
The rebels about it with
   Torturing guns were seen,
And chasms of death
   At once did intervene.
Then a fight was pressed, so close
   On those that were concerned,
If it had not been for Sherman
   None could have returned..
Some scenes about this expedition
   Were novel and exciting.
The gunboats pushing through the woods
   And soldiers chase in fighting.
The gunboats from the cypress limbs,
   Got many an awful drubbing,
And raked along their mailed sides,
   With one continuous rubbing.
There was many a scene fantastic,
   Scattered along the way.
Things burlesque and picturesque,
   Happening night and day.
By destruction among the rebels,
   Many a ginn and house was gotten,

          For them it also took away,
            Two thousand bales of cotton.
          The provisions then destroyed,
            To give it here I scorn.
          The most of it consisted
            In ten thousand barrels of corn.
          Private property was almost
            Universally respected,
          Although it was a fact that
            The rebels scarce expected.
All these expeditions proved elegant extremes,
They used up rebel power and wasted Yankee means,
At each expeditions start they each would pick the pie.
                              [deny,
But when they got back again, they were willing to
Was it the officers that led the warring men,
Or did the officers stay behind and follow after them.
They each defy, and all deny they ever had bad luck,
                              [they're struck
Until a sword cracks their gourd, or by cannon-balls
              Until it's such as,
            Death holds 'em in his clutches.
            With death so close they can't defy,
            Their tongue so stiff they can't deny.
            Soldiers hold a curious belief,
            The de'il or death's their only thief.
        Throughout the army from blade to blade,
        Providence assisted to work the trade.
        Upon both sides he killed and slayed.
        For some chaplain was always there,
        Ordering Providence to do and dare.
    E'en heaping on him the biggest share.[Mar. 1883.
              The armies wealth,
              In spirit and health,
Was highly rated throughout, around and before,

From the commonest soldier to the heaviest corps.
Of course there was a few on the sick list,
And it spread over the country in a frightful whist.
As no mail from the army could reach its friends,
Until the Vicksburg scheme came to solid ends.
As our mails might be captured by rebel power,
From whence facts might be learned in a critical hour.
The home friends of the Union and her cause

         [claws.
Were more to be dreaded than the rebels' bloody
         [loud.
O'er the sick that went home they howled long and
Fearing that Grant's army was dying in a crowd.
         [supplies.
They were afraid Grant was short and needed hospital
Thus it disturbed the weak, and horrified the wise.
But in such, he had all that could be needed.
His hospital in any branch could not be exceeded.
Now Grant combines his aid with Farragut and Porter,
         [court her.
Combined against Vicksburg with shot and shell to
Grant moved around Vicksburg to reach its lower side,
         [tide.
As Farragut runs Port Hudson's guns on Mississippi's
Now Grant and Vicksburg were by no means together,
         [other.
Vicksburg on one side of the river, and Grant upon the
It was in March's days, when run to twenty-nine,
Above Vicksburg then, Grant's forces marched in line.
The thirteenth corps led in marching to the scene,
Then seventeenth was followed by fifteen.
         [munication,
The sixteenth corps held watch o'er supplies and com-
While the others marched on to lead in devastation.
About this time Farragut went down the Mississipp',

To go up the Red River on a devastating trip.
Thus he did a part that was extremely wise,
For it always kills a foe in taking their supplies.
On March thirteen, the village of Richmond found,
That Yankees were marching o'er their sacred ground.
But the thirteenth corps spent two long hours in fight,
Ere they forced the daring rebs to flight
    Then on they pressed with vim and vigor,
    To cut the bonds that tied the nigger.
In reaching New Carthage they checked their vim.
For in getting there they had to boat it o'er or swim.
                [to build,
(Therefore they stopped, boats to collect and barges
And at it, many a long, weary day was killed.)
    Bayou Vidal's levee opened,
      To try the Yankee armies' fate,
    And placed the village of New Carthage
      In an isolated state.
    Therefore a question with this
      Vast Yankee army arose,
    How to convey their ordnance,
      And grub to fight their foes.
    Therefore the men laid hold
      With sufficient force amain,
    And men assumed the place of mules,
      To drag the heavy train.
    It was no use to go and strike
      A half supported blow.
    Therefore Grant got a giant's club
      To crush a daring foe.
    As Grant was performing those
      Long and muddy marches,
    Porter was preparing to pass
      Vicksburg's cannon tortures.
    On April sixteenth, Porter's fleet,

Combined with three transports,
Ran by Vicksburg's batteries,
  Fired on from all her forts.
And why not here confess,
  One was totally injured,
And the others more or less.
Then six transports were made ready,
  Against Vicksburg's balls to press,
No soldiers were ordered to travel
  With such a dangerous fleet,
But volunteers were called,
  To perform the daring feat.
To which officers and men responded,
  With unequalled enthusiasm,
To ferry this transport fleet,
  O'er Vicksburg's deadly chasm.
To each boat was attached
  Two barges loaded with forage.
To tug them along o'er water,
  Was much faster than by carage.
Upon their wooden hulls,
  The bombshells shrieked in clatteries,
On April twenty-second, five out of six,
  Got safe below the batteries.
Part of the barges and one boat,
  Got awfully in distress,
And all of them, both in and out,
  Were injured more or less.
The repairing of them
  Gives many glorious charms,
Porter had material,
  And the mechanics were men in arms.

Before leaving Vicksburg's northern side,
Grant cut all communications, never to be tied.

---

* The rebels attempting to scale Grant's sword.

Or at least, ordered Grierson to perform it,
Which he performed with the spryness of a hornet.
He captured, wounded, burned destroyed and slayed
With his cyclone mounted cavalry, first brigade.
It was April seventeen he started on his bout,
And wreck and ruin was scattered along his route.
   Colonel Grierson's raid was grand,
   The most successful in the land.
   It took wondrous wit to guide it,
   And force of arms to just decide it.
   Many a town they rummaged through,
   Fording many a creek and slough.
   Many a road they left in ruin,
   And many an engine out of tune.
   And many a rebel hid in brush,
   They went the rebel foe to crush.
   For they went through the rebels land,
   Their armies surrounded them on every hand.
   Skirmishes they oft took place,
   And the rebels always led in chase.
   Many a rebel in dust was laid,
   One thousand more as prisoners made.
   Two locomotives were knocked to smashes,
   Two hundred cars were burned to ashes.
   Three railway tracks in ruins laid,
   Nine bridges into ashes made.
   They cut two telegraphic wires,
   One tannery consumed by fire.
   Three important rebel mails destroyed,
   Three rebel camps to ruin decoyed.
   Rebel whisky often filled their tanks,
   Twelve thousand horses joined their ranks.
   It was four million dollars worth,
   That they swept from the face of earth.
   Eight hundred miles in meandering ways,

Was traveled in just fifteen days.
This bold and daring, adventurous band,
Hewed their way through a rebel land.
And often fought them hand to hand.
  And on the field, so its said,
  They left of foes unnumbered dead.
  The hewed their way to Baton Rouge,
  A daring scheme, tremendous huge.
  When the Union garrison by them was meeted,
  Long and loud the shouts that greeted.
  When at Baton Rouge, a surprise arose,
  How they could hew their way o'er so many foes.
  In fact, it was such a great surprise,
  The garrison scarce believed their eyes.
  This raid sorely injured the rebel cause,
  And as much it buoyed the Union laws.*

When Grant had reached his destination,
Which was Hard Times, a river station,
Which was seventy miles from Milliken's Bend,
When his supplies o'er ruined roads must wend.
But the ruined road, he repaired it, of course,
By a large and powerful pioneering force.
Thus the road was mended across the rebel border,
And men camped along it to keep it in order.
  When April twenty-ninth
    Had wound its day along,
  Grant's army was on transports,
    Concentrated fierce and strong.
  With Admiral Porter's fleet,
    Combined together,
  To rattle shot against

---

* Colonel Streight, and many more,
  O'er rebels wreaked a vengeance sore.
  In fact, they raided in every direction,
  And struck the rebels in every section.

The rebels' dusky leather.
Then for five long hours,
  Cannon-balls winged their flight,
They rode inspired
  On wings of dynamite.
But to fight those rebels
  In their den,
Was wasting ammunition,
  Without injuring them.
Grant on a tug boat,
  In the middle of the stream,
Took in the action
  Of all the naval scene.
At a time propitious
  To strike a fearful blow;
But at a time propitious,
  He didn't have a show.
For Grand Gulf was fixed
  For battle's dreadful storm,
And those who ventured near,
  Would be welcomed warm.
The transports to run those batteries
  In passing down below,
At Hard Times landed their troops,
  To shun the heavy blow.
As the soldiers moved by land,
  The transports moved by water;
Oh, it was a grand advance
  On the rebels front, to slaughter.
Then when the army got below
  Grand Gulf's deadly chasm,
All on board, shortly,
  Soon the transport has 'em.
  To those present it was a day,
    They'll ne'er forget it soon;

On that tropic first of May,
        Hot as the last of June.
Oh, those deadly ranks,
        That shoved their lines before,
Was McClernand's boys,
        The thirteenth army corps.
When they landed at Bruingburg
        In search of wild secessions,
There every man drew a supply,
        A three day's run of rations.
All were loaded light, and marched to fight
        Wherever chances
Overhauled, or stopped and called
        The rebels to the dances.
The baggage train they did restrain,
        None followed in their wake;
They went to fight, and travel light,
        Therefore none they take.*
They went their way o'er mud and clay,
        The bluffs among.
And there they found, rebs in the ground,
        By the tunes their bullets sung.
They captured them, disarmed their men,
        All that with ease;
To Fort Gibson then, pushed all the men,
        Still as a breeze.
There, Yankees wise, wished to surprise,
        A daring foe.
The Yankees through 'em, got near to 'em,
        In battle row.

The Yankees quick the rebels sized,
The armies met with none surprised.
Here's where Feds on rebels wrought,

* See book of "Remarkable Remarks on Grant."

When the battle of Thompson's Hill was fought.
Here muskets rattled and cannons boomed.
As a bayonet charge their lives consumed.
But the rebels were firm and strong,
And bore the contest well and long.
They bore it long enough to know,
They were inferior to their foe.
Four hundred and fifty wounded and killed,
With five hundred more as prisoners billed.
We un's got three great big guns,
From those southern warlike sons.
They fled through Port Gibson town,
And burnt Bayou Pierre's bridging down.
The Yankees followed the flying foe,
And hit him many a welting blow.
Many a racket and din was heard,
As on they flew towards Vicksburg.
It seemed it did delight the Fed's,
To butcher and to capture rebs.
But havoc with the Yanks they played,
When chances they had to ambuscade.
Of Grant it's said he traveled light,
On this campaign, the rebs to fight.
His example was so rich and rare,
To imitate him no privates dare.
He carried no weapons used in war,
His only baggage, toothpick and cigar.
Without a horse he started there,
His only brute was shanks' mare.
He had no servants along with him,
As servants are only a fickle whim.
All hardships he seemed to 'rive at,   .
Known or found by the soldiers private.
A low crowned citizen's hat he wore,
Two officer's stars, and nothing more.

(To distinguish his power and rank,
He had the style of a country crank.)
With other soldiers he took chow-chow,
Hard tack, with belly *de la* sow.
Many a night on the ground he spent,   [tent.
With a log for a pillow and the heavens for a
No wonder the troops he did inspire,
With such an enthusiastic fire.
With a fire so hot, and so fierce a frown,
It withered the rebel empire down.
The rebel foe thus was sounded,
By our six hundred killed and wounded.
And this time a glorious day,
After April, the first of May.   [1863.]
Dismay filled the rebel cranks,
Fleeing from the Federal ranks,
As on the rebels they bore down,
Within sixteen miles of Vicksburg town.
They vacated Grand Gulf, leaving guns and store,
But the most of it was destroyed before.

Some of our barges in running Vicksburg's batteries,
Got punctured into frightful tatteries.
It's said by those to whom it's known,
Their hulls were punctured like a honey-comb.
Thus, many barges loaded with stores,
Seemed to perish in twos and fours.
For cannon-balls played on their decks,
And canister swept o'er in pecks.
Many a tug boat blew a farewell shriek,   [leak.
And settled in the river from an over-indulging
Grant to deceive each rebel band,
And those who stood high in command,
Against every rebel camp the Union forces thundered
Along the railways all army supplies were plundered.

The rebels had no resting place from the Yankee's raid,
All the rebels felt the weight and whittle of his blade.
[while,
They had no forts that would restrain 'em only for a
[style.
For the northwestern's were born when warring was in
In feints that about Vicksburg ensued,
The pursuing were often chased and pursued.
But oftener the rebels were chased in flight,
And fierce devastation boomed day and night.
Grant with feints kept the rebels stirred,
Events whirled so fast that nature seemed blurred.
It was a scheme to make reinforcements come late,
A scheme which the Yankees found first-rate.
For the rebels knew not where to go,
Or where would strike the pending blow.
Which caused them many a march unuseful,
Which was to the Yankee cause produceful.
For the rebel cause to hold her slaves,
She robbed the cradle and her graves.
The rebel armies one with the other,
Were ranks of youth and age together.
They could not stand the Yankee chases,
In their long and tiresome races.
For the youths were too soft and tender,
And in the matured, age seemed to hinder.
But the southern infants seemed matured
When at their heels there dangled a sword.
(In the south, it seemed, ere the cloud was cast,
They were called to join in the fiery blast.)
And all the pluck of Marion's men,
Seemed two fold more produced in them.

Foregoing verses have described,
How Grand Gulf was occupied.

With the soldiers and their fashions.
Started out on three days rations.
Grant stopped in Grand Gulf long enough
To see to the army's ration stuff;
To have them clothed and fed on plenty,
And never 'low them to go scanty.
Always in person Grant superintended,
When things went wrong he had them mended
One can take soldiers into the field,
But to them no victory 'll yield,
Without clothing, bed and grub.
There's where always comes the rub.
The kitchen of an army is grand,
And big supplies must be at hand.
The shelter must be ample and plenty,
Where soldiers camp, the grounds are tenty.
That's why soldiers held Grant so dear,
And filled the rebel ranks with fear.
With every necessary secured,   [May, 1863.]
And every soldier had his board.
The army then got up and sped,
All in tune for flying lead.
And on the morn of the seventh day,
When blossoms proved the month was May,
At Hawkinson Ferry, there Grant quartered,
On Black River, where rebels loitered.
Sherman was left behind to guard
The supplies from suicidal retard.
For to an army it's a suicide,
To leave supplies without guard or guide.
That's where the hams are stowed away,
There's where the horses get their hay.
It is the common soldier's kitchen,
Which is the needle that does the stitchin'.
Here's where Grant manœuvred to fool the foe,

Brewing a plan to strike a blow.
While Sherman's corps with supplies advance,
Who are the main fiddles in the dance.

Now, John L. Pettus,　　Don't forget us,
Come and whet us,　　With daggers fret us,
　　The best you can.
The dying life of living death,
Seems to hover o,er each breath.
　　Hear how it sounds,
　　C-r-a-w-l-s, then rebounds.
Oh, living friends of a dying cause,
Come help support your country's laws.
Drive the foes from out the state,
And beat him at a merciless rate.
Come all ye Mississippians,
At the wheel of war try your hands.
The barbarian hordes must be driven.
No quarter asked, or none be given.
Fathers, brothers, sons and daughter,
Assist us on the fields of slaughter,
Assist us now, is all we ask,
To wrench from tyranny its brazen mask.
Come help your neighbors as designated,
To restore your homes so desecrated.
Come wrench our land from rapine and ruin,
Or in death, about our hearths be strewn.
Let it not by foes be said,
That our chivalrous country's dead.
The Federal army must be mastered,
Come, be a hero or a dastard.
　　This is the length and tune of the nip,
　　As sung by the governor of Mississip'.
　　Will the de'il get us,
　　Or John L. Pettus?

Now Grant congratulated his army,
For checking rebels in fields so stormy.
He rehearses all the last campaign,

And thanks them oft and o'er again.
For all the mighty deeds they've done,
And all the bloody battles they've won.
It was on the morn of this seventh day,
And time proclaimed it the month of May,
That a great advance then ensued,
Three army corps it did include.
And the army corps at which I mean,
McPherson led corps seventeen.
Then McClernand's thirteenth corps,
And Sherman's eleven added to four,
With Grand Gulf he severs communication,
And opens Yazoo Pass for recreation.
Grant followed up his army corps,
No threes could go in squads of fours.
As the army on its course pursued,
Long, bloody skirmishes oft ensued.
McPherson did into Raymond advance,
And met the rebels' armed expanse.
With Cregg and Walker to command,
And trees before each soldier to stand.
Logan's division did the routing, [John A]
While other brigades did the shouting.
It was a fight three hours sturdy,
The ground by human blood worked muddy.
Artillery swept the federal lines,
And mowed the limbs from neighboring pines.
But the rebels with sullen tread,
Left the field with unburied dead.
The rebel dead sneaked off to hell,
As the living back into Jackson fell.
The battle occurred in the month of May,[1]
Houred up to the dozenth day,   [11863.]
When fled from Raymond was secession.
The Federal lines then took possession.

Fifty-one of our soldiers into the grave were tipled,
While an hundred and eighty more were crippled.
Seventy-five of theirs were hid from sight,
Butchered in this stubborn fight.
And from the rebel's we have of his'n,
One–eighty–six[1] picked up for prison.　　　[1 186.]
This battle was fought at a great expense,
And many were wounded in its defense.
McPherson has now advanced to Clinton,
And Sherman's soldiers their tracks are printin'
Footsteps on the road to Jackson.
With his powerful army of Gael and Saxon.
So that his warring sons o' Gael
On rebel hearts can try their steel.
And many of them perhaps will fall
By swords, in fhe hands of the fiery Gaul.

　　　Now on to Jackson they move alike,
　　　Along the railway and o'er the pike.
　　　The seventeenth and the fifteenth corps,
　　　En route to pound the rebels sore.　　　[places.
　　　While the fourteenth garrisoned the vacant
　　　Where now are seen fierce warring traces.
　　　The bodies of horses and mules undone,
　　　Lies festering in the melting sun.
　　　Joseph E. Johnston was so cute and cunning,
　　　He came out to meet the Feds a-gunning.
　　　(I think it was a job quite tame,
　　　To go and show the Feds their game.)
　　　To hold the daring Yanks at bay,
　　　So that rebel plunder might be carried away·
　　　But Johnston's army was too weak,
　　　Again their rifle-pits they seek,
　　　The Yankees pressed 'em hard behind,
　　　Till Johnston was to foes consigned.

But it took two hours to drive them in,
  And death to many hummed a doleful din.*
The rebel property there was large,
Of which our government took charge.
Our officers to Jackson then restored,
Power unknown to the rebel horde.
All public property in waste was laid,
No railway thence plied their trade.
For all their ties for miles were burned,
And the rails around each other turned.
But private property was respected,
And by our army was protected.
About Clinton it was just the same,
No public property did remain.
They almost carried the pikes away,
So rebels o'er them couldn't convey.
From Jackson, the rebels fled elsewhere,
With coattails flying and a bloody spur.
But their swords were bright and clean,
As if they held them in high esteem.
  (Ah, cinnamon seed and sandy bottom,
  Along Dixie's road we'll often trot 'em.)
May our cannon-balls hum day and night,
Tearing along on wings of dynamite.
In Jackson, Grant learned something queer,
That made him for the rebels steer.
It seems that Johnson was sincere,
In ordering Pemberton to take the Federals' rear
    From Vicksburg.
But Grant turned round to kill and scare,
Which turned his front into a rear.
    Then danger bloomed.
The seventeenth moved back to Clinton,
In its hard blows were never stintin'.

See book of "Remarkable Remarks on Grant." "Old Abe," the eagle.

On the morn of the fifteenth, Bolton before,
Was occupied by a division of the thirteenth corps.
They captured a lot of prisoners, of course,
Which was merely done by the power of force.
The three corps all added together,
One and all, each supported the other.
McClernand with his thirteenth corps,
Pushed on to Edwards Station before.
Where he met the rebels all in trim,
Pouring forth to welcome him.   [May 16.]
With cannon-balls to cheer the scene,
And musketry to fill betwen.
Here manœuvring seemed to swing,
Men and arms and everything.
The right would fall upon the left,
The center, sure, would then be cleft.
Here Colonel Slack's Indianians, chased by rebs
Which finally turned to furious Feds,
Then fell on them in such vehement styles,
They left dead rebels stacked in piles.
Then when the rebels fled for cover,
Close on their flying heels they'd hover.
Thus many a rebel, unmercifully slayed,
Fell victims of the warring trade.
Bayonets probed many a hole
Through rebel hides, whence fled their soul.
Everything was left, in the murderous scrape,
The rebs only thought, was to escape.
Those rebels, in their frantic runs,
Lost e'en themselves and several guns,
Death reveled there in bloody bowers;
The battle raged for nine long hours.
Did blood and ruin here prevail,
On purpose to paint a hideous tale?
To the Big Black River the rebels fled,

Leaving behind their wounded and dead.
The dead to be placed in cavities that scoops
Had dug, in the hands of the union troops.
Over the Big Black River they ford,
With battle oaths and a drawn sword.
The railway bridge was their only means,
To cross the army without its teams.
McClernand pressed them hard behind,
As o'er the country in ranks they wind.
On Black River, beyond morasses,
They fortified themselves in masses.
The engineers used up their wits,
In well located rifle-pits.
On Black River's either side,
They were well posted for battle tide;
The railroad bridge in easy reach
Of their cannons, to open a yawning breech.
O'er which no Yankee foe could cross,
Without sustaining a frightful loss.
But Grant was equal for the occasion,
And laid a bridge of pontoon persuasion.
O'er which was taken corps thirteen,
The only one acting in this battle scene.
But the enemy's works had to be raided,
Charge a fort after a lagoon waded,
For it was the first, or basement story,
That blocked our way to Vicksburg glory.
The order to charge was greeted with cheers,
And will long be remembered in rivers of tears
The rebel guns swept with an angle,
One hundred and fifty at a blow to mangle.
Our soldiers here o'er death's river crossed,
In a volley, one hundred and fifty were lost.
But the bayou waded, the charge was made,
The fort was captured, which ended the raid.

The charge was made with rapid runs,   [May 17]
No time had the rebs to load their guns.
    The power of it was a surpriser,
    A gigantic underground tantalizer.
    Arms in quantity, seven thousand stands,
    With three thousand prisoners fell in our hands.
    Seventeen artillery, and stores in gobs,
    With a large supply of corn on cobs.
Attempts to cross the river in the afternoon were made,
But on the bluffs beyond, the sharpshooters forbade.
They were so thick, artillery it took to disperse them,
And artillery alone was the thing to coerce them.
    But they made it dangerous for all exposed,
    Till night with its mantle the warfare closed.
    Then sharpshooters and all, moved off togther.
    Traveling along in the dusk clad weather.
The army under Grant, without a pause,
Closer to Vicksburg, nigher draws.   [May 18,]
    Oh, what a grand sight, to just behold,
    So many men by one controlled.
    Who leads them on through battle scenes,
    Like fairy tales in novel dreams.
(A novel is something that always should attract
Its just a curious tale, an artificial fact.)
    About Vicksburg it does appear,
    The Yankee boys are drawing near.
    With all the caution of a creature,
    Drawing near a thing of a deadly feature.
At two P. M., Grant ordered a general assault,
But his men were murdered into a halt.   [May 19.]
The ground they passed was close contested,
As bullets through them sore digested.
    But to future ages here we'll tell them,
    They took the outer works and held them.
    In spite of rebel death broadcast,

They firmly stood the withering blast.
And by the commander it is affirmed,
That many a noble one, to mother dust returned.
           [centered,
They lost their point, around which their hopes were
The rebel's works they found impossible to be entered.*
    Porter also from his boats
      Hurled mighty cannon balls,
With stupendous shells
      Against the rebels mighty walls.
But these hellish missiles
      Just merely went a plunkin'
Like flipping beans against a mighty pun'kin,
The musicians got excited or very jubilant,
All their power to the instruments were lent.
    Great chunks of music,
      Of most ridiculous noise,
Were broken off in hunks
      And tossed among the boys,
To cheer them on their bloody course,
And bring their mighty arms in force,
For they fought a fiend, not to be greaned
      By sword or bomb,
From places that are old, in a country ne'er cold,
      They come from,

Death passed along the other day, [August 1886.]
As death in chancery often may ;
It passed along, but don't presume
It came too late or e'en soon,
For death it is an unexpector,
Taking all, e'en to a rector.
But death in coming this 'ere time,
Got something that was rare and fine.
     Ah ! hark,
Hear ye the wail from Gramercy Park,
There it was death passed along,
And killed the valiant, not the strong.
Ah, death alone, it was that that killed 'im,
The great and good Sammy Tilden.

Those rebel boys, they were no toys
          In war's disaster.
But situatious, and strong stations,
          They ne'er could master.
For the world was such a hummer,
With the the de'il for a drummer,
          They ne'er caught on to the hag
'Till their leaders were whipped,
And the Yankees had skipped,—
          With the swag.
House walls, by cannon balls,
Were torn down all o'er town ,
Wrecked entire, was many a sire, by blood and fire.
          Ah! Vicksburg,
Of such a siege who ever heard ?
          So thick they were in many a spot,
          It seemed the air was strained with shot.
And the ground, for miles around
          By shells were plowed.
Shells flew so thick, they raised old Nick
          In every crowd.
Thousands killed—what blood was spilled,
          Oh! what was it for ?
Each one fights, for his rights,
          So note the bloody war,
Until secesh times, no such lines,
          Ever appeared in slaughter;
Old Alex' the Great, at such a rate
          Never viewed the likes on land or water.
It would melt the heart of old Bonaparte
          To view such deadly work.
Guns and mules, are the tools
          That soldiers shirk.
When the boom of the gun replies
And reverberates along the skies,

To rebeldom a keen surprise,
Chattering the teeth in the heads of the wise,
    When bombshells break,
    And creations quake,
E'en cutting off men from earthly ties
Taking the foolish as well as the wise,
The ones unknown or of highest prize;
    With its hellish rake,
    And its murders and fake;
Such is the canon's deadly size,
To sever men from all earthly ties,
    Life is dangerous, sure to shake,
    For life we never can retake—
But death comes without if's and's or I's,
                    [surprise?
And why should death to a soldier be any great
Oh, Vicksburg, Vicksburg, the bloodiest scar,
'Till then recorded on the pages of war.
Old and rough, hard and tough,
        Dilapidated, aged rebels;
Tobacco smoked, rum soaked,
        Are still more hideous devils.
But Grant was a shaker at his trade,
He tried their muscles with his blade,
He shook the rebels out of town,
And e'en bombed their castles down;
Then with sword and bayonet fixed,
His soldiers among the rebels mixed.
Death and vengeance they e'en dared,
The rebels among them roughly fared.
Neither side their duty shirk,
The field was rife with deadly work.
After Grant had established his base of supplies.
Which was done after this fashion, and in this wise,
He done it as the troops before Vicksburg laid,

He done it as they rested, from activity stayed;
  It took him two long, active days,
  In skirmishing, and other peculiar ways.
At Young's Point the supplies were stayed.
As the soldiers heretofore had been living by raid,
Except five days from the commissary fed.
And stlll they had plenty, but short of bread,
 Now here is the point, to rebels a pity,
 Grant got his supplies from north of the city.
Now Grant determined the city to assault,
And close it in a conquest or a bloody halt.
Grant struck the blow from many a cause
Which, to tell it here I need not pause.
On the twenty-first his orders were given,
Then with animation stirred the livin'.
  For as the morning sun arose
  With deadly vim to strike their foes,
  First with artillery's heavy din.
  Then with the small arms to join in;
  Join in with bayonets extended,
  And Yank's among the rebels blended,
  To bayonet them from their ditches,
  Which is the bulk of rebel riches.
  Loud and fierce the cannons rattle,
  Then skirmishers bring on the battle.
 The general assault was fixed for ten,
 When men must slaughter their fellow-men,
 The charge was ordered in the teeth of the foe,
 To scale their walls and onward go,
 Sparing nought of the rebels power
 But slay them in the coming hour.
McClernand on the left, Sherman on the right,
McPherson in the centre, they charge into the fight.
 They charge the foe with vigor and vim,
 But with their force are not equal to him;

They mow the Yankees down in lines,
Like a cyclone in a forest of pines.
The rebels stood the Federal assault,
Like cliffs that cause an ocean to halt.
They drew their line of death so firm,
Few ever crossed it to return.
Some of our soldiers were very brave,
Climbing o'er the walls into their grave.
That assault it soon did fail,
Without weakening our power to assail.
Said Grant.
And to teach them we have the power,
To scoop them in some future hour.
Vicksburg is ours without a doubt,
They'll soon be at us to let them out.
It showed the quality of the men,
Who dared the rebels in their den.
Who fell advancing on their foes,
Whole companies cut down in rows,
When thus Grant saw his columns fade,
He vowed to put Vicksburg to the spade.
Which was a life economizer,
And was a feat a great deal wiser.
The gunboats on Vicksburg roar,
Ere the bloody day all night before.
Admiral Porter, the whole night long,
Bombarded Vicksburg fierce and strong.
Then in the morning doubled his zeal,
In flying balls of hardened steel.
And here is where the trouble's been,
He hit the foe, and the foe hit him.
After this assault, McClernand's boys,
Partook of their commander's joys;
They led the furthest in the advance,
And they waltzed the rebels in the dance.

Then a dissension here arose,
Who was the boldest before the foes.
The other corps launched out in a growl,
Long and fierce would have been the howl.
But Grant relieved him of his command,
Then ordered him to another land.
There, from Illinois, o'er her borders,
Report to him for future orders.
Now, remember McClernand was his right hand bower,
From the time he stepped into army power.
Now he's dismissed and ordered away,
For the help he's done, what glorious pay.
Then from a supply of Generals on hand,
E. O. C. Ord took McClernand's command.

There were two battles on one bill,
Black River bridge and Champion Hill.
Among the rebs it was reported,
That Pemberton on those battles sported.
And against all rebel laws,
He sold them to the Union cause.
Now listen to the speech he made,
To those that in his army stayed:
"You hear I am to treachery lent,
And in commanding, incompetent.
Perhaps you hear it oft in report,
To sell Vicksburg is now my forte.
Here's the fact and why not tell it?
Note ye Vicksburg, how dear I'll sell it.
Not till the army is forsaken,
By the last pound of beef and bacon;
Or as long as flour and corn remains,
Or blood pours through a creature's veins,
As long as a cow or hog can stand,
Or a horse or dog remains on hand.

Or as long as a man is in the trenches,
To oppose those marauding sons of wenches.
Or as long as a cannon near the ditches,
Can hurl a shell at the sons of bitches.
Then all of you may know full well,
The price at which Vicksburg I'll sell."

In the meantime Colonel Carnyn's cavalry brigade,
Served Uncle Sam in the wasting trade.
His raids into Alabama extended wide,
Showing ruinous waste on every side.
Communication lines were torn asunder,
And everything destroyed that was rebel plunder.
All private property was generally protected,
A thing that the rebels scarce expected.

The siege of Vicksburg now begins,
It's not the gun, but the spade that wins.
The troops being taught by blood and rupture,
That Vicksburg was a solid structure,
Takes up the spade with grim content, .
And a daring will that couldn't be bent,
To the rebel works Grant's lines did hug,
The ones who fought, and the ones who dug.
Till the rebel works were nigh invested,
And communication all but arrested.
Johnston and Pemberton oft communed,
About the things they wished repruned. ·
Which was a leak or mighty suction,
That would make long a short reduction.
The siege would be no siege at all,
Unless our lines ran around them all.
So General Herron withdrew from Arkans'
To help Grant scoop the big bonanz'.
Thus he went to pelt the rebels' rinds,

On the extreme left of the Union lines.
Which made the investment then complete,
From all outward traffic or retreat.
Here are some facts I'll give away,
Our army's position at the end of May.
They were well on to the fortification,
And were well securing their own foundation.
Artillery was planted* at various sites,
To assume the power of legal rights.
Which sent shells screaming through the air,
With vengeance of ruin to kill and tear.
Artillery duels grew fierce and hot,
When but a hundred yards to fling the shot.
And if a man popped up his head,
At it would fly a peck of lead.
It seems a leaden disease prevailed,
By it the whole army was assailed;
Haines' Bluff was held by Blair,
And a deal of country was under his care;

Pemberton to Johnston, sent word in haste,
That the Yankees, at once, had better be chased.
"Come with thirty thousand, my arms to assist;
Be here in ten days, or the job is missed;
And if you don't get here, you'd better retreat,
For my fifteen thousand will fall in defeat.
I've grub to bridge o'er but thirty days,
By using it in the most economical ways.
It makes my heart ache the facts to portray,
That my soldiers must live on but one meal a day.

---

* Planted artillery razed rebels dead,
But worse was musket's flying lead.
Such are the humming birds of war.
Dead men were all they were humming for.
On death those humming birds were fed;
Life was honey to their beaks of lead.

My ammunition is scarce, but caps in particular,
Which would be to the Feds a joyous tickler."
This was sent in the hands of Douglas the trusty,
A man, I presume, that was dangerous lusty;
His father, in Illinois, was called a big gun,
But he joined the rebels, from Texas he come.
But the message offered a golden chance,
To leave the rebels before the advance,
He walked straight into the hands of a picket,
To give the Federals a chance to punch his ticket.
His ticket was of the poorest kinds,
A pass from Pemberton, through his lines.
Douglas, to hades, should have been thrust,
He was a traitor to Pemberton's trust.
But Douglas brought something that was not stale,
To the Federals he volunteered an interesting tale.
Pemberton saw that the siege would be long,
That the balls of the Union would beat on him strong;
So each field and staff officer picked out a steed,
And the rest were turned out. Lo! the scarcity of feed
Gave the Federals thousands of horses and mules,
That once helped the rebels advance with their tools.

The big Black River crossings were guarded,
So that Johnston, in crossing, would be sorely retarded.
Which kept the rear of Grant's army secure,
That was all that was needed, enough and no more.
General Osterhaus's division is the one that guarded,
By him Joe Johnston would be retarded.   [27, 1863.
F. P. Blair started out with a racket and din,   [May
To shake up the rebels, the country within.
He was prepared with artillery, cavalry, and then
Each corps supplied him with its quota of men.
In a country ruled entirely by Madams,   [Adams.
Near Mechanicsburg they met, and defeated Wirt

[their arms,
Within twenty miles of Yazoo City they pressed with
Carrying off all the stock that was found on the farms
Of bacon, they met many sides that were fine,
And the Yankees mustered them all into line.
    All the beef-cattle joined in this big expedition,
    And the horses fell in, shunning all superstition
And when they turned back to their Vicksburg lair,
As they passed o'er bridges, they all caught afire.
    In returning they left the country forsaken,
    Short five hundred cattle and tons of bacon.
    Also for drawing their farming tools,
    They were short five hundred horses and mules.
    In short, the Federals left nothing behind,
    What they couldn't carry, to flames consigned.

    Grant kept his sappers and miners at work,
    Carrying powder and shoveling dirt.
    They worked upon eligible sites,
    As bombshells screamed in dizzy flights.
    The Federal guns in bombardal roar,
    Kept pounding away at the rebel's door.
    They pounded away with furious vim,
    Both night and day, in a deadly din.
    The fleet tossed in her heaviest shots,
    And the ditches gave them jobbing lots.
    Both armies following up old creeds,
    Each army defying the other's deeds,
    Till it seemed that death and ruin ran riot,
    And shells lit up the heavens by night,
    The shell inspired our men with vigor,
    To work the spade or pull the trigger.
    General Parker's ninth army corps,   [June 16.]
    Came to help Grant in the general roar.
    Also General Washburn, with part of sixteen,

Came around to help wind up the scene.
The Big Black River by them was guarded,
As Johnston again had to be retarded.
Johnston would not be hard corraled,
His army from the country swelled.
Old men into arms were rustled,
And children from the cradle hustled.
To arms! to arms! the Yankees come,
Resounded aloud, from many a drum.
A captured courier here reveals,
That the rebels will not show their heels.
Instead of carrying deadly knives,
He had rebel letters to soldiers' wives.
The letters, in sad tones were written down,
Showed how they felt in Vicksburg town.
But they seemed to the Lord resigned,
They in Joe Johnston comfort find.
Hoping the Yankees will not fleece them,
And that Joe Johnston will come and release them.
Here Grant sends Sherman to kill his kids,
Or murder his old, gray-headed nick-a-dids;
Or drive him away from threatening the rear,
And give him a thundering, old-fashioned scare.
So that's the way Joe Johnston was treated,
Till he finally found himself defeated;
But this taught Johnston to have a fear,
And that Grant was solid in the rear.
   So towards Jackson, he did retreat,
   Leaving Pemberton to a sure defeat.
The mines were dug and the powder planted,
O'er which the rebel fort so canted.   [June 25, 1863]
     Which caused the fort to sail up then,
     Turned to sticks and dirt and mangled men.
     Sharp-shooters kept the rebels downed,
     As the sappers mined into the ground.

The saps that led into the mines,
Were guarded from all outward signs.
No soldier could enter into that mine,
That ranked below a General's line.
Except the workmen there employed,
There, no visitors ever annoyed.
Three hundred yards they sapped their way,
To dig the mines for the powder to lay.
The men were chosen from the ranks,
Who had learned their lesson on foreign banks.
It took fifty men but forty hours
To plant the powder to get its powers.
Beneath the rebel fort 'twas laid,
Twenty-two hundred pounds it weighed.
The powder laid, the fuse attached,
A match upon the pants was scratched,
By which the match was therefore lighted,
The end of the fuse it then ignited. [June 25.]
It was the signal for frightful danger,
Then all our men got out of range, sir.
The forty-fifth infantry of Illinois,
Stood ready to charge the rebel boys ;
With the twenty-third Indiana, they all laid low,
To strike the rebels a withering blow.
Many of the boys laid off their coats,
Expecting warm work with the Pemberton bloats.
Carrying nothing with them but murdering tools,
An uncommon thing in common rules.
They all stood gazing along the lines,
Awaiting the explosion of the mines ;
Which meant throughout the lines, a blow
To be hurled against a powerful foe
Cannons were to fling their heaviest balls
Against the weakest place in the rebels' walls.
The minutes it took to consume the fuse,

Seemed like a ponderous age of blues.
Minutes, then held on like weeks,
As the hissing fuse the powder seeks.
At last the earth seemed raising high,
Hundreds of feet towards the sky;
Carrying in its columns sticks and stones,
With mangled flesh from rebel bones;
All kinds of *debris* with trucks for guns,
The air was filled with many tons.
Then the forty-fifth rushed for the breach.
Charging the rebels that were in reach.
It was a rush into the jaws of death,
Where many a brave one lost his breath;
Lost it through a rent or gaping wound,
Whose blood but fed the hungry ground
General Leggett led his boys in the charge,
Till it seemed that death on men would gorge
There a flying splinter laid Leggett low,
Stretched on the turf at a single blow;
But I'm glad to say it was only a stun,
A shell that exploded from a rebel gun.
The artillery opened on the line entire,
And roared with a constant, unbroken fire.
Our guns, their shells against the fort unloaded,
Striking the parapet, bounded o'er and exploded.
Exploding among a living mass,
Mowing a swath, like a scythe in grass.
The artillery roars and the muskets rattle,
And the cheering men o'er the din of battle;
With the ships' broad-siders, in wreaths of smoke,
With their thunderous noise and ponderous stroke;
The distant mortars, with deafening booms;
The solid shots' shrill whistling tunes;
With wreaths of smoke in various places,
And arching shells leaving fiery traces;

With a vigorous reply from the foe as well,
No wonder it holds in an awe-bound spell.
    Oh! it was a scene sublime,
    The rarest on the sheets of time.
    Oh! it was a fierce reception,
    That paralyzes all description.
    The effect was about the same,
    On either side, in wounded and slain;
And those Illinoisians, with murderous sport,
Drove back the rebels from the fort.

    Here, Grant puts General Ord
    Strictly on his military guard.
    He told him how McPherson stood.
    And posted him for general good.
    The powder explosion, a crater dug,
    Resembling a funnel-shaped, tapering mug.
And McPherson held the position secure
Against the rebel din of battle roar.
    And ere the morning sun can shine,
    His artillery will be mounted in line.
    Let Smith's division sleep under arms,
    To prevent surprise from rebel harms.
    It only needs strict vigilance,
    It is chief in siege advance.

Grant kept ringing his cannon knells,*
And advancing by way of his parallels;
Till thirteen hundred yards were gained,
From the lines the rebels first maintained.

---

* Grant protected the city as well as he could,
He protected it alone for the city's good;
And for the women and children helpless therein,
No cannon balls were thrown the city within.
If Grant on the city had aimed his fire,
He could have swept it away like ancient Tyre.

As the Yankees advance, the rebels retreat,
Until Pemberton's lines break up in defeat.
Then a long correspondence here arose
Between Grant and his conquered foes;
But Grant would receive no tender
But one, unconditional surrender;
To which Pemberton swore by the gods of hate,
That his men would fight them to the end of fate.
For protected well, they were with ditches,
And would fight for fame, and not for riches;
Unless Grant would change his station,
And give them some say in the capitulation.
The rebels fearing on July the fourth,
That they'd feel the fury of a furious north.
That they would work strong and hard,
And use their fire-works in bombard.
But ere the morn of the third was gone,
Many hours before the fourth would dawn,
A flag of truce from the "Johnny Johns"
Shows that John C. Pemberton now corresponds.
The messengers, now, advance they down,
Colonel Montgomery and General Bowen.
Then, they tread blindfolded among the Yanks,
Where once the balls played fearful pranks.
The message delivered, they then returned,
It seems that Grant the message spurned;
But, Grant admitted the rebels were brave,
And would lift them from the mire of an early grave;
If they, their arms then, would tender
To his terms, "Unconditional Surrender."
It seemed that here, the armistice would set,
They parted till the chieftains met.
So, they agreed to meet in the afternoon,
At three o'clock, so short and soon.
So the siege went on as it had before,

With moving dirt and cannon's roar;
But, as the meridian got under the sun,
There was not to be heard a single gun ;
And when the short hand on the face of the clock
Proved the afternoon had three hours in stock ;
Our signal shot rang clear in its ca'l,
Then a reply from the rebels rang over their wall.
Pemberton, on the works, then advanced in view,
In McPherson's front, full facing his crew.
A white rag was the shield that he bore,
A white rag on a stick, and nothing more.
Then Grant rode out to neutral land,
Dismounted, and shook that rebel's hand.
Here, deadly foes, each other grasped,
Hand in hand each other clasped.
They were beneath a giant oak,
The cannons were mute as the chieftains spoke.
It was Grant, A. J. Smith and McPherson,
The two first messengers and Pemberton in person.
With each chieftain, came his staff besides.
In full red tape, of army prides.
Pemberton talked surrender and war,
As Grant puffed at his black cigar.
After talking long, they turn their backs,
And each returns his former tracks.
Yet, undetermined how or when
Pemberton must give up his men.
But Grant was not to fire a gun,
Till morn showed its coming sun.
Pemberton, in the meantime, must interview
The mighty heads of his daring few ;
And report ere the sun's glorious ray
Can usher in the break of day.
But, ere then, many despatches passed,
And the armistice agreed upon at last.

But a great deal of this quibbling was for,
The rebels claimed the honors of war.
It seemed the place was sore becalmed,
When came no more bombshells from water or land.
 The two armies nigh, they almost mixed,
 A few pickets along, just stood betwixt,
 Till the capitulation stood at a fix.
  All rebels kept their private things,
  That could not soar on warring wings.
 Each mounted officer to be mounted still,
 With all their side-arms at their will;
 With all the grub they could take away;
 With thirty wagons the same to convey;
Allowing two horses or mules for a team,
Though sieged so long they must have been lean
 After all transactions were consoled,
 Each individual was then paroled.
On the Glorious Fourth, the surrender was complete,
It was a surrender, but not a defeat.
  It was at the hour of ten,
  The news was given to the sons of men.
 Not Vicksburg alone it did include,
 But the Mississippi Valley was then subdued.
  McPherson's corps was left to guard
  Vicksburg, that cost in blows so hard.
  Colonel J. A. Maltby's infantry boys,
  The forty-fifth from Illinois.
  It was for his heroic deed
  Grant placed him in the column's lead.
It was for heroic deeds, at Vicksburg rendered,
That he lead our column when it surrendered.
  The citizens were sullen and shy,
  As if Yankees they would defy.
They shut themselves close in their homes,
As if the Federals would crush their bones.

Colonel James Wilson, provost-marshal o' the corps,
And the provost guard were the boys that led before.
　After the rushing around with such vim and vigor,
　Working cocks and pulling the trigger.
　　　　Soon Vicksburg settled as quiet
　　　　As though there never had been a fight.
　　　　The abandon soldiers, of rebel hue,
　　　　Were the only misdemeaning crew.
　　　　In four hours after the capitulation,
　　　　Many steamboats took up their station ;
　　　　And as far as the eye could reach,
　　　　Steamers lined the river beach.
　　　　Commerce, at once sprang into life,
　　　　Right in the tracks of sullen strife :
　　　　Where cannon-balls a few hours before,
　　　　Blocked up the streets with human gore.
　　　　It seemed as if some magic wand
　　　　Lay hidden in some elfish hand ;
　　　　It seemed the city was too punily made,
　　　　To handle the stuff shipped there for trade.
　　　　For two long years, Vicksburg had stood
　　　　A fortified city, to little good.
　　　　Only to starve her people out,
　　　　And prove herself weak, when others are stout.
　　　　(Around Vicksburg's warring scene,
　　　　Fell Generals Tracy, Tilghman and Greene.)
　　　　Vicksburg's loss to the rebels was great,
　　　　And they had no way to retaliate.
　　　　Thirty thousand men it did consume,
　　　　And a thousand more it did entomb ;
　　　　Four thousand of them were left on crutches,
　　　　Of the ones that fell into our clutches.
　　　　Of Lieutenant-Generals, there was but one,
　　　　Which was the towering John C. Pemberton.
　　　　There were also other commanding seers,

Nineteen major-generals and brigadiers ;
Of commissioned officers there were many more,
At least two hundred and thirty score.
Guns and cannons and other supplies,
Enough to make one stretch his eyes.
It seems that Pemberton had fighting men,
Short of nothing (except more of them).
It seems as though in death's disaster,
One was not the other's master,
This is the price of Vicksburg's cost,
One thousand men, in death were lost.
   (But heaven is a glorious place,
     And filled with saints supernal,
   Who banish all the thoughts of hell,
     And things that are infernal.)
   Of course those figures do not contain
   The whole of Vicksburg's long campaign.

LINCOLN'S AUTOGRAPH LETTER TO GRANT.

Lincoln's letter to Grant was grand,
Thanking him, in the name of the land ;
Thanking him for the great deeds done ;
Thanking him for the battles won ;
Thanking him for the skill he used ;
Thanking him for the rebels bruised.
When Lincoln first read Grant's success,
Some comic jokes he did express.
Some gentlemen then standing by,
Complained that Grant used too much rye.
Then, Lincoln, to them did express,
Of Grant's using whisky to excess ;
Of which they deemed he surely did
Pour it down like the ancient Cid.
   Then Lincoln asked them of what kind,
   The General so revived his mind.

> Therefore, President, why ask you now,
> Then and therefore, when and how.
> I wish to know the kind he's on,
> To send each general a demijohn;
> If it can such victories afford,
> As the one o'er Vicksburg now secured.
> (Oh! give me country-folks,
>   For lively lads and lasses,
> But give me country-gentlemen,
>   For stupid fools and asses.)
> A cigar and Grant together wed,
> The army, into Vicksburg led.
> Rebel Frank Gardener was the chief that held
> Port Hudson, by his arms corraled.
>   But Port Hudson, with all its cranks,
>   Fell into the hands of General Banks.
>   (It was Federal pickets that first did call
>   Frank Gardener's attention to Vicksburg's fall.
> Port Hudson's surrender was a good excuse,
> For, without Vicksburg it was of no use).
> One major-general and a brigadier,
> With fifty-five hundred to bring up the rear;
> And all they had within their works,
> From artillery down to common dirks;
>   Of which they had a big supply,
>   Of everything needful to defy.

THE SECOND CAPTURE OF JACKSON.[*]

> Joe Johnston, into Jackson fell back, there to stay,
> Then Sherman advanced, to drive him away.
> When Johnston got to Jackson, he filled up its ditches,
> With a lot of old men who were fighting for riches:
> And kids who were called from the cradle to arms,
> To show northern men their infantile charms.

[*] See book of "Remarkable Remarks on Grant." "Old Abe," the eagle,

Whether kids or old men,
  They fought strong in the war,
  The kids didn't know, and the old
    Didn't care what they fought for.
But Sherman, at Jackson gave Johnston the bounce,
He did it with long, minie balls, weighing a short ounce.
Sherman, against Jackson, a siege there created,
Johnston stood it for a while, and then he vacated.
But destruction and ruin he spread over town,
The city, to ashes, he laid much of it down. [July 16.]
The Yankees found torpedoes after Johnston was gone,
Planted about, to explode when trodden on.
Johnston, towards Meriden, filed off with his men,
Stealing off from the Yankees, unexpected by them.
All his big heavy guns fell into our hands,
With much cotton that grew in the fair southern lands.

The Union soldiers, near Jackson found
Jeff Davis's letters on hostile ground.
This was when the siege commenced,
With the rebels inside, strongly defenced.
There were several bushels of them together,
Which served to pass away the weather.
  For many were carried to the lines,
    And served as novels to literary minds.
  They were most all, on war engaged,
    And how it would be commenced and waged.
They showed how rebelhood, on Jeff relied,
And that rebelhood had long been cut and dried.
There were also several gold-headed canes,
Some were inscribed with illustrious names.
One was from a soldier to a soldier friend,
One from Franklin Pierce, to the greatest of men.

Grant, at Vicksburg, laid on his oars,
As his daring boys patched up their sores;

Which were gifts from the sons of men,
Some, in after years, proved to be a gem.

A gem to draw a pension on,
When only one arm or leg was gone;
But, if by chance, a head was taken.
The poor body was then forsaken.
But, all this time, Grant was not idle:
He was forcing the rebs to take a bridle.

Against Yazoo City he plotted and planned,
Then sent General Herron along to command.
Where almost three hundred men,
At that place, was captured then.
For the rebels beat a hasty retreat,
And they captured only the tail end of defeat;
With all the munitions, or warring wear,
Leaving four noble steamers on fire.
The rebels burned them, just because
They wished to keep them out of our claws.
General Ransom, by Grant was sent to Natchez,
                      [scratches.
To chase the rebels there, and give them particular
For they were crossing cattle, regular beefing beasts,
To drive them to the rebels, a-fighting in the east.
                      [rattle,
When Ransom got to Natchez, he surely made them
                      [cattle:
He captured many prisoners, and five thousand Texan
And, of ammunition, more than two million rounds,
Besides a thundering sight destroyed on the grounds.
This, ends the campaign in the Mississippi Valley.
The rebels were so ruined they never more could rally.

Here Grant thanks Porter
For his assistance rendered,
He helped Grant in many battles,
Wind up in victory, splendid.
He was, to Grant, a pillar and support,

Grant worked in the rear,
As he forced the guns o' the fort,
Could the government have hired
A better to support her
Than this fearless Admiral,
David Daniel Porter?

Grant, in gaining victories, nailed them by a power
That would protect them, now, and at every hour.
His head-quarters, at Vicksburg was located,
And peace in his department, at once was consecrated.

Grant's department, now, was wider in its grip,
For it extended all o'er the State of Mississipp'.
Grant, now, took some rest, of which he sorely needed,
Before another campaign, by him was superseded.

Here, Grant was given
A fine and gorgeous tool,
Which monarchs would love to own,
When tyrants want to rule.

It was a gorgeous sword, of magnificent brand,
Given to him, by officers, placed under his command.
The inscription on that tool, was beautiful and grand,
A young giant crushing rebellion from a land.
The scabbard was of solid silver, pure,
Just wrought of solid silver, silver, and nothing more.

About this sword, a rose-wood case was found,
Whose outer surface, with ivory was bound.
(Ah! it was a blade that would tickle any tinner),
Ivory-covered the outside. satin-lined the inner.
On the interior of the lid, the General's name in silk,
Crimson letters on a ground, pure and white as milk.

Here, Lincoln, on him conferred his share,
Made him officer of regulars, instead of volunteer.
With commission dating from the fourth of July,
The day the rebels lost their bold defy.
Now, his madam goes to meet him,

With sweet, flattering words to greet him.
Now, Grant's soldiers, so strict to duty's sound,
Took relaxation in furloughs, homeward bound.
　　All the honored ones,
　　　　Took their chance in turns,
　　For every true soldier's heart,
　　　　With family pleasure burns.
　　The southern sympathizers
　　　　That dwelt about our forts,
　　Hated the Union soldiers,
　　　　But begged them for supports.
　　Oh, them rebel planters
　　　　Were such hideous swiggers,
　　They got the Union army
　　　　To support their starving niggers.
　　But, Grant, restrained his rations,
　　　　As much as it could be done,
　　To benefit the cause,
　　　　And every southern son.
　　The traders 'neath our flag,
　　　　Were treacherous to the cause,
　　They traded to suit themselves,
　　　　Regardless of the laws.
　　All trading with the rebels,
　　　　Was weakening to our lines,
　　Because, it could not be restricted
　　　　By any legal fines.
　　Grant proposed to let them stand
　　　　The terrors of the war;
　　Then, when peace came 'round,
　　　　They'd know what peace was for.
　　Trade not with the southern states,
　　　　In dealings great or small,
　　Then, when peace unfurls its wings,
　　　　They'll greet it one and all.

From Vicksburg, down, now Grant controls
The river, by gunboats and mounted patrols.
  Soon, everything was snug and quiet,
  The country was free from bloody riot.
  Furloughs, to good soldiers were given,
  And mean ones from the ranks were driven.
  The sick ones had the greatest care,
  And in furloughs had their share.
  The crippled ones, for life disabled,
  In the invalids' corps was stabled;
  Or discharged to wend their way
  With money, their expenses to defray.
  Grant's orders, to steamboats forbade
  To swindle soldiers in their trade.
  Grant set the price that they should charge,
  If they charged over, they must disgorge.
  Which was in one particular, the case,
  They had to refund, to the boat's disgrace.
  Five dollars to Cairo, from Vicksburg, then,
  Was the fare of the private men;
  But, if a man held a commission,
  He had to pay two dollars in addition.
  But these fresh water captains were sharks,
  They'd triple on the dollar marks;
  And e'en sometimes, twice that, and more,
  They'd gouge the soldiers to the core;
  At which Grant's eyes would kindle fire,
  And he'd clench his fists to smother his ire.
  But in every case where the captains bummed,
  If caught by Grant, they were made to refund,
  Or have their boats confiscated,
  And they themselves as prisoners rated.
  No wonder Grant had such a team,
  And by it held in such high esteem.

The first of August, sixty-three,
  Grant's Vicksburg orders,
That to the ears of rebeldom,
  Went rushing o'er their borders.
All usurpers of legal rights,
Will be treated like vultured kites.
All irregular laddies must learn to know,
If caught, they're among a dangerous foe ;
All banded pillaging must cease,
All conscripters must leave in peace ;
All citizens, in their vocation,
Can follow their trade or occupatian ;
And they shall, by Uncle Sam,
Be protected wherever I can.
    All negroes must be recognized
    As citizens, howe'er despised.
All private property must be respected,
And by Uncle Sammy's boys protected.
The county of Warren, laid waste by war,
Where the foe so often dragged his car;
Where the foe so often advanced or fled,
But now the survivors must be fed.
  Sherman, of the fifteenth, and
    McPherson's seventeenth army corps,
  Let each one set apart
    Proper commissary stores.
  Prime necessities must be given
    To those that cannot buy,
  Issue to them. at the proper time,
    Enough, and no more, or try.
  All cavalry, in dirty work,
    At once must be restrained,
  For no dirty work, within our lines,
    Can ever be maintained.
Punish all with vim and vigor

Both the white man and the nigger,
    That don't obey.
The officers with long commissions,
Must rule their men, or lose positions.
Every crooked door must be punched,
Beneath the wheel of justice crunched.
Here, Lincoln's proclamation
  Freed the niggers o' the nation,
But, it did not enrich them,
    Nor give them occupation.
      And jawbone currency
        Had yet to come in vogue,
      As every nigger was a thief,
        Who happened to be a rogue.
Our army established camps,
    Purposely to feed them,
The poor whites were taken in
    As well as colored freedmen.
The government worked them.
    Wher'er a chance occurred,
Or hired them out to white men,
    Just as the nigs preferred.
After the department was made secure,
Fore and aft and long before,
With McPherson in command,
With local duties in his hand,
He went to view his district afar,
Where rebeldom dragged their car.
He went to view the army gems,
From Memphis down to New Orleans.
(Grant arrives at Memphis, Tennessee,
August twenty-fifth, sixty-three.)
At Memphis, those southern sinners,
Bloated Grant on gorgeous dinners.
He was toasted, praised and boasted,

(And e'en by the rebels roasted).
He passed his visit gay and grand,
With delicious things on every hand.
The champagne batteries shot erect,
Such gorgeous things, could one expect?
Wine and women together mingled,
Bottles and glasses clinked and jingled.
Every thing was done first-class,
To make the moments gaily pass.
Toasts were said, both loud and strong,
Some were witty, short, and long;
Grant took it in, he list'd and heard,
But never toasted them a word.
He was the great and silent man,
The counterpart of the Ritter Bann,
It was a glorious day to him,
Mixed with women, wine and sin.
But as the morning sun arose,
Grant's return, it did disclose.   [Aug. 27]
The "City of Alton" bore him down
To Vicksburg city, of late renown.
His letter to Memphis, was surely grand,
It showed the power of a chieftain's hand.
He thanked them for their loyal action,
In breaking off the rebel faction.
There was nothing in it, sharp or witty,
But thanks profuse, to Memphis city,
And to its long and kind committee:
Messrs. R. Hough and many others,
The thrifty sons of southern mothers.
He did not long in Vicksburg, stay,
But to New Orleans, he rushed away.
He stopped at various places along,
To see that garrisons were strong.
General Banks, at New Orleans,

Grant classed him among his friends.
When Grant into the city, drew,
September days had slid to two.
Next day it was sounded in New Orleans,
That she could trade with her northern friends.
Of her wealth she could disgorge,
And trade with Uncle Sam at large:
      Where'er her boats could sail,
      Or transportation, carry mail.
Here, Grant presents himself before
His glorious old thirteenth corps;
Which was transferred from Vicksburg ranks,
To join the command of General Banks.
(After Vicksburg had lost her hold,
And the Mississippi ran uncontrolled;
From its fountain to its source,
No rebel guns hauled o'er its course.
At Carrolton, the review began,
Dressed in his best, was every man.
   An undress uniform, he wore,
   No sword, sash or belt he bore;
   A low, soft felt hat, he wore with ease,
   His coat flung open to the breeze;
   With a cigar between his teeth,
   Curling up its odorous wreath.
   (To here tell it, had I need,
   He puffed unbroken, the noxious weed.)
   He used a luxury that none forbids,
   On his hands a pair of kids.
On a big horse, fierce and strong,
Borne o'er the fields, the lines among;
Grant, from his horse's back was hurled,
Almost into the other world.
His breast-bone was slightly crushed,
Three ribs into six were rushed;

One side of him was paralyzed,
And a continent was sore surprised.
From a litter, he was stowed away,
On the steamer "Franklin," all O. K.
 It was in a critical time,
 Almost at a point sublime;
When he was needed to command
The three grand armies of the land.
The Ohio, Cumberland and Tennessee.
Were combined to make the rebels flee;
And he was needed at its head,
But misery held him in her bed.
It was thought he would never wield
A drawn blade on a battle-field;
But, thanks to the doctor's skill,
They brought him around again to kill.
But, it took them four long weeks
To chase away the painful streaks.

ENLARGED COMMAND "MILITARY DIVISION OF THE MISS-
ISSIPPI."

As soon as Grant had made amends,
He pushed out to see his friends;
And voyaged up to Vicksburg town,
Planning to tear rebellion down;
And fixing his armies to combine
In Chattanooga at the proper time.
While in Vicksburg, there he stayed,
He ordered his army to be paid.
All detached men were ordered in,
With full descriptions to draw their tin.
He also spoiled the wealthy job
Of the steamboat's charging mob.
He tackled them like tons of niggers,
And scheduled them to price and figures.

The military civic jurisdiction.
About Vicksburg and vicinity had no friction.
Everything ran with ease and quiet,
As though everything was panning right.
The seventeenth corps, Grant placed upon her,
For their worth so glorious, an "ensignia of honor."
They fought the foe with all their might,
They led the army in every fight.
They were the first to come,
The last to run,
For they always won.
The officers and men together,
All drew badges, one like the other;
Except it was a few straggling hards,
That served as anchors or retards,
The awarding committee did consist
Of a long, well-chosen list.
After the repulse of Chickamauga,
Way down in the land of Conasauga,
Where big sweet potatoes grow,
And people learn things very slow;
Where Chattanooga boldly stands,
With a river washing her fertile lands
This is the scene we'll now describe,
Where warriors met in death and pride,
And many a sick one lingered and died.
Here, Sherman got his boys together,
To storm the rebels and the weather.
Now the rebels soon must meet before
Sherman's noble, daring fifteenth corps.
But, ere Sherman got into position,
He met with long, deadly opposition.
Near the town of Cherokee Station,
He met the horded rebels of a nation.
But he advanced steady and strong,

With a deadly sword, keen and long :
Until Chattanooga before was gained,
Where terror, for a season reigned.
While Sherman, thus, his troops deployed,
A trip up the river, Grant enjoyed ;
To the City of Cairo, up the Mississipp',
Grant went on a long, reviewing trip.
As along that mighty stream he coasted,
At Washington he kept them posted.
He posted them through storm and calms,
O'er electric wires, by telegrams.
By telegraphic apparatus,
Grant met his superior at Indianapolis ;
It was the secretary of war,
The chieftain Grant was working for.
Together, their whistles were never wet,
It was the first they had ever met.
He met Grant, and gave him orders to take
Command, of the greatest army 'tween gulf and lake ;
The three great departments, all combined,
To Grant's command, they are consigned.
The " Ohio," " Cumberland " and " Tennessee,"
    All ready for motion,
    That spans the interior to the ocean.
Then General Thomas, he stepped in
The place where Rosecrans had been.
For Rosecrans had no help at all,
When Bragg nailed him to the wall.
Then Grant and the secretary, to Louisville go,
That once was filled with the rebel foe.
When Grant, his way to the city wended,
A crowd on every hand, extended,
And at the Gault House, where he stopped,
Heads from every window popped.
The big Kentuckians, with goggle eyes,

Looked on this little man, with big surprise.
Poor fellow, was so weak and lame,
He traveled 'tween a crutch and cane.
The Vicksburg hero was the rage
Of this and every seeming age.*
About Louisville, he rode with leisure,
Taking in the city at his pleasure;
But he had no time to follow it long,
For the war was sounding its deadly gong;
And his great, big, new command,
Was the most stupendous in the land.†
   And no general, in any nation,
   Ever held so grand a station.
   No general below a general-in-chief,
   Ever sailed with such a reef.
   The entire zone of operation,
   Was held beneath his occupation.
   The "Military Division of the Mississipp',"
   The largest beneath a single grip;
      Added to his great army,
         Under his supervision,
      Was the Cumberland, Ohio,
         And Hooker's grand division.
      Now, fighting Joe Hooker
         Was the one that shook them;
      When he went for rebels,
         He generally took them.
      This Joe Hooker division
         Was surely a pander,‡
      When onto its ear,

---

* Said one Kentuckian, tall and gaunt,
   The very image of a spectral haunt,
     "A small chance for fighting he'd be no good,
     Around this neighboring Kentucky-hood.

† See book, "Remarkable Remarks on Grant," for curious facts.

‡ Signifies an exquisite, double-refined two-edged penetrating terror.

A frightful expander.
Thus, beneath Grant,
  A galaxy of marshals played,
No wonder they were successful,
  A delving in their trade.
His army commanders knew
  All about their work,
And would such men as Sherman,
  Burnside, Thomas or Hooker shirk?
To retreat, such men,
  Would truly be the last,
While each and every one of their men
  Feared no fiery blast.
The soldiers under Grant's command,
  According to nature's law,
Was composed of the best material
  The world ever saw.
(Added to it afterwards,
  Was General Foster's lines,
Which strengthened up our army,
  At least, in outward signs.)
How, then, could the southerners,
  With their puny dwarf,
Drive such a giant
  From their infamous wharf.
Now, each and every corps I'll draw in proper line,
And each and every general, to his proper place consign.
Granger had the fourth, Potter had the nine,
Howard had the eleventh, the twelfth was Slocum's line.
  The twenty-third was Manson's,
    McPherson's seventeen;
  The blood those ranks have shed,
    Enriched many a green.
  The sixteenth was Hurlburt's,
    The fourteenth, Palmer's corps,

Which never would travel behind,
　　When they were going before.
The fifteenth army corps, they never went a-boggin',
For it was commanded by General John A. Logan.
　　Now, here's a fact that I must not skip,
　　The great "Military Division of the Mississipp';"
　　　　It took Michigan, Illinois,
　　　　　Indiana, Ohio and Kentucky,
　　　　If it had stopped here,
　　　　　They would have been unlucky.
　　　　But yet, it took more of Uncle Sam,
　　　　　Mississippi, Tennessee,
　　　　North-western Georgia and Alabam'.
The opposing force was some less grand,
With well-trained generals in command.
There was Bragg's army of well-tried vets,
That would force the deal with bayonets.
Then joined with Bragg, to fight and kill,
Was Longstreet's force, combined with Hill.
Also Pemberton's army, which was exchanged,
Under Bragg's command, they were arranged.
Then, there's Joe Johnston close at hand,
With thirty thousand in his command.
Then, between the Black and Jackson there stayed,
L. D. Lee, with his six thousand cavalry brigade.
　　(But for all of that, it seems they felt
　　That the Union cause would wear the belt;
　　　And here is where I gleaned the facts,
　　　From rebel papers' long extracts.
　　　Says one paper " Give us corn and wool,
　　　Then we'll clip the horns of the northern bull."
Nail this to your door-post to read at leisure,
If we had grub and clothes we'd lick them with pleasure.
　　　But they've got one army more,
　　　Let's wipe that out, then victory's sure,

Let's go at them with all our "pizen,"
And give that army a pulverizin'.
Drive them into the river's flood,
Let water mingle with their blood.
There in Chattanooga, lies Rosecrans,
With pleasure, he and his commands.
Destroy and crush that over-plus,
Then by-and-by, we'll settle the fuss.
Readers of these verses, note
The mighty budget Grant must tote.
The Chickamauga army defeated,
Back into Chattanooga retreated;
And was shut in by General Bragg,
The bull-dog of the rebel rag;
Where he laid and licked his sores,
Received on Chickamauga's moors.
He laid there, watching Rosecrans,
Expecting him to fall into his hands.
Then he heard of the change of Grant,
Which made the rebel hero pant;
Then, his remarks, he cast them forth,
That smote the armies of the north;
"Saying, the hero, Rosecrans, was shaken.
Then, by two fools his place was taken."
Grant and Thomas, was it their share,
They seemed to be the lauded pair?
Hear ye Lincoln's remark, the southern rebel hater:
"If one fool is great, two fools are surely greater."
Ho! ye rebels! lo! ye rebels! listen to my song,
I really cannot understand how you can stand it long.
Soon, Grant left the kind Louisvillians,
With their treasured wealth of millions;
And down to Nashville, did repair,   [Oct. 20]
The lion in his den to dare.
For, Grant would ne'er stand still,

With a rebel growling o'er a distant hill.
Of course, at Nashville, they offered him pleasure,
Which seemed to abound in endless treasure.
 For there the citizens are grand,
 And would honor one high in command.
 But they drew from him no wrangling boast,
 He offered them no speech or toast.
 But he re-arranged his forces there,
 With all the strictness of a general's care.
 To make sure, his communications,
 That may be needed from other stations.
Then the rail, from Chattanooga, to the Ohio River,
Where floods of commerce flows forever.
 He ordered that line to be re-gauged
 For military purposes, when wars are waged.
 For soon, Chattanooga must feel the power
 Of General Grant, in his exalted hour.
  For all the Union ranks within it,
  Seemed as transient as a linnet
  That may have to get up, and soar away,
  Or grow to a lion in a night or day.
 On half rations, the soldiers fed,
 They were scarce of meat, and had little bread.
The horses' frames, it's said would rattle,
They had nothing to drag their guns to battle.
The horses and mules were starved so weak,
When they moved forth, their joints would creak.
 Then, Grant arrived upon the scene, [Oct. 23]
 With fatness, instead of added lean;
 For he came with power immense,
 The starving soldiers to recompense.
 But during the time those soldiers were cooped,
 They were high-spirited and never drooped.
In a few more days, the gem they prize,
Would lay complete before their eyes,

They'd open the gate to northern supplies.
  (But, Grant came a few days too soon,
  And changed the music with the tune.)
    Hooker climbed the mountains,
      And gave them a rakin',
    When the rebels awoke,
      Their works were taken.
The works that severed communication
Between Chattanooga and Bridgeport station.
But, when Hooker went out on this midnight grazin',
He was combined with Brigadier-General W. B. Hazen.
It was no child's play, the art of chasing a reb,
And every soldier knew it, that was a legal Fed.
    There were no cowards in either army line,
    Only the ones that straggled out behin'.
    And from the earliest, it proved to the last,
    The soldiers obeyed the loyal blast.
    Every soldier, to the lowest position,
    Fought up to the general's highest wishin'.
Davis! Jeff Davis! came to view the rebel means,
And look down on the Yankee scenes.
      Where Davis came to talk with Bragg,
      Was on Lookout Mountain's loftiest crag.
      Where a clear view into four states may atone,
      For the dim view of the fifth alone.
Davis viewed Grant's army, before which he stood,
Working like beavers, making their earth-works good.
    Then, with joy, his hands he clapped,
    Saying "I've got Grant's army now entrapped."
    General Pemberton, on horse-back, standing by,
    To the assertion of Davis, he did reply.
    He thus did address him, in the words of a sage,
    That should be honored in a future age:
"You're commander-in-chief and present here,
By a vigorous assault, you think they'd scare?

Now, o'er yon valley, charge our whole concern,
Not a living man will ever return.
Only those that the Yankees have saved
As prisoners of war, to their cause enslaved.

LONGSTREET'S ADVANCE ON KNOXVILLE.

Chattanooga had assumed her right,
And everything was settled and quiet;
Stores of all kind that were needed,
O'er nothingness was superseded.
The jolly officers flashed their blades
In various drills and dress parades.
While above, on the lofty heights,
The rebels viewed the splendid sights.
Grant moved about, was unattended,
He e'en with the people blended.
In a Chattanooga cottage he dwelt,
With all the pride its owner felt.
   He e'en enjoyed the scenes so good,
   With his pipe of briar-wood.
   He and his leading marshal men,
   Long they sat in council then.
   The evening gloom showed morning stars,
   Still they consulted on the wars.
   As peace in agitation slept,
   A mighty cyclone forward crept.
   Sherman's advance, now appears
   In regimental long drawn tiers.
(The raiding rebels destroyed the Feds,
Wherever they bobbed up their heads.
Though unarmed, they lived in peace,
The raiding devilment never ceased.
     Grant at last got satiated,
     Then drew his pen and retaliated.
Wherever the rebel raids annoyed,

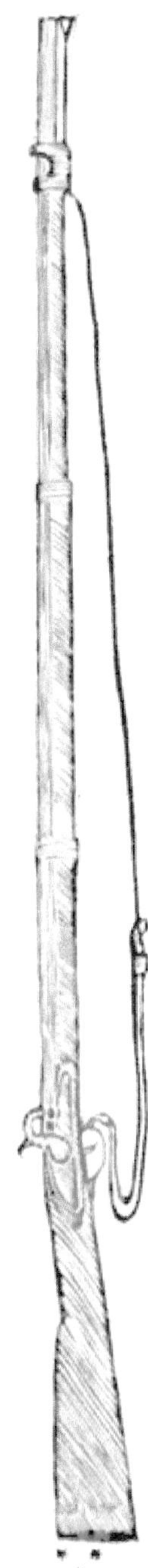

Likewise secession was destroyed.
Whatever the Feds in damage lost,
Secession planters paid the cost.
For every Feddy's horse they stoled,
On some secession purse it told.
Feds must be bruised and battered,
Though among the rebels scattered.
Retaliation, here must stand,
To conquer, or destroy the land.
Rebs must pay the Federal dues,
Even down to horses' shoes.
That their own good horses cast
In fleeing from the rebel blast.)
To Chattanooga, he came to fight,
He settled down on Thomas's right.
They laid for all that might transpire,
To advance, as the rebel lines retire.
But, ere Sherman brought on his force,
Longstreet was pursuing his course.
And, to Knoxville was his lay,
To drive the Yankee troops away.
Many a soldier bled *en route*,
And many a soldier died devout.
Along that route, no living fled,
The road was strewn with the dead.
Burnside could have stopped Longstreet,
And never have led him in retreat.
But he was luring him away,
From where they wished him not to stay.
Burnside fought a long retreat,
And Longstreet thought it was defeat.
They fought Longstreet, some time to gain,
So they could secure their wagon train.
Then, when at last they had succeded,

⁎ Long range "life extinguisher," used by the Yankees.

Then, into Knoxville they retreated.
Then, on the nineteenth of Novem',
Knoxville was besieged by Longstreet's men.
Grant had them now where he desired,
From the proper place, retired.
Now, Lookout Mountain must be taken,
Her massive rocks, by artillery shaken.
The Chattanooga siege must end,
Beyond the power of Bragg to mend.
So Grant drew up his plans to fit,
And his commanders sanctioned it.
Backed by an army, fierce and strong,
With dangerous blades, keen and long ;
Ready to meet foes, unnumbered,
In each soldier's arm a cyclone slumbered.
Each soldier was restless for the fight,
Each hand a keg of dynamite.
Bragg's lines were stretched at either extreme,
Till scarcely nothing remained between.
But Lookout Mountain was his hold,
And Missionary Ridge must not be sold.
Grant was to tackle his both extremes,
With all the furor of infernal fiends,
General Sherman was to attack the right,
While Hooker should put the left to flight.
With Lookout Mountain for a stand,
If the rebels left it in his hand.
The center was to Thomas given,
That must, by bayonets be riven.

BEFORE CHATTANOOGA'S FIRST DAY'S BATTLE. [Nov. 23]

Now, everything was ready made,
The troops advanced, as on parade,
The rebels thought it was a review,
Till heavy losses proved it untrue.

The losses of important places,
The bamboozled idea it soon erases.
The Yankee lines were never shaken,
Till Orchard Knob and works were taken.
Here it was, that General Wood
Led his soldiers firm and good ;
And in the evening, entrenched his men,
So bombshells would not pester them.

THE SECOND DAY AT LOOKOUT MOUNTAIN.   [Nov. 24]

Sherman got as good a posish',
As any general could ever wish.
The place he seemed to hold and fill,
Was near the place called Tunnel Hill.
Around the hill, he then possessed,
He e'en fortified its crest.
Hooker had been engaged all day,
In fire and sword's most deadly play.
Cannon-balls shrieked o'er his head,
Unmindful of the fallen dead.
But on, he climbed the mountain's side,
In a vast, ascending human tide.
To those lines of moving Feds,
The rocks and trees gave up their rebs.
You bet the Yankees made them rattle,
They had no time to e'en skedaddle.
By Hooker's movements, queer arranged,
(He took many old prisoners unexchanged.
That had been at Vicksburg taken,
That stood so long by bombs unshaken.
By their officers, it was arranged,
To make them believe they'd been exchanged.)
On Lookout Mountain's summit high,
Artillery seemed growling from the sky.
On its summit, the battling crowds,

Fought their battle above the clouds.
Joe Hooker did some deadly work,
Which only ended in the evening murk.
The point of the mountain, it was taken,
Where the rebel fire was long and rakin',
And on the eastern slope, all the livin'
Rebels from it were killed or driven.

THIRD DAY.—TUNNEL HILL AND MISSION RIDGE. [Nov. 25]

Hooker chased the rebels, with all his fiery zeal,
For they were well aware his was a dangerous steel.
Before Hooker, not a rebel showed his face,
But during the night, they'd sought a safer place.
Lookout Mountain was wrenched from rebel powers,
And it was snugly held by the army that was ours.
Hooker drove everything over to Mission Ridge,
And arrived at proper time, in rear of Breckenridge.
Sherman had some guns placed in good position,
To bombard Fort Buckner, showed his disposition.
But Buckner replied with sheets of lurid flame,
Then, on Sherman's lines, there fell a metal rain.
In the brush there sat three patriots at their ease,
Scribbling in a note book, placed upon their knees.

> They were all scribbling away
>   Like clerks put out on hire,
> They never even seemed to notice
>   The fierce and growling fire.
> The bombshells above them,
>   Through the bushes brushed,
> But, they wrote away as though
>   Everything was hushed.
> Well, it seems they wrote a hand,
>   Legible and plain,
> As Buckner poured over them,
>   His canisterial rain.

Travel o'er the world,
    In every land beside,
You'll never see it any place,
    Beyond our nation tide.
It is a sight that one,
    Would scarce ever expect,
It is a point, o'er which a man
    Can well and long reflect.
Fort Buckner, on Tunnel Hill,
Was a hard and bitter pill;
It was there that Sherman's lines,
Got repulsed a dozen times.
Every time that Sherman charged,
It seemed that death, with blood was gorged.
It seemed the men, their part would wield,
Iron-hearted, with nerves of steel,
Men, against fate dare not contend,
For a deadened man we ne'er can mend.
May future bards, on this take hold,
Deal us warm and never cold.
Rig ye derrick of mighty lore,
To raise tales ne'er told before.
Sharper than hunger-clad Anderson's prison,
Sharper than the sword that Grant called his'n.
Rig a derrick, by your might and main,
To drag peace back to our country again.
Soldiers, by shell torn and rended,
By flesh-carpenters sewed and mended.
By sword and saw, knife and gun,
It seems the country thus was run.
Fierce and marauding bands,
Pillaged rich and fertile lands.
Life was in danger to be owned,
Many an unshot freeman moaned.
Moaned at the bloody ruction,

Of the wide and sad destruction.
Destruction lurked in every waif,
It was deemed dangerous to be safe.
Even swords leaped from their sheath,
A common thing was general death.
Lead woke up from its long slumber,
Like fire reaped up in sheets of slumber.
Looking for blood, it mightily strode,
On wings of powder, it must have rode.
Death prevailed in every race,
Death always held the highest place.
His breast, from crotch to chin,
Was hung with medal's worthless tin.
He took cannon of ponderous size,
To whet his blade, to win the prize.
  Everything he did abuse,
  From man down to holy shoes.
He came with power to break to smashes,
Nothing could stand his furious slashes.
Bullets flew by powder's expanse,
The bullets led in smoke's advance.
Unlike Britons or the Hessians,
No dreamy man could quell secessions.
It took a sword whetted to an edge,
With an arm able to swing a sledge.
To make the dashing rebels feel,
Or to a foe show up their heel.
It took the Yankees' might and main,
To make them feel a battle's pain.
And leaden balls with points of steel,
To make the rebel chieftains feel.
Lightning itself, was appalled by them,
To see what deeds were done by men.
Then came Gordon Granger's dash,
A wild and fearless, murderous crash.

Three long half miles, o'er stones and ditches,
Ere he got to the murderous wretches.
Enough to terrify the strong
A weak man never would have gone.
But on they go, with steady tread,
They mark the field with their mangled dead.
The divisions of Sheridan and Wood,
Wade breast deep in fire and blood.
Oh, the scene—with the battle's gone—
By painters and sculptors never drawn.
A pen or tongue can not describe,
A chasm of death so vast and wide.
They push on, they never swerve,
Well knowing behind there's no reserve.
They push on to the hill before,
Where long and loud artillery roar,
To climb o'er ridges, rocks and dale,
It seems too strong for a truthful tale.
But think ye not my pen has lied,
It is too strong to be described.
The grape and canister, shot and shell,
In long rows of death did tell.
Fort Woods and Negley, with mighty strokes,
O'er the rebels' heads mowed off the oaks.
Then, opened up Fort Palmer and King,
Their artillery made the mountains ring;
Also Moccasin Point and Orchard Knob,
Joined in with the fortish mob.
From base to summit of Mission Ridge,
They battered the rebels like a giant sledge.
But on and on marched our troops,
Like demons onto deadly brutes;
To get to the rebels was their desire,
They burned and rolled like a prairie fire.
Their trail was marked with blue and red.

Their bravest were numbered with the dead,
Mission Ridge had looks satanic,
Her whole surface seemed volcanic.
Mission Ridge, with its racket and roar,
Never jarred to such music before.
Oh! will this battle with death ne'er clog
This sounding board of Chickamaug'.
The old army of the Cumberland, here,
The boys all led, there was no rear'
Think ye, it's a battle with no death in it,
With sixty heavy guns a minute.
The work of the Ridge's base, in the storm,
Was swept as by a giant's arm.
Now up the craggy hill they sweep,
O'er the rock-strewn, stumpy, frightful steep.
Each man, here takes himself in command,
And towards the foe crawls hand o'er hand.
Of all the battles ever fought,
This episode's the most startling ever wrought.
Thus, with the Ridge they wrestle long,
With power it seems, sufficient strong.
Their blood pours down the mountain side,
Made slippery by the crimson tide.
By all the strength of manly powers,
Mission Ridge at last was ours.
The men shook hands, laughed and cried,
Then, to hug themselves, they e'en tried.

> Turned a somersault, and then,
> Done the whole thing o'er again.
> Then the pursuing and pursued,
> At each others' heels they hewed.
> Till down Chickamauga stream,
> Rolls the last of the battle scene.
> Four thousand men, in battle slain,
> Except the ones that lived again.

But, for the dead it has no charms,
The ten thousand captured stands of arms
With fifty-two big, heavy guns,
That once served the southern sons.
And of rebel prisoners, be it said,
Seven thousand besides the dead,
Tennessee rebellion is o'er,
Kentucky kicks it from her shore.

Oh! the wave of battle, see it rage and roll,
The earth is reeking in blood, it e'en tries man's soul
Hear ye the cannons' loud and deadly roar,
Shot and shell raining destruction where'er they pour
A thousand soldiers dead, a hundred more may bleed,
But soldiers fighting, to them can pay no heed.
Oh! ye human race, have ye become imbruted?
The rebel soldiers wounded, and the doctors executed.
The soldiers that stood the charge of bayonet,
Couldn't stand the doctors to whittle, mend and set.
The doctors with lancet, saw and knife,
'Reft many a soldier of a sweet and precious life.

THE PURSUIT.—FIGHT AT RINGGOLD.

Much of the task was done,
　But much of it uncompleted,
It did not prove we'd wrecked them,
　Because they so retreated.
Sherman, Hooker and Palmer,
　Then followed in pursuit,
The harvest that they gathered,
　Was surely tempting fruit.
We'll name some of the things here,
　The rebels lost a-main,
Scuds of bacon, molasses and corn
　And an entire pontoon train,
Also swords, guns and meal,

Small arms and straggling men,
And it was at Chicamauga depot,
Where they got the most of them.
The rebels tried hard to destroy
What they could not carry away.
But somehow or other, the time
And chance rudely skipped away,
But on and on to Pigeon Ridge,
The rebels they were driven,
But here they stopped to fight,
According to orders given.
And from their position, they were
Shortly afterwards bouted,
And, then they slid along,
As if completely routed.
The enemy, slowly through Ringgold, ooze,
As the Yankees hard after them pursue,
The Ringgold gap is finally gained,
And by the rebels, long maintained.
Then hear the bullets, hear them hum,
Oh, how the shells would come bum.
Here the Yankees fled from their wrath,
Down from the gap, along Ringgold's path.
Then when the Yankees turned and fled,
The rebels followed with sword and lead.
But Osterhaus's division was brave,
They rallied and made the rebels cave.
But ere the rebels would give in,
Geary's division joined the din.
(Yes, Geary's division of the twelfth corps,
Helped rock the rebels out before.)
But ere the Yankees did retreat,
Before they felt it was defeat;
The seventh Ohio was fearfully shaken;
All of its officers were taken.

They went into the fight, bold and stout,
They fell back, with only a lieutenant to lead them out.
It took many a long and patient toil,
Before the rebels would recoil.
But when they broke, they broke for good,
With all the fleetness of noble blood.
These are the spoils they then took back,
From this wild and weird sack:
They captured no wealth in gold or lead,
But they captured three hundred rebs instead.
They were a docile lot of cranks,
High privates in the rear ranks.
At Dalton the rebs made a stand,
Far from General Sherman's command.
The railroad from Cleveland to Red Clay,
By Yankee troops was swept away.
Here the rebel government missed 'em,
Ruined was their mighty railroad system.
When those mighty things took hold,
Grant was quartered at Ringgold.
He was tickled o'er the things,
That made the rebels so take wings.
He showed it in his tickled mood,
As if by war, he then was wooed.

KNOXVILLE RELIEVED.

When General Bragg was chased,
    By Grant and his command,
Longstreet, before Knoxville,
    Determined to retrieve his land.
(More of his name he thought,
    Than all his country wide,
He did not want to waste his name
    Upon misfortune's tide.)
Therefore, at Fort Sanders,

He struck with might and main,
There he tried to dash
The Union lines in twain.
But the Union lines were not so tender,
Or easily torn asunder,
And if ever he saw it lightning,
Here he heard it thunder.
It was here he was repulsed,
With such a bloody hand,
It was some time before
He had power to stand.
But ere he could recover,
The Yankees gathered 'round him,
And with their swords and guns,
They were prepared to pound him.
For from Chattanooga, Foster, Granger
And Sherman's men poured around,
Like a wave from the ocean deep,
O'er a soft and treacherous ground.
Then Longstreet got up and fled,
With all his power lent,
Then Foster and Sherman's cavalry
Pursued with vast destruction meant.
The siege was raised, and Knoxville sound.
To Washington was hurled,
Then in the works that Longstreet held,
The stars and stripes unfurled.
(Lincoln, then, according
To strong religious living,
December seventh, sixty-three,
Ordered a thhnksgiving.
December eighth o'er Grant he poured
Long and fervent thanks,
And every soldier that e'er tread
The Mississippi banks;

Where the chains of slavery beat
  With loud and erring clanks,
Grant had Lincoln's thanks,
  Put in an order grand,
And read to every regiment
  Throughout his big command.)
Then Halleck in his annual report,
Followed him through dale and court;
Where the enemy was chased and killed,
How many graves by Grant were filled.
Was all given in language clear,
The words of which I quote not here.

THE REBELS SERIOUSLY WORRIED.

Said a rebel correspondent that knows
Where Grant will strike the coming blows:
"Towards Atlanta, Yankees cannot go,
The roads are bad and footing slow;
The ferries are all poor concerns,
And bridges into ashes burns;
And of railroads they have none;
And not a car beneath the sun."
Now this is what that correspondent heard,
And the conversation that occured.
Our idea of the Vicksburg take,
Proved to us a vital mistake.
We thought our climate they couldn't stand,
That our water would purge them from the land,
With Pemberton's guns to decimate,
Would surely seal the Yankees fate.
All seemed to be a lubrication,
Not as we deemed it, a decimation.
In ninety days see what he done,
Took all Vicksburg, e'en Pemberton.
They will not sleep like dromedaries,

They'll bridge the streams that have no ferries,
Our correspondents may figure wise and canty.
It'll take men, not mud, to save Atlanta.
Yankee activity supplies Grant's needs,
And such activity always succeeds.
　　Now, what is to be done,
　　　Must be done without delay,
　　Or we'll find Grant in Atlanta,
　　　Ere the eve of Christmas day.
　　　Our country raked,
　　　Our cotton faked,
　　　　Or all of it destroyed."
Richmond, (Va.) Whig. Dec., 1863.

Here Grant rehearses o'er again,
The bloody fields of his last campaign,
Which commenced at Bridgeport town,
And ended at Knoxville with such renown.
He thanked them for the deeds done,
He thanked them for the battles won ;
He thanked them for all their service did.
From the highest command, to the drummer kid.
He praised their heroic, daring acts,
And the steadiness of their fierce attacks.
　When advancing in your wrath,
　No obstacle can bar your path.
Oh ! glorious were the words he said,
Thanks to the living, and praise to the dead.
When the order by Grant was given,
He was a weak one among the livin'.
His fall had worked him serious harms,
The skin hung loose upon his arms.
Stooping forward, his shoulders bent
Like a sapling, to a hurricane lent.
When Grant was informed that Hardee commanded,
In place of Bragg, for Bragg's being stranded ;

He quietly remarked it was his choice,
O'er it, both armies seemed to rejoice.
For Hardee had no bull-dog nature,
But more like the poodle creature.
Now here's the figures showing for
The deeds that Grant has done in war.
Grant did some business to awaken
Four hundred and seventy-two cannons taken,
Ninety thousand prisoners joined to his plunder,
With small arms, to tedious to number.*

But this Indian orion never told
How dear that rebel plunder sold;
How many soldiers' lives were lost,
Nor nothing of the general cost.

GRANT'S FEARLESSNESS.

At Ringgold's short battle rage,
Almost obscure on history's page.
For half a mile, he faced the balls,
More solid than a mason's walls;
And I don't think he thought it out
How much danger rode about.
In this place, so fearful hot,
He rushed not, only in a trot.
Here, our men were awfully killed,
Their life-blood down the mountain rilled.
Close he studied the ground beyond,
And how to make the rebs abscond.
He had no escort, heavy or slight,
Only a staff, strung out like the tail of a kite;

---

* Those figures are by Colonel Ely S. Parker,
A Sachem chief, an Indian corker.
High he ranked in exalted station,
O'er the Tonawanda tribe and Seneca nation.
By his Chattanooga conduct, so giraffe,
He became a member of the general's staff.

That is when he's rushing around,
  To roads in particular, he's never bound.
But over fences, floods, fields and ditches,
Forth he sails, like the king of witches.
Now, here it comes to the ticklish part,
He never cares for daylight or dark.
He will ride from breakfast away,
Till next morn's peep of day.
  Without a single thing to chew,
  Unless it is a cigar or two.
Then when the sun dispels the murk,
He'll repeat the dose. till he ends the work.
  As often times he does to boot,
  Take a few whiffs at his briar-root.

AN INCIDENT.

This is an incident, which is alleged,
To have happened in Chattanooga, when besieged.
Which happened in the days of that city,s gloom,
When many stood on the verge of the tomb.
It was when Meigs and Grant arrived,
When hunger alone was all that thrived.
  They took a horse-back airing one afternoon,
  About the city so wrapped in gloom:
They passed a huge mule, so wrapped in stench,
That it might stifle a nigger, or smother a wench.
It seemed the hero of Vicksburg was shaken,
The briar root from his lips was taken.
Then solemnly spoke he to Quartermaster Meigs,
"There's a soldier of your's totally off his legs."
    Dolefully spoke General Meigs,
      "He was once expensive,
    Poor old vet, he lies so quiet,
      But still assuming the offensive."

A SCENE ON LOOKOUT MOUNTAIN.

On Mission Ridge, 'neath the rebel rag,
Sustained and honored by General Bragg,
Near where Breckenridge's headquarters stood,
A rebel of noble, southern blood,
There dwelt a woman on that height,
Upon the scene of that bloody fight.
She asked Bragg where should she go,
To shun the furore of the coming foe.
"Lord! Madam, to shun them Yankee Feds,
Why, up here, they dare not show their heads."
With a blubber she added to a Yankee seer,
Less than fifteen minutes you all were here.
Now again,
Grant prepares for a new campaign.
And it was plain to be Grant's course,
To crush the south by overwhelming force.
And for Uncle Sam to break each prison,
And take the men that now are his'n.
(Oh, Andersonville, the latest type of hell!
What's been suffered there, no mortal can tell,
And the fiend who ran that prison,
May hell's hottest part be his'n.
Where vermin is as the sand, unnumbered,
The very dust by them encumbered.
No such prisons were ever ran,
Where man so punished fellow-man.
Men were so starved their bones would rattle,
Like skeletons once lost in battle.
Whose hip bones, worn through the skin,
Were more fearful than battle din.
They looked like some horrid dummy,
The image of an Egyptian mummy.
There, hundreds upon hundreds died,

It seemed the brutal warden's pride.
To that unprotected horde,
He was more deadly than the sword.
This prison work, what a burning shame,
My pen point's heated, till it's lame.
And this was not the only place,
Where man so punished his brother race.)
One million men Grant recommended,
Thus to have our lines extended.

"Headquarters in the field,
(May victory, ruin and rebels yield).
Chattanooga, Tennessee.
December twelfth, sixty-three.
"Military Division of the Mississippi."
(May rebeldom not grow too lippy).
Read ye this, all brave men,
General order, number ten.
All rebeldom was now displeased,
By dissatisfaction sore, diseased.
They had been whipped too oft and long,
And pounded at so fierce and strong.
That the common soldiers were disgusted.
And the leading men were sore mistrusted.
So they deserted in squads and gangs,
To shun turmoil and battle clangs;
And came within the Yankee lines,
With all the show of peaceful signs.
Although Uncle Sam did not expect them,
He was determined to protect them;
Protect them from the rebel power,
To punish them in a future hour.
Read ye, the disposition made,
How they from rebel power were stayed.
When rebels desert their arms and surrender,
Their arms at once, they then must tender.
The commanders of division or brigade,
When rebel deserters quit their trade,
Can protect them within our line,
If they find the desertion genuine.

> But to protect us both,
> Swear them to the following oath ;
> 'May heaven my soul eternally damn,
> If I don't stick hereafter, to Uncle Sam ;
> I'll stick to him through thick and thin ;
> To congress, and to all her sin ;
> I'll do whatever it may ask,
> No matter what may be the task.
> I swear to this, by the God of war,
> To all God's worth, and what he's for ;
> I swear by God, and all in reason ;
> By everything in and out of season.
> Thus I'll swear, as I have begun,
> So help me God, till the thing is done.'
> Now this is an oath for all it's worth,
> From the death of Christ, to the devil's birth ;
> Oh, twist it around, to make it level,
> From the birth of Christ, to the death of the devil.

> No oath is false, when it is real,
> Note ye this, my hand and seal,
> John Nicholas Snyder,
> And old man Rider,
> With witnesses in
> Albert Ezery Shinn."

Rebel deserters may obtain passes free,
And rations to take them home, wherever it may be,
> Or by quartermasters, they may be employed,
> So, by old acquaintance, they cannot be annoyed.
> Or by engineers' department, they
> Can choose the one, whiche'er they may,
>   If there is room.
But to protect them from old contempt,
From military service, they are exempt.
> All army traders were hustled out,
> That did not follow the legal route.
Grant ordered all rentals to the government, paid,
That the rental of "secesh" property made.

Grant expected his officers to collect the few
Taxes, to the government due.
When no other way can reach them,
And no other way will teach them
    To ante up their taxes.
Tax commissioners went out reckoning,
All o'er the southern states collecting.
They were Uncle Sam's collectors,
Uncle Sammy's tax protectors.
Rebel property was not abused,
But for storage and quarters used.
Grant allowed none of his soldiers supplies
To fall behind in any wise.
Grant, watched his supplies, with due extremes,
They were his soldiers' fighting means.
    He gave his quarter-master control,
    To make the railway rollers roll;
And to set steamboats in motion,
Whether they be on river or ocean.
From Chattanooga to Nashville, Tenn.,
Grant travels down with river men;
Aboard of "Point Rock," a government packet,
Which was propelled by a Boiler racket.
Grant has not yet recovered all,
    From last summer's horseback fall.
    He now walks slowly, oft with a cane,
    It will be long ere he's well again.
From the Nashville correspondent, undone in rhyme,
Shipped east a purpose for *The New York Times*,
    And in that paper it occurred,
    In sixty-three, December twenty-third.
In this city, right here in town.
Is the first soldier of warring renown;
Quartered on High street, a beautiful place,
The man who designed it, was the chief of his race.

That residence is the rebel George Cunningham's
That once was the quarters of Rosecrans.
Grant is not short in general liking,
But there's nothing about him, the least bit striking.
    A rather spare built man, of medium size,
    With dark brown hair, and sharp blue eyes;
    His chin was covered with short, red hair;
    His brow above was straight and square,
    A nose almost Grecian, delicate and fine,
    But boldly set with a firm outline.
    He was far from looking dangerous or wild,
    But modest, unassuming, simple as a child.
        No one would take him for a taker,
        No one would think him such a rebel fakir.
            He was a dandy in his deals,
            Corpse-strewn were his battle-fields.
            He often saw the rebels' heels.
    (The more of a bum,*
    The longer one will last for ages to come.)
                To work on land,
                He was no hand;
                To reap and mow,
                Prune and sow
                    For others.
    At Nashville, he stayed not long about,
    Only to rush the Chattanooga railway route;
    Then, to Knoxville, he steered his course,
    To look at the roads and view his force.
            Of Grant, it is claimed,
            In trades he was famed,
            But never in battle maimed.
            He was a killer,

----

* Hear what Sherman of him said :
  "Grant was a man, short of a head,
  Glorious bum, illustrious dead,"

A tinker and tiller ;
A blacksmith and a miller.
And like Black Maria,
A curious terrifier,
Still wondrous to inspire.
Cool in construction,
Fearless in reduction,
And wondrous in a ruction.
He worked his men with vigor,
In pulling cocks and trigger
In work, to free the nigger.
Grant's men worked in rows,
A-hewing on their foes,
With fierce and deadly blows.
All his men worked in ranks,
Using hand and shanks,
A climbing hill and banks.
To catch men, or fetch them
As prisoners of war.

CHARACTER AND TRAITS OF GRANT.

Grant was modest, reticent and shy,
He was rather light, five feet, eight inches high
He had no looks of the heroic cast,
A face that would lull a cyclone's blast.
Perhaps, I here may miss my standing,
His a face was face far from commanding,
On the battle-field he had a peculiar vim,
Which seemed to inspire all to obey him.
Was their anything striking about him ?   (My, no,
Unless it was when he struck the rebels a blow).
His brow it was straight and square,
About him, there was nothing lofty there.
His nose, it does somewhat slightly incline,
To not be a Grecian, but an aquiline.

This is the only feature about him suggestive,
His eyes are blue, sharp and expressive.
An extract from a letter of Grant's,
To a friend of his, who never wore pants.
The postscript that the letter bore,
I'll name it, as I've not before:

> Chattanooga, Tennessee,
> December thirteenth, sixty-three.

Dear Madam, before me the letter of your husband lays,
My friend and class-mate in collegiate days,
From me he asks a lock of my hair,
As relics to be sold at the Rochester fair.
(That is, if the article's not scarce on my head,
Caused by age, more wearing than rebel lead.)
I'm glad to say it's as thick as ever.
And the last hair from my head I would sever,
To aid in raising sanitary money,
For our mangled boys in the south so sunny.
I hope lots of cash from it you'll make,
I wish you success for the soldiers' sake.
Though in it you'll find age holds its mark,
By the silver threads among the dark.
It proves that boyish youth has passed and gone,
And that age o'er manhood's began to dawn.

> Oh! think ye of the soldier's pain.
> Very truly, your friend I remain.

Oh!   say,   it's   U. S. Grant, M. G., U. S. A.

THANKS OF CONGRESS—A GOLD MEDAL.

The thanks of Congress to Grant was given,
The greatest American general livin'.
It was Washburn, of Galena town,
Who first worked the bills aroun'.
The reason he to Congress those bills presented,
Was that Galena by him was represented.
What the bills were I will here portray,
Those bills so offered in a determined way.
One was to revive the lieutenant-general's grade.

An office long banished in the warring trade.
Near the time Washington had sheathed his blade.
The thanks of Congress was in a medal fine,
Portrayed and engraved with a proper design.
The medal and thanks to Grant soon passed,
It seemed with important things to be classed.
This bill got through all rushingly straight,
At the very first session of Congress thirty-eight.
Then a committee took the thing in charge,
And viewed the designs of draftsmen at large.
Leutze was the man with the lucky design,
Something fit for coinage, gold, rare and fine.
On the obverse side, profilely portrayed,
Was Grant with the year of his chief battle trade.
On the reverse side were legions of history.
Wrapped close in truth, and tied up in mystery.

   To Grant was given honorary chances,
   To stand in the lead of all advances;
   And memberships for life were given,
   To him, by whom the Johnnys were driven,
   He received them with pleasures fained,
   And the same for glory long retained.
   He could have lived as well without them,
   And never thought a thought about them.

   Herein there comes another year,
     To change the date upon us,
   Eighteen hundred and sixty-four
     Flourishes her hand upon us;
   New York for Grant and his army,
     Legislated thanks, [Jan. 17]
   For what he did for rebeldom,
     In clipping off her shanks.
   Ohio followed New York,
     In line of legal thanking,

Somehow or another, it's done up,
  As merchants do their banking.
At Colt's armory, at Hartford,
  A working in the shops,
At least a dozen men or more,
  Upon an inlaid pair of pops.*
The handles are of black horn,
  Polished smooth and slick,
In which it takes a workman fine
  To e'en perform the trick.
The barrels and magazines
  Are all inlaid with gold,
Which, from solid chunks of ore,
  Are hammered, beaten or rolled.
The trigger-guards, and all such thing,
  From chunks of gold were hammered
In revolvers; o'er such another pair,
  No workman ever clamored.
The cartridge-boxes were fine enough
  For e'en a priest to purloin,
They were made of metal
  The same as silver coin.
The whole was then encased
  In a casing rich and rare,
Velvet on the inside,
  And rosewood for the wear.
They say they are the finest
  That's ever yet been made,
By gentlemen of honor,
  That're working at the trade.
        At last
The lieutenant-general bill was passed.
On March the second, sixty-four,

* Mr. Colt, like all the rest of the fools,
Presented him with a deadly pair of tools.

> Grant was major-general no more;
> For he was by act of congress, made
> Lieutenant-general in his trade.
> From ville to ville, he now proceeds
> Delivering out his warring creeds.
> From Knoxville, he to Louisville rushes,
> As the winter winds o'er the mountain brushes
> The snow laid deep upon the ground,
> The fiercest weather upon him frowned.
> Oh, it was a journey, 'twould make none laugh,
> This cold campaign, by him and his staff.
> The winter blew her coldest gust,
> Frost filled the air in place of dust.
> The most of this journey on foot they bore,
> Walking, and driving their horses before.
> Through Barboursville's big hill and Cumberland Gap,
> Through Lexington, (look on your map).
> Along that route, Grant was embraced,
> Fierce cold, by warm meals was chased.
> The reason Grant came by this route,
> Was to know exactly what he was about.
> See the importance of its size,
> O'er it travels Foster's supplies.
> That's what makes Grant so great and wise,
> He'll stoop, small things to supervise.
> His blue clothes were fully sized,
> He was embraced and lionized.
> Into Louisville, unnoticed he entered,
> But soon the city around him centered.
> Then for Nashville, on the morrow,   [Jan 12]
> Pleasures from to-day they borrow.
> The frost may turn to frozen rain,
> And snow-storms pelt their pelts in vain.
> All such hurts then sadly fails,
> When riding wheels o'er rattling rails.,

The Chattanooga railway's done,
The cars upon her rails are run.
To build it up from Bridgeport town,
Was a scheme of great renown.
It was just one long string of schemes,
Hewing through mountains, and bridging streams.
It was a road immense to build,
It was all, either cut or filled.
When the first train o'er this road drew,
From Bridgeport into Chattanoo';
There was some big rejoicing done,
By every warring mother's son.
For heretofore they had half rations,
To fight the warring, fierce secessions.
But this road it promised plenty,
No more would the Yankee boys be scanty.
Here Grant began collecting supplies,
With arms, the rebels to tantalize.
For in the spring, war must open again,
With a long, determined, strong campaign.
We find on January's thirteenth day,
Grant, in Nashville, presumed to stay.
He'd been around his department, all over it sir,
In the most inclement season of the year,
Thus, by superintending all minor things,
It bore him aloft, on superior wings,
That's what made him so terrible in battle,
That's what made his arms so successfully rattle.

GRANT AT ST. LOUIS.—PUBLIC DINNER.

Grant came to St. Louis, far from his pleasure,
To see a sick child, a fond waif of his treasure.
He came to St. Louis, and registered where he stayed,
"U. S. Grant, Chattanooga," was the entry he made.
Volumes laid wrapped in that name far below,

As the top of it showed with a diamond-hue glow.
It was found out soon, by inspecting the books.
That all were astonished, from the chief to the cooks.
They thought that such a man,
With a high-honored name,
Couldn't slip into town,
Without blowing the same
By the blasts of a trumpet,
And the toots of a horn,
And the roll of a drum,
That no princess could scorn.
Then, like fire, of the wildest description,
It spread o'er the city, in every direction.
The doctors, with his child, did do as they please,
And he was recovering with a ruined disease.
A long invitation, to Grant at once went,   [Jan. 27]
From the great and the good of St. Louis it was sent.
To invite him to dine with old friends, not a few,
And to get acquainted with some that were new.
By a letter he accepted, the long invitation
From the St. Louis folks, backed up by a nation.
The City University, he examined it all,
From the boys that recited to the outer wall.
The St. Louis Theater that evening caught him,
I think a free ride and a ticket brought him.
More eyes from the house, Grant and his family drew,
Than the grand old play of dear, old "Richelieu."
Grant with "Richelieu," no glory shared,
Between the acts, he was lustily cheered.
"Hail! Columbia!" made the orchestra pant,
Then "Yankee Doodle" was played for Grant.
At the "Lindel," then the dinner spread,
Old acquaintances, with the new, were fed.
Many, many there were seated,
No use their names here repeated;

Unless I bring F. Dent to life,
The aged sire of the hero's wife.
Grant was the great now, and has been,
All eyes of the feasters were turned on him.
The devil by such, would be harassed,
Then Grant, you know, was easily embarassed.
  After the merry party was fed,
    Long council documents were read.
Long documents by the council bruled,
The council that o'er the city ruled.
Then long and gaunt came many toasts,
As horrid as old satan's ghost.
To here rehearse them, they're too long,
They'd jar like the notes of a broken gong.
    Then before him music paraded,
    He was honored, toasted and serenaded:
    And time will not permit me here,
    With his many invitations to interfere.
    Some of them were better than the best,
    But the most of them were very grotesque.
    The general a letter to some of them sent,
    They merely prove how his opinions leant.
(His opinions were all easily got,
As few of them crumbled while they were hot.)
At St. Louis, the western sanitary commission,
Among themselves, voted him a high position.
Grant to his department rushed off again,   [Feb. 1]
To carry out his plans of the spring campaign,
        Which is to rend the rebel cause,
        To destroy it and its hellish laws.

LIEUTENANT-GENERAL.—CONGRESSIONAL NOMINATION.

    If ever I used inspired musings,
    Here, heaven help me in my choosings:
    Here, help me tell just what it is,

With all the fancy of a poet's "biz."
For here's a great bill to be voted,
Which will make this congress noted.
It was by Washburn introduced,
To have the lieutenant-general reproduced;
And there were none within the nation,
But knew who'd get the nomination.
On the passage of that bill for   [Feb. 1, '64]
All knew it would be the champion of the war.
Farnsworth wanted to make that bill a law that morn,
But long and loud against it, Garfield blew his horn.
The appointment of Grant was recommended,
And thus, the bill was so amended.
First by Ross, it was submitted,
Then by the house it was admitted.
Then followed debates, at furious rates.
Let us take Washburn's speech, to sample by,
And pick its bones, the meat to try.
Here, Washburn's speech I'll introduce,
I'll not the original hero produce;
I'll just extract its sweetest parts,
And cast aside the keener darts.
Washburn delivered a long and glorious speech,
The hearts of his fellow-men to reach,
He rehearsed Grant's life all o'er and o'er,
Telling what he had done, and a great deal more.
He went on to show that Vicksburg gunning,
Was dangerous to battery running;
That without an exception, all the boating crews,
To run the batteries did refuse.
Then men of war, who'd served their years,
Blew their horns for volunteers.
Then triple the needed number came,
To a glorious cause, to sign their name.
They came, the rebel cause to fight,

They, whom no rebel balls could fright.
The " Lead Mine Regiment " of my place,
Proved the boldness of its race.
One hundred and sixteen of her men,
Offer they, their service then;
With commissioned officers, sixteen,
To join in that daring, deadly scene.
Where the breath of death shall breathe,
Where the hurricanes of death shall seethe
They were all eager to join in the affray,
Let scathing death work as it may.
Then by lot each place was chose,
To run the gauntlet of the foes.
Thus each boat secured her crew,
Each one assigned the place he drew.
Each lot drew seemed a suicide,
On every wave death seemed to ride.
One noble boy of Galena, drew
The most dangerous place in that daring few.
Other men of daring and vim,
Offered to buy the chance from him.
One hundred greenback dollars new,
Was offered for the prize he drew.
But with a manner fierce and bold,
He refused the offer, stern and cold.
(Each soldier was a hero born,
That a world of Cæsars ne'er could scorn.
Each soldier himself was a noble commander,
Which would astonish old Alexander.
Each individual was a daring host,
Such as Napoleon's arms could never boast.
It seems they were true sons of Mars,
Each individal born for wars.)
He safely passed the Vicksburg guns,
 Where metal flew to the weight of tons;

Then at Grand Gulf, the same performed,
Thus, death's seething chasm he passed unharmed.
 His disposition is like a child,
 He is never excited, but always mild.
 He was slouchy in his dress,
 As much as others were in excess.
 He was a plain man, of common sense.
 He run himself on light expense.
  No ding fringals,
  Hob worked hingles
  Ever bored him,
  Cut or scored him.
  He was plain to excess,
  In all his actions, e'en his dress.
His soft hat stuck up before, and down behind,
In heart he was tender and very kind.
He showed it when Colonel O'Meara fell,
And on other occasions, just as well.
(O'Meara was colonel of the "Irish Legion,"
A brace and a stay in that rebel region.
 He was the one on the trestle-work,
  Near Holly Springs,
 That checked Van Dorn,
  And saved Grant's things.
 There, he did a big thing
  For the Federal nation,
 He saved Grant's army
  From sure starvation.
 It was in December, sixty-two,
  When he saved those things,
 From Van Dorn,
  When raiding 'round Holly Springs.
Grant never forgot that daring feat,
Where hundreds from thousands would not retreat.
 As the colonel's coffin at the landing laid,

To it, at once, Grant immediately strayed.
He ordered it opened so he could behold
The face of one so daring and bold.
A man, whom he'd honored with public thanks,
In less than two months after joining his ranks.
To the hero dead, from the hero livin',
A sad and touching farewell was given.
   Given to a soldier who had forfeited life,
   To quell his adopted country's strife.
   In support of the flag, a flag of the brave,
   That o'er so many Irish exiles wave.
The flag that waves o'er such glorious things,
That waves o'er a country, peopled with kings.
Where writers appear in poetry and prose,
And painters file past, in long, solid rows.
The home of inventions and great machines,
Till Uncle Sammy 's a giant behind the scenes).
            Grant was bold,
For the love of victory, and not for gold.
   Shot could hum about his head,
   But he heard nothing about them to dread.
   He would coolly smoke his black cigar,
   As if reposing in a palace car.
   Here's about Sherman's promotion,
   Grant urged it almost to devotion.
   He respectfully, but sternly urged
   That Sherman's name to honor verged.
   Here's what he of Sherman says,
   About the man and his warring ways:
       It was Sherman's promptness,
          That made Donelson yield,
       By rushing men and
          Munition into the field;
   And at Shiloh's bloody bout,
   He's the one that saved us 'rom a rout.

It was there with troops entirely raw,
He performed a feat, uncommon to nature's law.
With the raw troops under his commanding,
He held the keystone to that landing.
>   It was there he, with his troops,
>   Withstood the rebels' deadly swoops.
>   There, three horses beneath him fell,
>   Twice he, himself was hit as well.
>   No other general could have done it,
>   From the way the Johnnies begun it.
At Chickasaw Bluff, and Arkansaw Post,
Are movements, o'er which any general can boast.
>   All his moves, why here rehearse them ?
>   Where rebels swarmed, he'd there coerce them.
>   He would cause a Napoleon to blush,
>   He was so stern at a rebel crush.
>   He would crush them in a fight,
>   Then prune their rear when in flight.
>   He was so decisive, fierce and bold,
>   He makes one think of the warriors of old.
When fields are red, and the country stormy,
To promote such men is strength to an army.
That same day, McPherson came in for a share,
'Sixty- three, July twenty-third of that year.
McPherson's been with me in every battle ruse,

>   [blues;
Except at Belmont, where the grays were chased by
And a better engineer than him never yet arose,
To draw a line or dig a ditch to intercept the foes.
And as a general, there's none can ever reach him,
He's so complete, the world combined can't teach him,
Throughout his art, in every part, he knows it well,

>   [have fell.
The rebel knows, and dreads his blows, wherever they
Among the dead that's passed, and the present livin',

No such genius was ever to one man given.
    The whole warring trade, in one combined,
    The likes in no other man on earth we'll find.
    No pen on earth can e'en describe,
    What's hid beneath McPherson's hide.
      His genius is as rich and rare
      As diamonds at a country fair.
      There is no place here to enumerate
      His points in genius, grand and great.
      The report of Grant was closely noted,
      Each in his turn was then promoted.
      Grant was extremely mute and modes',
      As mum as the statue of our Goddess.
      There's where all his wisdom laid,
      Because his lips were mute and staid.
      He could be drawn into no conversation,
      About the future welfare of the nation,
      To mummery he was devout,
      No political affair could draw him out.
      On his name they insisted to use
      Him as President, the people to choose.
    Said he, " let us settle the war, then it's time
    To look after an office in the president line.
  To one political office, I do aspire,
(And how in the world could one climb any higher).
      But that I'll be, when the war is o'er,
      And rebelry is rebs no more.
      As mayor of Galena, I wish to run,
      And I hope to be the lucky one.
      Then, a sidewalk I will have fixed,
      From my house to the depot (in betwixt)."
      Great military men of every age,
      That did in bloody war engage,
      When nation at a nation flew,
      With drawn swords, to cut and hew,

They all had a peculiar mode of their own,
That no other nation or race had known.
But, with all of them, strategy stood
More powerful than walls of wood.
For strategy disarms a foe,
They know not where to parry the blow;
         But Grant,
In strategy was scarce and scant.
Hear him, his strategy explain:
I don't believe in it as others claim,
I use it in laying low, or crawling up to a foe.
Then up guards, and at 'em with your heaviest blow.

CANTO.

Grant's last campaign, the war ends,
The north and south again are friends;
The old feud, so long a-brewin',
Is wrecked, scattered and laid in ruin;
The southern lord, no slaves are his'n,
The nigger to a free man's risen.
In this canto, now we'll close
The bloody chasm 'tween two foes.

SIXTH.

After, Grant by Lincoln was appointed,
He, by the senate was anointed.
Anointed with the legal oils,
O'er which the country cauldron boils.
An order then to Grant was sent,   [March 6]
Himself at Washington, to present.
Then he and his son, thirteen years old,
Eastward, o'er the country rolled.
Rolled on wheels of locomotion,
Facing towards the Atlantic Ocean.
At Covington he stopped entire,
And paid a visit to his sire.   [Jesse R. Grant.]

Thence to Harrisburg, Pennsylvan',
Then to Baltimore, on the morning train ;   [Mar. 8]
        Where he stopped in a roaring noise,
        Cheer upon cheer from Yankee boys ;
        Then, with the next train's humming wheels,
        Grinding o'er the endless steels ;
    Off to Washington, he whirled,
    Like a ball, from the mouth of a cannon hurled.
  Then off to Willard's hotel, he racked, [17 o'clock]
  Himself, from his traveling attire unpacked.
        Then, without a staff or stay,
        To the dining-room, he wound his way.
        Without rank or title, attended
        Among the common plebes, he blended.
        Undiscovered, he sat for dinner,
        To recuperate the *a la* inner.
        Among the guests, of several hundred,
        At his rusty uniform, none wondered:
        Until his name was finally learned,
        All in that uniform, were then concerned.
        Introductions, looks and cheers
        Then ushered in the long arrears.
        His quiet was entirely taken,
        His appetite for dinner shaken.
        Embarassment then lent her wings,
        To make him do some awkward things.
    Then, when the evening sun was low,
    To give the lamps a chance to glow,
    Then, to the White House he repaired,
    To enter unannounced, he even dared.
    Where a big reception, in lengthy rows,
    Showed people in their finest clothes.
    Soon, Lincoln, on him spilt his eyes,
    At once the hero to recognize.
    The greeting then was long and warm,

Which no pencil can the scene perform.
Mrs. Lincoln, then, in his company aired?
But from the room he soon retired.
He has repeated it oft a-main,
It was his warmest, best campaign.
The freedom of Washington, was given him,
With its hospitalities thrown in.
This welcome was a series of resolutions,
Handsomely written, with its fine executions.
To him, by the Mayor it was presented,
The city at large, the Mayor represented.
Now, here's a grand thing right at hand,
Lincoln presented Grant with a high command.
    A lieutenant-general, the highest given
    To any officer in the Union livin'.
It was a grand and high commission.
A stupendous long and wide position.
Present at the presentation we find,
Lincoln, with his cabinet combined;
With his private secretary and Lovejoy too,
And the general-in-chief of the warring crew.
Then Grant with his staff and his son was all
That ever can the scene recall.
Lincoln's words were few and simple,
Each was a priest within a temple.
They arose at the presentation,   [13 o'clock.]
The highest gift to a soldier of the nation.
Grant's acceptance was simple and crude,
Hovering almost on the verge of the rude.
Grant to the cabinet, was then introduced,   .
Then a half hour's chat was well produced.
Then on the morrow, Grant did proceed
To visit the army of the Potomac with General Meade.
Then, to the west he bounded away,
When March had reached its eleventh day.

In March, the day of three times four,
In eighteen hundred and sixty-four,
Read how the President's order ran,　　[No. 88]
Read letter for letter, if you can.
Halleck, at his own request in brief
Was hauled down from commander-in-chief,
For Grant, then stood in his stead,
Grant was the army's tail and head.
For the head-quarters of the army, you see,
Was where Grant might prone to be.
Also, in Washington it was the same,
Such power with Halleck did remain ;
For on Grant's staff he was the chief,
To worry the rebels into grief,
For they'll worry them most damnable sure,
Great holes through them, with guns they'll bore.
Then W. T. Sherman takes up his grip,
Commanding the "Military Division of the Mississipp'."
Then J. B. McPherson is commander, you see
Of the " Department and Army of the Tennessee."
Now here's to Halleck, thanks in brief,
For the duty he did as general-in-chief.
His arduous task, he with zeal performed,
A man of his work that was well informed.
E. D. Townsend, A. A. G.
It was the greatest military order of the war,
For all it aimed and what it was for.
It had no draw-back in reaction,
It was a big hunk of long satisfaction.
Grant was well informed of all the troops,
And Sherman advised as to future swoops.
Then the Virginia campaign he undertook,
With that daring Lee in his front to brook,
A soldier, equal to all his skill.
To march and flank, to cripple and kill,

Grant brought overwhelming forces to bear,
The rebel ranks from earth to tear.
He took his soldiers big, with gun,
O'er Lee, he had a score to one.
The great armies, against Lee were hurled,
The mightiest army in the known world.
The armies of the Shenandoah, Potomac and James,
The three were joined for the coming games.
The games that Grant and Lee must play,
One or the other must be swept away.
The great Yankee force, to one center drew,
On the Richmond rebels, to cut and hew.
Lee and his force, south to the Rapidan,
There laid entrenched, both horse and man;
Laid entrenched for further use,
Till Yankees should their swords produce.
In front of Lee, across the stream,
Laid Meade, with dirt to intervene.
In front of Lee, there really stood
Two hundred thousand men for blood;
And still they come from every quarter,
Invited to the Richmond slaughter.
There thousands of prophets stood
In waiting for each other's blood,
Like old Mose at Horeb's Rock,
There was one, but here's a flock.
And each one, with his magic wand,
To start a stream, at the word of command.
More curious than what Moses done
Causing water from dry rocks to run.
But here, a hole, at a distance is dug,
By powder behind a leaden bug.
That issues forth a dying stream,
That no Mosinian ever seen.
A daring "sheence," was that old Mose.

To just toot rams' horns at his foes.
His rams' horns tumbled stupendous walls,
Much easier than our cannon-balls.
    Old Moses was a cankershin
    In a regular warring, murderous din.
But that old "sheenee," it is plain to me,
With a telegraph pole, couldn't reach to Lee.
But Lee was so far in advance of his times,
As we kill men now, would then've been crimes.
The leaders of the Union forces were good,
As ever stood in waiting for blood.
Hancock, Sedgwick, Warren and such,
There was Sheridan, the very de'il, on a crutch,
Also Butler, *de la* cockeyed Ben,
Was there with his army of nigger men.
Who stayed so close to the whites in fight,
As dusk does to the gloom of night.
Yes, the nigger followed in the bloody affray,
Like darkness following the last sun's ray.
They always were there when the fighting was done,
Grimly grinning o'er their polished gun.
It was Burnside's force, forty thousand strong,
They opened up this campaign, so bloody and long.
    Now, Bermuda Hundred must be seized,
    By adroit movements it must be squeezed.
    Till every rebel from it is pushed,
    And their rebel trickery ever hushed.
    Between Petersburg and Richmond it stands,
    Communication 'tween the two it commands.
    Now, this job, old Benny bossed,
    With those eyes of his that nature crossed.
    This was to keep the places apart,
    So Yankees could probe their stony heart.
    The army of Shenandoah by Sigel was led,
    Sigel, the dutchman, at the army's head.

Lee's supplies he was to infest,
And cut them off, that came from the west.
And protect the Shenandoah valley,
With Maryland and Pennsylvania, from rebel rally
While those moves were being made,
South, Sherman went on a gigantic raid.
With his three armies, often tried,
The glory of the nation's pride.
With glorious generals to assist,
Mighty generals formed the list.
Howard, Hooker, Logan, McPherson and Schofie'd
Drew their blades for the battle-field.
Atlanta was the place to go,
Georgia soon must feel the blow.
Such was the gigantic scheme,
To interest the rebel team.
Interest them everywhere,
Pin them down, so they can't stir.
The army of the Potomac, horse and man,
Crossed the river of Rapidan ;   [May 4]
Striking Lee's right, with metal by the ten,
Strongly entrenched at Mine's Run.
But ere Lee's army can be bossed,
The "Wilderness," it must be crossed.
It was a wilderness broad and wide,
Five miles it stretched from side to side ;
And its densely treed, wild longitude
Twenty miles it did protrude.
In it the "boys in blue" were met   [May 5,
By Longstreet's furious rebel set.
Longstreet struck a staggering blow,
But Sedgwick twice repulsed the foe.
Then the center, under Warren's command,
Felt the power of Longstreet's hand.
But Longstreet struck, and struck again,

But all his strikes were struck in vain.
It was a stubborn, staunch old fight.
And long it lasted, far into the night.
Then at four on the morrow's morn,　[May 6]
The battle opened with a storm.
　Lee it was who lead the rebs,
　Trying to break the right of the Feds ;
　To ruin the right or break the center,
　So the rebel force our lines could enter.
　But Hancock there, with terror swayed,
　Tried all the arts known in his trade.
　(Except the art, to fly in retreat,
　To which no Yankee had trained their feet.)
　Back, the rebels at first were beaten,
　Then the Yankees were found retreatin'.
　It was a bloody day to all concerned,
　Grant's extreme right was finally turned.
　The right was turned, completely flanked,
　Where rebs against his lines were banked.
　But this was in the dusk of eve,
　When each, their foe could not perceive.
　To Grant it was a critical time,
　So much it was almost sublime.
　Grant was turned, but was not licked,
　So safely out of danger he picked.
　A new position, at once he chose,
　Then in turn he flanked his foes.
　When Lee, his plans had disarranged,
　His operative base was changed.
　Which brought him from the wilderness,
　More fully his cannon to express.
　Express them, so their shot would tell
　By rebels, that unnumbered fell,
　The souls of thousands went to hell.
　To Spottsylvania court house, then,

Lee went hither with his men;
Where Grant found him, and there engaged,
For three long days then, war was waged.
Then Grant and Lee, both in surprise,
Found each the other had no flies.
Grant was good, but Lee was better,
Lee knew his business to a letter.
Grant was good, but not so well
Prepared to give the rebels hell.
As Lee, in his contesting power,
Proved to the Yankees, each fighting hour.
He was the foe's most bloody fiend,
A genius that should be well esteemed.
For genius should be recognized,
Though its acts he sore despised.
Around Richmond, thousands bled,
Unnumbered were the mangled dead.
Together Feds and rebels laid,
As they each other, in battle slayed.
Grand manœuvers were then performed,
First Lee was injured, then Grant was harmed.
Till on the thirty-first of May,
It was a noted, glorious day.
Then fifteen miles, ah! what a pity,
It held Grant off from Richmond City.
It was not miles that kept him back,
But Lee lay stretched across his track,
For wherever Grant would move to score,
Lee was found in his path, direct before.
Then skirmishes, for days together,
Would neither stop for wind or weather.
Till the sixth corps found with pride,
Cold Harbor laid along its side.   [June 1]
Where it was joined by a detachment soon,
That came from the lines of "silver spoon." [Butler.]

Who is known better, now or then,
Than the illustrious, stanch old cock-eyed Ben.
Then Cold Harbor battle ensued,   [June 3]
Where thousands upon thousands hewed.
They down upon each other bore,
With stubbornness unknown before.
But facts are facts, and no digression,
The Union troops, there took possession.
Then Grant tried the rebel ditches,   [June 3]
To drive forth the living riches.
But Grant found he had no power,
To race the rebels, or make them cower.
Without a slaughter so immense,
'Twould paralyze the human sense.
   So at once he desisted,
    And left them as they then existed.
    Then Grant executed a movement bold,
    By which the rebels were sweetly sold.
But they, in turn, played him a tune,
Which showed he was discovered soon.
Heed ye Grant's bold, daring scheme,
He crossed the James, a river stream,
Though by the rebels, he was unseen,
Where long before Butler had been ;
And scooped Bermuda Hundred in.
There's where he in ease had laid.
He fortified the place and stayed.
Sure it was by shovels and spades,
He resisted the rebel raids ;
Then Fort Darling he did press,
But never reached the point, success.
Then on Petersburg, he dashed.
But nothing by his force was smashed.
By him, Grant was much assisted,
By him the rebels were resisted.

But Siegel's army was rebuffed,
In Shenandoah Valley, sorely cuffed.*
Then Hunter took the dutch command,
And drove Sam Jones from Staunton's land.
From whom he took several guns,
And chased the rebels in furious runs.
Many a rebel by death was felled,
Many a prisoner by him was held.
Then finally General Early came,
The power of rebeldom to maintain.
Then Hunter, in his turn must fly,
Need I the reasons tell you why?
Until the mountains of western Virgin'
Arose around, and fenced him in.
But his suffering was immense,
Before he found a safe defence.
So close General Early came at last,
That Washington and Baltimore stood aghast.
But the nineteenth corps, from New Orleans
Laid in front of the advancing fiends;
And the Potomac's sixth army corps
Laid stretched out long and strong before;
While Colonel Couch, from Pennsylvan',
Advanced onto the rear in vain.
For he got up and slid asunder,
Carrying off tons after tons of plunder.
But Sheridan, with his ranks of fire,
Swept around Lee's lines entire.
Their outer lines he e'en crossed,
From his ranks, scarce a man was lost.
He struck the rebels with surprise,
Burning railways and supplies.

* It was to-day, in South Carolina, Charleston shook hands with hell,
  Which, so terrified the earth, it shook till her houses fell.
  Yes, all o'er the streets, huge houses everywhere were spilled,
  Hundreds were crippled, and dozens more were killed. [Aug. 31, '86.]

He captured rebel boys for prison.
Releasing many that once were his'n.
In five days this raid was done,
Around the rebel lines entire it run.
 Now, to Grant, we will return,
 View him and the whole concern.
 Petersburg, he now infested,   [June 22]

As o'er and o'er it was contested.
But that place could not be bound,
Only on two sides, half way around.
Then the Weldon railway was destroyed,
And the rebels at every chance annoyed.
But the rebels were good in a purloin,
And always paid in sterling coin.
The rebels were no spurious wits,
In debts they used no counterfeits.
But debts, they paid them every time,
In payments strong and genuine.
Around Richmond fights ensued,
Ranks on ranks eternally hewed.
Each army it seemed in executing,
Did its work in musket-shooting.

 Now a season of quiet rest
 Let the siege its course digest.
The Union lines in trenches stayed,
Before Petersburg, in waiting laid.
In a smothering dust and blistering sun,
The bombshells hummed their doleful hum,
And carried off many to kingdom's come.

 It is a work, a soldier's fate,
 It is a work that soldiers hate;
 No chances are lost to retaliate.
There was a mine, five hundred feet,
Dug beneath the rebels strong retreat.
From Petersburg, two hundred yards it stood,
Built up of dirt, with stones and wood.
Beneath it, four tons of powder laid,]
Ere matches to its power strayed.
What power a match could here assume,
In sweeping hundreds to the tomb.
It was done, to the rebels unknown,
Til heavenwards the fort was blown.

But ere a match to the powder strayed,
On Lee, by Grant a scheme was played.
Pontoons, o'er the James they lay,
Muffling it all soft with hay.
The second corps and Sheridan they passed o'er,
On distant rebs their lines to pour;
In line of battle, to beat them sore,
To stab the rebel line in corps,
Or all secession that looms before.
At Strawberry Plains, they work the fake,
A battery and line of entrenchments they take.
(It was in twelve miles of Richmond City,
Them miles intervening, oh! what a pity.)
Lee met this unexpected, daring blow
With fifteen thousand of the foe.
Then the Union force slipped back again,
On July nights, twenty-seven, 'eight and 'nine,
In front of Petersburg. in battle line.
Then, when the morning sun arose,   [July 30]
A smoking fuse it did disclose,
Which soon tore up all rebel repose.
Which raised two hundred rebs aloft,
Or to hades, rushed them off.
A yawning crater where the fort had stood,
Showed dying rebels in dust and blood.
But ere the sound had died away,
A hundred guns o'er the scenery play.
All Yankeedom then in reach.
Rushed to this deadly open breach.
But Yankees were not slow to learn
That the rebels met them strong and firm.
To the Yankees it was a wasting blow,
Four thousand of their men laid low.
But Union forces to victory led,
Around that scene where hundreds bled.

Thus, the rebels held on in state,
Whose losses were one-fourth as great.
At last the Union from blood withdrew.
A thing they were compelled to do.
Then came the battle of deep bottom, [Aug. 12]
Where Federals surely got 'em.
In captured prisoners, five hundred strong,
They took six cannon, with two mortars along.
Soon other battles then ensued,
The pursuing often were pursued.
At Reme's Station, and other places
Where rebels dared to show their faces,
Grant, his choice movements made,
Covering an attack by a distant raid.
Then came Ord to Chafen's farm,
To wreak o'er rebeldom a harm.
Fort Harrison was carried then,
We carried and captured three hundred men.
Our loss to theirs, it was immense,
Eight hundred to carry Fort Harrison's 'fence.
General Birney, also killed rebels too,
Where their entrenchments showed but few.
Then o'er the roads, the Yankees spill,
Up and onto Laurel Hill.
Then Cavalry-Generals Kautz and Terry,
Chased the rebels till they were weary. [Oct. 1]
Wearied by the blood they'd shed,
Weary of the unnumbered dead.
The summer past, experience showed
The Yankees learned things they never knowed.
Pennsylvania and Maryland felt
The blows that General Early dealt;
For Early was devilish in a raid,
The rebel cause he braced and stayed.
He was a fiend to strike a blow,

He generally went where he wished to go.
He supplied Lee's big army kitchen,
Which kept him and his raiders twitchin'.
He went where farming was the thickest,
And grub was obtained the quickest.
Then the government, to block this bum,
Made several divisions into one.
So that one general could command,
And have more territory under hand.
It was called the "Middle Military Division,"
Under General Sheridan's supervision.
Or, the "Department of Shenandoah,"
The finest valley the world can know,
Where grain and fruit in luxury grow.
    Grant suggested all the changes,
    All the moves and rearranges.
Early's raids were raids no more,
As Sheridans guns had a larger bore,
Early was oft by Sheridan beaten sore.*
Sheridan ruined Early's pastime pleasure,
In raiding Shenandoah of its treasure.
At Oquequan Creek, Sheridan got of his'n   [Sep. 19]
Two thousand men scooped in for prison.
    Also several guns and large supplies,
    As in dire confusion the rebel flies.
    Then again at Fisher's Hill,   [Sept. 22]

---

* By malaria now I'm overtaken,
By it unmercifully I'm shaken;
Malaria of the damnedest type,
In all its pains and achings ripe.
Oh, badly, badly used up I am,
Till scarcely am I worth a damn. [Sept. 22, 1886.]
Oh, frightful pains of wild malaria,
Like hellish paths so dark and dreary.
Oh, would that I could break its grip.
In safety from its shackles slip.
It seems as if by pains I'm cursed,
Or is it because I'm green, and it is my first?

He routed the rebels to prune and kill.
Then General Rosser was repulsed,
Till his rebel army was convulsed.
Then Early fell onto Sheridan's men
At Cedar Creek, and routed them.   [Oct. 19]
But Sheridan, at Washington was far away,
When Early so routed his men that day.
But at Winchester, he met with them,
His wildly flying, shattered men.
With swinging cap and furious whoops,
To catch the ear of his flying troops,
He, like a cyclone forward borne,
As when mighty oaks from rocks are torn.
"Face the other way, boys," he said, and then
Stopped and turned the flying men.
They followed him, like hounds their master,
To victory, from a fierce disaster;
    And captured all that they had lost
    In bloodshed, at rebel cost.
    Sherman, meanwhile, had taken possession,
    Of Atlanta, from the secession;
    And to the sea, commenced his march,
    To win the land by sword and torch;
    And Thomas took care of Hood, for see,
    Hood exploited in Tennessee.
But, to Grant and Richmond I must return,
To the marches and fights of that vast concern.
As about Hatcher's Run we reconnoitered, [Oct. 29]
By rebels, our troops in gobs were slaughtered.
    Now North Carolina's strong Wilmington,
    Must be! shall be captured, man and gun.
    The rebels, through Wilmington were supplied,
    All blockades she e'en defied.
Against it Grant sent a big expedition,   [Dec. 12]
With long swords, for rebels a-fishin'.

Fort Fisher was bombarded strong,　　[Dec. 24]
She was shelled, at least nine hours long,
By our fleet she was racked both fore and aft,
Shelled by every Union gun-bearing craft.
　　But beyond the facts that none expect,
　　Our shot was fired to no effect.
But on the morrow, in spite of wind and weather,
Land force and sea must strike together.
　　The navy, by Porter was supervised,
　　As the land force went as Butler advised.
　　　The navy struck, as it had agreed,
　　　But Butler did not well succeed.
　　　The works was viewed before assaulting,
　　　Which bluffed old Butler into halting.
　　　He thought it suicidal to strike 'em thus,
　　　Thinking death and rebels must win the muss.
　　　　At which he re-embarked to ride,
　　　　Then Porter was greatly dissatisfied.
　　　　Then all, all then returned?
　　　　Wasted in vain, the powder they burned.
Then Butler was relieved of the army of the James,
To General A. H. Terry were given its reins.

Behold another year, with its twelve months in line,
Now sets forth, upon the tally-board of time.
It is the year EIGHTEEN HUNDRED SIXTY-FIVE,
With rebels all hearty, and most of them alive.

　　　Then Fort Fisher again they try,　　[Jan. 13]
　　　A fort that did their ranks defy.
　　　There Porter's boats played a bombard,
　　　The fiercest that time ever stopped to record.
　　　For every second of time that expired,
　　　Four shots into Fort Fisher were fired.

For one hour and a half it was maintained,
Thus solid shot o'er Fisher rained.
Then Terry brought his troops to land,
To crush Fort Fisher's walls of sand.
    Then again the fight renews,   [Jan. 15]
    The gunboats on Fort Fisher hews.
As sixteen hundred sailors land,
On its seaward face to try their hand.
Joined by four hundred old marines,
So fierce, two would equal seven fiends.
Oh! viewers of a fierce assault,
This was butchery, butchered to a halt.
It was a hand to hand long stubborn fight,
From in the day.[3 p. m.]till deep midnight.
It would curdle a man's blood till its chilled,
To there note the men that vengeance killed.
    Oh, fierce scenes of cruel war,
    Let us drop those scenes of horror.
Six blockade runners there were capped,
By skilful cunning they were entrapped.
Two rebel gunboats were also mugged,
Which were into Yankee service tugged.
Forts Anderson and Coswell then evacuated, [Jan 19]
Soon Wilmington from the rebels was extricated. [21]
    On Hatcher's Run another movement begun,
    Which by the sun, was a long and desperate one.
There for three days, two armies bled,
Until the field, with blood ran red.
First the reb, and then the Fed before each other fled,
Till thousands would not number the limit of the dead.
Against Fort Steadman, the rebels massed a blow,
Taking the whole concern, garrison and foe. [Mar 25]
    But here, surely I must book it,
    The Yankees rallied, rallied and retook it.
The rebels were driven back from their place before,

And their place was taken by the sixth and seventh corps.
Now Grant makes changes in many of his lines,
To keep up with the rebels and fashion of the times.
Now about Richmond, General Lee is hustled,
Then, again, in turn General Grant is rustled.
One general will go out upon the other fakin',
                                        [retaken.
And capture a line of trenches, then have' the thing
            One is good, and stronger
                Than the other,
            Now which one is the best,
                Is where comes in the bother.
            Lee was just as good
                As ever tread a soil,
            And Grant was just as good
                In fierce and wild turmoil.
            All around Richmond
                Was a fierce and bloody hole,
            Grant with his long blade,
                Kept stirring in the bowl.
            Grant upon one side,
                With Lee upon the other,
            They were the mighty chieftains,
                Bucking at one another.
        Around the court-house of Dinwiddie,
        Was a scene, both dark and bloody.
        Along Hatcher's Run and Boydton road,
        Death in long daring phalanx strode.
        The rebels from Five Forks were beaten,[Apr 1]
        Which showed out in long lines retreatin'.
        All round and round the rebels were driven,
        With dead and crippled mixed with the livin'.
            Along the Appomattox River road
                In dishonored glory, rebels strode ;
                Strode with all their vim and vigor,

To shun the Yankee sword and trigger.
Around Fair Oaks and Malvern Hill,
It seems that death delighted to kill.
Then artillery opened to lines of pain,   [April 2]
In numbering the dead by hundreds slain.

All along the Union lines they howl,
At Petersburg, in front they growl.
   And as the day to battle warms,
   Death its deadly work performs.
   Yankees for the rebels reach ahead,
   Till both lines are strewn with dead.

The rebel forts by Yanks were scooped,
The rebels from their ditches whooped,
But blood about in torrents fell,
Earth it seemed was turned to hell.
To the Southside railway the Yankees go,
Sweeping everything in a deadly blow.
They tore up the railway bars,
To stop the progress of coming cars.
As in this charge the Yankee comes,
They took several prisoners and many guns.
It was a day, a day of wild digression,
Destructive to the fierce secession.

This was a day of widespread shifting around,
A day of indescribable, tumultuous roaring sound.
Every step it seemed by human blood was washed,
Blood upon the living from the dying soldier sloshed.
But the fate of Richmond and Petersburg was sealed.
They were no longer tenable for soldiers in the field.
For all communication was severed around the places
Starvation now at last stared rebels in the faces.
Also the Federal troops commanded the city at that
But ere they got there, one third were *hors du combat*

Lee sees no chance for retaliation
So the night is spent in evacuation.   [April 2]
O'er Richmond, then, the old flag waves,
The emblem of unnumbered graves.
O'er many a battlefield she's stood,
Cheering men o'er seas of blood.
When that old flag o'er Richmond waved,
It proved to the world the republic's saved.
All o'er the Union lightning told,
What arms at Richmond had controlled.*

* But there's no time to moralize in,
Time goes so fast, it is surprisin'.
For the typesetters chase my pen,

Here Grant not a moment wastes,
But Lee at once by him is chased.
Here Lee's retreat bears bitter fruit,
By Grant's remorseless, pitiless pursuit.
Lee's retreat was soon a rout,
All his army's courage fast oozing out.
At the fast repeated, frightful blows,
That the Union hurled upon her foes.
The Federals on the rebels rattle,
The retreat was one long flying battle.
The pursuing Feds stopped not for plunder,
That the retreating rebels hurled asunder.
They never stopped to count the ones for prison,
That the Yankee boys had got of his'n.
The rebel army pushed on as if possessed,
The Yankees followed as if cyclone dressed.
Till Grant in a letter to General Lee,   [April 7.
Asked him to stop the murderous melee.
Several letters then were passed,
And that bloody chasm closed at last.
Lee by Grant was then controlled,
All officers and men paroled.
When rebeldom at last did cease,
Both armies cheered the dawn of peace.
The rebels were so hard pursued,
No grub their haversacks include.
For haversacks they'd none at all,
They were so close pushed to the wall.
Here the Yankees showed their kind of men,
Their scanty grub was shared with them.
Private property was private still,
The officers retained their arms to kill.
At Appomattox station peace was tendered,
For there's where Lee to Grant surrendered. [April 9

For the work it gives to each of them.
For they're as close upon my flying pen,   [Sunday, Sept. 26, '86]
As Grant to the heels of Lee's retreating men.

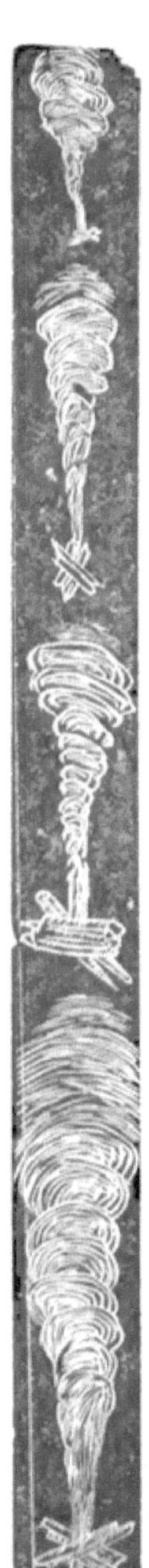

In Lee's army stretched out then,
Were twenty-two thousand officers and
  men.
Grant to Washington hastened then,
To stop expenses and enlistment of men.
Some government expenses then were
  stopped,
And officers from the army cropped.
Trade and commerce then renewed,
There no military should intrude.
As along the railway line he wound,
To Burlington, New Jersey bound.   [on a
  family visit.   April 14.]
There a despatch to the general told
That Lincoln's life by fiends was stole.
And that Secretary Seward's life,
Had just escaped a murderous knife.
Then in the trial 'twas afterwards shown,
That early movements saved his own.
Then back to Washington, at once he come,
To view the deeds that Booth had done.
But Booth! oh Booth! where could he be?
Broken-legged, flying was he.
From the men that were pursuing,
While he, his horrid deeds were rueing.
The war now comes to its close,
In every field were beaten foes,
Sherman swept the southern land,
With his long and fierce command.
Johnston's blade to Sherman given,
Showed rebeldom's last cords were riven.
Dick Taylor then, and Kirby Smith were
  taken,

* Those distant camp-fires loom a glow,
  There is some one camping there I know.

Showed the rebel cause asleep, never more to waken.
Then Jeff Davis fell into our hands,
Oh, Jeff Davis! Jeff Davis! where thy scattered bands?
    Here Grant spent his summer months,
        Rushing o'er the nation,
    In his mighty office's
        Stupendous occupation.
    At Philadelphia, on West Chestnut street,
        To General Grant was given,
    A thirty thousand dollar house,
        For him and his folks to live in.
    Then, on the third of May,
        There, they took possession,
    It was a gift from the people,
        For quelling fierce secession.
    Where so many shot
        Against his lines were hurled,
    That carried off so many boys
        From this to the other world.
At Washington, Grant was present then,
When from war returned our glorious men.
When that great and grand discharge
Was given to the army of the republic at large.
But ere this discharge, a grand review,
The grandest that ere from battle drew.
Grant's old neighbors at Galen',
Served him well, and never mean.
    For, to Grant, in Galena,
        A house to him was given,
    A sixteen thousand dollar house
        For him and his to live in.
    To where he went
        With joyous cannons' boom,
    With all the bells in the city
        Joined in the welcome tune,

Wherever Grant
    Throughout the nation went,
It seems the people, before him,
    In furious homage bent.
But in New York City,   [Nov. 10]
    The greatest reception was spread,
At the "Fifth Avenue Hotel,"
    The greatest of soldiers fed.
Then Grant's path ran smooth
    As any 'neath the heaven,
Until the summer months
    Of eighteen sixty-seven.
Then Johnston, him and Stanton
    All got in a wrangle,
Which almost got the government
    Into a fearful tangle.
In that Johnston racket
    There were no heads or tails,
It was like a circular fence
    Built out of hickory rails.
But Johnston gave Grant
    And Uncle Sam to know
That he was a statesman,
    And knew how things should go.
Now the papers, republic
    All o'er the country howled
Grant for President ;
    As no stern democrat then growled.
Then millionnaires of New York
    Launched his mighty boat,
Which must upon the stream
    Of moneyed millions float.*

* Yesterday, Professor H. L. Williams died,   [Sunday, Sept. 26, 1886]
The one that set up this book, or at least the one that tried,
The poor old man worked all the week for leisure time on Sunday,
On Saturday he had no time, and couldn't wait till Monday.

Twas money paved his path to power,
From millionaires in a jubilant hour.
All who tried into Grant's politics to pry,
Were answered promptly with a mum reply.
When he was nominated, then came the trying hour,
In which mummery proved the sweetness of its power.
That's what made Grant so everlasting sharp,
He used mummery, mummery alone for a dart.
Under Johnston, Grant was secretary, *ad interim*,
Still commander-in-chief, the thing was bad on 'im.

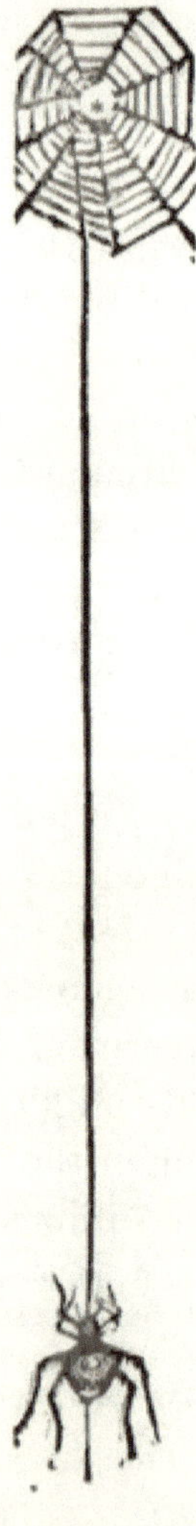

Grant Elected President.

Grant at Chicago was nominated for presidential tracks,
To make a team of black horses, he and Schuyler Colfax.
[there,
The time was June, and in New York, the place was
[to run with Francis Blair.
Where by democrats Horatio Seymour was nominated
[together.
To elect Grant, the majority and minority joined hands
[weather.
Which left poor Seymour and Blair, out in the stormy
1869.]
Grant was inaugurated upon the usual day,*[March 4,
With all the pomp a nation could display.
E. B. Washburn, of Illinois, as secretary first did dance
[ister to France.
Then Hamilton Fish got the posish, as he went min-
And there that Fish stayed through thick and thin,
Through both the terms that Grant was in.

    He was the leader of that concern,
    He could teach lessons for others to learn.
    He worked that "Alabama" claim,
    That great arbitration of worth and fame.
    Which pointed out to all warring men,

---

* That day's a day, I'll long remember it,
For on that day, from off a sleigh, was buried Charley Hitt
He was a true man, a man, sir, with all its filial love,
And I hope that sire of mine's enjoying himself above.
For in those days rank and title gave no man his worth,
For a gentleman, husband and father is known around his hearth
For about a hearth, no sham character can be played,
All shammery in that sacred place must fade.

That swords must wither before the pen.
That arbitration was a scheme gigantic,
Which was settled at Vienna, beyond the Atlantic.
May that new lesson in the world long live,
Here, the details of which I cannot give,
That arbitration between two nations so big and strong
Surprised the world at large, and surprised it long.
That two such nations with such deadly tools,
Should set in arbitration like common fools.

But lord of lords, and king of kings,
It was the greatest of all earthly things.
Grant's manogenius hods of hashion,
Did all the curious things in fashion.
He patronized all other nations,
Using all their grades and stations.
Anything that in our nation helped,
Uncle Sam, the cub by England whelped.

Under his administration in peaceful power lent,
The great Pacific railway across the country went.
It was a railway, a railway for the best,   [west.
It was a tie that brought the east much closer to the
Nearly two thousand miles, it ran through lands forlorn
From Omaha, Nebraska, to "Frisco," Californ'.

[tethered,
The Pacific to the Atlantic, by a string of iron was
[gathered.
Which, to the plains of the west, all nationalities
With people from that old, and curious Bohemi',
A land so far away, so far away and dreamy.   [such,
With Prussians, Russians, Hessians, antipodes and
[clutch.*
That are serving now as slaves, to dollars devilish

---

* Hi-o-ho, Geronimo has surrendered to the foe,   [Oct. 11, 1886.]
Upon a reservation in some future time to go.
To work the spade and shovelplow, and train himself to hoe,
Which are the proper things for a bloody savage to know.

Oh, fame! thou art a ladder, by genius made sublime;
Which few of the many, e'er have the nerve to climb,
To cut the cables of life from the wharves of time.
(All o'er the mighty west, its plains long and broad,
Over much of it I've tramped, o'er all of it I've trod.
                                        [pleasure,
In my wandering o'er the west, it was not done for
I was looking o'er the west, a-searching for a treasure.
Ah, treasure there I found, in wild, stupendous clogs,
But it all happened to be snakes and prairie dogs.
But the coyote's are the most hideous of all hids,
                                        [katydids.
Whose noise ranges no place between the lion and
                                        [pert,
Oh, their howl it is so strange, lonesome, weird and
It's like at least a score of de'ils howling in concert.

    They're as doleful as that criminal pile,
    Prison covered Blackwell's Isle.
    Though beauty o'er its landscape stretches,
    A beautiful scene for criminal wretches.)*

Grant taught the south to bow to an iron-clad rule,
That never weakened before a southern tool.

    Civil service, he made it civil,
    As civil as the very devil.
    Things were brought to a solid basis,
    Whether they had or hadn't faces.
    Whether fact or fiction was ushered in,
    The weak all perished in the din.

---

* Good and glorious, luscious Samp,   [Oct. 11, 1886.]
Good to learn a man to tramp.
Thou mayest some day successfully went,
It was then thy force was successfully spent.
But why now on me vent thy spleen,
To take my dimes and treat me mean,
Oh, "Arty," read this to ease your cares,   [ares
And call back the times when we were blooming into million-
In samp speculation, oh, what a gorge!
I've lost confidence in it and the world at large,

Who, and which and what, about his nomenclature,
This tin lined, curious money-snatcher.
The financiering was bridged o'er boggy ground,
Then specie payment was safely brought around.
Brought around till it stood the test,
And paper money proved the best.*
Such a thing was never known of old,   [gold.†
A dollar's worth of currency worth a hundred cents in

---

* Oh, what a nasty morn! rain enough to cool us, [Oct. 28, 1886.]
But for all that, we must unveil the Goddess.
For the poor old orphan stands out on Bedloe's Isle,
Holding her torch aloft, upon a stony pile.
Her father, the Frenchman's here, ready for the ceremony,
O'er his copper-iron child, that never can grow bony.
Sired by a Frenchman, forth the Goddess came,
Fire and smoke and metal was the lonely orphan's dame.
Her nose is pointing to the east, her back turned to the west,
And where her bubbies ought to be, she has but half a breast.

† This poem was commenced at No. 68 York street, Jersey City,
shortly after the death of Grant, and there it was partly written; also at
Saybrook Point, Conn., and at 45 Grand street, Jersey City, and finished
at No. 126 Monticello avenue, October 28, 1886. Monticello avenue, recol-
lect it, the Samp Factory.

Grant's Tour Around the World.

No man ever held a higher hand,
Or went around the world so grand.
He hob-nobbed with kings and priests,
And dined with nabobs in the east ;
He traveled in steamship, coach and cars,
And viewed the princes, knaves and czars.
For to the world Grant was made known
By furious trumpets, loudly blown;
O'er which many a printing press
Wore itself into sore distress.
The presses bugled up his name,
Till it wore cosmetic fame.
But they never mentioned in their raillery,
The whisky fraud, or grab of salary.
But, as to who, and how and when,
Around the world's went many men.
Each pursuing his emotions and desire,
Plowing the oceans by steam and fire.
But how and who, and which and when,
Have nothing to do with other men.
The first of our statesmen that e'er tried,
Around the world, in pomp to ride.
That is, a statesman of consequence,

A real genius, a man of sense.
William H. Seward was the great erratic,
Known only to the classes diplomatic.
He was received like a hundred million,
Though only a statesman and civilian.
He was celebrated as our state secretary,
While the south was on her big contrary.
Then the Union's reconstruction aga'n,
Fall most entire on this great man.
In circumnavigating this ball,
The ovations to him beat them all.
But they were far behind the ones to Grant,
As could is ahead of can't. .
But over it one need not be surprised,
While one was not, the other was advertised.
The greatest crowds were of the lower plebe,
That were ready to worship any ruler's creed.
Of course he was the president centennial,
(But who will be the president millenial?)
Of course he asked the rulers of every other nation
To come over and help work the celebration.
In this case Grant proved uncommonly wise,
To catch on to the chance to work an advertise'.
Of course it was a rare chance,
In an unique celebration,
To be the chief majesty
And ruler of a nation.
Grant, with all those honors
Piled upon his name,
When they were laid aside,
Was loved and honored the same.
Heed ye the diplomatic circular hurled across the sea.
Our diplomatic circulars
Beyond the seas abroad,
Bid our officials everywhere

To raise a grand applaud.
This despatch was started May the twenty-third,
Six days after Grant's sailing had occurred.

Read ye {Reception and dinners
{Amid officials, priests and sinners.

From Philadelphia, the home of the brave,
Grant determined his passage o'er the wave.
The steamer "Indiana," was the chosen tool,
To carry him o'er the seas to Liverpool.
One of our only sea-crossing line,
That the United States men run at that time.
       The seven days
Ere he started on his long, wandering ways.
The city where the cradle of freedom first rocked,
At which the tongues of the bells ratified and knocked.
The city's hospitality was high-toned and grand,
Without regard to politics, one object of the land.
    Associations, clubs and guards
       Of different occupations,
    Minglifications e'en hards,
       For Grant's recreation.
    They loosed their leather,came together,
       A-purpose to be merry,
    In freedom dressed, tho' once oppressed,
       Forgotten is the worry.
    Added to ovations, were congratulations
       And good wishes,
    Also wining and dining
       From very fine dishes.
    Matches and scratches, cigars and dispatches,
       Flew fast,
    The smoke would choke an ordinary bloke
       As it passed.   [answers.
    But the waltzers and dancers, dispatches and
       Why.

You needn't to fear that I'll put
    Them in here, or attempt to try.

The embarkation} of Grant.
Or fork-ation }

        On the seventeenth of May
            Grant and family got aboard,
        As the crowd on the Delaware wharves
            Louder and louder roared.
        The tug-boats and steam-boats,
            And smaller of the streams,
        Whistled an accompaniment
            To the crowd's enthusiastic screams.
Each craft was in bunting wound,
Like fairy-tales in pictures bound.
        To Grant was it a sin?
        His old misses accompanied him.
With her body.guard of loyal sons,
Bibles for weapons, instead of guns.
Their names must they go among seers?
They'll be forgotten in a hundred years.
For what will brace them o'er years to come?
Only the ladder their father clumb.
            Frederick D.,
        The eldest son of General G.;
The next, Ulysses S. Jr.,
And Jesse's all the sons there are,
        They have no fame,
But their father's sword will brace their name.
That will only bridge them o'er years,
But never make them sage or seers.
Will the world by them grow better?
Will they forge a chisel to cut a fetter?
The pen that wrote their father's book,
May give their aged years an easy nook.
            Then eleven days,
            Of storm and haze;

And whether it was hot or cool,
We know they landed at Liverpool.
For Uncle Sam and England are close together fixed,
Are welded close together, by fire and water mixed.
On the first morn far out at sea,
The general felt relaxed and free.
No letters to read,
Or dispatches to heed.
Which for sixteen years had been,
 A canker worm a-gnawing in.
Great hunks of kindness then began,
To tumble from this silent man.
Silent because afraid to utter
Something that might make others mutter.
(But few people of this nation,
Ever held so high a station,
But what they found some recreation.
When hirelings can be procured,
To work so hard, who can afford?
They say that Grant worked hard and long,
Bright and early, from dark to dawn.
All of this, I have never believed,
His biographer has just deceived.)
While he served as president,
His time like his predecessors' went.
Like a leader to a mob,
His secretary did the job.
But be it said as he ferried o'er
From Uncle Sam's to England's shore.
He grew congenial, free and easy,
And e'en inclined to be some breezy.
Into amusements proposed, he entered with zest,
To have his share, and assist the rest.
His conversation on all topics ran,
Except the political power of man.

His politeness and manners were uniform,
   He was never gross, and could seldom charm.
In sailing o'er the seas so deep, blue and dreamy,
He thought of Sucker Dam and far away Galena.
He was a soldier cut loose from pomp and pride,
And on his nation's war-vessel around the world to ride.

Grant at Queenstown }
With his renown.   } And his ways.

   As the "Indiana" did
      The Queenstown harbor enter,
   All attention, at once,
      To that great point did center.
   A tug-boat, then and there
      Pushed out from the shore,
   A deputation of citizens,
      And John Russel Young it bore.
   John Russel Young to be
      Grant's companion on the way,
   The deputation was to invite
      Grant and his folks to stay.
   Grant, with courtesy,
      The invitation declined,
   Saying, "My route at present
      Is marked out and confined."
   He promised those Irish,
      That in some future while,
   He would visit their people
      And their fair, lovely isle.
   The Atlantic cable,
      That carries mind so fast,
   Got there before Grant,
      To blow an eastern blast.
   Of course the cable told his route,
      And all the facts about it,
   Thus it clothed the paper in,
      A curious way to spout it,

Thus England, with her lordly knave,
  Peasant, priest and slave,
All of them, to Grant
  A letter of welcome gave.
They, awaiting Grant,
  In Queenstown office lay,
And of wining and dining
  They all had something to say.
The general ignored self,
  In all of his replies,
Those letters struck him hard
  A billet of surprise.   .
It showed the things before,
  On each and every hand,
It gave him a foretaste
  Of welcome in " Merry England."

Where he { Arrived at the Mersey stream,
            { Where Liverpool calm and serene
            { Hovers on an ancient green

When Grant arrived at Liverpool,
He found the day bright, clear and cool;
No clouds above to intervene,
It was a rare and gorgeous scene.
Each vessel rivaled to extremes,
To display their regal scenes.
They wanted to prove to Ulysses G.
That they had a big thing o'er the sea.
Flags of every nation, there
Waved their colors in the air.
Conspicuously, our lovely banner
Waved its folds before the tanner.
A. R. Walker, the mayor of the city,
Met Grant, with sayings long and witty.
The courtesies of Liverpool at large,
Was given to Grant, free of charge.
Thus, the mayor addressed the tanner

In a dignified, lordly manner:
"High on fame's bulletin board,
You've dug your name with a mighty sword;
Dug it deep, dug it to stay,
Till this, our country wastes away;
And when the war and carnage did cease,
You were a statesman, sir, in peace."
Then Grant without a stutter or sigh;
Made an appropriate, fine reply.
In his state carriage, the mayor then took them,
To a hotel for a dinner to book them;
Then after that, six miles into the country they went,
And spent the night in the mayor's own residence.
They spent two days in Liverpool, to be explicit,
To see places of interest, in receptions and visit.
Then a requester from Manchester,
    Invited him o'er;
At the mayor's hand, a welcome grand,
    He got to be sure.
They boasted him, and toasted him.
    In war and renown;   [guest,
He was a soldier in trust, to Mayor Haywood a
    While in Manchester town.
Curious facts, always attracts,
    Wherever found.   [truded
Thus Haywood alluded to things that pro-
    On forbidden ground.
The things that he alluded to,
    I give them in brief,
"George Griswold," to working-men,
    Was a ship of relief.
For the working-men
    That were out of a trade,
Caused by the shortage of cotton,
    That our rebellion had made.

Uncle Sam sent the vessel
  Freighted down with grub,
Presented to the lion
  A gift from its cub.
As Mayor Haywood was
  Receiving that vessel of victuals,
(To help the poor men,
  By filling their kettles,)
The English "Alabama,"
  And many of her kind,
They sought o'er the deep,
  American vessels to find.
They looked for American merchants,
  Not those that dealt in shot,
For of old Jones and Perry
  They had not yet forgot.
England looked for our vessels
  To capture and destroy,
For seamen of England,
  Love to fret and annoy,
We've treated old England
  Just like a brother.
We fed her on one side
  As she stole from the other.
But England, to nations that quarrel, is a curse,
For she'll hang on their verge, to rob their commerce,
    Too bold to go home, and stay away;
    And too big a coward to join the affray.
  So thus, she hangs on the verge of disaster,
  And of the poor crippled ones makes itself master.
As we fed their starving, so they wouldn't go under,
They roamed o'er the seas, our merchants to plunder.
    After our merchants,
      They'd never went splashin',
    But our nation was at war,

And it therefore, was their fashion.
They thought to rob us,
    With old fashioned glee,
As we shot the south,
    In eighteen sixty-three.
"Alabama," at our merchants,
    Threw many a deadly missile,
But England paid dear in after years,
    For Alabama's whistle.
Then Grant's reply to the mayor,
Was a solid, staunch old stayer.
Towards manufacturing he did lean,
Work and working-men was his theme.
In behalf of the sons of Uncle Sam,
He loudly thanked every Manchester man,
For their sympathy with them in their cause,
Which was done nobly in support of our laws.
Thus Grant got up o'er England, and blessed her,
Some for England, but more for Manchester.
One M. P.—Jacob Bright,
Remarked that Grant did fight,
        Not for fame,
Or conquest, or name ;
But to join the people's hand
Into a union of his native land.
In all his conduct, power and strength,
Drew his sword to a deadly length.
Then when the fire sons of Mars
Proved rebels' swords were poor in wars,
Who drove them oft in wild retreat,
And conquered them in sure defeat?
Then he asked his country for generous terms,
    To lavish on those vanquished worms.
        Such was Grant.
The American merchant,

Who in Manchester resides,
　Presented the general an address,
　　With a welcome presides.
All o'er the kingdom,
　　Throughout the cities.
Letters of invitation came to him,
　From peasants, lords and witties.
To G. W. Childs of Philadelphia,
　Grant letters this information:
"The English show their respect to me,
　For the love they have of our nation.
Between Uncle Sam and England,
　I wish the jealousness dead,
In civilization and commerce,
　They are the powers to spread.
Among all other nations on earth combined,
Such civilizing powers we cannot find.
Combined, we can our own wars decrease,
And keep the world at large in peace.
We can draw our swords, and paint them red,
And cross them o'er the warring nations' head;
And make foes shake hands with foes,
In long, double-columned rows."
　　　Then Grant went down
　　　From Manchester to London town.
(Where hammers beat in modern clang,
And many a bard in rhythm sang;
Where Shakespeare did his deeds in lore,
And finished what Marlow had done before;
Where rare Ben Johnson did his deeds,
But scarcely e'er could meet his needs.
His stomach, his dearest friend, still a dreadful foe,
That struck his pocket many a dangerous blow.
　　He was long a champion of the stage,
　　A rock of power in a literary age.

Green, Nash, Peele, Messenger, Webster and Kidd,
All, through poetic London slid.
They all slid in play or verse,
Some of which we still on stage rehearse.
Then we came down to more modern times,
To where Goldsmith drew a scribbler's lines.
And many others as great as he,
That launched on thought's fathomless sea.)
The Midland railway's Chairman Ellis, and
General Superintendent Allport show their hand.
They were peculiar Grant-loving fellows,
And over him long and loud blew their bellows.
And along that road they loudly roared,
On a special train, with Grant aboard.
As to London, the train run down,
They stopped at Leicester and Bedford town.
They only stopped a few minutes they say,
So that the mayors could their addresses pay.
Grant's London visit surely paid,
For only thirty days he stayed.
In the middle of which time he went,
And some of it with his daughter spent.
In Southampton is her abode,
Where winds many an antique road.
Along which roads the general spent
Many a day, to pleasure lent.
Looking at the curious scenes
Of feudal lore, and modern themes.
Netley's Abbey was among the score,
They viewed its ruins o'er and o'er;
Which rested him and his family well
From dinners and receptions, to cease a spell.
Bidding farewell to Mrs. Sartoris, then
He sought London's busy marts of men.
The great and witty

> Proud London city,
> Her freedom gave,
> To Grant, a slave
>   She bowed.
> To serve or treat,
> Or wash his feet.
> She owned him God
> Of English sod,
> Who came from the surf
> To wash the turf
>   With blood.
> All his coming tour,
> And that before,
> Was not so grand
> As the scene at hand.
> For sure as you're livin',
> To few are given
>   The freedom of London.
> For on none it rests
> But distinguished guests;
> And it's offered to none
> But the largest gun.
> The ceremonies grand
> And stately in hand.

The highest honor that London can
Confer upon a fellow-man.
The way that Sammy with England stands,
It was very significant at London's hands.
The aldermen gave Grant his seat right
Beside Lord Mayor Sir Thomas White.
On the side where warring swords were dangled,
When nations get into a bloody wrangle.

> The lord mayor came in state,
> On our citizen Grant to wait.
>   And all

The ceremony was in Guild Hall.
After the common council did its routine,
The Chamberlain, B. Scott, addressed Grant fine.
Alluding to our "Pilgrim Fathers" grand,
That brought freedom to this land;
And may the landing of the pilgrims be
A sacred spot beside the sea.

THE PILGRIM'S LANDING.

Ah! easy, for now you tread
Where freedom to the world were wed.
Here's where men first shunned sceptered power,
And worshipped God in nature's bower.
It is from Plymouth stones we trace
Freedom of a mighty race.
The foundation laid in song and prayer,
Was ever a landing more rich or rare.
The wooded slopes beyond this scene,
The trees loomed tall and dark between.
They came not with pomp and power,
With whetted swords, sharp, to devour.
  Nor were they banished from a land,
  For disobeying some king's command.
  They came not in convict bands,
  Imported there, from foreign lands.
  They were workmen of a common station,
  Proper guardsmen of an infant nation.
  They came not with roll of drum,
  But as true conquerors, they come.
  They came, they came to stay,
  Though every country should pass away.
  They came in solemn song and prayer,
  And braved all hardships men could dare.
  The barren limbs on the winter trees,
  A rocky coast and a foreign breeze,

Were all the scenes to welcome them,
With the wild beasts and savage men.
Old age and youth together mixed,
Love and truth the scene transfixed.
Lovely women in fearless devotion,
Dared the storms of land and ocean.
What sought they on a rock-bound coast,
Clad in its mail of hoary frost'
Where winter winds the tree-tops tossed ?
What sought they in a land so far ?
The wealth of seas, the spoils of war ?
Or, was it jewels of a mine ?
They sought a faith's pure shrine !
Its holy soil, where first they trod,
Left in unstained freedom to worship God.
Such was the birth of England's cub,
Which in after years she tried to drub.
But got badly drubbed in turn,
The English, Scotch and whole concern.
The ugly whelp, to thus disdain,
England, its dear old dame;
But that was in years past and gone,
When freedom first began to dawn.
Then he alluded too, with care,
How Uncle Sam received the British heir.
That is, when old Queen Victori',
Steps down from her seat of glory.
Then he can the throne assume,
If unseen fate don't seal its doom.
Also Prince Arthur, in Grant's reign,
Was welcomed kindly from o'er the main.
To all those things he alluded,
The facts from the fiction protruded.
For all you did for heir and prince,
Stands like the coins from ancient mints.

Now in giving the freedom of London we claim,
The coins we now return again.
The privilege we grant and make,
To you, for your country's sake.
Hoping our country's to be one,
In mighty deeds that's to be done.
    May all of our rivalry be square
    On both sides honest and fair.
After the chamberlain ended his speech,
A copy of the resolutions to Grant did reach,
    Which were illumed and fine,
    Bearing an engraved design.
With a casket of gold, strong and good,
On the back of which an American eagle stood.
The design of which was elaborate,
Which here I cannot communicate.
Then after all of this complete,
Grant, in fellowship they greet,
June thirteenth, of Grant it's said,
He became a citizen. to London wed.
Then Grant to them reciprocated,
The following facts communicated.
Part of his speech, I'll here rehearse it,
Though fools in after years may curse it.
Curse him, and then curse me,
Then wish themselves cast in the sea.
Because they were not noted,
And for great things often quoted.
It is a hard thing to quote a fool,
And is seldom done, as a general rule.
He thanked old London, kind and calm,
For their love shown towards Uncle Sam,
Saying, "Although a soldier bred,
I'd rather, by far, make peace instead;
I have no love for war at all,

Only for the trouble that it may appall;
And I hope the trouble between our nations
Can always be settled by arbitrations."
Then after all bombastication,
He signed his name to the corporation.
To the roll of members, honorary,
(Which has no members on a contrary.)
The last act its prudence deem,
An ending ceremony closed the scene.
Regal power in splendor serene,
Grant stoops to dine with England's queen.
The queen invited her adopted vassal,
To view her splendor in Windsor castle.
While in the Marlborough house,
The Prince of Wales and he carouse.
They play the regal splendor fine,
Chewing rare dinners and drinking wine.
The Brazilian Imperior, then,
Hob-nobbed with those mighty men.
Royal maidens, dames and Queen,
With lords and earls mixed between.
With those men of wisdom, wit and lore,
Such did adorn the royal floor.
The laboring skeletons back in the rear,
To view such scenes dare not draw near.
Let American fancy view those things,
Then long for his country full of kings.
Each lady that treads Uncle Sammy's green,
Is powerful as a foreign queen.
And all the maidens throughout this land,
Are sceptered princesses right at hand.
Bless our land of kings and queens,
Where no vassals mar the scenes.

 A dinner at Liverpool,
  Where sumptuous power deigns to rule,

Then Grant accepted an invitation
From the mayor and corporation,
To help stuff the inner man
On all the dainties mortal can.
It was by mayor and gentlemen led,
It was a delicious public spread.
There was, perhaps, some less or more
Of gentlemen, two dozen score.
Honored Liverpool citizens, square and just,
Grant and his son were the mayor's guests.
Toasts, they were taken, and freely given,
To remember the dead and arouse the livin'.
General Grant in his toasts alluded,
How his reception beyond his expectations protruded,
And of the relations
Between the two nations.
Ye should hark
To his remark.
"Our nation it begun
In kindred and blood were one;
In language and occupation;
We are one in civilization.
But our nation being young and strong,
Ahead of its aged parent has gone.
A leading off from ancient Briton,
As a lion should lead a kitten."
The last clause
Caused
A pause
For merriment.
Oh! London fair,
So rich and rare,
When Grant returns
Thy honor burns.
It burns to greet,

The general to meet.
Where sages and sinners,
In receptions and dinners,
    All dined together.
The associations
In representations,
Invited him to dine,
And bib of their wine.
The journalists in lead,
And editors indeed,
All hovered around
As though to drown.
With questions
And suggestions
They bored him,
The working-men;
His name attend:
Presented their claim
To honor the same.
Among which were the great iron overseers,
Iron-founders, miners and engineers.
    To honor our man of fame,
    The "Workingmen's League" came;
    The "Iron-workers' Society" was there.
    To participate in a thing so rare.
They all came General Grant to caress,
To whom they offered a flattering address.
        Oh! Soy!
Read ye General Grant's reply:
"I have received attentions, free hand-shakin's,
        Ovations,
        Presentations,
        Acclamations,
        Invitations
          From associations

And the nations
    Highest rulers.
But no reception,
Without exception,
Am I prouder of than this.
    Where workers great,
    At a social fete.
All the greatness of the United States,
Alone, from labor it rates.
Not Uncle Sam, but every land,
Labor holds all greatness in her hand;
It's the world's foundation,
And the world's demand.
All that exists, we have or enjoy,
Are only products of labor's employ;
All the great things into existence charmed,
Are only the facts of labor performed."
    Oh, work! work!
    May you forever lurk;
      In future ages,
      May seers and sages,
      On their respective stages,
Act in vast performing,
To make the coming world more charming.
Telegraphing, labor guides her,
All steam inventions, labor strides her.
All machinery of labor-saving styles,
Labor up around them piles.
For all the labor one tries to stop.
Five times stronger grows the crop.
It takes two laborers to attend,
Where but half a one's to mend.
Labor, dear labor in her station,
Is the guardian watch-dog of a nation.
Also the United service club,

Came to pay its rubby-dub;
Representing the army and navy combined,
Founded when wisdom to wit resigned.
A dinner and reception spread,
Grant by them was bounteously fed.
Then the American Embassy tried
To spread before him native pride.
There many an American, London stayed,
Before the hero came to parade.
Of course the reception was very grand,
There Grant shook many a native hand
Just introduced.
Grant goes to see, ere he returns,
The Scotchly home of Robert Burns;
The greatest peasant of his line,
The first to tune up " Auld Lang Syne ,"
And sent "Tam O' Shanter" homeward flyin',
With clang and clatter,
And his mare short a tail, where the fiends got at her.
But ere the general to Scotland went,
He made a short run to the continent,
Where love and luxury to him spent
In curious feast.
Everything to splendor lent
As in the east.
Mahomet himself, would be astonished
Himself by Yankee kings admonished.
For Yankees in this latter age,
Are patrons of every rage.
To imitate,
Create,
And so,
The Yankees surely are not slow.
To Edinburgh with many charms,
The mayor welcomed with opened arms.

The freedom of the city, also here,
Upon Grant they did confer.
When Grant was by this blessing cursed,
Was on August day the thirty-first.
(Here, be it on thy memory pressed,
Grant was the mayor's welcome guest.)
Then Grant to the mayor made reply,
O'er a dinner that was not dry:
"I am filled up with emotion so,
How, to reply in thanks, I hardly know.
I thank you in a hundred fold,
For making me a burgher of your city old.
It is a compliment that's grand
To me and my native land.
From a land of sages and seers,
That's bridged its name o'er a thousand years.
We are proud of citizens that are Scotchmen,
They benefit us, and it's profitable to them.
    (Here, the rattling of the doors
    Proves that laughter loudly roars.)
    Here the juncture now sets in,
    How to end and where begin.
    For a feast is so diverting,
    And an over-fill ends in hurting.
(The lord-provost of Glasgow town.
May his speech live in annals renown:
"Lincoln struck down the Upas tree,
And Grant killed the roots of slavery.
The Americans are a christian host,
The likes no other nation can boast.
Of a grander and sublimer scene,
Till then the world dared never dream.
Until the south the north had whipped,
But never once the vanquished kicked.

The north and south shook hands together,
Then never molested one another.
Revenge got not a drop of blood,
But peace and quiet was understood.
In peace, each side decorated their graves,
That fell in battle o'er the slaves;
Then united and free, again they stood,
To learn from evil, lessons of good.")
All his sight-seeing we cannot trace,
In this short, limited space.
　　In the commendations freely given,
　　Proved him one of the greatest livin'.
　　When he his presidency led,
　　Peace, to the world was truly wed.
In adjustment of the Alabama claims,
He bound the world in golden chains.
Peace was his motto, from end to end,
And made him many a lasting friend,
In Geneva's renowned old place,
To there, Alabama claims we trace ;
Where settled was that wordy faction,
And history celebrates the action.
Honor to our nation it did descry,
And bound the world in a holier tie.
And may the world hold in renown,
The actions at ancient, honored Geneva town.
There's where millennium age was born,
It was the age's progressive morn.
It was where swords' annihilation
Assumed the power of arbitration.
It was an achievement of civilization,
A stay and brace to every nation.
　　　　Again,
　　　In England.
　　　More explicits,

Rounds and visits.
As Grant from Albion, passed o'er
To Ireland's down-trodden shore;
Where tyrranic powers hold
A grip o'er a nation's fold.
As he passed out that way.
His route through manufacturing England lay.
Newcastle, Sunderland, Sheffield and such,
Birmingham and others, that make as much.
His ovations along that way were grand,
The Newcastle one gives the style at hand.
It was the working people massed,
Which run to eighty thousand or past.
Which moved in one long stream of banners,
Representing all trades, from soldiers to tanners.
In this long stream of general union,
Where workingmen were in communion.
They bore a long stream of red and blue banners,
With mottoes complimentary, in different manners:
" Welcome Hero of Freedom," to our heart,
" Let us Have Peace," " Welcome from Arms to Art."
Then they, all together,
Wound up on "Nothing Like Leather;"
With many others thrown between,
Which to the comic side may lean.
The banners, badges and ensignia'
Clogged the streets along their way.
Elaborate were their addresses,
Gotten up to go on slow expresses.
Each speaker in bold amends,
Praised the day that they were friends.
Grant now visits Erin's shore,
A land chock full of ancient lore.
Where lore abounds,
In stacks and mounds.

Its wit is without an end,
Which no nation can amend.
Ah, it was a while,
Since Grant promised to view the isle.
One year and two months lay between,
Grant's promise, and this very scene.
Mrs. Grant shunned this parade ;
She with her daughter, in England stayed.
Grant and his friends from London sped,
July the second, for Holyhead.
There the mail steamer in its line,
At Kingstown landed them on time.
They reached Dublin the next morn,
(Where lynching powers first were born.
The de'il his power to Dublin lent,
For who but the de'il such could invent.)
Lord Mayor Barrington, Sir J.,
Met Grant at the landing on his way.
And in the carriage of the Dublin mayor,
Who become for a time Grant's chief drayer.
He drayed him off to the Shelburn Hotel,
Where Grant and he put on a swell.
It was a swell no fellow-mortal could excel.
It was a swell of square wrought deeds,
It was a swell of the country's needs.
                Then nex',
The American consul paid his respects.
Then when the clock on the mantel tree,
Had ticked along four hours till three,
The mayor with his carriage came,
For Grant to occupy the same.
So they could go and see the town,
And its ancient things wrapped in renown.
Academies, museums and halls,
Also where art decorated its walls,

The chambers of commerce, stock exchange and banks,
That holds the wealth of Ireland's money cranks.
Then the fine streets they went to view,
Of which they looked at a dozen or two.
Along which many a loud and lusty cheer,
Fell soothing on the general's ear.
Then the carriage, like a bounding ball,
Drew up before the city hall.
The freedom of the city, in resolution,
Was read to Grant in execution.
The one in whom the elocution lay,
Was the lord Mayor, yes, Sir J.
The certificate to Grant he handed,
Which no power on earth demanded;
But when to courtesy we allude,
It never was known to protrude,
The certificate was richly illuminated and faced,
In a casket of carved bog oak encased.
Then the usual addresses,
Came forth in Irish messes.
To which the general held his side,
In facts, not fiction, he replied.
He did it up in language tony,
All the thanking ceremony;
Then said,
In tones as heavy as tons of lead.
(I mean in facts, void of fiction,
Beyond the fact of contradiction.)
"While in office, Irish I represented more,
Than the majestic English Queen Victor'.
For in Uncle Sam, with truth it's said,
There are more foreign or native bred,
Than all this Emerald Isle can boast,
Or probably double such a host."
Next morn, in a foggish rain,

The mayor took him to the train.
Then in that morning's foggish dew,
They bid each other a kind adieu.
Then, on the rail that hums so merry,
Grant boarded the train for Londonderry.
Great crowds along at the stations cheered,
But it's not on record where any sneered.
He was received with enthusiasm,
In each Irishman's face, yawned a roaring chasm.
Hand-shakings, addresses and a' o' that,
Were gi'en and taken in the land o' Pat.
Then to the city hall, he was driven,
As the mass all warned him they were livin';
(For the Irish plebe came out in wads,
Lords, bog-trotters and common plods,
In the scene, all mixed together,
One could not tell which from 'tother.
Like the scum on a western lake,
The streets were crowded to a cake.
They were so thick they could not stir,
The front was crowded by the rear.)
Here the general was enrolled,
By certain ceremonies controlled;
Which in the end entitled be,
An Ulster Irishman was he.
Next morn they saw the sights,
Made noted by Irish lords and knights.
Also old 'derry's historic walls,
Wrecked as though by cannon-balls.
Relics of historic dead,
Left from the scenes past and fled.
Fleeting scenes can never last,
But like a stream, they drift apast.
Till in the distance loom at last,
Tall and sharp,

The towering steeples of old Belfast,
  Like a dart.
Then in that old and ancient town,
To shower honor on Grant's renown.
The linen shops and mills shut down.
  The working people in a thousand score,
  Welcomed him o'er and o'er;
  They welcomed him in legend lore,
No other place, without exception,
Here they gave a grand reception.
'Neath the American collars and English rags,
Which hung suspended o'er the flags,
All the public buildings there,
Of eternal flags wore their share.
The lord mayor, and others of his persuasion,
Did the honors of the occasion.
On the next day a gang of prominenters,
Including merchants, editors, but no inventors,
They paid their respects, and visited places,
Where mighty men ran mighty races.
  As the general's carriage drove along,
  It was cheered so much it made a song.
  At a railway station along the way,
  A little lassie, bright and gay,
  Asked Grant a message of love to give,
  To her aunt that did in America live.
  Grant's reply I never learned,
  Or that he ever felt concerned.
  Then to London just the same,
  He returned the way he came.
  That is on his Dublin run,
  He went back the way he come.
    (It is so sentimental,
    That part of Europe continental.
In the land where Rinaldo Winkeriff fell,

Where lived tyrant Gessler and patriot William Tell.)
Many lines back in this poem, I am sure,
Of Grant's continental visit, they've told long before.
But time and particulars, it stood not upon them,

        [con them.
For days were full of pleasure, and hadn't time to
   There it was, three long weeks he stayed
   And in that time, one corner-stone he laid
Of an Episcopal church, with creeds improved,

        [moved.
To accommodate the folks, who, hitherwards had
     Folks of the land
     Where Grant and his band
     Performed heroic deeds
     To back the creeds
     Of human needs.
  This happened in Geneva town,
  Celebrated in arbitrary renown ;
  Which Uncle Sammy did first propose,
  And that's the way the scheme arose.
  For well old England knew our hordes
  Carried long, deadly, dangerous swords ;
And once she was acquainted with our commodores,
So held in terror around her shores.
  Let us note the stone that Grant here laid,
  He struck it, and since then it stayed.
  The hammer he used, was dressed in a rag,
  The glorious, noble, American flag.
  Whether flag or testament was honored the most,
  It was laid in the Father, Son and Holy Ghost.
The American flag, on the hammer stocked it,
But on that stone there, not a testament knocked it.
Or did Grant and the clergy have one in their head,
Or was it carried in their pockets instead.
Here flags and creeds were mingled together,

With bibles carried in lids of leather.
(If any,
There were none too many.)
I'll hold my pen, for it shows my size,
And this is no place to criticise.
Then a brief address,
And a fond caress,
Then all was done,
Ended where it begun.
With July twenty-seven for a date,
And the year before, seventy-eight.
Grant replied to the welcome given,
He was the proudest man a-livin'.
To be in a place where "Alabama Claims" were smo'red
By the power of arbitration, instead of sword.
It was a great art given to the nations,
This shield from war, in arbitrations.
Then here's another fact that's grand.
Among fellow-Americans, in a foreign land.
It scatters news,
Knocks the blues
In fours and twos,
Like snakes in shoes
If nothing more

Explanation. {In this lengthy song of songs,
{This at its proper place belongs.

Geneva's visit is no good here,
But look back in the poem, two months and a year.

October the twentieth, from Folkstone,
We find him landing at Boulogne;
Himself, wife and son,
Accompanied by John Russel Young,
Who, from evidence, it's clear,
Became the touring chronicler.

Just declare us
Off to Paris;
Rushing along on a train of cars,
To view Paris in splendor and horrors.
The car-wheels restless in their rattle and bang,
Still a lullaby tune they sang;
And at every way-side station,
They stopped as if for recreation;
But maybe it's a turn in their vocation.
But at one of these way-side slacks,
A lot of grandees drove up in hacks;
And when the cars started off again,
The grandees were aboard of the train
They all came out from Paris town,
To meet the man of great renown.
General Noyes and Torbert, our men official,
And McMahon, *aide de camp* as well;
The *aide* to welcome in his master's name,
The others loved him for his glorious fame.
When Grant arrived at Paris station,
He met a number of Americans in high occupation.
(For 'round about Paris, America's not spurious,
Are not so scarce, as to be curious.)
To the Hotel Bristol, he was conveyed,
To join in dining receptions' long parade;
To which the Americans gave one grand,
With three hundred natives, all on hand.

Official receptions, then
Were held by the mighty men.
President McMahon most cordially received him,
He astonished Grant so that Grant hardly believed him.
Grant to him, had many endearing charms,
So he received him as a fellow-soldier-in-arms.
Therefore, President McMahon soon prepared a day,

To give Grant a show of military display.
    But Grant was an odd one, here I'll say,
    He had a strong aversion to military display.
    And was sure to keep away from it,
    Just as far as courtesy would permit.
      (For he had seen enough of war,
      Clothed in all its wretched horror.
    Which never comes to the gaze,
    In the glitter of military displays.)
    They visited each other close and warm,
    Each for the other bore a charm.
    Of course the French's different factions,
    Took their stand on different actions.
    In the Franco-Prussian war,
    Which few went against and many for.
    American minister, General Noyes,
    Gave a reception to Grant and other boys.
    Grant gave Paris a two months' stay,
    And then packed up and moved away.
    For Italy and the Holy Land,
    And Egypt 'mid the burning sand.
    The Grant family were three in number,
    Besides carpet-bags and traveling plunder.
      Mrs. and Mr. and Jesse R.,
      Boarded Uncle Sammy's man-of-war.
    The " Vandalia," a Mediterranean cruiser,
    Was detached, so General Grant could use her.

    When from Villa Franché they started away,
    It was December's thirteenth day;
And the fourth day found them in Nalpes Bay,
        With anchor cast,
In sight of Vesuvius, on placid waters lay
        Tight and fast.
Next morning, to Vesuvius they ambled,

Grant threw coins, and beggars scrambled.
　　Around the curve of Naples Bay,
　　Carriages rolled them out that way.
　　For they were late in landing soon,
　　For official visits reached nigh to noon.
　　In reaching the volcanic mountain's crest.
　　They rode part of the way and walked the rest.
The scene from the crest is broad and grand,
Stretches city or bay on either hand.
　　The next day the general went,
　　And sometime o'er Pompeii's ruins spent.
　　Which, two thousand years ago,
　　Was buried in an ashy flow ;
　　Where Vesuvius threw its ashes down,
　　And made a sepulchre of a town.
　　　　Beneath ashes twenty feet,
　　　　Ten thousand persons sleep.
　　It has a fascination for men,
　　The modern, who are exhuming them.
　　Imagine a city of so long ago,
　　Buried at a single blow.
　　It is inspiring, to one that views,
　　And awes the thinker into a muse,
　　　When Grant viewed Pompeii's scene,
　　　It was December's day nineteen.
　　To Egypt, now it was time to start,
　　And with awe-inspiring Pompeii part.
So thus at Malta, on their way,
They anchored on December, twenty-eighth day.
Into Malta, she came with steam and sail,
And anchored 'mid the rustling of a gale.
But as the sea's bottom, by her anchor was riven,
A salute of twenty-one guns was given.
　　(Yes, a salute aroused the hour,
　　Long and strong twenty-one gun power.)

The "Vandalia" dipped
  Her anchor in the sand,
Near the "Sultan," under
  The Duke of Edinburgh's command.
The "Sultan" was an iron-clad,
  That wore a coat of mail,
She could cleave the waters
  In steaming through a gale.
The Duke visited Grant,
  In a pleasant, informal style,
And invited him to luncheon,
  At his palace on the Isle.
Grant and his party
  Were received cordially, such as
Can be afforded
  By a duke and a duchess.
From the beach to San Antonio
  It is four mile,
Where lives the duke with his duchess,
  In his palace on the isle.
Where walls and orange groves
  Break the monotony of nature,
With the garden of San Antonio
  Is a fair and lovely feature.
Around the castle, the duke placed upon her,
Drawn up in front, a regimental guard of honor.

Off to the land where Joseph went,
And the infant days of Christ were spent.
(At this point, the years change date,
From 'seventy-seven to 'seventy-eight.)
So when January days numbered five,
At Alexandria, they did arrive.
At once the governors, pachas and beys
Called upon him in their Egyptian ways.

They were there, the same as in other land,
They all press to grip a hero's hand.
Americans, officials and all,
Upon him, here and elsewhere call.
Henceforth, American callings are tame,
And I shall not mention them or their name.
 This was Grant's first time in all his while,
 To be entertained in Oriental style;
And the entertainment was regal that they gave.
All classes were at it, from Khedive to slave.

   At one of those dines,
   'Mid luxury and wines;
  Grant first met, Henry M. Stanley.
   Of course one can guess
   Their tones of address.
   One from an African tour,
   In a complete explore,
  By a chief man of the manly.
   Now, its to Cairo en route,
   Like a sausage on kraut ;
   Or quail on toast ;
   Or a mighty man's boast ;
    For it's grand
   When things all work to hand.
  So Grant, o'er the plain,
  In the Khedive's free train
   Sped along.

From Alexandria to Cairo it's four hours apart,
To the time you arrive from the time you start.
 So therefore, I think they got there soon,
 It was three o'clock in the afternoon.
A guard of honor, officers and civilian,
With the owners of nothing and the owners of a million
 All ready to receive Grant and his party,
 In ways to show it strong and hearty.

There Grant met two West Point friends, of course ·
They were generals in the Khedive's force.
General Loring, of the rebel cause,
And General Stone of the Union laws.
General Stone purposely came
To welcome Grant, in the Khedive's name.
Then Grant and party to a palace went,
Which the Khedive, free to him had lent;
For the Khedive was the general's friend,
His servants in the palace, on Grant attend.
The Oriental styles here,
Reign summer, winter and throughout the year.

Just hold a while,
Grant's on the Nile,
Or soon will be. Started January 18th.
That flows into a delta, from a delta to the sea.

About a week in Cairo spent,
In viewing curious things were lent.
Oriental dines,
And rare old wines.
Then for a while,
Up the famous Nile,
They steam along.
Now this thing note,
It was Khedive's boat,
Free and strong.
Then the Khedive showed his forethought again,
By sending a guide that knew antiquities by name,
And in reading hieroglyphics was an expert man,
Professor Emile B-r-u-g-s-c-h pronounce it if you can.

At Siout,
A place of caravan renown,
It is upper Egypt's ruling or capital town.
Here, Grant got dinners, and n' o' that,
That whets the dull and makes the hungry fat.
They praised our country with grand emotion,

Which hovered o'er the edge of sacred devotion.
Uncle Sam's a giant of all the nations
In manly art and true vocations.
  No wonder she should supersede,
  For she's the youngest of all we read.
  It is youth that gives us sprightly motion,
  Age only tends to stern devotion.
  Uncle Sam was born just to amaze,
  Therefore, the world upon him gaze.
  Uncle Sam's a nation without foes,
  For he's awed the world into repose.
    It is a nation quite surprising,
    The infant nation leads in civilizing.
      Here now, you have my version
      Of the Abydos excursion.
      At Girgal first they landed,
      Where the banks were highly sanded;
      And it was January, you see,
      Seven multiplied by three.
Here, ass-drivers beset the party,
And to hire their asses, clamored hearty.
The drivers summed up the party, net,
And an American name, on each donkey set.
  As an example, here it is,
  All men should profit by their biz.:
  " Yankee Doodle," was the ass's name
  They offered to our man of fame.
  The ass' name suits the nation.
  That they meet in their occupation.
When they before Abydos' Temple stand,
The oldest relic in the land;
Their hats ornament their hand'
      Instead their head,
For awe holds one at its command
      Before the dead.

They have it well with ages spiced,
Four thousand years from the birth of Christ.
The fountain head of civilization,
The art and science of all creation.
Let monks of old and ancient glory,
Doctor up the hideous story.
It gives the ass-boys recreation,
When pilgrims view the situation.
In ambling to it through the nation.
Then up to view ruined Thebe's glory,
'Hundred gated, as sung in Homer's story.
Therefore, why should we refute it,
When there is nothing to dispute it.
   There is where gigantic art
   Awes one to paralyze the heart.
   Here is no place to delineate,
   Or tell of things that are great
   Or I could write a thousand pages
   To illumine the future ages.
   Here, the largest obelisk is found,
   On this old and ancient ground.
It's the only stone, which of women's virtue teaches,
And in one gigantic piece, ninety feet it reaches.
        Then up the Nile
        To the ruins of Philœ.
        Near where pours,
        Along Nile's shores,
        Cataract first;
        Where rocks immersed,
        Churns it to foam,
        In roars and moan;
        To waste it o'er
        The deserted moor.
        One thousand miles,
        From the Nile's

Deltaed mouth.

Then turn back, turn back, boating machinery,
And carry us back to Cairo's first scenery.
Where the Khedive will meet us in pantomime gesture,
And give us a dinner to fill out our vesture.

Give us a dinner in style Orient,
Which for kindness, alone shall be meant.
It was done, all and more, then a farewell bade,
And the party in joy passed on to Port Said.
Which they reached in plenty of time,
Along in February dayed to nine.

There, the "Vandalia" met and received them,
She was always on time, and never deceived them.

Then they started for Palestine,
To view that rare and holy scene;
Where all the Testamental course,
Was laid down in living force.
Therefore, its a holy land,
Where Christ the angry waters calmed.
They at Jaffa shortly entered,
For Jerusalem, where they centered.
Even at Jaffa they were readily detected,
Which the general had not expected.
He was received as in other places,
But with much less flaring graces.
And in letters rare and scant,
O'er an archway, "Welcome, General Grant."
Then they went in a modern manner,
And viewed the house of Simon, the tanner.
Then for Jerusalem they start,
Jerusalem and Jaffa, forty miles apart.
Three clumsy wagons with open tops,
With jogging rattle and frequent stops.
To Jerusalem conveyed them.
There, I suppose, the general paid them.

They viewed Jerusalem in all her parts,
Held sacred in the christian hearts,
Here, for Mrs. Grant, a monk so tame,
Gathered some flowers from Gethsemane.
All the noted places were seen,
On the plains of Palestine.
Then at Jaffa they arrived at eleven,
February's day, number twenty-seven.

    It was March five,
    They did arrive.

Then CONSTANTINOPLE
        Was taken in,
With all her mixed and curious din.
Bazaars and horrors, and all of them,
Common to Constantinople men.
    Grant was sustained,
      Entertained,
    Wined and dined
With all the luxuries they could find.

    Grant left Constantinople in peace,
    To view the grandeur of Athens, Greece.
    In that city of classic scene,
    He was received by king and queen.
Then Grant looked around with stern decision,
On the classic scenes of old tradition.
Grant in nothing, was a fanatic,
But in sight-seeing was systematic.
In sight-seeing, great and small,
He learnt their whys, wherefore and all.

    Then he hastened on to ROME,
    Around the world, to get back home.
    It was to Grant there, unexpected,

Pope Leo, thirteenth, just elected.
There, New York's Cardinal McCloskey, then,
As a Roman Catholic, he represented them.
He arranged an interview between Grant and the Pope,
For which King Humbert did also hope.
He gave a state dinner to Grant, it is seen,
On a lovely spring day, April fifteen.
Then after sight-seeing, and dining with kings,
And all such grand and transient things.
When April had chased her days to twenty,
Grant, in Florence, saw Americans plenty.

Then to Venice and Milan, they
To Holland, pass on their way,
And reach Paris the seventh of May.
There Grant visited the exhibition,
According to McMahon's requisition.
Then, in a few days Grant left them all,
Who invited him to dine, or asked him to call.
On to Holland, he then pressed,
To gain recreation in rest.
At Hague, first they landed,
And then o'er Holland they expanded.
At Amsterdam, Grant dined and ate
A dinner noted for its costly plate.
Grant never saw a grander before,
On his world-encircling tour.
Then to Brock, a visit they did address,
A town, oppressive for cleanliness;
Then through the Dutch country whirlin',
They railway themselves to Berlin.
They in the streets of Berlin mix,
The day of June called twenty-six.
Grant loved the city with rare extremes,
And rambled o'er it to view the scenes.

There Bismarck called on Grant,
To perform what peasants can't.
Then Grant, unattended went;
And a social chat with Bismarck spent.
Now remember, in Dutchland wide,
There were dinners and receptions on every side.
From Berlin, on July's second day,
For Hamburg, Grant steamed away.
There, General Grant, to memories lent,
The fourth of July in Hamburg spent;
Then he left the Dutchman's land,
Where freedom reigns on every hand.
Then on July sixth, the general started
To Copenhagen, from Hamburg parted.
In Denmark, Sweden and Norway,
The general passed three weeks away
In ways and means
To viewing scenes.
The time was rich and rarely spent,
And the people are very intelligent.
They knew Grant's whole history through,
And they knew him as tried and true.

To St. Petersburg, the tourists starts,
With open eyes, and anxious hearts.
So on July's thirtieth day,
They reach it in a grand array.
Easy St. Petersburg is to come at,
First one must land at Cronstadt.
To Grant the old Russian Imperior,
Swore by inside and exterior.
That his love would never grow inferior
For the United States.
And no other king-love like his stood superior,
Or in finer rates.

Then he halts, to truly tell
Between them, peace shall ever dwell.
This action shows the Imperior's thought.
He lent Grant the royal yacht.
Then to Moscow, Grant went seeing,
Where Russia sprang into national being.
The railroad that connects the capitals, old and new,
Is an American structure, on a bee-line through.
Grant, in Moscow, met Americans in numbers,
And their cheering voices roared like distant thunders.
The Russians treated Grant in splendor,
No more to one can a nation tender.
Grant goes to Warsaw, Poland, then,
Where lived and died patriotic men.
But dear old place, she's bound in chains,
A ruined relic of her old remains.
Then off to Vienna, Grant went away,
Where he arrived on August's eighteenth day.
In the south of France, Portugal and Spain,
Three joyous months Grant did remain ;
In sight-seeing, receptions and such,
And other good things that pleased as much.
Sight-seeing was his recreation,
A studious, staunch, hard occupation,
Which ran to extremes in deviation.
Now Grant from those scenes will soon abscond,
For the Red Sea, and India beyond.
For a new year and a month, marks the time,
January twenty-four, in the year 'seventy-nine.
We find him ready to travel by sails,
On board of "Labourdonnais," from Versailles.
This is the first account in his trip,
That he traveled on board of a Frenchman's ship
Now I'll give you an invoice of Grant and his band,
The ones who accompanied him to India's land.

Grant's own family ain't large, one can see,
Himself and his mistress, and her son, Frederick D.,
And a Philadelphia man, E. A. Barie by name.
With John Russell Young to accompany the same ·
And one or two others, no matter who they be,
Together in a ship, they all sailed o'er the sea.
They went by Alexandria, o'er to Suez,
Where they took in the country, and read the late news.
    Here, the "Venitia" they had to wait for,
    After 'lighting from their steam rushing car.
    But soon the "Venitia" hove into sight,
    A powerful ship, and rapid in flight.
    They boarded her, as the sun set low,
    And shed a radiance o'er the sands below.
    Through the Red Sea, o'er the Indian Ocean,
    The clanking machinery kept the vessel in motion.
    Now remember, on February's thirteenth day,
    Grant was received in romantic Bombay.
    The addresses and receptions were grand,
    Such as one seldom meets in a foreign land.
    Dinners, receptions, all that and more,
    Resembled those, on old England's shore ;
    As India is run in manner and styles,
    Like her ruling country, the British Isles.
    To the General's eyes, it was a great feast,
    The Bombayic things, in the land of the east.
        So he took them all in.
        Without loss to his tin.
Then the governor lent him two cars, to convey
Him and his party away from Bombay ;
O'er the country where he saw fit to stray,
Where railroads happened in that direction to lay.
        So they rummed,
        And they bummed
Through Allahabad, Agri, to Delhi, where,

From Mahomet's beard, they saved a hair,
The greatest thing that's guarded there.
By Mahommedan saints in prayer.
To Lucknow, on they roar,
Through Calcutta and Malacca, to Singapore ;
Where he met the American consul Struder, a Swiss,
And the curious part of that is this,
He was a lieutenant, under Grant's commanding,
Down at Pittsburg's bloody landing.
Grant got to Singapore in time,
To date, March twenty-nine.
From Singapore
The young king of Siam invited him o'er ;
For he'd seen all the sights,
The wrongs and the rights
That lay along the way,
From Singapore back to Bombay.
He embarked for Siam,
In the midst of a calm,
And away,
Straight for Bangkok Bay.
And they paddled and puffed for five long days,
'Mid weather so clear, it was tinted with haze.
And the day they arrived on Bangkok's scene.
Was the day of April that's called fourteen ;
And the scene that ensued,
Why figure it out rude
In a fashion that's nude ;
When it's more pleasant than one could expect,
With royal scenes, in splendor decked.
For it's grand for one to come
Into a country as its ruler's chum ;
And a palace to live in, ah, wasn't it fine,
With his brother as servant, and a princely routine.
Now, young Americans, ye need take no alarm,

Mrs. Grant and the prince walk arm in arm.
That landing reception, you bet it was grand,
With our "Hail! Columbia" played by their band.
  The king entertained Grant rich and rare,
  The royal things he did not spare.
  A king in the regal rights,
  That kept pace with the advancing whites.
    He was a king in his royal station,
    Far in advance of his heathen nation.
Grant's Bangkok visit was some days long,
Then he went to Singapore from Hong Kong;
     Where the meeting was grand,
     For a Chinaman's land.
The Hong Kong visit was a pleasant stay,
Where Grant was done up in the usual way.
The Chinaman there, took curious pains,
To spread before Grant their vast domains.
  Then at Pekin, an order ensued
  To entertain Grant in a way to protrude
     O'er any given
  To white men dead, or dark ones livin'.
  Then Canton looms up to view,
  It must be visited and courted too.
  Where sedan chairs were brought in play,
  To travel in a royal way.
     Grant unassuming,
     With name a-booming,
  Dressed plain in the extreme,
  No jewels about him, were ever seen
  Upon his hands or breast to gleam.
They expected to see him in diamonds dressed,
A barbarous chief, from the distant west;
Dressed up in feathers, gaudily dyed,
To strut before them in regal pride.
One cannot imagine their vast dismay,

When the thoughts of their thinker were given away.
    A single Tartar officer led the procession,
    Bawling to the crowd in a hideous fashion,
    To pay respects to the "foreign Barbarian,"
    As though he was a wild Siberian.
    But little of Canton was visited or seen,
    Little time had they entertainment between.
    Then back to Hong Kong, they did return,
    More about that realm to learn.
        Then they go
        A short visit to Macao.
        It was May nine,
        In that Chinese clime,
        The weather was fine,
        Almost divine.
Then to Swatow away, Shanghai to Tientsin,
At each place, a day or two spent glancin';
    Glancing at the odd and curious,
    New things made old but spurious.
    Then up to Pekin, Grant must go,
    Along the excuse of a river, Peiho.
    It was a long, tiresome night and day row.
    Till Pekin it reached, I think it is now
    Got to by way of village Tung Chow.
    Then in state, to ride the sedan,
    Lugged along by the Chinese man.
    Mandarins were lots and plenty,
    Scores of them, and a dozen and twenty.
    Grant led in a sedan chair for a wagon,
    Eight coolies bore it, instead of a dragon,
    Grant for curious things went seekin',
And was highly entertained at the City of Pekin.
    Princes and kings, kungs and lungs,
    Changs and Wangs, Tungs and Bungs;
        All come to meet,

The great to greet.
Here Prince Kung
Asked Grant, as an arb'ator, to lend him a lung;
For old Japan
Was growling at him like a dog in a pan.
Each government hanging on the verge of spiles,
Almost ready to war o'er Loochoo's Isles.
So Grant promised him, in terms very good,
To help the governments all that he could,
When the scenes begun
In Pekin, were done,
To Tientsin, then,
Grant went, when
Twelve days in June had fled,
And there, a few days in luxury led.
Where Madam *de la* Li Hung Chang.
Got up dinner for a ladies' gang;
And none but ladies partook of the feast,
A brand new thing for the ancient east.
It was gotten up on purpose you see,
To honor the mother of Frederick D.
Six other American ladies were there,
The luxurious dinner, with Mrs. Grant to share.
A piano was ordered by the mister—it came,
The first ever seen by the curious old dame.
She sent for her guests in chairs sedan,
And thus returned them home again.
Each lady was presented
A roll of silk in her chair;
All the native-born friends
Of the hostess were there.
It seems, at this feast
Sociability was fixed,
The first time the two classes
Ever had mixed.

Aboard our man-of-war, " Richmond," the party
           Left, to go
Across the bosom of the Yellow Sea, to the
           Harbor of Chefoo ;
Where dinners grand, they did expand,
           And all of such,
There Grant partook, where bowls and nook
           Were filled with much.
Then for Nagasaki the " Richmond " steamed on,
When half of the night had fled and gone.
Safe, she reached her destination, soon,
When twenty-one days had fled in June.
Where she fired twenty-one guns,
An honorary salute to Japanese sons;
To which the Japanese forts replied,
That stood on the coast, with the city alongside.
The Japs called their minister, from Washington, home,
So Yoshide could meet Grant when he come ;
       For in Washington, they served together,
       Grant the higher, ruled o'er the other.
       The Japs took the general on trust,
       And simply made him the nation's guest.
       The governor of Nagasaki, a true Japanee,
       Asked Grant and his wife to both plant a tree.
         He gave them a place and settled a mark
         In Nagasaki's broad and pleasant park.
Grant and his wife set the trees, so they own,
And wrote an inscription for a tablet of stone ;
           To be placed near the trees,
Or where Governor Utsumi Togatsu may please.
Then the citizens gave Grant a unique dinner,
Elaborate enough to christianize a sinner.
         For with them it's not this or that,
         But " a man's a man for a' that."
Their dinner seemed to be in forces,

And was composed of sixty courses.
No wonder it was a strain,
On seven hours to entertain.
Then they boarded the "Richmond,"
  And soon did fix,
And sailed away on that June twenty-six.
Along the coast to Yokohama, for five long days,
They sailed at ease, in leisurely ways;
Where July the third, in joy they landed,
With all the glory that ever attended;
Or rank and power that ever befriended.
  The vessels took a hand,
  As well as the land,
   In shooting,
   And tooting,
  And hoisting their flags.
   And I'll say,
   Of vessels their lay,
   A whole world in one bay.
Where a special train stood ready to go,
And carry Grant to the capital, called Tokio.
  Which it did by steam power,
  In less than an hour.
  Where crowds were gathered,
  And dinners were weathered,
  Where he met some old Japs,
  Who were Washington chaps,
  That went there to ratify
  Treaty first; to gratify.
  Imakura was one,
  An old government gun;
  Second minister prime,
  That graded his line.
Then Grant and his party on the fourth of July,
With the Japs assistants, had a big ratify.

"Hail! Columbia!" was played on a silver-toned band,
 Way out in the Japanese rice-covered land.
   With a talk to the kings,
   And a great many things
   Too numerous to note.
   Or book-lids to tote.
   Then Mrs. Grant and the queen
   Had their little side scene,
  All to themselves with the rest,
  And their two languages stood a hard test;
   Which they often tried over again;
    Which many have seen,
    With an interpreter between.
    The Imperior, be it true,
    Was a man of broad view,
   In love with his nation.
The Imperior asked Grant of the wherefore and whiles,
His Chinese dispute o'er the Loochoo Isles.
   Grant merely suggested,
   (And there the case rested,)
    To settle in peace.
  They discussed education, tariff and tax,
  With agriculture, its reeds and its facts.
The above conversation was all so curiously made,
          [stayed.
The Imperior sought Grant in the palace where he
   During the Tokio lay
   Of a two months' stay,
   Festivities alone
   Was all that was known.
   Then leave was taken,
   In a big hand-shakin'.
   Grant wrote an address
   To Imperior and Empress;
   Which was highly admired,

Then they retired.
Then soon it will be, with clatter and sound,
On the rails they'll be traveling, homeward bound.
For the engine, now, stands dressed in flags,
Well decking herself in national rags ;
And what other colors would the old hussy seize,
But the beautiful American and wild Japanese.
Around the station, gathered a vast horde,
By the prime minister they were ushered aboard.
The old ruler dealt them rare and genteel,
For he lent them his car, and that was imperial.
And aboard was Mrs. Mari and Mrs. Yoshide,
Who once in Washington, did reside.
Then all the samee,
They soon got o'er to Yokohama ;
And then homeward bound,
From the wide world around.
Then they fired-up, and made the sky smokey, oh,
And started to 'Frisco, on the " City of Tokio."

HOMEWARD BOUND.

GRANT'S SONG.

Turn rapid ! turn rapid ! oh ! wheels in your motion,
And carry me back to my dear, native ocean ;
Carry me back, carry me back o'er the wide rolling sea,
It's the land, dear land of all others for me.
So let us return to the nation of which the world sings,
In the land of freedom, where all are born kings.
So let us return to that part of the earth,
Where greatness is severed from chances of birth;
Where nothing is placed on birth whatever,
And the merit of man is a national lever.

Then Mr. Grant asked his mistress to sing
Some countrified, lovely old-fashioned thing ;

As she used to sing in days gone by,
When the snows meandered through the sky.
Cheery
And merry
Were the songs that she sang,
'Mid the clatter and clang
Of machinery.
Till 'Frisco towned them,
And home was around them.
"Home!" what a volume in a word confined,
It cannot be comprehended by a common mind.
And may 'Frisco, with pleasure ever remember
The twentieth day of that lovely September,
When Grant was received with stupendous ovation,
[nation.
More than a king could receive from a crown-headed
Thus, Grant's tour around the world was completed,
In one grand run of ovations he feted.

CHINEE-ISCO.

The Chinese of 'Frisco gave Grant an address,
It was a good thing, may he never get less.
Their address, written in whole,
On a worked silken scroll,
Was grand,
In Chinese characters
To stand.
To which Grant made reply,
In regard to whiches, wherefore and why;
Of their home and place,
Their grade and race.
Then to Grant's mistress,
For helping their sisters
In hewing away
The prop and stay

To domestic seclusion,
To freedom's infusion
A casket of ivory they gave her.
So visiting the mighty
Big trees, and Yosemite,
And all the great places, great or forlorn,
That could be seen in Californ';
Then he turned around o'er Oregon, why?
In memory of the days gone by;
For he saw it once as a territory,
Where Indians reigned in all their glory.
The general must have been surprised
At how the place was colonized.
Then o'er the home-stretch, on a tour continental,
He wished to travel unobserved, but it was sentimental,
As one ovation,
From station to station
Greeted him.

A-HOME.

Out of a home, he long had been,
Only those that he rented,
Or the government consented
To lend him.
So in New York's vast human hive,
Where folks have settled too thick to thrive.
He settled too.
It was in the upper part of town,
Where things are not so tumbled down;
And in a place where things combine,
To make the city rare and fine.
His residence looks handsome and neat:
Three, East Sixty-sixth street.
And here, his life run on its line,
Uneventful for a time.
But soon, into various schemes,

He entered with might and means.
In the Mexican Southern railway plan,
He was in it an important man.
He served in it as incorporator,
And was its president somewhat later.
Then went down and viewed the scenes,   [1881]
In regard to the country's means.
    Then when the two oceans joined their hands
    Across the face of Nicaragua's lands,
His name on the bill, ran as incorporator,
And he served as commissioner, somewhat later.
To negotiate a Mexican trade,   [1882-83]
Where the canal might be surveyed.
    Of course it was a government affair,
    As President Arthur sent him there.
    Then the Wall street scenes loomed high,
    In burning flames that would not die,
    That glorious name, it seems was marred,
    Under the title of Grant and Ward.
    It was Grant and Ward to deal in stocks,
    And face the world in commercial knocks.
    But Ferdinand Ward proved a villain,
    And James D. Fish the worst in a million.
    By James D. Fish the funds were sank,
    While he served as president of Marine Bank.
    He swamped General U. S. Grant and all,
    Then alone he was left to fall.
Their swindling schemes were more gigantic
Than Satan could be o'er men tyrranic.
It seems the company hellwards ran,
Each one to lead his fellow-man.
One hundred and fifty thousand then,
Grant borrowed from his fellow-men.
And Vanderbilt's the man that lent,
But all those dollars they were spent,

In Ward a-patching up the rent;
  Which was indeed so mighty vast,
  Beyond a patching, it had passed.
It proved as the people did suspect,
Grant, wife and son were totally wrecked.
      On Wall street slew,
      And others too.
Then Vanderbilt, he must be paid,
And transfer deeds were quickly made.
Vanderbilt offered to cancel the debt,
But the generous offering Grant would not let.
So Grant and wife gave all they owned,
And scarcely then was the debt atoned.
Grant's war relics, held so dear,
With home, the debt would scarcely clear.
But Vanderbilt, the relics returned,
Not to Grant, but those concerned.
  They were given, and really meant,
  As relics to the government.
  Among them were the general's blades,
  Tools of the barbarous trades.
  At those blades he would not tug,
  In time of war would scarcely lug.
  But cigars were his delight,
  He carried them both day and night,
      And smoked them, too,
      As well as chew,
        As some assert.

FISH.

Well, James D. Fish, what about him,
Wrapped about in his cloak of sin.
Ah, that portion, it was his'n,
To stay ten years in Sing Sing prison,
      And Ward,

They dealt him a portion just as hard.
As Grant supported the stripes and stars,
So he supported the stripes in bars.
The wall street racket, misfortune smiled on ;
Then soon it was wrecked, and to ruin gone.

TURNS AUTHOR.

Then for the Century Magazines,
He wrote four articles on bloody scenes.
It was the Century editor's command,
And that's the way Grant showed his hand.
It was the dollars that laid behind,
And the employment was to ease his mind.
In the preface to his " History of the Civil War,"
He tells what he did his writing for.
His page of life then was opposite the sunny,
And life was lived on, through borrowed money.
More than half of Grant's book was a death-bed scene,
He wrote it, the fits of suffering between.
His sons looked the records for the greatest of men,
As he dictated comments to an amanuensis' pen.
For nine long months he suffered dire,
Almost the torture of martyr's fire.
For his suffering was internal,
Close akin to things infernal.
It was a cancer rooted fast,
At the root of his tongue it gnawed its last.
In no part of his life was it shown so nude,
As his life's last act in fortitude.
The general was moved to Drexel's cot,
On Mt. McGregor's lovely plot.
From Mt McGregor lies stretched to sight,
The scenes where Fenimore Cooper's wits ran riot.
And where Burgoyne lost his tyrannic blade,
Lies in the distant scene of the woodland shade

On Mt. McGregor, it is there,
One breathes the dust of freedom's air.
Near Mt. McGregor, is where Stark
Among the Hessians hewed his mark.
Hewed them till no more were found;
Till blood and corses strewed the ground.
So that cool air's refreshing breeze,
Might crush the general's sore disease.
But seven long weeks he lingered there,
Attended with the tenderest care.
Ere he spread his sable sail,
Before life's rapid, fading gale,
For that sweet country of repose,
Beyond this clime of daring foes.
And when his start for the unknown occurred,
Was on July the twenty-third.
In the year 'eighty-five, our dating age,
Grand curtains fell around his stage.
A country mourned its general's loss,
That dealt o'er rebeldom so cross.
Condolence to the family from every direction,
All over the Union, in every section
   Came pouring in,
   From various creeds,
   In different leads.
   From the mighty and grand,
   And best in the land.
And as the general laid low and prone,
The nation with him seemed to moan.
To him, sympathizing letters came,
From all 'sociations one could name.
The very church, her 'pistles drew,
And sent their sympathizings too.
Such was the sympathizers' way,
They averaged several times a day.

To politics, they shut their eyes,
And all joined hands to sympathize.
Born in a valley, died in a mountain,
At the source of fame's bright fountain.
　Scarcely had the general died,
　And bid adieu to this world of pride;
　Ere the lightning, it drew near,
　And the storm played around his bier.
　It seems that the lightning scorned
　All the living, that about him mourned.
　It leaped around with lurid flash.
　And thunder echoed with a crash!
　　Bonaparte was a slaughterer,
　　　Because he had the might,
　　Alexander loved to conquer,
　　　Because he loved to fight.
　　Cæsar was a buccaneer
　　　Upon a spacious plan,
　　But Grant was a soldier
　　　For the sake of his fellow-man.

That warrior statesman, Grant is dead,
　And soon he'll be entombed,
He's gone where bombshells never scream,
　Nor musket-balls ne'er wound.

He's gone to the grand reunion,
　The reunion of the brave,
Far beyond life's troubles,
　But just beyond the grave.

He has reviewed Alexander,
　And all his mighty host;
Alexander conquered a world,
　But that was all his boast.

Or, perhaps, he's wandering among
　The soldiers of Julius Cæsar,

The earth's greatest tyrant,
  Freedom's unbeliever.

He forged fetters strong,
  To bind his fellow-man ;
But they were broken asunder,
  Like tender ropes of san'.

Or perhaps, it may be
  With Napoleon, he's talking war,
Napoleon, the illustrious bandit,
  Whose name looms up afar.

The heavens he illumed with fire
  Of cities burning red ;
Oh, his hand was mighty,
  Ten thousand soldiers bled.

Oh, he was a bandit,
  With war's rampagent wrath ;
For death and destruction
  Was scattered along his path.

In death and destruction,
  His hand was never stayed.
For he was an adept
  In whittling with the blade.

Or maybe he's with Washington,
  Reviewing the revolution ;
How he drove the Britons
  In tyrany's execution.

I imagine the Americans about him,
  That once were living heroes ;
Telling of freedom's cost,
  And all its savage blows.

By Washington and our country,
  Freedom first was moored,

Lincoln was its stay,
    Grant braced it with his sword.

A hero, without a scar,
A general through a noted war.
The grandest thing that in human power lay,
Cannot be transferred nor given away;
It is a mixture that will stay
      With none.
It is confined to one tenement of clay,
    Its original one.

Oh, why do we leave our friends possessed
Of all we have but the richest and best,
That must forever be wrapped in one breast,
       To stay?
And when we are laid in the tomb to rest,
      There it must lay.

Oh, worth cannot be given to others,
Cannot be transferred to friends or brothers;
Cannot be given to sons, by rich and valiant mothers,
     It is a gift
From God, direct to man, which age ne'er smothers,
     But time can lift.

CHARACTER.

Grant's fame must rest upon his sword,
In blood it was bathed, as cannons roared.
It led the charge in many a din,
Where few came out where many went in.
It was he that whetted his sword,
On the hearts of the rebel horde;
And he followed the rebels as close to kill,
As the endorsement on the back of a bill.
Grant was a champion in all that's good and great,
And was a proper man to be ruler of state.

It was at Lee's surrender Grant showed a tender heart,
By every southern soldier, he did a manly part.
    He was feared and hated by the southern soldier,
        As they did no other,
    But after the surrender,
        They loved him as a brother.
He conquered them, to prove to them in the end
He was no foe, but their and their country's friend.
    So let Grant on his sword hang up his fame,
    He has left behind, a perpetual name.
    Uncle Sam may grow old in historic ages.
    But Grant will illume its glorious pages.
    Grant, in war was seldom shaken,
    And never lost a point once taken.
    Retreating was something he never learned,
    To flee from a foe was a thing he spurned.
    Grant never rose at once, if you please,
    But gradually, by well-tried degrees.
    He was a man possessed of vast reserve,
    And integrity that would never swerve.
    His eye, he trained it well in vigil,
    For it was as keen as that of an eagle.
In military strategy, far-sighted, in execution bold;
Energetic and deliberate, plain, by duty controlled.
        Though mild
        As a sportive child,
      Or calm as the seas
      When lulled by the sportive breeze;
    But fierce as the cyclone's wasting power,
    When called by his country in a perilous hour.
      Jealousy o'er him, ne'er drew a rein,
      Or even caused the slightest pain.
      For he gloried in a subordinate's raise,
      And on them, lavished unstinted praise.
      And in his praise, he never was swerving,

If the one for praise had a just deserving.
  All of his warring goes to show,
  He never humiliated a vanquished foe.
With courtesy and magnanimity they were greeted,
And never in his presence, was one mistreated.
  And to him, the happiest, grandest thing,
  Was the magic domestic circle ring.
  As a father, none ever surpassed him,
  And as a husband, 'way up they classed him.
  His wife and children, he loved the concern,
  And by them, was loved back in return.

CLASSING MEN.

          We can
  Say he was moderate in classing man.
  The facts are great and many,
  He knew military men best of any,

FRIENDSHIP.

Grant in friendship never dickered,
A friend once, he never flickered;
And like the adamantine rock,
Would almost stand the rudest shock.

FUNERAL OBSERVANCES.

Unlike the winter's winds that roar,
Mild August days had run to four.
And morning hours had numbered ten,
Assembled then the sons of men.
Around the piazza hotel fronting,
Cottage Drexel dressed in bunting.
Within its walls, the general dead,
And a human mass about it spread.
The great and small together mixed,
With sorrow on each visage fixed.

The high and low together jammed,
With visages crooked, as if they were damned
There several scores of clergymen,
Mixed with the common people then.
The doctors of divine graces,
Got up to talk with long, wry faces.
To see those doctors would amuse,
With faces long as dummy Jews;
As if the de'il would come that way,
And steal the spirit of the dead away.
When those diviners in pulpits stand,
Devils face them on every hand.
Diviners for devils were made alone,
From the soul's sepulcher to roll the stone.
Now let us go on with the funeral din,
With brother Agnew to usher it in.
Of Bishop Harris, as he's there,
We ask him to give a proper prayer.
Then J. P. Newman discoursed long,
In painting Grant divine and strong.
He even tore our Lord away,
Now, to Grant, the world must pray.
Here, true christian belief was spurned,
Grant, e'en to a Christ was turned.
(Christ is a gauge, to gauge men by,
So as he lived, so let us die.)
May heaven draw on lads and lasses,
As ministers are fools or asses.
For bible bigots do exist,
Not yet from earth to hell dismissed.
After things had resumed restriction,
And said and done was the benediction;
Then all of Grant that on earth remain'
Was processioned to the waiting train.
It was when ten had stretched to one,

And o'er the meridian, passed the sun;
Then the funeral engine winds
　Her course, among the mountain pines.
As down the mountain side she wound,
Seven cars to her were bound,
The engine's top, her sides and fronting,
Were snugly wrapped in proper bunting.
And as she traveled by water and flame,
The funeral car was dressed the same.
The minute guns kept one in mind,
That soldiers are to graves consigned.
Then at sunset, thirty-eight,
A roaring charge for every state.
Soon that road, to the mountain confined,
Her burden to the New York Central consigned.
There at the junction, no racket or din
Marked the start of a new journey to begin.
In a special train, carred up to nine,
Dressed in flags and emblems, rare and fine;
Thus, the corpse of Grant was borne,
As the nation, did an ex-chief mourn.
And in Albany's capitoled halls,
He laid within their gorgeous walls.
The people, to him, homage render,
Borne hither in pomp and splendor.
And during the twenty-one hours that he laid in state,
For the New York-bound train to wait;
To view the remains, a constant stream,
Eighty thousand persons came and seen.

SERVICES IN WESTMINSTER ABBEY.

Simultaneous with Mount McGregor service scene,
One was held in London with an ocean between;
It was an arrangement grand and sublime,
The electric cables gave them the time.

That vast edifice, Westminster Abbey, oh,
It was packed full, and to overflow ;
And in that edifice was seen
The royal household, all, to the queen.
Lords and ladies, dukes and dame.
Kingly princes unknown to fame.
    The English soldier, chief-at-arms,
    And ladies of the rarest charms;
And other officers, without number,
That vast edifice did encumber.
Gladstone was there with his children's dame,
From the house of commons, many came.
With embassadors from various climes,
And perhaps, some dealers in graded wines ;
And of United States men too,
There were several of a choice few.
Senator Edmunds, Hawley and Waite,
And others equally in power to mate.
The music was appropriate and fine,
And the discourse rare, almost divine.
Canon Farrar was the organ
That talked as by a special bargain.
The Church of England was the creed,
The burial portion they did read.
General Grant and our institution,
He lauded them and our constitution,
Hear what Canon Farrar said
About our country's lamented dead :
"Grant was the greatest soldier born,
The American continent to adorn ;
Whose sun set, while yet 'twas day,
In peace and quiet he passed away ;
In whose land now, ten thousands mourn,
With grief their breasts are rent and torn.
They gather at this soldier's obsequies, a'

To mourn with his friends a few hours awa'.
Uncle Sam, as a nation, has stayed his trade,
Laid down his saws, hammers and shaving blade.
They've laid away tools of all occupation,
And gather to mourn throughout the nation ;
And now, in England, here we stand,
To mourn with them hand in hand.

His monument, o'erlooking the Hudson, will stand
To tell future ages the deeds of his hand.
The deeds of his land, so dark and so drear,
With a mighty hand he helped to make clear.

Grant's glory is an American career,
For no man there, holds his neighbor in fear.
No one there is honored by accident of birth.
But God grants each one a patent of worth.
So at the top or bottom, or middle livin',
Each one stands where his patent is given.
America is the land of all other lands,
For each one there on his merit stands.
So let the British Lion and American Eagle,
Freedom o'er the world inveigle.
It is a spectacle vast and grand,
Where freedom stretches on either hand.
It makes a land happy and blest,
Where all are free and none oppressed.
For all men are born the same,
Without regard to wealth or fame.
During the abbey service memorial,
The flags royal were lowered temporal.
Yes, the flags on the royal places,
Were lowly hung in mourning traces.
The service was English, without amend,
English throughout, from end to end.

ALBANY TO NEW YORK CITY.

At thirty minutes after noon,
The train that bore Grant started soon ;
And the remains of that noted tanner,
Was escorted to the train, in the usual manner;
With pall-bearers from the highest station
That people hold, within our nation.
With a procession deep and long,
Like an army wide and strong.
The train that bore the general's remains,
Had the right of way o'er other trains.
To every child the fact was known,
Where'er the train passed, respect was shown.
And only at West Point it slacked its speed,
The presence of cadets there to heed.
Where all that Academic race,
Presented arms in a lineal space.
While across the river, the cannon's boom,
Proved a soldier was nearing the tomb.
The Grand Central in New York city on time
Was reached, by the clock, four hours till nine.
It was the month when farmers thrive,
And August numbered her days to five.
An imposing procession, this one of them all,
To escort the remains to the City Hall ;
Where the usual customary lying in state,
For two long days, he then did wait.
Where thousands went to view,
The soldier who so many slew.

RIVERSIDE PARK.

Grant chose no certain burial-place,
His was a very peculiar case.
West Point, Galena or New York,
Thus, he set his burial mark,

"New York," said he, "was a friend in need,
Which truly proves a friend indeed."
                    So Mayor Grace
Gave Riverside Park as a burial place.
To all of which the family consented,
To bury a chieftain so lamented.
For him mourning cloth, the nation o'er,
Wrapped the country from shore to shore.
          (E'en Paris and Mexico,
            All, all, their mourning show.)
Riverside Park is the finest of all,
That Manhattan's Isle her own can call.
It is a ridge along Hudson's tide,
The glorious Park of the river side.
And on its highest elevation,
There Grant's tomb takes up its station.
Far up and down old Hudson's stream,
One can view her watery sheen.
For New York city lies below,
And Jersey 'neath the western glow.
And in the background it is found,
Jersey's hills loom up around:
Then east, o'er the city and sound.
All descriptions they are mean;
To be appreciated, it must be seen.

LYING IN STATE.

It was an extra lot of pains,
To take a look at Grant's remains.
And some never viewed them at all,
Lying in state at the city hall.*

---

* I myself filed past in the long procession,   [Aug. 7, 1885
To see the cor'se of the man who killed secession.
The procession was a two mile one,
Four ranks wide past the Stewart building strung,
And it wound around with many a crook,

Men were scanty in that force,
That went to view the chieftain's cor'se.
New York city few did lend,
This great procession to attend.
Few men there cared to intrude;
Two-thirds were women who came and viewed.
Three hundred and thirty thousand came,
To view the one with an illustrious name.
The procession in double column tends,
On either side a column wends.
On either side the coffin goes,
The procession makes two single rows.
From six in the morn till one again,
Continued this viewing caravan.

THE MOTTO OVER THE CITY HALL ENTRANCE.

THE TREAD OF HIS BANNERED ARMIES SHOOK THE WORLD;
HIS GENIUS PRESERVED TO LIBERTY HER DIADEM, AND PER-
PETUATED TO COMING GENERATIONS, AMERICA'S EXAMPLE OF
A FREE AND INVULNERABLE GOVERNMENT.

THE NAVAL CEREMONIES.

In proportions it was grand,
The most elaborate of our land.
The flagship "Despatch" her pennants wore,
Half mast, draped, and nothing more.
That ship, with quite a government fleet,
At this grand funeral service meet.
They took their position alongside the park,
The evening before, while it was dark.
When the catafalque its journey begun,
The "Despatch" fired a gun salute of twenty-one.
The men-of-war the same repeated,

Like some wild, meandering mountain brook,
Where thousands upon thousands viewed him in state,
From ragpicker down to the mighty and great.

For to great soldiers, such is meted.
And as the procession wound its way,
Half hour guns kept up their play.
The stream was packed with crafts so various,
Its surface looked like one mass calcareous.
Each craft was packed with human beings,
Who came to view the various seeings.
It's the greatest funeral we ever manned,
It was a funeral by sea and land.

THE PROCESSION.

As the procession was leaving the city hall,
With its sombreus draped, emblemed wall,
An impressive funeral hymn by the Liederkranz,
Was sung, in voice's power, one hundred men's.
  The catafalque was drawn along
  By horse power, twelve couples strong.
  Then, to cut a swelling figure,
  Each horse was guided by a nigger.
  The niggers', like the horses' hair ;
  Each couple was a sombreus pair.
  (A nigger at a white man's tomb,
  Must have lent to the scene a hideous gloom.
  With teeth to shine and eyes to glitter,
  A fiend for heli, no subject fitter.
  May my clay, when inanimate,
  Ne'er be touched by fiends I hate
  May my flesh rot on the clay,
  Ere by Afric's sons be hid away.
  May swine and dogs gnaw at my bones,
  Ere they should cover me with stones.
  The nigger is a fiend that's damned,
  The nigger is the de'il diagramed.)
The military portion of the procession grand,
Moved to the plaintive strains of a mighty band.

Amid church bells' toll,
And cannons' roll.
Trinity chimed proper tunes in her glorious ways,
At midnight and mid-day, at sunset and sun-raise.
And many other towers shed forth their chimes,
In low, sweet, melodious, yet plaintive rhymes.
A long, mournful train the procession did mark,
Eight miles from the city hall to Riverside Park.
A point in passing, so long the procession,
It took five hours, in its funeral fashion.
It was a human stream, tremendous long,
Calculated to make five hundred thousand strong.
That is, counting the many, and numbering the few,
Those in the funeral parade, and those on the view.
Sixteen governors, some with their staff, came,
From distant Minnesota, and the frosty state of Maine.
And of associations, nearly fifty kinds,
Were mixed among those far extending lines.
Associations of all kinds, political and civil,
Each and all tried his neighbor to outrival.
And many associations came from distant states,
       [cut-throat rates.
It was rich for the railroads, with their murderous,
    An'
The New York soldiery turned out to a man.
    The route,
By dense public mourning was marked out.
    Emblems, they
Were vast and many along the way.
    To mourn—
Some elaborate, others humble, their sorrows to adorn.
    The weather,
It was the finest ever raked together.
For the rain, with all its fluid might,
Rained throughout the livelong night.

And when the morning sun arose,
A scene of beauty it did disclose.
It found zephyr on her sweetest wings,
Lending grandeur to all other things.
Cool and pleasant was this eighth August morn,
Such a day as youthful springs adorn.
Oh, the air it was so clear and bright,
Renovated by the showers of the night.
Fleecy clouds on airy wings sailed by,
Through a beautiful blue etherial sky.
And the green was of a greener cast,
Than when the sun set on it last.
Behold the morning of his birth,
Was like this farewell day on earth.
Then old time when he's timed his last,
Swamped in eternity where he's mired fast.
When this world and all that's in it's burned,
Then free again his spirit shall be returned.
   Where time ne'er mars,
And cannon balls sing to lull the wars;
   All, all are burned,
And sin can never be returned.
For in the testament there Christ has 'em.
All the stays to bridge o'er death's dark chasm.
   The tombs last rites,
   To the man of many fights.
On a gentle slope in the park of Riverside,
There his temporary tombery does abide.

  Hard by there soon will rise,
  A monument to pierce the skies.
  Beneath which his bones will rest;
  But by a stone he'll ne'er be pressed,
  Hid in that mighty, steely chest.
  Of red brick the tomb is made,

With strips of black among them laid.
While throughout, the interior is lined,
With white-glazed bricks of a beautiful kind.

The casket was rich and rare, purple velvet covered,
And o'er it in various places silver trimming hovered.
Then the casket was enclosed in a box of cedar wood,
Then all in a box of steel, riveted strong and good.
This great overcoat was wove in a woof of steel,
[unreal.
Wove so strong by fire and hammer, that it really seems
It is wrought steel of great, sonorous sounds,
And in heft it reaches o'er thirty thousand pounds.
With the last rites of the ceremony consumed,
The steel case was riveted, and Grant was entombed.
Of course it sealed him away to time's eternal end,
[rend.
Or till rust's cankering jaws its ponderous steel shall
Or gnaw the rivets, to expose
The end, that's riveted to enclose.
The casket, they buried it doubly secure,
So heaven and hell it could endure.
Can Gabriel wake that soldier's slumber,
Or the de'il add him to his horrid number?*
On two marble pedestals the case was left to rest,
Till time its contents should digest.
The procession arrived at Riverside Park,
At five o'clock, between dinner and dark.
With the family near the tomb there stood,
The wise and beautiful, brave and good.
There was the president, also the vice,
With Hayes and Arthur to entice.
With ex-presidents we can also rate,
Mr. Bayard, the secretary of state.

* See book of " Remarkable Remarks on Grant," [his coffin.]

Sherman and Johnston, Sheridan and Buckner, lo,
Here they're paired off as they should go.

> His pall-bearers, then,
> Were great and mighty men.
> Governors and senators, U. S.,
> And ministers of high address.
> In different deeds,
> And various creeds.
> Also other men were there,
> To lend a hand in a thing so rare.

The Grand Army of the Republic its ritual read,
Then part of the Methodist burial service was said.
"I am the resurrection and the life," saith the Lord,
Your earthly stay and heavenly guard.

> Then read they other scriptures that begun,
> At first Corinthians, fifteenth, forty-one.
> By Bishop Harris it was mumbled,
> As before the general himself he humbled.
> Then J. P. Newman to him prayed.
> Then after the benediction said,
> The casket in the grave was laid.
> Then the bugle gave the signal note,
> Clear and distinct on the ear it smote.
> Then the seventh New York fired a volley strong,
> Deep and wide as it was long.
> Then several others did the same,
> Then last of all the artillery came.
> This consumed all the ceremonies at hand,
> Of a pageantry so vast and grand.

There the mortal remains of U. S. Grant were laid,
Around which a guard of government soldiers stayed.

> I thank the reader for reading so far,
> Viewing Grant in peace and war.

May howling critics here abuse,
Let each line, their silly mind peruse.
Ah! critics! critics, may they be damned,
Head first into hades jammed!
Critics? ah! what love and justice,
The damnedest fiends that ever cu'sed us!
Such fiends should have no tongues to wag,
Hellwards a fellow man to drag.
Now tie your apron strings to fit,
On your humble servant,

Adrian Hitt.

9 783744 711654